**"DEAR LORD. SOUNDS LIKE HALF THE ROOF
JUST CAME DOWN THE CHIMNEY
INTO THE DINING ROOM FIREPLACE."**

Hannah turned and headed straight back through the door to the veranda, to the set of open French doors, where she was immediately grabbed by both arms and tugged sideways, pinned between the open door and a warm, damp, and very hard chest.

"Watch out," came a deep voice next to her ear, followed a split second later by the sound of heavy debris rolling off the roof and bouncing into the yard just a dozen feet away.

"Oh!" she said, jumping at the loud sound it made, the word muffled against the hard, T-shirt-clad shoulder as he instinctively jerked her closer and turned to shield her from the falling stone, brick, and other debris. Her body reacted instantly—and quite favorably—to the sudden, full-body contact. It took her mind a few seconds longer to catch up. Will McCall, he of her rooftop fantasies, had her pinned to her own French door. So she could be excused for being a little muddled.

Also by Bestselling Author Donna Kauffman

Published by Kensington Publishing Corporation

Lavender Blue

DONNA KAUFFMAN

ZEBRA BOOKS
KENSINGTON PUBLISHING CORP.
www.kensingtonbooks.com

ZEBRA BOOKS are published by

Kensington Publishing Corp.
119 West 40th Street
New York, NY 10018

All Kensington titles, imprints, and distributed lines are available at special quantity discounts for bulk purchases for sales promotion, premiums, fund-raising, educational, or institutional use.

Special book excerpts or customized printings can also be created to fit specific needs. For details, write or phone the office of the Kensington Sales Manager: Attn.: Sales Department. Kensington Publishing Corp., 119 West 40th Street, New York, NY 10018. Phone: 1-800-221-2647.

Zebra and the Z logo Reg. U.S. Pat. & TM Off.

First Printing: February 2019
ISBN-13: 978-1-4201-4549-6
ISBN-10: 1-4201-4549-5

ISBN-13: 978-1-4201-4550-2 (eBook)
ISBN-10: 1-4201-4550-9 (eBook)

10 9 8 7 6 5 4 3 2 1

Printed in the United States of America

For those Moran fellas . . .
John, Austin, & Will.
Thank you for the joy you bring to my world, every day.

Chapter One

It wasn't every day Hannah Montgomery got to pick lavender and watch a half-naked man rebuild her bluestone fireplace. Four fireplaces, actually. *Be still, my heart.* "But I'll take all of those I can get," she murmured as she walked from the fields toward what was once known as March House. Now it was the Lavender Blue Farmhouse & Tea Room. *Or soon-to-be tearoom,* she thought, a happy, satisfied smile curving her lips.

Hannah swore she wouldn't stare this time. He was up on the roof again today, under a blazing, late May sun, restoring the stone chimneys to those four beautiful fireplaces. Well, they would be beautiful. As would the rest of the place. *All in due time,* she thought, surprised at how serene she felt about the whole thing, this monstrously enormous task that she and her three closest friends had undertaken.

She had goals now. Clear, direct-line-to-the-finish goals. It felt good and a little terrifying all at the same time. But even the fear of the risk she'd taken by selling her home in Alexandria, along with most of her worldly possessions, to move lock, stock, and paintbrushes to the Blue Ridge Mountains of Virginia felt good. Taking the risk made her feel alive. And that had been precisely why she'd done it.

He didn't look up—or down, as the case might be—as she drew near the four sets of French doors that lined the south-facing side of the sprawling farmhouse. Originally built during the Civil War, the house had been renovated, restored, and refurbished many times. There had been several additions built onto it, including the deep veranda. When the four sets of French doors that lined the exterior wall of the enclosed veranda were all opened and latched against the house, it turned the space into a porch, with an unparalleled view of the lavender fields and the mountains beyond. The veranda would be the setting for their tearoom. Eventually.

She did glance up again. *One last time.* Aside from being aware he was the only stonemason in Blue Hollow Falls, Hannah didn't know much about Wilson McCall. Well, other than that he did amazing things to a sweat-soaked, white T-shirt. He lifted a large, flat piece of bluestone from the chimney and balanced it carefully on the roof. The motion had her glance turning into a protracted and very appreciative gaze. *My, my, my.*

Vivi had been the one to hire him and he certainly seemed to have a good work ethic. Unlike most of the folks Hannah had met since moving to the Falls, Will wasn't the chatty type. Or the talk-at-all type, really.

She climbed the steps to the veranda, then turned to look back out over the fields. She could feel her heart swell inside her chest at the panoramic view of the Blue Ridge Mountains, laid out before her. Their timeworn, ancient tumble, the endless rippling of granite and slate, pine and cedar, never ceased to move her. In the months since she'd moved in, she'd watched in awe as the fields that spread out before her began to regain their color with the advent of spring. That awe deepened further as the proof-of-life green had slowly marched its way up into the hills, higher and higher in elevation as spring moved toward summer. Around boulders, into every fold, through every nook and cranny, color bloomed, bright and bold, cheerful and happy, as new shoots reached for the sun. If that hadn't been a sign of hope and proof of the resilience of the life she'd come to champion, she didn't know what was.

She actually laid a hand over her heart, feeling the thumping beat of it. She'd lived in the newly christened Lavender Blue Farmhouse for five months now, and she already knew she'd never, not ever, take that view, that confirmation of life, for granted. "Look at it, Liam," she whispered. "Look what we're doing here. Can you believe it?"

"You going to bring those stalks into the house or do I have to wait until you quit mooning over those hills?"

Hannah laughed and turned to find her friend, fellow life warrior, and new business partner, Vivienne Baudin, standing in the doorway that led from the broad veranda into the biggest kitchen Hannah had ever seen in her life. Born in New Orleans, Vivienne had known early on she was destined for the bright lights of Broadway, where she'd happily spent more than forty of her sixty-seven years. A former Broadway showgirl turned costume designer, now lavender farmer, she tackled every part of her life with gusto. One only had to glance at the wild swirl of carefully arranged, lavender-hued, silver curls piled up on top of her head like a showgirl headpiece to know that while the showgirl might have left New York, she would never quite be leaving Vivi. And Hannah wouldn't have it any other way.

"I tried to pick the ones that were just opening, like Avery's chart showed," Hannah said, handing the big basket over to Vivi. "Let me know if I'm not getting the right ones."

Vivi grinned. "Honey, like I could tell the difference." She took the basket and leaned down to breathe in their scent. "We'll do something with you, my pretties," she said, closing her eyes in momentary appreciation. Then she straightened and let out that marvelous, smoky, infectious laugh of hers as she added, "Even if it's wrong, we'll have fun figuring out how to make it right." And that, Hannah thought, pretty much summed up Vivi's entire worldview, which was why they'd become such fast, if unlikely friends.

Hannah—thirty years Vivi's junior—was a painter, a former children's book illustrator, and now, too, a lavender farmer. As recently as Christmas, neither of them could have told anyone a thing about how to make tea, soap, essential oils, or anything else from stalks of lavender.

But they could now.

Time would tell if the end result was anything worth crowing about. Much less packaging up and selling. But that didn't matter. Not yet. Now was the time for building and restoring, for repairing and learning. The time for opening their doors, their lavender fields, their tearoom, and welcoming the world into their new home would come soon enough. Hannah didn't want to rush any of it.

A loud crash on the roof above made both women jump and look up. A moment later a rumbling reverberation came from the dining room that made the black-and-white tiled floor of the kitchen vibrate beneath their feet. "What in the world?" Hannah said, pressing her hand over her racing heart.

"Dear Lord. Sounds like half the roof just came down the chimney into the dining room fireplace," Vivi said, her hands also clasped against her chest. "I'll go that way," she said, motioning toward the door to the dining room. "You go on out there and find out what on earth is happening."

Hannah nodded, still processing the sudden turn of events. "Be careful," she told Vivi. She turned and headed straight back through the door to the veranda, to the set of open French doors, where she was immediately grabbed by both arms and tugged sideways, pinned between the open door and a warm, damp, and very hard chest.

"Watch out," came a deep voice next to her ear, followed

a split second later by the sound of heavy debris rolling off the roof and bouncing into the yard just a dozen feet away.

"Oh!" she said, jumping at the loud sound it made, the word muffled against the hard, T-shirt-clad shoulder as he instinctively jerked her closer and turned to shield her from the falling stone, brick, and other debris. Her body reacted instantly—and quite favorably—to the sudden, full-body contact. It took her mind a few seconds longer to catch up. Will McCall, he of her rooftop fantasies, had her pinned to her own French door. So she could be excused for being a little muddled.

"Chimney's coming down," he said by way of explanation, not letting her go quite yet.

"Intentionally?" she asked, her voice still a bit high pitched, her body and mind at odds over the clamor happening on the rooftop and the one happening inside her own body. The sudden change to her previously uninhabited personal space was as jarring as the pieces of chimney thumping into the side yard. Likely because it had been a very, *very* long time since her personal space had been so thoroughly . . . inhabited.

"No," he said, as succinct as always. "Sorry for the scare. You okay?"

"Startled, but yes, I think so," she said, knowing she sounded a bit breathless, and perhaps not entirely due to almost being pummeled to death by falling chimney debris. "I might not have been if it wasn't for your quick reflexes." She lifted her gaze to his. "Thank you."

Now that the immediate danger had been averted, she tried not to stare. Again. Of course, she'd been trying and failing to not stare at the man for two weeks running now, and this moment proved to be no different. But now that all of him was right up close and personal with all of her, it was kind of impossible not to. Her first thought was that he was older than she'd realized. Closer to her own age, maybe even a few years older. There were lines at the corners of his eyes, which might have come from working in the sun. *Not from smiling,* she thought. At least she couldn't recall seeing him look anything other than serious and focused on his work. *Green,* she noted, as her gaze got hung up in his, filling in another detail she'd wondered about. Beautiful, dark, almost gemstone-rich, green eyes.

His hair was dark—which she'd already surmised—and average in length, cut close on the sides and back, a little longer on top. But now she could see how thick it was, and just on the side of unruly, maybe because of the heat. Maybe because he raked his hands through it. Her fingers itched to do the same. He was clean shaven, though there was a hint of shadow already coming through on the hard lines of his jaw, and it wasn't two in the afternoon yet.

She already knew the way his T-shirt clung to every ripple and curve of the muscles in his back, chest, and shoulders. Shoulders she was now getting intimately acquainted with, given her palms were plastered to both of them. Throwing around big chunks of granite and bluestone all day long apparently did a body good. *Really, really good.* That led her to wonder what he'd look like with that dirty, white T-shirt stripped off and—

"Ma'am?"

She jerked her gaze back to his, feeling a hot flush rise to her cheeks at being caught staring. Only he didn't look amused. Or insulted, for that matter. Just concerned. Clearly, he wasn't experiencing the same awakening of the senses she was. The "ma'am" part should have made her feel ancient, only from him it had merely sounded polite. The kind of politeness instilled by generations of southern mamas . . . or maybe by the military, since he had no southern accent that she could discern.

"I'm sorry—I'm fine," she assured him, quick to smile, while trying not to get lost in those emerald-green eyes of his again. They really were something. "You—this just caught me more off guard than I thought," she said, having completely forgotten about her close brush with the falling chimney until that moment. "And it's Hannah, please."

"Will," he replied, not quite gruffly, but close. He finally, carefully set her back a step, keeping hold of her elbows, concern still clear on his face. He was taller than she'd expected, too. Though why she'd expected anything one way or the other, she couldn't have said. He was a good three inches taller than her own five-foot-nine, which was nice. Even if it didn't matter. At all.

His concerned look didn't ease, but he did turn his attention toward the side yard.

She glanced past him and gasped at the array of broken stone and brick that littered the side yard she'd traversed less than thirty minutes ago. "What happened?" She automatically started to slide out from her spot between him and the pinned back door, only to have him hold her right where she was.

"Don't," he warned. "There's more to come down yet."

Trying hard to ignore his broad, warm palm wrapped around her bare arm, and the feeling of her chest rubbing up against his chest, and the skitter of sensations that sent through her, she shifted her gaze past his shoulder to the yard again. "We heard a loud crash and a rumbling sound in the dining room, but I had no idea what—" She broke off and her eyes widened as she looked at him again. "Wait, are you okay?" She looked him up and down, or as much as she could given the tight quarters, searching for signs of injury. "You didn't tumble off—"

"No," he assured her. "I thought I could contain it, but when I realized the whole chimney was going to go, I climbed down to warn you not to go outside for a bit. Only it followed me down before I could knock on the door."

"I think it came down inside as well," she told him,

relieved that he hadn't been hurt. "It sounded like the Thunderdome opened up a location in our dining room."

The corner of his mouth might have curved the slightest bit for the briefest of moments at her *Mad Max* reference, but she wasn't sure because a second later he was shaking his head, his jaw flexing, possibly due to the words he looked ready to mutter, but didn't, in deference to her presence. "I'll head in and check that out, but you'll all need to use the front entrance to the house until I give the all clear."

Hannah nodded her assent, then grew worried again. "Wait, Vivi went to check the dining room fireplace. Should she not be in there? Is there a chance——"

But Will was already moving her safely inside the enclosed veranda, then letting her go and heading through the door into the kitchen. She followed right behind him. "Stay here," he told her in a tone that left zero opening for argument, then cut through the spacious kitchen toward the arched doorway that led into the formal dining room. "Ms. Baudin," he called out as he went. "You shouldn't be——"

Vivi met him in the arched doorway, bringing him up short. "I'm fine, I'm fine. And I believe I've mentioned, it's Vivienne," she told him. "Or Vivi. Sounds like you're calling my mama otherwise. God rest her soul."

Hannah's worry immediately lifted. She hid her amusement at the abashed look on Will's dirt-streaked face. A moment ago he'd looked like a five-star general commanding the troops. Only Vivi could reduce a general to a chastised schoolboy.

"Sorry, ma'am." At her perfectly arched eyebrow, he said, "Miss Vivienne."

Vivi accepted the polite, southern form of address with a smile and a regal nod that did her showgirl background proud. She always carried herself as if she was casually balancing a thirty-pound headpiece. In heels. "As I was about to say, it appears half the chimney is now filling the fireplace grate and a good part of the stone hearth. What on earth happened?"

"It collapsed," Hannah said. "Almost took Will with it."

Vivi's eyes traveled from Will to Hannah, paused consideringly, then moved back to Will. "You're okay, though?"

Will nodded. "The stonework on the front room chimney that I restored first was bluestone veneer on block, redone from the original brick back in the mid-eighties. It was just as stated on the plans I got from the county. Supposedly all four had been redone the same way. Only when I went to re-point the joints on the dining room chimney, I learned—too late—that they had just slapped the stone to the front of the brick, which had been crumbling due to leaks that weakened the structure from the top down. Hence the remodel in the eighties. For some reason, they didn't replace the brick on that one, just put the stone over it. Only whoever did the job didn't do anything to shore up the disintegrating brick joints first. Maybe they thought attaching stone to it would do the trick, and, I'll admit, it's held up for a long time. But once I started to remove the stone, they all started to go. The brick behind the stone essentially crumbled. There was no way to know until the stone being removed revealed the brick, and by then it was already too late."

"Well, I don't see how you could have known otherwise," Vivi said, seeming calm about this unexpected state of affairs. "I'm just grateful you weren't injured. Will you be able to rebuild using the bluestone?"

At the same time, Hannah asked, "Are the other two chimneys like that one? Or the first one?"

"Yes," he told Vivi, "only it will be a more extensive repair. For that one, at least, you're looking at a full replacement. And I don't know what that will mean for the fireplace inside, but I imagine it will have to be rebuilt from top to bottom. You wanted the hearth and mantel redone on that one anyway, so it's not quite as bad as it sounds." Will turned to Hannah. "I don't know yet. I'm going to brace them before I go further, so at least if they start to go they won't fall into the yard. The dining room chimney will have to be dismantled the rest of the way and removed." He looked back to Vivi. "I'll do a full assessment and give you a revised estimate; then you can let me know how you want to proceed."

"Well, we need functioning chimneys," Vivi told him. "I'm not closing them off. So, do whatever needs doing."

"You'll want to look over the cost analysis," he told her, looking surprised at her casual reaction. "My previous bid wouldn't cover—"

Vivi merely waved her beringed hands at him, the many gold and silver bangles she wore on her wrists making a jingling sound at the motion that sounded like wind chimes. "As I said, do what needs doing. I trust you're charging a fair price, despite not having any competition."

Will frowned at that last part. Hannah knew that Vivi was never quite as casual about things as she let on. Nor was she stupid. Far from. Though the lavender hair and over-the-top accessories might lead one to think otherwise, Vivienne Baudin was shrewd about finances and a keen judge of character. That didn't mean she didn't test the waters from time to time, just to make certain.

Thanks to both of those finely tuned traits, along with a very successful career in stage costuming and alimony from two wealthy ex-husbands, money wasn't an issue for Vivi. Most recently, she had also received a substantial inheritance—part of which had been March House—from the man she'd thought of as her soul mate. That didn't mean she wasn't smart about her finances, but her cushion was such that when she decided she wanted something, she found the right person for the job, then rarely let any obstacle come between her and getting the desired end result.

Hannah smiled. Will McCall was about to find that out.

"There are other tradesmen down in Turtle Springs," Will began, and Hannah could see his jaw was a bit tighter, though his voice was as calm and smooth as it had been all along. "I can recommend two who work with me on bigger projects. I'm sure they'd be happy to come give you a new—" He fell silent when Vivi arched one perfectly penciled brow, causing Hannah to fake a cough to cover the laugh she'd unsuccessfully tried to swallow.

"Must have swallowed a little dust from the debris," she claimed when the two looked at her. The slight narrowing of Will's gaze told her he knew it wasn't dust. As did Vivi's amused look.

"Are you trying to wiggle out of your contract?" Vivi asked him.

"No, ma'am," Will said, then immediately added, "Miss Vivienne," before she could stare him down again. "But if you'd like to get other bids—"

"What I'd like is for you to stand by your word and deliver me the four new fireplaces we agreed upon. I trust you'll put together a bid that is fair to both of us. Particularly as there are the walkways, the stone well down by the paddocks, the stables—though we'll have to talk to Chey about them a bit more before we embark on that adventure—and Lord knows what other items I haven't discovered yet. This place is nothing if not a scavenger hunt of what needs restoring next." She waved her hands again. "My point being that in a place this old, which has been sitting empty for as long as it has, there are bound to be a few surprises and more than a few hurdles. I hope you won't let that discourage you. I had really hoped you'd be up to the job."

"No, ma—" Will stopped mid "ma'am," and for the first

time ever, Hannah spied the barest hint of a curve at the corners of his no-nonsense mouth.

She felt some internal part of her all but lean in his direction, urging that smile to continue to emerge. Even the promise of one had done amazing things to those oh-so-serious eyes of his. *What would they be like, sparkling with laughter?* she wondered, instantly entranced by the idea of finding out.

"I mean, yes, I can handle the job," he finished, the serious expression returning to match his tone. "I'll rework the schedule once I've gone over the extent of the deterioration and give you a new bid."

"Excellent," Vivi said, beaming once again. "Do what is needed, keep me apprised, and bill me when you need to. I trust you can get someone in here to clear out the debris from the dining room? Is it safe to go in there? The wall and roof aren't going to come down, are they? I had that architectural firm do a complete analysis when we drew up the renovation plans, so they'll be getting a call from me regarding those chimneys."

"Don't be too hard on them," Will said. "I don't see how they could have known, either. I have copies of all the plans filed with Rockfish County for this place, and according to them, all four chimneys were renovated the same way."

"Sounds like someone might have been cutting corners," Hannah offered.

"Most likely," Will replied, and looked her way again.

She thought he'd glance back at Vivi, only his gaze stayed on hers, as if he expected her to continue the conversation. She should be well past the shock of the brick shower by now, but darn if her pulse rate wasn't still *thump-thump-thumping* right along. The temperature felt like it was climbing by the minute. *Sure, blame it on the broken chunks of brick.* Made her wish she had one of those hand-painted, Japanese silk fans that Vivi favored.

When she didn't add anything further, Will looked back to Vivi and Hannah let out the breath she hadn't been aware she'd been holding.

"Yes, I'll get the dining room cleaned out, but it would be best if you all steered clear of that room until the work on that chimney and fireplace is done. We may have to do the same for the remaining two. I'll let you know."

One of the remaining fireplaces was in the library, just off the foyer, on the opposite side of the house from the kitchen and dining room. That room was still empty, save for a few moving boxes that the four of them had stored in there, so staying out of the library wouldn't be an issue. However, Hannah knew that the final fireplace was in Vivi's master suite upstairs, but decided not to bring that up. The two of them could negotiate that situation when the time came.

The entire second floor of the house was Vivienne's private lodgings, so it wasn't as if she'd have nowhere to go. But Hannah knew the other rooms were still empty or filled with moving boxes and a few dust-cloth-draped pieces of furniture, until Vivi decided how she wanted to renovate and decorate them.

Even though Vivi had inherited the house and all the property it sat on, including the acreage already planted with lavender, the deal the other three of them had struck when deciding to take on this new life venture was that they would each invest in the farm. That meant they had each bought a quarter of the farm property, and their own private quarters.

Avery's residence was the one-story addition that had originally been added off the back of the house at the turn of the twentieth century. Its original function had been to accommodate live-in help, but somewhere in the mid-fifties or sixties when live-in help was no longer required by the owner at that time, the wing had been refurbished into what was called a mother-in-law suite. It was a fairly big apartment, with its own small kitchen, two full baths, two bedrooms, a decent-sized living area, and a small study.

Avery had turned the latter into her own little chemistry lab, where she'd been figuring out how to make the various items they planned to produce and sell from their lavender crop.

Cheyenne, the fourth member of their fearsome foursome—as she'd tagged them back when they'd all befriended one another—had claimed the stables and the small attached stone cottage that had been built for the stable manager some decades back. As she'd come with three horses, that had made perfect sense.

Hannah's investment had netted her the converted loft space over the garage. It was more spacious than it sounded, given the garage had been built to hold several horse-drawn buggies, along with a variety of the first models of automobiles. They all used it for their vehicles and had room for a tractor besides. When they bought one. The loft had its own galley-style kitchen and a lovely full bath with an old claw-foot tub. The main area was an open floor plan that included her living space and bedroom. What had sealed the deal for her was the huge floor-to-ceiling windows that made up the rear-facing wall of the oversized room, facing the fields and the mountains. Two additional skylights set in the high-peaked, open-beam ceiling overhead filled the space with the perfect natural light. Hannah had set up her easels and unboxed all of her paints and brushes before she'd even unpacked her clothes.

"If your deadline for the chimney and fireplace restoration isn't flexible due to other work you're having done, we can bring in more help," Will went on, drawing Hannah from her thoughts. "But that would increase the price."

His voice was deep, the cadence steady, almost soothing. He was the epitome of unruffled, calm, and confident. The kind of man who engendered trust just by his bearing. Her mind darted to that moment he'd pulled her to safety, right up against the hard length of his body, then instinctively sheltered her when more debris had rained down from the roof. He'd taken charge as naturally as if he'd been been born to it. Or trained for it. She wondered again if he was former military.

"Use the front door only for now," he said, then nodded toward the mudroom that jutted off the opposite side of the kitchen from the veranda. "Steer clear of the doors exiting either side of the house. Until I can get the rest of the chimney torn down, I can't guarantee which way the debris will roll."

Hannah turned to Vivi. "Avery should be back shortly and she'll be coming around to the mudroom side. I'll wait for her on the front porch, get her to park up there."

"How long do you think that will be?" Vivi asked Will. "Not using these doors, I mean."

"I have to get back up there to determine that," Will replied. "I'll need to check on the other two chimneys as well. Might be just a few hours or could be a day or two, depending. That much I'll know today."

"We'll be here," Vivi told him. "Just let yourself in when you're ready."

He nodded.

"I'm going to head out front," Hannah said.

"I'll follow you out," Will added, surprising her.

She walked down the hall leading to the front foyer, assuming he wanted a word with her, and wondering what for. Maybe he was worried that Vivi didn't truly appreciate how the crumbled chimney was going to change the bottom line and he wanted to tell her separately, get her to talk to Vivi.

She opened the heavy oak door with the beautiful, floral pattern inset in leaded glass that formed an oval-shaped pane.

The door itself was badly weathered and the lead around several of the glass panes needed to be resoldered as well, but it was stunning craftsmanship and deserved a full restoration. *So many items left on the to-do list,* she thought, trying not to let the magnitude of everything they had yet to do discourage her.

Just because they each had the financial wherewithal to finance the work didn't lift the burden of needing to get it all done. And that was in addition to learning to run the farm and educating themselves on how to turn it into their joint business venture. And now the chimneys were going to be a bigger deal than they'd thought. *But what else is new?* There were times she thought they'd never get it all done.

She stepped back out into the spring sunshine and let the warmth and beauty smooth the edges off her worries. She turned, expecting Will to pause and say whatever he'd followed her out to say. She braced herself for the impact of being pinned under that gaze again, feeling a little foolish for her reaction. Only to feel even more ridiculous when he merely nodded and walked right on past her and down the steps. She laughed at herself, realizing he'd followed her out because he couldn't safely exit through any other door.

That didn't stop her from watching his long-legged stride as he headed back around to where his ladder was propped against the roof. Or the way he filled out the back of those canvas work pants he favored.

"You waiting on Avery or simply admiring the scenery," came Vivi's amused voice behind her. "Not that I can blame you," she added, a knowing twinkle in her bright blue eyes. "I hired him because he seemed to know what he was about, and he came highly recommended." She sighed and fanned her face with her hand, setting her bangles to jingling. "But I readily admit the view certainly was a point in his favor."

Hannah nodded, not embarrassed at being caught ogling.

Not by Vivi, at any rate. Vivi, Avery, Chey, and Hannah knew one another right down to the core and marrow. They were closer than family, their understanding of one another running as deep as was humanly possible. So, there was no point in pretending or trying to hide anything from one another. Nor did she want to.

To other people, the idea that the four of them—who'd only met one another six years ago—would each up and leave their lives behind to start on this crazy joint venture had seemed just that: crazy. Most people couldn't understand the level of trust or the unique sisterhood that came with the particular bond the four of them shared, and Hannah, for one, was grateful they couldn't.

Because that meant they hadn't been where she and the three women nearest and dearest to her heart had been. That meant they had never experienced the depths of grief so deep and all-consuming that they hadn't known how to climb back toward the light, much less the land of the living.

Hannah slid her arm around Vivi's waist and Vivi draped her arm over Hannah's shoulder. They watched Will disappear around the side of the house, then looked at each other. Vivi wiggled her perfect brows, making Hannah snicker; then they both full-out laughed.

Yeah, maybe they were a bit crazy, the four of them. But Hannah would take their kind of crazy, and the joy they'd figured out how to reclaim for themselves, every single day. No regrets and no looking back. Except to the ones they'd loved so deeply and lost.

They'd learned that, for them, the way to manage their grief, and their survivor's guilt, was to bring the ones they'd lost forward with them. To tackle new goals, take new risks, jump into life, full on, and experience everything it had to offer.

As Chey had said the day the four of them had walked

out of the Friday Morning Grief Group they'd each joined and instantly hated, they were not going to be wallowers. They were going to be warriors. Life warriors.

They would pay tribute to their loved ones rather than mourn them, by being the bringers of light, of positive thinking, the spreaders of joy. The better they did, the better they were doing by the loved ones they brought along with them on the journey, in each of their hearts. Showgirl Vivi and her lifelong benefactor and soul mate, Harold. Brilliant child prodigy Avery and her college professor mother, Lisbeth, and poet laureate father, Bernard. Barrel-racer Chey and her bull-riding brother, Cody. Painter and illustrator Hannah and her seven-year-old son and only child, Liam.

It hadn't been an easy climb. They had been with one another at their lowest, their rawest, their weakest, and most vulnerable. They had cried together, raged together, feared together, and, ultimately, grown together. Warriors didn't simply appear fully formed; they were forged.

Hannah looked out at the fields of lavender, row upon row riffled by the warm afternoon breeze, and took in a deep breath as Vivi squeezed her shoulder, likely reading her thoughts. *Battle-tested,* Hannah thought, *but not bulletproof.*

She had no idea what new tests awaited them, awaited her, only that she knew there would be more of them. That was the scariest part. Exciting, too. But still scary. Understandably, none of them wanted to be hurt again. In any way. But that's not how things worked. Not how life worked. Not if you planned to live it fully. She owed a full life to Liam, promised him that every morning when she woke up—promised herself, too.

Hannah and Vivi both jumped as more stone and brick rolled and banged down the roof and off the side of the house, then shook their heads and winked at each other.

A new adventure, and the new tests that would come with it. The farm, their big plans for it, their ongoing plans for themselves as well. Hannah's mind went to Will. Was he going to be one of those life tests, too? Was she even ready to find out?

Some big, bad warrior you are, Hannah thought wryly. *Yeah, but even warriors carried shields.*

Chapter Two

Hannah waved as she saw Avery's little Prius start down the long, winding lane that led to their farmhouse. She returned Vivi's squeeze before the older woman headed back inside the house to begin prepping the lavender buds for their big afternoon experiment.

Hannah heard Will's heavy work boots on the roof above and rubbed her arms as if she could erase how it had felt to have his hands on her. It had been so very long since she'd felt a man's touch. And longer still since a man's touch had made her feel something. Anything.

She walked down the steps and motioned for Avery to park in front of the house instead of in the dirt and gravel lot around the side. Hannah made a mental note to tell Vivi that they all should move their cars to the garage or driveway loop in front of the house for the time being. That's all they needed—for their cars to get bashed in.

Hannah found herself glancing back up at the roof again, at the man in the white T-shirt with the green eyes and too-serious face. She thought about that flash of an almost smile, about wanting to see if she could get a full one out of him. *Yeah, you're just begging to put a few more dings in that shield.*

She tried not to think about that as she watched Avery park and get out. Avery Kent, at twenty-four, was the youngest of the fearsome foursome. Hannah might have had the most boring life, but Avery had inarguably led the most sheltered one of the four. Avery was a child prodigy, having earned her PhD in statistical analysis at fifteen, and a second one in library science just three years later. She also had an eidetic memory, which meant she could recall every single thing she'd ever done, seen, read, or heard, down to the tiniest detail. It was both freakishly impressive and not a little daunting to those who spent any amount of time with her.

To date, everything Hannah, Vivi, and Cheyenne knew about lavender farming, they knew because Avery had read up on the subject, and then taught them like a boss.

But book-learning and creating the products was one thing. Making what they'd learned into a business, they were each discovering, was another thing entirely. Today, they were going to learn how to make an essential oil. Hannah hoped. Avery had gone to pick up the necessary supplies that could be sourced locally, or down in the valley, anyway. Everything else had been ordered online. Hannah was hoping this experiment went better than their first attempt at making lavender-scented soap. They'd come close to needing a full kitchen remodel after that escapade.

Hannah jumped when she heard another piece of chimney roll down the roofing and plunk into the side yard, but was proud of herself for resisting the urge to take one last look. "Maybe you need to get some essential parts of yourself oiled," she murmured under her breath, then grinned as she hurried around the back of the car when Avery popped the latch.

"I wasn't able to get the exact tubing I'd hoped to find," Avery said without preamble, as was her way. "I wanted glass but settled on heavily tinned copper that I found at Jansen's hardware. You'd be amazed what they have in there.

Everything from old rotary phone parts to Red Flyer wagons. It was like stepping into a different century, but with on-premises Wi-Fi and a catalog they've compiled over the years listing every part from every . . . well, everything that has parts." She grinned. "I loved everything about it."

She lifted a box from the back and handed it to Hannah. "It's doubtful we'll get the same distillate levels, but for the purposes of this test run, that won't matter. If this comes out remotely well, I'll see if I can find a suitable resource for wholesale ordering when it comes time to make bigger batches." She pulled another smaller box and two handled bags from the back, then hitched them on her slim hip so she could close the hatch.

Avery was pretty much Hannah's opposite in every way. Where Hannah was tall, with light brown hair and just enough extra curve in her hips and boobs to make finding proper-fitting clothes a bit of a challenge, Avery was short and boyishly slender. Hannah favored keeping her hair in a long, loosely woven French braid, and was forever tucking stray wisps behind her ears as she worked. Avery wore her ruler straight, thick dark hair in a swingy, razor-sharp bob that fell just below her chin. Her big, round, red-framed glasses only served to emphasize her serious hazel eyes and cute little upturned nose. And Hannah loved her like the little sister she'd always wanted but never had.

Along with Avery's outrageous book smarts and her mile-a-minute brain, she had a mile-a-minute mouth to match, and a bubbly enthusiasm about, well, pretty much everything. She was endlessly curious, and wanted to see, read, and do it all. Hannah thought if anyone could accomplish such a thing, Avery would be the one to pull it off.

"We should probably figure out whether the process is worth the effort before we invest in too much gear," Hannah said, as the two lugged the supplies up the front steps.

"I've done the development charts on that, and it will be,"

Avery assured her. "If we produce oils, soap, and sachets, then the expenditure on supplies will easily be outweighed by even minimal sales in as early as eighteen months. And if my projections are accurate—and I based them at the low end of the performance scale and potential customer base, formulated using the overall population of Blue Hollow Falls, adjusted to the percentage of those who regularly shop at the Bluebird Crafters Guild booths at the restored mill, and adding in the increased consumer flow of new tourists that will likely occur when the new music amphitheater opens in August—we'll be operating in the black by our second season. Possibly one-and-a-half if we go ahead with the off-season, holiday-oriented events I outlined in the prospectus I e-mailed to each of you last week. You have reviewed those, right?"

Hannah opened the front door and held it so Avery could navigate herself and her box and bags into the house, then went in behind her, shaking her head, an amused smile on her face. Avery's always active mind and Vivi's sheer force of will combined to make an energy field that alone ought to make Lavender Blue a success.

"I did look it over, yes," Hannah said truthfully. "And your forecast on our long-term potential definitely gives me hope. But you'll recall how the soap-making venture went our first time out, so—"

"Entirely avoidable," Avery said matter-of-factly, as if almost burning half the house down had been nothing more than a minor lab accident. "We couldn't have known that the industrial stainless steel mixer would short the circuits and cause the wall to catch on fire. Well, we might have had some advance warning on the circuit aspect had I done an analysis first, but there was no way to know that the space behind the wall had long since been turned into a mouse condo and veritable tinderbox. Anything could have set that off." She walked on into the kitchen and set her box and bags down on the large, plank-top workstation that dominated the center of the sun-filled room. "Frankly, we were fortunate to find out when we did, and with all of us present to help put out the sparks before the whole wall went up."

"Yes, well, when you put it like that," Hannah said dryly as she slid her box onto the table next to Avery's bundles. She opened the box she'd been carrying and lifted out a big pressure cooker. Frowning, she set it on the worktable. "So, this looks alarming," she said, not bothering to mask her concern. "I thought we just picked the buds and covered them in alcohol."

"That's how you get an extract or tincture," Avery told her. "To get a true essential oil, you have to distill it. And that means making lavender steam." She gave Hannah a disappointed, but not entirely surprised look. "It was all detailed in the step-by-step guide I put together and sent each of you."

Hannah watched as Avery opened the other boxes, including the ones that had been mailed to them, and pulled out what looked like an unusually formulated glass laboratory bottle, a long piece of tubing, and a big bucket. "This looks complicated."

"Not really," Avery assured her. She was the brains behind all four of the products they had decided they wanted to offer to their eventual customers. Lavender tea, soap, essential oil, and bath salts. Avery had also found a recipe for a body scrub, but Hannah thought they were being pretty ambitious as it was. They also planned to set up outdoor workstations during harvesting season, so the people who came to pick their own lavender and tour the farm could also make their own sachets, small wreaths, and dried flower bundles.

They each had specific areas they intended to oversee. Vivi would run the tearoom, Cheyenne the farming, Hannah the workstations and tours, and Avery would head up the actual production of the products. There would be employees in all of those areas eventually, as well, but first they'd agreed that each of them should fully understand all areas of the business, including hands-on experience. Right now, that meant learning how to make each of their future products.

"Where is Chey?" Avery asked as she finished assembling the various pieces. Picking up the tray of buds that Vivi had removed from the stems Hannah had picked, Avery examined it.

"She had to take one of her horses to the vet," Hannah said.

Avery looked up, concerned. "Foster?" she asked, referring to one of Chey's two rescue geldings.

Hannah nodded. "She's had the vet out twice now, but Foster never displays the issues he's having when Doc Fraser is here, so he asked her to bring Foster in and board him there for a day or two so they could observe him on camera. I'm not sure how long all that will take. Chey said she'd call when she was heading back."

Avery and Hannah shared a dry smile. Chey wasn't exactly . . . punctual. Or good at staying in contact. To say she was an independent spirit was underselling Chey's aptitude for going her own way.

"Good selection," Avery said as she went back to examining the buds, plucking three out of every four buds and tossing them in a separate bowl.

Hannah was proud of herself until Avery handed her that bowl and said, "Keep these for making the tincture."

Hannah sighed. "Will do. Should I go pick more? I'm not sure we'll have enough."

Avery glanced at the basket of cut lavender Vivi had been working her way through before going upstairs to take a call from another contractor she'd hired to do some painting. "That's all you got?"

Hannah nodded, trying not to feel dispirited. "We have a field full of them, though," she offered gamely. "I'll go cut more." She picked up one of the stems from the basket. "Show me which ones look best and I'll try to do better with my selection."

Avery pointed to one of the buds. "See how this one is just opening, but this one"—she pointed to one higher on the stem—"shows more of the individual segments?"

They looked exactly the same to Hannah, but she nodded before Avery went to get a microscope to give her the full lecture. "Which one is better?"

Avery pointed to the second one.

Hannah gave her a little salute. "I'll do my best, captain."

"Take this with you," Avery said, handing her the stalk they'd just been looking at. Her droll expression made it clear she knew Hannah had no idea what she was supposed to look for. "To use as a guide."

"Thanks," Hannah said with a grin, then peered at the two buds again.

"Just pick a lot," Avery told her with a sigh as Hannah headed for the door to the veranda. "They won't go to waste."

"Front door," Vivi reminded Hannah as she strolled back into the kitchen. The satisfied look on her face said the call had been productive, so Hannah took heart that at least one thing was going right that day. Hannah gave Vivi a little salute with her lavender stem and changed course to head for the front hall. "We should probably put signs up on both doors reminding us until we get the all clear. Or reminding me, at any rate," she added with a laugh.

"Don't linger too long out there," Vivi added mildly as she emptied the basket onto the workstation and handed it to Hannah, a knowing twinkle in her eyes.

"Ha-ha," Hannah said, knowing exactly what Vivi was getting at and not bothering to pretend otherwise. "I think we all have enough on our respective plates not to be worrying about distractions."

Vivi laughed. "Honey, don't you know that's exactly when the best distractions happen?"

Chapter Three

Will McCall was not a Peeping Tom. Nor did he eavesdrop. Not intentionally. But as he continued clearing the chimney debris from the yard, it was next to impossible not to notice what the women of the soon-to-be Lavender Blue Farmhouse & Tea Room venture were doing in their big, sunlit kitchen. *You mean it's impossible not to notice what Hannah Montgomery is doing,* his little voice prodded.

He ignored it. Just as he'd been trying to ignore pretty much everything about Hannah Montgomery for the past two weeks. Ever since the first time he'd spied her out in the lavender fields, basket over one arm, filled with clippings of the newly budding stems. The ankle-length floral skirts she seemed to favor alternately billowed around or clung to her long legs, depending on which way the breeze was blowing. The pale yellow T-shirt she was wearing today was soft and loose, a size or two too big, as he'd noted was her custom. She'd rolled up the sleeves and tied a scarf around her waist, and another around the brim of her wide straw hat. She favored those, too. The shirt still hung loosely over her curves, but he knew they were there. He'd felt every one of them pressed against him earlier. She'd felt soft and warm, and, well, good. She was taller than he'd estimated,

which appealed to him. He hadn't held a woman in his arms
since . . . well, for a very long time. "Maybe it's like riding
a bike," he muttered, realizing he was once again off day-
dreaming instead of getting the job done. That was as unlike
him as his newly wandering eye.

As if taunting his determination, the front door opened
and she emerged with an empty basket over her arm, heading back out to the fields. She took the long way, avoiding
the side yard and walking around the driveway where it
looped in front of the house instead. He watched as she let
herself through one of the gates in the fence-line about
twenty yards down the long stretch of driveway that headed
out to the main road, if you could call it that. Maybe a dozen
cars a day would pass by at best. He suspected that number
would increase sharply when the farm opened for business.

Most days she wore her light brown hair as it was now,
woven into some kind of complicated-looking braid that
hung a fair way down her back. It swung as she walked,
keeping counter-time to the graceful sway of her hips.
Strands of her hair had come loose and danced around her
face in the late afternoon breeze. He found himself thinking
about what it would be like to slide the elastic band off the
end and slowly unweave each and every plait until the long,
rippling waves ran through his fingers.

He realized he was standing there, straight-out staring at
her like a teenager mooning over a new crush, and jerked
his attention back to the task at hand. He bent down and
grabbed a few more pieces of broken brick and stone, tossing
them into the wheelbarrow he'd loaded several times now.
He heard a hint of something on the breeze as he pushed the
wheelbarrow over to his truck to unload the debris. Realizing it was coming from the fields, not the house, he paused,
listening. She was humming, or maybe singing. Just loudly
enough that the breeze carried it all the way from the rows
of lavender to him. It was like the fates were tormenting him

or something. "Well, I hope you're enjoying yourselves," he murmured, resolutely turning his back to the field and to her. But the lilt of her voice reached him anyway, if not the precise words.

She had a wide smile that was frequently on display. Somehow it didn't surprise him that she could carry a tune. She laughed easily, too, sweet and melodic, the kind that pulled a person right on in. Her eyes had been a surprise to him, though he couldn't say why. He would have guessed . . . well, he didn't rightly know what he would have guessed. A sunny blue most likely. But it turned out she had the softest, warmest gray eyes he'd ever seen. He hadn't known gray could be a warm color, but it was on her. The light sprinkle of freckles across the bridge of her nose had been unexpected as well. She was a tall woman, almost statuesque, so the freckles should have seemed incongruous somehow. And yet they suited her perfectly.

He tossed another armful of stone into the bed of his truck with perhaps a little more force than was absolutely necessary, causing the happy chatter emanating from the kitchen to come to an abrupt stop.

Vivi had opened all four sets of French doors and the kitchen windows once the sun had started to edge toward the horizon. The air cooled quickly at this elevation and the heat of day was already receding. He glanced over to find Avery and Vivi both looking his way in concern. He made a motion that all was fine and went back to work. He purposely did not look toward the fields. At least she'd stopped singing.

He wasn't used to having his head turned so easily. Or at all, to be honest. Will's focus for the past seven years since his mom had passed had been on providing a life for and single-handedly raising his now fourteen-year-old son, Jacob. Will's mom had been born and raised in the Falls and had come back there to live full time after Will's dad had been killed in combat in Iraq. So everyone in the Falls knew Will's story even before he'd processed out of the marines and moved to Blue Hollow Falls full time.

They knew he was a widower. Hard not to know since Jake had come to stay with his mom after Zoey's death, while Will had still been deployed. And most of them probably thought he was something of a sad or pathetic figure for still carrying a torch for his wife all these years later, despite having lost her when Jake was barely old enough to walk. It wasn't like he'd planned to feel that way or thought he should or shouldn't feel that way. But even though Zoey was no longer by his side, the spot she'd always occupied in his heart was still hers. It was as simple as that, really.

The very, very few times he'd made an effort to move on, he just couldn't find it in himself to get past coffee, or dinner. Not even for his son, to give him the benefit of a woman's nurturing kindness in his life. It just hadn't felt right.

He smiled briefly and shook his head. Zoey would be horrified that he'd gone on all this time alone. His wife would have been the first one to tell him that life was for the living and to get on with it already. He got that. He'd have wanted the same for her if the situation had been reversed. It was still shocking to him that it hadn't been the other way around, given the tours of duty he'd done in some of the most unstable places in the world. He'd been doing just that, in fact, when she'd been killed in that car accident. So, in his head, he knew moving forward was the right thing, or at least the healthy thing to do. He just had never figured out how to make his heart okay with it. After a while, it had just become easier not to try.

Despite that, he was a happy man. Or a contented one, at any rate. He had a son he was proud of and loved with every part of himself. He and Jake were both fit and healthy. Will had a job that allowed him to work with his hands, something he was good at and that gave him a strong sense of fulfillment, as well as allowing him to provide for himself and his son. Jake was a good kid who was turning into a wonderful young man. Will was biased in that regard of course, but his son was well-liked by everyone who knew him, and that was a balm to Will's soul.

Will and Jacob had both come to love Blue Hollow Falls, so putting down his own roots where his mom had grown up, and her parents before her, hadn't been as much of a challenge for Will as he'd feared, given his own military brat upbringing.

The Falls had quickly come to be more than just a place he'd spent the occasional summer as a child, visiting his grandparents while his parents packed up and moved all of his stuff to yet another military base. It was truly home to him now. He'd wanted to put down roots to create a strong foundation for Jake, given the boy had lost both of the women who had helped to raise him. Certainly more stability than Will had had as a child, moving all around the world, then enlisting himself as an adult. Blue Hollow Falls had a way of pulling a person in, and the people of the Falls held on to the ones they cared about. They had with his mother, and with his son, and now with Will. He couldn't imagine living anywhere else.

He straightened and wheeled the now-empty barrow back out into the yard and saw Hannah had come back in from the fields while he'd been unloading the debris, lost in his thoughts. Mercifully, she hadn't caught him staring after her like a lost puppy, so there was that. She'd just crossed the front landing and let herself into the house as he set the wheelbarrow down again.

Laughter from the kitchen followed soon thereafter, drawing his attention back to the French doors and the women inside. He'd done about all he could do outside for the time being. He needed to get inside and at least check out the dining room fireplace before calling it a day. He would put in a longer day if he could, but he had to pick up Jake. He washed his hands with some of the water from the big jug he always kept on his job sites, getting a layer or two of soot and grime off them.

He'd just crossed the veranda and was about to announce his presence to the women before opening the screen door when his phone rang. Vivi, Hannah, and Avery, who had all been bent over studying some sort of contraption that was set up on the edge of the kitchen's big center workstation, turned, looking momentarily startled.

"Sorry," he said, then turned his back to the door so he could take the call from his son without interrupting them further. "Hey, Jake. Almost done here. Tell Seth and Pippa I'll be up there in about an hour." He checked the time on the phone. "Sorry, I'm running late. We had a bit of a problem with one of the chimneys coming down."

"Seth and Pippa just left to go down to the music venue for some meeting and Bailey has already been picked up," Jake told him. "They offered me a ride but I thought you were on the way. I can just hang out in the stone barn—"

"No, I'll come and get you. Sorry, buddy, it's just been a day."

"Can I help?"

Will turned to find Hannah standing behind him in the doorway.

"I'm sorry," she said, appearing a bit abashed. "I wasn't trying to eavesdrop."

Welcome to the club, he wanted to tell her. "Hold on, Jake," Will told his son, then lowered the phone for a moment. "No, that's okay. I've got to go pick up Jake—my son—at Bluestone and Vine."

"Seth's winery?" she asked, her expression brightening.

"I've been up there and met him and his wife. Beautiful place. Your son . . . does he work for them?"

She seemed surprised. Whether it was by the fact that he had a son who was old enough to work, or by the fact that he had a son at all, he wasn't sure. "Something like that," Will told her. "And thank you for the offer, but that's not something you need to—"

"If it will help, I honestly don't mind." She gestured behind her. "I know today has had some unwelcome surprises that have probably really screwed up your schedule with all this." She gestured behind her. "We're done with our little chemistry experiment in there, and I wouldn't mind getting out for a bit."

"Dad," came Jake's voice through Will's phone. "Dad?"

Will lifted the phone back to his ear. "Just another moment."

"If it helps you and she doesn't mind, I'm good with that," Jake told him. "I could introduce her to Dexter and the gang if she'd like."

"Dexter?" Hannah asked, then appeared a bit sheepish when Will looked at her. "Sorry. The McCall men's voices carry, I guess."

"Excellent," Jake said happily. "So, we're all set. Tell her I said thanks."

Will just shook his head, a smile ghosting his lips. "Apparently I'm not even in this conversation. You can tell her yourself shortly. Hold tight," he told Jake. "I'll call you back in a minute." He ended the conversation with his son, then turned to Hannah. "Thank you for the assist. I—we—appreciate it."

"Happy to do it," she said. "Who is Dexter?"

"Seth's llama," Will told her, then found himself smiling in full when her pretty gray eyes widened with delight.

"And 'the gang'?"

"A variety of farm animals. Jake and one of his friends

help Seth out by taking care of them after school and in the summer. If you don't have time for the tour, just tell him. You're already going above and beyond."

"It's not that far from here and sounds like the perfect break."

"Break," he repeated. "You all have more experiments lined up this evening?" He glanced past her into the kitchen, where he saw Avery still hovering over what looked like some kind of miniature distilling setup.

She followed his gaze and laughed. "No, I think we've risked life and limb enough today. Essential oils," she said when she looked back at him and saw the questioning expression on his face. "A few weeks ago we tried making soap, shorted a circuit, and almost set the wall on fire. That was before you started working out here, which is lucky for you. It smelled awful. Today was far more successful." She beamed. "Our menu of future lavender products is coming together. Slowly. But we're going to get there."

"Sounds like you've got things planned out," he said, and got all caught up in the sparkle of unabashed joy that filled her eyes. Hannah Montgomery wore her emotions right on her sleeve, or at least it seemed that way to him. He was more the guarded type. Partly by training, thanks to the US Marine Corp, and partly by nature. "That explains the wall behind the stove being stripped down to the beams, I guess." He'd noticed that when he'd come in earlier.

She nodded. "Apparently the mice had created quite a homestead in the walls, filled it with all kinds of shredded stuff. So maybe it was just as well we found that out. The restoration isn't as bad as we feared, but hopefully there will be no more surprises when they check behind the other walls."

Will tried not to look dubious about that. Mice were

opportunistic marauders and the house had sat empty a very long time.

She caught his look and her tone turned wry. "Basically, we're just hoping the place won't crumble down around us." She grinned. "Or on top of us, as the case may be."

He smiled briefly at that. "I'll have the remaining two chimneys shored up tomorrow and will be able to give you a better idea of what you're looking at."

"Vivi—we all—appreciate that," she told him. "We knew that a house this old would come with all sorts of issues, but . . ." She trailed off, her gaze traveling from the kitchen to the roof, to the veranda, and back to him. She folded her arms and sort of hugged herself, her eyes sparkling again. "I love it already. It's an adventure I wouldn't miss for the world. None of us would."

He was tempted to ask her how the whole enterprise had come about, but he resisted the urge. In a town as small as Blue Hollow Falls, he was somewhat surprised he didn't know the answer already. He wasn't one for poking his nose in, quite the opposite, but knowing everyone's business was a staple of Blue Hollow Falls life. He didn't have to participate in gossip for it to find its way to him.

This was different, though. He did want to know. About how they'd decided to take on an overgrown, long-abandoned lavender farm, how the four of them—a more different group of women he was never likely to meet—had come together in the first place. They weren't just running a business together; they were all living together as well. Well, living on the same property together, at any rate. He hadn't exactly known what to expect when Seth had passed on the word that the new owner of the old March place was in need of some masonry repair. Running a lavender farm and opening up some kind of café or coffeehouse, or whatever a tearoom was, wasn't the oddest thing he'd ever heard of, but nor was four women settling in a new place all together under one extended roof a particularly normal thing, either.

He'd yet to speak directly to the youngest one—Avery, he knew now—or the one with the horses, but as an outside observer looking in, they seemed a pretty levelheaded, straightforward bunch. Purple hair and an excess of jewelry notwithstanding, he thought, as he pictured Ms. Baudin. She was a character, but she was no dummy. Which meant she'd fit right in with the folks in the Falls.

"Actually, Vivi is going to be working on a recipe she's developing for tea and lavender-infused cupcakes and cookies later," Hannah said as she turned her attention from gazing adoringly at her new venture to beaming at him. "She's the baker of our fearsome foursome."

"Fearsome foursome, are you?"

Hannah's eyes widened instantly when he smiled. Or her pupils did. In that way a woman's eyes widened when she was attracted to something. Or someone. It had been a very long time since he'd stood close enough to a woman to notice such a thing. And an even longer time since that look was directed at him. He'd have thought it would have made him uncomfortable, or at the very least prodded him to end the conversation and get on with his work. He wasn't one for wasting time with small talk, much less encouraging more of it, and yet, there he stood. And his immediate instinct wasn't to find a way to extract himself from the conversation. No, his immediate instinct had been to take a step closer. Find out what kind of response his nearness would elicit in those expressive eyes of hers.

It was that reaction to her that had his expression faltering and him taking a step back. As if he'd done something or felt something he should feel guilty about. Which was nonsense, but there it was anyway. "I should get on inside and start on the fireplace in the dining room," he said, not intending to sound curt, but the surprise on her face, followed by her own smile shifting to one of polite friendliness made it clear he had been. "Sorry," he said, feeling contrite. And confused. Neither of which helped him in the comfort department. "I'm just—"

"No need to apologize," she told him, her tone easy enough, but her soft eyes telegraphing the sting she'd felt at his abrupt shift. "I'm keeping you from your work. I'll go on up and get Jake. Do you need him back here at any certain time? If he wants to introduce me to Dexter and the rest, that's okay?"

"More than," Will told her, feeling like an out-of-practice idiot. *Get it together, man.* "I've got at least an hour inside, more if you don't mind Jake staying here for a bit. He'll be helping me, so he won't be underfoot."

Her eyes warmed again. "That's no bother at all. We'll need a taste tester for the cupcakes and cookies."

Will relaxed a little and his smile came naturally again. "You might be sorry you offered that. He eats like, well, like a fourteen-year-old boy."

Something flashed through Hannah's eyes at that, something he couldn't quite put his finger on—surprise, sadness—it didn't make any sense, but he quickly added, "You don't have to—"

"Vivi always cooks like she's feeding an army," Hannah said with a laugh, recovering so quickly Will wondered if he'd misread the moment. She held her arms out. "Clearly, I know of what I speak."

Will automatically glanced down at her body, as invited, both surprised and charmed by her easy, open way of owning who she was. She'd said it without any hint of digging for some kind of compliment or other affirmation that women sometimes did. Which he was thankful for. Given his plainspoken way, situations like that often left him feeling clumsy and inadequate. Taking a beat too long to formulate a smooth, sincere reply had been his downfall on more than one occasion.

So, he surprised himself by responding without giving it a second thought. "I don't think she could ask for a more flattering advertisement." The moment the words were out of his mouth, he realized she might not take them as intended, and silently cursed himself for once again putting his foot in it. "What I meant to say—"

"I know what you meant," she said, a shade abashed now, the most delightful rosy shade coloring her cheeks. Then she laughed. "At least that's the way I'm going to choose to take it."

"Good," he said, feeling his lips curving again. She did that to him, and he wasn't sure how he felt about it. He didn't think of himself as a particularly dour or overly serious man. Quiet, perhaps. Introspective. Maybe he should smile more. Laugh more. "I—I should get on inside."

"Right," she said, and the moment between them—if there had been one—quickly dissipated. "I promise not to be too long up there. I appreciate your staying to start on the dining room today. Vivi passes it off like she's unbothered by the whole thing, but I know it rattled her a little bit. Having you in there assessing things before we close up the house for the night will allow her to sleep better."

"Not to worry," he said. "Thanks again. For getting Jacob."

"Anytime," she told him.

They stood there a moment longer; then Hannah turned. "I'll just go get my keys." She disappeared into the house.

Will stood for another long moment on the porch, looking out across the fields, to the mountains beyond. Trying to talk himself out of what the rest of his body was trying to talk him into. And not entirely sure why.

Chapter Four

Hannah pulled her old Jeep Cherokee into the small dirt and gravel lot by the bluestone barn. It was a beautifully restored building that sat just beyond Seth's gorgeous mountain home, with its soaring A-frame, the glass front glistening in the early evening sun. She got out and turned in a full circle to take it all in. If the view from her farmhouse made her heart swell, the view from up here took her breath away. "Stunning" didn't do the vista justice.

She took another moment, then another, then silently chastised herself for stalling. She'd come a very long way in the seven years since she'd lost Liam, and while she still missed her son every single day, she'd worked hard to get to this point. She felt good and positive and strong about how she'd decided to go forward with her life, carrying him forward with her, rather than letting his loss hold her back. But that didn't mean there weren't still hiccups. Sometimes, like now, they were obvious and expected; other times—most times—they came out of nowhere.

Like on the veranda with Will, when he'd casually mentioned that his son Jake was fourteen. Liam would be the same age now. It had just caught at her, not surprisingly, but the reaction required a determined response. As an illustrator for two popular series of children's books, she'd met with many young people during the years since the accident. Most times she was able to prepare herself for those occasions, knew they would make her both sad and happy. Sad because they naturally made her miss her son more than ever. Happy because her work as an illustrator brought joy to other children the same way it had to her child. And that was a good, positive thing to be doing. For herself, and for Liam.

"Ms. Montgomery?"

Hannah didn't have time to brace herself before turning. She didn't want to feel those pangs, but she knew that there would always be moments like this. It was all in how she handled them, how she let them handle her. And in that regard, she felt a lot more confident these days. She'd learned the best way to handle the hiccups was to put herself in the mindset of her child. What would he want her to do, what would make him proud of her? And then it was easy. Or easier, at any rate. "Hello," she said as she turned to greet Will's son, an honest, welcoming smile on her face. "You must be Jacob. You can call me Hannah."

"Jake," he said with a nod.

Jake was tall for his age, matching her in height, and gangly. He had his father's dark hair and serious green eyes. The open, cheerful grin, she decided, must come from his mom. Vivi had mentioned she'd heard Will was one of the Falls' most eligible bachelors back when she'd hired him. Hannah hadn't known then that he had a son, so naturally she wondered what the story was there, where Jake's mom fit in the picture, but pushed all that aside when Jake extended his hand.

"Pleasure to meet you, Miss Hannah," he said with an easy politeness, then jerked his hand away at the last second and wiped it on his pants, before extending it again. "Sorry, I've been out in the fields." His voice was pitched in that place between childhood and manhood, which made him all the more instantly endearing. That and the slight blush that colored his cheeks at his last-minute hand-wiping. "Would you like to see some of the place? I checked with Mr. B— Seth," he clarified, "and he said it was okay. Unless Dad needs me back at your place."

"You dad is fine with me taking the tour," Hannah told him. She knew it was normal, natural, to compare, to wonder. Would her son be that tall? Would his voice be changing like that? It made her heart twinge, but that didn't deter her. If anything, it made her more determined. "I'd love to meet Dexter," she went on. "I've never seen a llama up close. If it wouldn't be a bother, that is. I've been up here before, to introduce myself to Seth and his wife, Pippa, after we all moved into the farmhouse. They seem like a great pair, but they were busy at the time, and I didn't want to bother them to show me around."

"They're the best," Jake agreed. "And I know this place like the back of my hand, so whatever you'd like to see, I'm game." He glanced down at her feet. "It's a bit muddy though, so maybe . . ."

Laughing, she looked at the sandals she'd changed into before heading out. "Right. Hold on. I've got it covered." She went around the back of her Jeep, opened the rear window hatch, and pulled out a pair of well-loved, purple rubber garden boots. She caught his dubious expression and said, "What other color would a lavender farmer wear?"

"Makes sense," he said, smiling.

She looked at his beat-up brown leather boots and said, "You know, you work in a vineyard, and grapes are purple." She wiggled her eyebrows. "I could hook you up. In case, you know, you want to be hip like me."

Jake laughed outright then, and she grinned.

"I think I might have to work my way up to that level of cool," he told her, making her laugh even as he blushed when he realized he might have insulted her.

He seemed to be an endearing combination of earnest politeness and engaging teenager, all at the same time. She suspected once he got to know someone, he was funny and outgoing all the time. *Certainly more so than his father, at any rate.* Amused at the thought, Hannah slipped out of her sandals and tucked her feet into the clunky boots, careful to keep the edge of her long skirt from getting tucked inside them. She grabbed a hoodie from the back and slipped that on, too. With the sun setting, and the winery being up at an even higher elevation than her farm, it had already gotten quite cool. She zipped up the front of the oversized gray-and-pink striped garment, then struck a glamour pose, with one purple-booted toe pointed in front of her. "And to think they rejected my modeling application."

They both laughed, then Jake led the way to the barn. "The goats are in here," he told her, much more relaxed now. "We have a bunch of new babies. Dexter is out guarding the sheep in the lower pasture. We can go see him next. We used to bring him in at night because llamas can overeat, but Mr. B found something you can give them to keep that from happening. So now he stays out with his flock."

"Dexter guards them?" Hannah said. "I didn't know llamas did that."

Jake nodded. "They're used all over the country that way. Keeps the coyotes and other predators away. We don't have much of a coyote problem here, but they are around." He slid the barn door open, then stepped aside, allowing her to enter first. "In this case, Mr. B sort of bought the sheep for Dexter more than the other way around. He came with the place when Mr. B bought it. Dex had been abused before the previous owners of the vineyard got him, but they didn't have him long enough to do much more than rescue him. Mr. B tried to get him a few buddies from an alpaca breeder down in the valley, but that didn't go over too well. The breeder suggested Dex might like to be kept with sheep, who wouldn't be so threatening to him. He said llamas had natural protective tendencies, so he'd likely bond with them and look out for them once they'd spent some time together. And it worked. Dex is super attached to the sheep now, like they're his family. It's pretty cool, actually."

"It sounds amazing," Hannah said, charmed. "What a lovely thing for Seth to do. I already liked him but now I like him even more." She paused to let her eyes adjust to the dim interior of the barn.

"This is also our tasting room now," Jake said, motioning to her left.

A row of stalls lined the far side of the spacious interior, but the rest of the barn had been converted into a tasting room for the winery, separated by a wall made of log and stone, with its own entrance. From what she could see beyond the double glass doors, beautiful, big oak wine barrels lined the near wall. Hardwood flooring had been installed and there was a long, polished bar of sorts in front of the space, with stools lined up along the front side. A few café-style tables and chairs dotted the space directly in front of the bar.

Outside the tasting room, there was a small office near the door they'd entered through that appeared to have at one point been one of the stalls. It had been closed in and remodeled and, from what she could see, it was nicely appointed inside, but the door was still the original stall door. She loved it. The combination of the nicely appointed tasting area and the original barn, complete with stalls and beautiful stone walls, made the place unique and inviting. All with a whiff of *eau de farm animal*, of course, but somehow it worked.

Speaking of farm animals, she heard rustling and quiet bleats coming from the stalls on the far side of the place. She looked back at Jake. "Your dad said you and one of your friends come up to help take care of the sheep and the goats?"

He nodded. "Yeah, me and Bailey. Bailey Sutton," he added. "She's eleven and used to be a foster kid, but now she lives with Addie Pearl Whitaker. They're family. Sort of." He smiled. "It's kind of a long story, but Miss Addie also runs the Bluebird Crafters Guild that operates out of the restored mill."

"Yes, we've met," Hannah said. "Addie Pearl, I mean. She's a wonder. My friends and I have talked about opening up a stall in the mill for our lavender products when the time comes. It's unbelievable what you all did with that old silk mill. I didn't even know such a thing existed."

"Most folks don't. It's a great place. My dad, Mr. B, and their friend Mr. Hartwell—Sawyer, he owns part of the place—are the ones who headed up the renovation. It was a lot of work."

Hannah heard the note of pride, and sensed Jake felt more ownership of the place than simply being the son of the guy who'd helped renovate it. "Did you pitch in, too?"

"The whole community did," he said, not taking individual credit, but she saw the way he stood a little taller.

"I'm guessing with your dad being one of the ones spearheading the operation, you likely put in more than your fair share."

"We all worked hard," he said. "Honestly, sometimes I look at it and still can't believe we got it all done."

"What a wonderful accomplishment for the whole community, then," Hannah said, charmed by his sincere humility. "I feel pretty strongly about the power of teamwork. It's amazing what people can do when they put their heads together."

"And their hands, and their backs," Jake added with a laugh. "I don't know how my dad does what he does every day. I didn't do half of what he did, and I was dog tired at the end of the day."

Hannah liked seeing the pride Jake felt for his dad. She didn't know the full story of their family dynamic and

she might never know—it was certainly none of her
business—but whatever their story was, Will had done right
by his son, there was no doubting that. He could and should
be proud.

"So, I'm guessing you don't see yourself following in
your father's footsteps, then?" Hannah asked, her tone
gently teasing.

"No," Jake said easily, taking the comment as intended.
"But Dad isn't hung up on that. I mean, if it was what I
wanted, he'd do whatever he could to help. I appreciate what
he does, more now since the renovation, and I help him out
as grunt labor from time to time, but I don't know if I see
myself going the same direction. We've talked a lot about
that in the past year or so. Ultimately, he wants me to follow
my own path. He supports that."

Hannah had been right about Jake being chatty and open
once he relaxed, and then some. She liked it. A lot. He'd be
hard not to like. "That's really good. Sounds like you two
have a good relationship."

Jake nodded. "We have our moments, but yeah. We're all
we've got. End of the day, that's what matters most."

Hannah's smile came easily, but she turned as if glancing
around the interior of the place again, hoping he hadn't noticed the quick sheen that came to her eyes just then. *Out of
nowhere.* She couldn't always hide the unexpected little
clutches. Around people she knew, she didn't bother, but
Jake didn't know her story, nor did he need to. She was truly
happy for Jake and his dad. That kind of bond was what
she wished all kids had, all parents, too. She'd have liked
to have had that bond herself growing up. She certainly
would have done her best to have had that kind of relationship with Liam. "You said 'our tasting room' earlier." She
looked back at Jake. "Is there a future vintner standing here
before me?"

Jake shrugged, but he instantly warmed to the subject.

"Maybe. Mr. B is showing me the ropes. I've been helping him more in the fields this past year. I really like the science of it all," he said, "and figuring out how the same exact steps can create a great product, or something that tastes like vinegar. Mr. B let me tend to my own section of the vineyard last year—he didn't tell me he was doing that specifically, but in the end, after harvest, he let me learn how to make grape juice from my grapes. Not fermented," he hurried to add. "My first batch was awful." He let out a short laugh. "So was my second batch. But the third one wasn't too bad. I think I've figured out a better way to prune the vines and a better extracting process, but—" He stopped then and just sort of shrugged, like maybe he'd revealed too much about his geekier side. He was an adorable mix of confident young man and shy teenager. And she'd bet he would be mortified if he knew she'd thought of him as adorable for any reason.

The notion made her smile widen. "I know exactly what you mean. I've learned more about botanical sciences in the past five months than I knew my entire life. I'm not as good at it as Avery, one of my partners in our lavender farm—she's a genius, literally—but it's still all very fascinating. We just learned to make an essential oil today. You have to distill it and capture the steam inside this tube and funnel it into a dark glass container." She paused, realizing she was the one geeking out now, and grinned.

But it had the desired effect of loosening him up again. "That sounds pretty cool," he said, and seemed to really mean it.

"You're welcome to come check it all out, anytime. Avery would be happy to give you the tour of the lab she's set up. We're learning how to make essential oils, tinctures, soap, tea. In fact, I was telling your dad that Vivi—another partner and friend of mine, who actually owns the farmhouse—is making lavender-infused cupcakes and cookies today.

As we speak, actually. She's hoping to add them to the menu for our tearoom when we get it up and running. She'd love to have another guinea pig to try them out." Hannah leaned in. "She was born in New Orleans and is an amazing— ah-mazing—cook. So, they're probably incredible."

"I'd give them a try," Jake told her, not sounding entirely sold on the idea of eating cookies made with flowers, but too polite to say so.

"You can always take a plate in to your dad and try them without her watching," Hannah told him. "Just give me a thumbs-up or -down and I'll only pass your vote along if it's good."

"I wouldn't expect you to do that."

"I'll be happy to give your grape juice a try in return," she said. "We can share our thumbs-up or -down at the same time. No harm, no foul?"

Jake laughed. "I don't know if I'm ready for that yet," he said, and she admired his honesty. "It's definitely still a work in progress. I'm not even sure I want to make wine yet. I'm interested in music, too."

"A man of many talents," she said admiringly.

He grinned. "Well, I did give up the astronaut dream, so that narrows it down a little."

Hannah laughed outright. "I don't know, maybe you could be the first man to grow grapes on Mars."

Jake's hoot of laughter was half high pitched, half croak, and entirely adorable. "I don't know, but I will say, if they ever figure out private space travel, all bets on the astronaut dream staying off the table are totally off."

Hannah raised her hand. "I'm in. I'll grow lavender in the field next to your grapes. Or in our growing pods. Or whatever they have for greenhouses on our new home planet."

"Deal," Jake said, and gave her a fist bump and they both did the exploding gesture, then laughed.

"Now I feel hip," Hannah said, still grinning. Jake was a

great kid, and she was enjoying his company immensely. Sure, there were twinges, thoughts of Liam, but she was truly glad she'd made the offer to come pick Jake up.

"So, you and—Bailey, you said her name was? I haven't met her yet. How did you two come to help out Seth with the farm animals?"

"We met when she and her sister, Sunny, came to live in the Falls. They never knew each other before then." At Hannah's surprised look, he added, "Like I said, it's a long story. Anyway, Sunny is with Sawyer now, and Bailey lives with Miss Addie. I guess it's been almost two years now or will be this fall. Seems like I've known her a lot longer."

Jake led Hannah over to the row of closed stalls. "So, Bailey was in foster care her whole life before coming here and part of that time she spent living on a farm. Sunny knew Bailey really missed that, so she got her some sheep, which she keeps up at her and Miss Addie's place. My dad, Mr. B, and Mr. Hartwell helped build and repair the pens where the sheep stay and she was at the mill a lot when we were finishing it up." He shrugged. "There aren't too many kids in the Falls, and . . . I don't know, we just became friends. She used to raise goats on the farm she lived on, so Mr. B got her a few to keep up here. I started helping Mr. B then, too, with the goats and with the sheep he got for Dex. Bailey's goats started having babies, and people wanted them. So, they worked out a deal where Mr. B pays her for her work up here with goat feed and stuff, and the money she makes from selling the goats goes to Miss Addie for Bailey's college fund. It's all cool."

Hannah nodded, truly impressed. "She sounds like an amazing girl."

"Miss Addie calls her a 'force of nature' and that's pretty much it. Bailey is very determined once she sets her mind to something, and she has this weird ability to just know things about you by looking at you. Mr. B says she's an 'old soul,' whatever that means. I guess to me she's just like my kid sister now." His tone turned dry. "But don't tell her I said that." He walked over to one of the closed stalls. "The babies are in here. She won't mind you seeing them. They're pygmy goats, so they stay pretty little—"

"Oh my goodness, look at them," Hannah said, crooning as she leaned over the stall door. The goats were tiny, not more than a foot or two tall, in varying shades of white, brown, and gray, some of them all three colors. Their coat was short but their ears were adorably fluffy, and they had little nubs on their heads. They immediately began bleating and stumbling over themselves to get to the door. Some began to hop, surprising Hannah with how high they could leap. "Oh! Oh no," she said, still laughing. She glanced at Jake. "Are they hungry? Should we not be looking in? I don't want to tease them and make them think they're going to be fed."

"They're always hungry," Jake said with an eye roll, but his tone was affectionate. He reached over the door with his long arms and plucked up one of the smaller ones. "This is Sherwin." Jake put him on the dirt floor and the baby immediately raced around the big open space, hopping and bleating.

Hannah laughed, utterly delighted. "Would you look at him! He's so adorable, I want to take him home with me."

Sherwin bounced over to them, then started nibbling on the cord of Jake's boot. He leaned down to gently pull the cord away, then scooped the little thing up in his arms. "Well, Bailey does sell them; in fact most of them are sold before they're even born. This little guy is already spoken for. Bailey never names them. She lets the new owners do that." He suddenly looked apologetic. "I'm sorry, maybe I shouldn't have picked one that wasn't—"

Hannah looked from the goat to Jake. "Oh, no, don't worry. I was only joking. Well, dreaming, more like, but that's pretty amazing. Eleven years old and she has her own goat-breeding business."

"Like I said, Bailey might be eleven in calendar years, but she's . . . well, she's like Yoda or something. Like she knows a lot more about everything than anyone else, but in a good way. She's a good judge of people, too. She sees a lot more than I do."

Hannah liked how respectful Jake was of his younger friend. "I hope I get a chance to meet her."

Jake nodded, then paused, then said, "Well, I probably shouldn't say this, but she's dying to learn how to ride. Horses, I mean. I heard your other friend—Miss McCafferty? I've heard she's maybe going to start giving lessons sometime?"

Hannah still hadn't gotten used to how everyone in Blue Hollow Falls seemed to know everything, especially when they all lived so far apart. She was surprised that anyone was paying attention to what they were doing out at the farmhouse. "She's talking about it, yes. I don't think she's decided on anything yet, though, but I'll let her know. Maybe having some local interest lined up will help sway her."

Jake nodded at that, then looked a little worried. "The thing is, Bailey doesn't have a lot of money. Like I said, what she makes with the goats—"

"Don't worry about that," Hannah interrupted gently, not wanting him to feel bad for trying to help his friend. "If and when the time comes, Cheyenne will make it work. She's great like that. If Bailey wants to ride, she'll ride. You can trust Chey."

Jake looked relieved. "Thanks. That would be awesome. I won't say anything to Bailey, though. Not until Miss McCafferty makes it official."

"Good plan," Hannah agreed. "I'll be sure to let you know one way or the other."

Jake walked over and gently deposited the baby back in with his fellow stall mates.

Hannah followed him and peered inside the stall one last time. "I never knew goats could be so darling," she said.

"They seem to have that effect on girls," Jake said, starting to walk toward another, smaller door at the rear of the barn.

"Just girls, huh?" Hannah teased, following him.

Jake glanced over to her, grinned. "They're little pieces of work, if you ask me, but I can see the appeal. I know girls like little things."

Hannah nodded, then stepped through the door that Jake held open for her. She figured he was a few years away from having girlfriends, but Hannah suspected someone was going to be very lucky to have Jake McCall looking her way.

It wasn't until she drove the two of them down the long driveway to the farmhouse an hour later that she realized she'd spent the rest of her time with Jake, including the drive back, chatting and laughing, without a single twinge about Liam. Jake got out and rolled up one of the garage doors for her. Hannah and the others had all agreed to park inside for the time being, and leave the front loop of the driveway open for the various contractors who would have to park there until the chimney situation got resolved.

She pulled in and parked, waved to Jake as he went around the side of the house to find his dad, and she went on upstairs to her loft to change her clothes, which had gotten a bit muddy tromping in the field with Dexter and the sheep. She felt good about being able to keep everything in such clear perspective, and also a tiny bit guilty. Part of her wondered how dare she lose sight of her own child while in the company of another. It was silly, that latter part, she knew. She went for long stretches without actively thinking about her loss, or of Liam, at least directly, and that was as it should be. She'd worked hard to get herself to that place.

Today, spending time with a boy who was the same age her son would be now, there was simply no avoiding the twinges, but it was also okay that she'd been able spend time with Jake without that awareness being a constant undercurrent. She walked over to the big windows at the far end of the loft and looked out at the farmhouse in time to see father and son give each other a welcome half hug, half clap-on-the-back. The guilty feeling dissipated. She looked from them out to the fields and beyond. She'd come a long way, figuratively and literally.

"And you're going to keep on going," she murmured, looking back at the house, but Will and Jake were no longer in view. "Here's to new adventures and future achievements. Whatever they may be." She gave the window a little fist bump, then did the exploding gesture. Laughing at herself, she turned away and went in search of a fresh set of clothes.

Chapter Five

"So, what do you think? Can we save it?"

Will straightened from his crouched position and took another walk around the old, stacked stone well. He turned toward Addie Pearl. "I think so. Doesn't mean it'll be functioning, though."

"Oh, I checked that out before I called you," Addie said, waving away his concern. "Didn't want you making the trip down here for nothing. I tossed a stone in, heard water when it finally hit bottom. The springs are still feeding it."

Sometimes it was just that simple, Will thought. "As overgrown as this was before you cleared away the brambles and vines, I imagine there's a fair bit of nature down in there, too."

She nodded. "That was my next question. Do you have any connections or recommendations on who I could get up here to clear the thing out? Once we've got it restored, with a new crank and handle, I'll make a cover for it."

"I can clear it out for you," he told her. It would be a pain, but for Addie, he'd do that and a lot more.

Addie Pearl was Addison Pearl Whitaker, born and raised in the Falls, and lifelong friend to Will's mom, Dorothy. At seventy-four, she could still exhaust most folks half her age with her stamina and determination. She was a master weaver, among other things, and had been the driving force behind launching the Bluebird Crafters Guild. The town largely had her to thank for seeing to it that the centuries-old, abandoned silk mill she partially owned was renovated and turned into something useful. Now an artisan center and soon-to-be music venue thanks to Seth's wife, Pippa, the mill at Blue Hollow Falls was a thriving community for the artist colony Addie Pearl had slowly been cultivating in the area. It was also a growing tourist boon and source of increased income to the entire town.

Will had done a large part of that renovation himself. It had been back-breaking labor, all of it contributed as a volunteer. Happily so. But he could still remember those times when he'd be dragging himself out to his truck after putting in a full day tacking down that slate roof, or rebuilding the stone wall that partly surrounded the place, and Addie, who'd been up since before dawn, running ragged herself, was still just as spry as she'd been when she'd brought them all coffee just after sunrise that morning. Oftentimes, she'd be heading home to start work on her latest loom-weaving project, while Will wanted nothing more than to eat, shower, and face plant into bed.

"Wonderful," Addie said, looking satisfied. "I truly appreciate the effort. Let me know if there's anything I can do, or tools I can provide to make it easier to clear out."

She turned and looked at the small pasture that ran down the slope in front of them. Her log-on-log, cabin-style house was perched up the steep incline of pines, boulders, and woods behind them, almost directly overhead. Several sections of the pasture before them had been fenced off, and there were a few outbuildings dotting the edges. One old stone building, one shed—both recently restored—and two newer buildings that had just been put up in the past year.

Will knew all this, because he'd helped Sawyer and Seth build them.

The fenced-in areas held Bailey's Herdwick sheep, with the stone building doubling as a place to keep the new babies that had started to come. The shed held the feed and other supplies, and the new buildings held fully enclosed pens that acted as a stable of sorts during extreme bad weather. Herdwicks were native to England's Lake District, on the small end, size-wise, and hardy, making them the perfect breed to handle the elevation, the terrain, and the elements here. Addie's place was at a higher elevation than both the mill and Seth's winery, up close to the peak of Hawk's Nest Ridge, which soared above them in all its jagged, granite glory. Sawyer and Sunny's place was just down the ridgeline, nestled in a beautiful, high pocket meadow. The view up here never ceased to fill his heart.

"The well will come in handy," Will told her, turning back to it. "You won't have to run hose all the way from that tapped spring."

"My thoughts exactly. Would be worth the effort, most assuredly." She ran a hand along the partially tumbled stone along one side of the well rim. "And it's a piece of history. The hands that laid these stones made use of this land long before I was born into it. Seems right."

Will nodded. "Agreed."

She beamed up at him and nodded, the matter settled. She wore her long hair pulled back in a skinny gray braid that hung all the way to her belt loops. Her face was weathered, lined, and tanned, a beautiful testament to a life happily lived. What caught and held most folks' attention, though, wasn't that she was short, just an inch or two past the five-foot mark, with broad hips bracketed by narrow shoulders above and skinny, but sturdy, legs below. Nor was it that she favored tie-dyed shirts tucked into army shorts that hung down below those knobby knees, their frayed, cut-off edges stopping just above her well-worn leather boots. Or even the variety of old beat-up hats she favored, season-depending. At the moment, she was wearing an old, soil-and-sweat-stained canvas hat that looked like it had come straight off an Australian cattle station. One half of the brim was tacked up on the side, and the knotted cord fell below her bony chin. And every part of the getup suited her to a tee.

No, what caught and held one's attention, even when cast in the shadows beneath the wonky brim of that hat, were her lavender eyes. They were pale, but crystalline sharp, like sunlight piercing through amethysts. Will had always thought she had some kind of special powers that enabled her to see far beyond the gaze of the mere mortal eye. Everything he'd learned since moving to the Falls had only cemented that belief.

"Work me up an estimate and I'll cut you a check for materials," she told him.

He nodded. "You know I've got that chimney and fireplace work out at the old March place to finish up first. Turns out there's more to do there than I realized, and it's put me behind a bit on two other jobs I've already committed to doing. I've been rotating among the three. The other two will be done by end of next week, weather permitting, so I can rotate you in then, if that's okay by you."

Addie nodded and they turned to head back up the steep trail to her house. Today she was using a hand-hewn hiking stick made from a hickory tree. She had a whole umbrella stand full of hiking sticks on her porch and another one, equally full, inside her house. The knob of this one had been carved into the head of a pileated woodpecker, probably a gift from one of the guild members. They had a few woodcarvers who did amazing work. Addie never went anywhere without one of her sticks, despite the fact that Will had never once seen her breathing hard, or covering ground in anything less than a determined stride. Now was no different.

"I heard about that chimney coming down," she said. "Not a surprise, I suppose, but a shame. How are things going out at Lavender Blue otherwise?" She made steady progress, chatting easily as they traversed the steep incline. "I'm happy to see new life being breathed into that old place. Sat empty for far too long. Drove by and was amazed they were able to recover as much of the planted fields as they have. Lavender is pretty hardy, though, so they lucked out with that. Not so much with the old house I'm guessing."

She's part Sherpa, Will decided with an inner head shake, pacing his words when he replied so he wouldn't sound like he was wheezing. *And you thought you were fit.* "You guessed right," he said. "Going well, though. The chimney work, anyway."

"That's good to hear. They've been working so hard since they took over the place. I've been meaning to get back out there once everything started blooming, meet the rest of them. I've only met Vivienne and Hannah so far. But with the music venue about to open at the mill, I just haven't had time."

Will didn't want to talk about the music venue. He heard enough about it from Jake. It was still a tough subject for Will. Jake honored his sensitivity as best he could, but Will knew his son was excited about his opportunity to perform there with Seth's wife, Pippa, during the festival that was set to launch the place in late August. Will was supportive of his son's new passion for music, proud of him for wanting to follow in his mother's footsteps, and his own as well, but that didn't mean Will was handling it any better now than he had when he'd first heard his son sing and play the fiddle the previous summer.

Jake sounded just like Zoey. And he seemed to have Will's own talent on the fiddle. Will had been teaching Zoey to play when she'd died and knew he should have had a hand in teaching his own son to play. He told himself that Jake had gotten a far better deal learning from Pippa, who happened to be one of the best fiddle players on earth. Most days that assuaged his guilt over not participating directly in his son's musical discovery. Most days. Will hadn't touched a fiddle, much less made one, in a very, very long time. *Twelve years ago. Twelve and a half, actually.*

He shut all of that down, and the memories that would come along with it, shoving them back up on a dark shelf where they belonged. With all the rest of the things he didn't want to think about. Or deal with. Jake was happy; he was getting to do what he loved. That was what mattered. "I know they'd like to see you out there," he told Addie. "They seem to be taking all the work and repairs in stride. Things are going as planned, at least as much as I can tell. We've only talked about the repairs to the house, so I don't really know."

As they hit a switchback on the trail Addie paused and looked at him. "You've been out there for what, three weeks now? A month?"

"About that. Three of the four chimneys needed a full rebuild. Takes time." He was thankful for the pause and tried not to look like he was sucking air.

"No doubt," she said, then pinned him with that crystalline gaze of hers. "Wasn't my point."

Will swallowed a sigh. This was another thing he didn't want to deal with, but he suspected he wasn't going to have the luxury of shoving it on a shelf, as he did with the memories of his late wife, something that had become harder and harder now that his son had gotten older and wanted to know more about her. Will's mother had shared a great many stories with Jake when he was little, but he was eager to hear the stories only Will would know. "I'm not much for small talk, Addie."

She snorted. "Tell me something I don't know." She

shifted her weight and leaned both hands on the head of her stick, clearly not planning to move on until she'd had her say.

Will knew better than to hurry her up. Better to let her get it out so they could go on with their day. It would just postpone the inevitable if he didn't. He sensed she'd been building up to speaking her mind for some time. This wasn't the first pointed hint she'd dropped. She'd helped him with Jake since his mother had passed, so she had ample opportunity to make her opinions known to him. *She's certainly never shy about it, either,* he thought with an inward sigh, and braced himself for what was about to come.

"You take after your daddy that way," Addie said. "Only met the man one time, the day he married your mama, but Dottie used to say that trying to get that man to have a decent conversation was like pulling teeth."

Will flashed a brief smile at that. "She might have mentioned that a time or two to me as well." Had it been left up to him, Will couldn't have said if he would ever have gotten past being a polite acquaintance of his mother's dearest, lifelong friend. He'd met her first as a child when he'd come to stay with his grandparents, but Addie had just been another adult neighbor to him at the time.

Addie Pearl, however, had made up her mind on that subject the moment Will had moved to the Falls full time to help care for his mother in her final days. Addie had already gotten to know Jake quite well by then, seeing as he'd come to live with Will's mother five years earlier, after Zoey's death. Will had come to the Falls in between missions, but his stretches stateside had been brief, and he'd spent most of those times focused on being with Jake and helping his mom, knocking down the lengthy to-do list that always built up while he was gone. Those had been some of the best times of his life back then. He'd missed Jake so much. And his mom had been a parent, ally, and friend to him, which had helped ground him. Because those had also been some of the hardest times for him. "The colonel was better at giving orders," Will told Addie, referring to his father. "He preferred 'discussing' things rather than talking about them, which meant he lectured and we listened."

"Sounds about right," Addie said with a laugh, her expression one of fond reminiscence. "From what I heard, she was pretty good at getting your daddy to do her bidding, though. She just had to learn how to make him think it was his idea all along." Addie gave him a sideways look. "Might have said the same about you, once or twice."

Will chuckled then. "Sounds about right," he said, echoing her earlier comment. They both shared a laugh. For all that the colonel had been a gruff sort who didn't suffer fools gladly, there had never been a single doubt in Will's mind that his father was head-over-heels in love with his wife. Will's mother had a way of smiling at his father, or saying just the right thing, usually something that meant nothing to Will, but was clearly some kind of private thing between the two of them, and his big bear of a father would grin and let out a rarely heard belly laugh . . . then do whatever she asked of him.

Will was certain it would shock the men who had served under his father, but the colonel had staged some elaborate surprises for his wife and for Will when he'd been stationed for long stretches in places where they couldn't accompany him, always thoughtful and perfect. At the same time, the colonel had been hard on his only son, expecting the best, and Will had always worked very hard to give it to him. His father had been both his hero and his mentor, and Will had wanted nothing more than to follow in the colonel's footsteps. And he had. To a point, anyway. The colonel had loved Zoey, and it was Will's deepest regret that he hadn't lived long enough to meet Jake. Will would have enjoyed nothing more than seeing his old man play grandpa.

"Your mama was the opposite of him," Addie Pearl said

on a happy sigh. "Dottie could chat up anyone. Even when we were all back in school, I used to say she could make a lifelong friend just standing on line at the grocery."

Will nodded, warmed by the memory. "That was definitely true. She had more friends than I could count. I remember when she was first diagnosed. I shipped home not forty-eight hours later, and the dining room table, the kitchen counter, the fridge, the freezer, you name it, were full of more casseroles and covered dishes than I'd ever seen. I didn't even know there were that many people in the Falls."

"I believe it," Addie Pearl said, her eyes misting over a bit. "Your mama was well loved, and you can't ask for a better thing than that in this life. I'm glad she moved back home after your daddy passed. I think it was the best thing she could have done for herself. Even after all those years she spent traipsing around the globe, we missed her so much and were so happy to have her back. I miss her all the time." Addie looked at Will. "I know how proud she'd be of you, the life you've built, that you stayed on here to raise Jake in the only place he really knows."

Will glanced down then, thinking he wasn't so sure about that. His mom would be proud of Jacob, certainly, and happy Will had stayed in the home that his grandfather had built with help from his own father. But Will suspected his mom would have long since lost patience with her only child's lack of progress in his personal life. She'd been prodding him even before she'd taken ill. Toward the end, it had been a constant topic of conversation. One he'd ducked as often as she'd brought it up. He smiled then, thinking that she'd outsmarted him there, too. She'd left behind a grandson to take care of that mission for her. Jake was gradually tearing down all those walls Will had so carefully built up after Zoey died, one stubborn brick at a time. *Maybe you should work a little harder at helping him out with that.*

"Don't think you're distracting me from my point," Addie told him.

Will sighed and chuckled at the same time, then lifted his gaze to hers. "Which is?"

"Even for someone who thinks one complete sentence is all the conversation he needs, how can you spend a month around those lovely women out at Lavender Blue and not glean at least some information? Through observation if nothing else?"

"Practice," Will replied solemnly, his lips curving when Addie swatted his shoulder. "Okay, okay." He closed his eyes briefly, picturing the farm. "The house needs a lot of work still. They get one thing done, and something else falls apart, or springs a leak. I've seen electricians out there, plumbers, a drywall crew, and a few new appliances getting hauled in. Nothing surprising, given the age of the place. As I said, Ms. Baudin does take it all in stride. They all do. I think they knew, or at least had an inkling, what they were getting into."

"See?" Addie said, rubbing the spot where she'd swatted him, then giving it a little pat. "That wasn't so hard."

Amused, Will shook his head. "Haven't a clue about their business plans, though."

"They must be excited about it all. Surely they're discussing it."

Will thought about the excited sparkle in Hannah's eyes when she'd told him about their experiments with the products they wanted to sell, about almost burning down the kitchen, and how none of that daunted her enthusiasm or love for the place. In fact, he thought it just made her feel more attached. "Oh, they talk nonstop," he said to Addie, sidestepping that little conversation they'd shared. "I just don't listen." He held up a hand when Addie would have interrupted. "I focus on my work and try not to get in their way."

Addie made a "mm-hmm," sound, but kept studying him.

"What?" he asked at length, half annoyed, but also half amused, knowing she'd tell him anyway.

"Lately, when Jake's been here, every other sentence out of his mouth starts with 'Miss Hannah said' or 'Miss Hannah told me.'"

Will didn't have to be told that. He'd been on the receiving end of much the same. He smiled at Addie. "Maybe you should get him to be your gossip spy then."

"Don't be smart with me now," she said, pointing the knob of her cane at him, only half teasing.

"Yes, ma'am," Will said sincerely, though the smile was still there. "He would be the one to ask, though. I've had him working with me helping to clear out the chimney and fireplace rubble from inside the house and I swear every time he passes through the kitchen, someone is feeding him something or asking him to give them his opinion on some product they're making. If you want to know anything and everything about Lavender Blue, he's your guy."

"He's told me a little about what they're working on," she admitted. "Apparently they have something of a lab set up there. Sounds very scientific and all. I'm more for just grinding things up or boiling them down. But though he talks about all four of the women, he seems mostly taken with Miss Montgomery. Said something about giving her a tour of Seth's winery when she came to pick him up last week. Sounds as if they hit it off like champs."

"She was kind enough to do me a favor the day the chimney came down. And you know how Jake is about the winery. My guess is they bonded over farming or something, given they're both new to the process of growing things." Anything that encouraged his son to focus more on farming and less on endless discussions of the new outdoor amphitheater got Will's vote.

"What about you? What's your opinion of Miss Montgomery?"

"I think she's a little old for him," Will said dryly, then lifted his hands before Addie could swat him again. "She seems nice," he said, relenting, trying—and failing—not to think about how Hannah had felt in his arms, how that gray-eyed gaze of hers had met his and just held on, reached in. "I don't know much about her, really." That much was true. Not that it had stopped him from thinking about her. All the damn time. He'd tried telling himself it was just because he hadn't held any woman in his arms in such a long time. *Yeah, and how is that working out for you?*

"Neither do I," Addie said, clearly a bit put out by that fact, drawing his attention back to the moment at hand.

Will knew better than to smile. Truth was, Addie wasn't much for spreading gossip. If you told her something, and asked her to keep it to herself, she'd go to the grave with it. No one was more trustworthy. But spreading gossip wasn't the same as listening to it, or perhaps asking a few leading questions here and there, to get folks to reveal what they knew. Consequently, if you wanted to know anything about anything, or anyone, Addie Pearl would be your first stop. Of course, she'd only tell you if she thought it was something you needed to know.

"I did look up her work online," Addie said. "Lovely illustrations. She's quite talented."

"Illustrations?"

Addie Pearl looked surprised. "Well, I thought you'd have learned at least that much. She is—or was—a children's book illustrator. Two different series of picture books, one for prereaders, about a precocious rabbit, and one for young readers, about a girl who has big adventures right in her own backyard. Quite popular from what I can tell. Won some awards, did quite well for themselves if the number of glowing reviews mean anything."

"You said 'was,'" he said. "She doesn't illustrate anymore?" Too late, he realized that by asking any question about Hannah, he'd given away his interest. Or his . . . something. He wasn't sure what it was he thought or felt about Hannah Montgomery. "Interesting profession," he said, trying to pass it off as casual curiosity, but Addie saw right through that.

"I'm not sure. From what little I saw, it seems that both of those children's book series have been completed. If she's working on anything else, something new, I couldn't say. There was a lot of information on the authors of both of the series, but nothing much on her. Which, I suppose, isn't all that odd. Most folks probably think the authors do the drawings. She doesn't have a Web site, or even a Facebook page. Rather an enigma." Addie lifted a shoulder, as if it was neither here nor there to her, but her gaze had remained steady and unwaveringly on Will as she spoke.

He should be used to Addie's spooky, penetrating looks by now, but he wasn't. Doubted he'd ever be. It was those eyes of hers. "Maybe she just likes her privacy," Will said, sending a little pointed look of his own.

To her credit, Addie Pearl's expression was both knowing and a bit abashed. "Well, if you're truly not interested, I'll let the topic be." She turned to continue their hike up the trail.

"Why would you think I'm interested?" Will wasn't sure why he'd continued the conversation. One thing he knew about Addie Pearl, though, was that she didn't do anything on a whim, or without forethought. He was sincerely curious about what had spurred this conversation, and he doubted it was his son's preoccupation with the pretty illustrator-turned-farmer.

Addie paused, turned, and didn't look remotely surprised by his question. To her credit, she didn't look smug, either. "Jake said you've talked to Hannah yourself a few times."

"About the repairs, yes."

"Wouldn't that be something you'd take up with Ms. Baudin?"

"I do that, too. She's not always around." Will walked closer, and they both turned and continued their hike upward. When Addie didn't say anything, clearly expecting more from him, Will finally relented. "She seems like a very nice person. She was kind enough to help me out, and she and Jake did hit it off. He's . . . he's changed a lot in the last year or two. Not as shy as he was, more confident. I think his friendship with Bailey has a lot to do with that. She's drawn him out of his shell, expecting—well, demanding, in her own way—that he keep up with her." He smiled. "All for the good if you ask me. And probably also because he's just growing up."

"He is indeed," Addie said. She laid a hand on Will's arm and added, "I know you don't want to hear this, or talk about it, but his fiddle playing and his singing have had a lot to do with that, too." She waited until Will turned his head to meet her gaze.

He felt sucker-punched, so it took him a moment longer than he'd wanted it to.

"Aw, honey," she said at whatever it was she saw in his eyes. Then she did something that few others would have ever taken the liberty to do, but she'd done since first laying eyes on him—she slid her arm around his waist and hugged him. Not a polite hug, but the tight hold of one person comforting another. And she held on until he felt compelled to hug her back. "I know it's hard," she said quietly, but surprisingly firmly, her cheek pressed against his chest as she rubbed his back with the palm of her free hand.

"It was a long time ago," he said, his voice a shade rougher than he'd have hoped. She said nothing, just kept holding on. "I should be past it," he heard himself say, not wanting to, just . . . compelled to. "I know that."

"Jacob sings like an angel," Addie Pearl said. "Plays like one, too." She finally released her hold enough to look up at him. At least he felt her shift away. His eyes were closed. "I know hearing him has to fill you with equal parts joy and pain. Maybe it would help to put yourself in Zoey's place. I don't mean to do what she would do, but to take it all in, hear Jacob, let his pure passion fill you, so you can pass it on up to her. You're not doing it for her, or in place of her, but sharing it directly with her. Maybe it won't make you feel her loss so much that way. Does that make sense?"

Will had already tensed and started throwing walls up, even before Addie had spoken. He'd heard variations on "what would Zoey want you to do" more times than he cared to count, and the bulk of those times had come from his own inner voice. But Addie's words, her take on it, caught him by surprise.

And he spoke before he had a chance to rein himself in. "I want Jake to feel connected to his mom," Will told her, quite truthfully. "He was too young when she passed to have any direct memories of her. My mom told him hundreds of stories, shared all the photos we have, so Jake knows a lot about his mother, even if he doesn't remember her. All the scrapbooks are still in the house. He can look through them whenever he wants." Will paused, then sighed, and said, "That used to be enough."

Addie slid her arms free, then rubbed her palm over Will's heart, before giving it a gentle pat and stepping back. "I know he wants things from you that are painful to give— all the stories you know that his grandma didn't. Stories about the three of you that only you could share. They're up to you to tell, or not. Just know that he'll be fine with them and without them. Don't pressure yourself so hard on that."

Surprised again, Will met her gaze. "It's not that I don't want him to know. It just . . . brings it all back to the front again."

"I know." And somehow, Will knew she did.

"I should have found a way to deal with it back then," he admitted. "When it happened. I just . . ." He looked away, trying to push it all back down, but now that they'd started, the words just seemed to force their way up and out, no longer willing to be contained. "I missed her so damn much. I felt lost without her, and not a little terrified of how I was going to handle raising our son. Not the day-to-day, but the emotional part of it. She was wonderful at that, a fantastic mom, it was all just so natural to her. And I . . . am more like my dad, I guess. I worried that I wouldn't be enough. That I'd screw up all the good she'd done with Jacob already."

He looked away, hoping, praying, Addie Pearl would step in. Say something, anything. He never talked about this. Not ever. Not even with his mother, who'd tried, but had eventually respected his decision to handle it his own way. Now that he'd opened the gates, he felt as though he was standing on the edge of a black, yawning hole that wanted to just suck him down right inside it. And he had no way of knowing if he'd ever be able to climb out again.

But Addie didn't say anything, and the words were all there now, like a force, gathering strength in his gut, in the back of his throat, and it was as if he had to say them, or risk choking on them. "She was my rock," he said, his voice rough with the tension gripping his throat. "My friend, my ally, my cohort. She was my wife, and Jake's mom. I felt anchored, tethered to the best things that life could offer. I was happy, and so damn grateful. I didn't just feel like the luckiest man on earth, I *knew* I was."

He paused, his throat threatening to close over. "When we lost her, just like that, I . . . I couldn't process it. I was half a world away, and I couldn't save her. It was Christmas

Eve, and I couldn't be there when they called to tell my mom about the car accident. That she'd been—" He did stop then, ducking his chin, closing his eyes, wanting to grab his heart and just yank it out. Maybe then it wouldn't hurt so damn much. "I . . . I couldn't get a grip on the fact that I'd never see her again, never talk to her again." His voice was gravel now. "There were so many things I hadn't said, wanted to say, so many things left for us to do together. And I just couldn't . . . I couldn't find my way out of that grief. I felt like I'd been ripped in two. And that terrified me, too. It was my job to be in charge of men whose lives depended on me. And I couldn't save the one person who meant more to me than anyone in this world." He pressed the bridge of his nose, at the corners of his eyes, then dropped his hand away, his eyes damp.

He'd cried exactly once since Zoey died. The night he first heard Jake sing and play the fiddle. That had been almost a year ago, and he'd tried—he truly had—to open up more, to be more willing to get in touch with the grief he'd buried so deeply, to find a way to make peace with it. But . . . old habits died hard, and he just couldn't manage to face the hell he needed to crawl through, when there was no promise that peace would be waiting for him on the other side. He'd been managing just fine, for a long, long time. Why couldn't he keep on doing it his way?

"It was having Jake that made me keep it together. I couldn't fall apart. I had to go on, I had to be able to do my job, to take care of him. So . . . I just shoved the pain down, assuming in time I'd find a way through it. After a while, that becomes second nature. And I have moved on. I've built a good life, managed to do okay by Jake, with a lot of help from my mom, and now from you. He's a good kid, and I feel, well, not confident, but less terrified." The corners of his mouth twitched. "Most days." He let out a sigh, then, and regained a bit of a grip on his control. Thinking about

Jake always steadied him. That had become second nature, too. That much, at least, was a good thing. "I handled my mom's illness, and her passing. It was merciful when it finally came. I miss her, but the grief is different there. I've made peace with it. So, I know I can do it. I just . . . we had plenty of time to say all that needed saying, to say good-bye. It wasn't like that with Zoey. No warning, no chance to do anything, say anything."

"That's the first time you've ever said her name to me. Do you know that?"

Startled, he said, "No, I'm sure I—"

Addie shook her head. "So that's a good thing, you know? Some things don't get better in time, but some things do. And I know you want things to be better. Or easier. Jake's a dear, and he doesn't want to hurt you. I think he really wants you to be proud of what he's doing. It's a tribute to you, to your skill at fiddle playing, at fiddle making, as much as it is to his mom and her singing."

"I am proud," Will said, his throat tightening up all over again. "Very. I've told him that. He knows he has my full support. I just . . . don't listen to his music much." *Or at all, not if you can help it.* It wasn't something he was proud of. "He sounds so much like her. And that's a good thing in this world, a great thing. Her—Zoey's—voice, was how we met," he said. "She was singing the night I met her, with a little trio, just off base. I was playing with a few of my buddies after her set." He sighed again, this time in fond remembrance. "I think I fell in love that night. But as I got to know her, those feelings only got stronger. Music was always a strong bond between us. I know it doesn't seem like it, but I am . . ." He searched for the right words to do justice to the immenseness of what Jake's gift meant to him. "I'm thrilled, relieved, so many things too big to name with words, that a part of her—of Zoey—" he said, making himself say her name out loud, realizing Addie was right. He hadn't known that he'd protected himself so deeply, buried his grief so deeply, he couldn't even say her name. It made him feel ashamed. And cowardly. Zoey deserved so much better than that, so much better than him.

Addie laid her hand on his arm again, then pressed her palm to his heart once more, and waited until he could open his eyes and look at her. "Because in Jake, part of her is still here, walking this earth," Addie said. "I know you have felt saved by that, and terrified by it, too, in equal measure. Maybe . . . just maybe, now is the time to find a way to start celebrating it, too."

He looked at Addie, knowing his expression was bleak. "I don't know how, Addie Pearl. If time was going to heal me, wouldn't it have happened already?"

She didn't look at him with pity, or even sorrow. What he saw on her face looked more like . . . determination.

She took in a long, easy breath and let it out the same way. He felt himself doing the same, willing a calmness to enter him, to soothe some of the ragged edges.

A smile creased her weathered face, filling her ancient-as-the-hills eyes with a clear, beatific glow. "So, here's the thing about time, and about healing," she said quietly, gently, and kindly.

Will waited for her to tell him he needed to find a good counselor and work through the grief he'd bottled up for way too long. He might shock her by telling her he'd already been considering that very thing, quite seriously. He wasn't ashamed to admit he could use some help. He just had no idea where to turn to find it. *And maybe you could have worked a little harder to figure it out.*

"Sometimes we just get stuck," Addie told him. "Or a part of us does. Doesn't keep us from going on about our daily lives, living, working, appreciating our blessings, overcoming the obstacles. That's how life is. But sometimes those little parts just stay stuck in the convenient cubbyholes we've put them into so we can ignore them. For them, time stands still. We don't work on them, try not to think about them. Sometimes with neglect, by starving them from being fed any fear, or anger, or pain, they wither and die all on their own. In those cases, time, all by itself, does heal. And when we do take them out and examine them later on, we discover that we have truly moved on and they have no power over us any longer." She tucked her walking stick in the crook of her arm and brushed her palms together, as if whisking away the last of a few crumbs.

She didn't have to tell him that his wasn't one of those cases.

"In my seventy-some-odd years on this earth, I've become a firm believer that not everything that's ever happened to us in life needs to be worked on or sorted out." She put the tip of her stick back on the ground. "Sometimes the very best thing—the kindest thing—you can do for yourself, is to just forget it, or at least shove it in some dark place and leave it be. Bad things, sad things, doesn't matter. Let them shrivel up and die." She leaned both hands on the knob of her hiking stick and held his gaze purposefully, but easily. "Not everything festers if left unattended. And if it's not affecting your life, your ability to live it as you please, then"—she shrugged—"who cares? The past is the past is the past. Focus on the now, look toward the future."

"Okay," Will said, even though he wasn't sure that that was okay at all. Which made no sense since she sounded like she was making his case for him.

She lifted a hand when he opened his mouth to speak. "The thing is," she went on, "sometimes, they just stay sealed up, as fresh as they were when we put them there. You can go on getting by for a very long time, with those things boxed up and forgotten, and all is well. Then something comes along and jerks them out of that cubbyhole, rips off the lid, and there they are, just as fresh and alive and powerful as they were the day you stuck them there. That's the downside, the risk of not dealing with stuff when it happens. Because you can't always know which ones will die, and which ones won't, until they get sprung on you, and knock your world sideways all over again."

"It's not that I don't want help, Addie," Will said.

"I'm not here advocating for help," Addie Pearl said flatly. "As far I can tell, you'll either spend time dealing with loss when it happens, or later on when it gets sprung on you. It's rarely a convenient time, then or now. And hey, maybe you can get away with never dealing with it, so sticking it in that dark, airless cubbyhole can be a risk worth taking."

He was just plain confused now. "Then what are you advocating?"

Her expression softened. "The thing is, sometimes you think you're going along, living your best life, content to leave those cubbyholes all sealed up, when the truth is, you're really not."

"If this is about Jake needing more of a connection to Zoey—"

"Jake is fine," she said, waving her hand. "He'll do fine whether you talk to him about his mom or not. I'm talking about you."

"Me?" Will said. "I'm fine. My only concern is for Jake. I don't want to let him down. I—"

"Then don't," she said matter-of-factly. "From the sound of it, you aren't. He's doing what he loves, finding fulfillment in that. You can't always be everything he needs you to be, and he can't always be everything you wish he would be. You're giving him all the tools he needs, all the love, all the support. He knows it, too. He's fine. Better than."

"Then what—"

"*You're* not fine." She stepped closer, reached up and cupped his cheek, and looked deeply into his eyes. "Honey,

Jake will be all grown up and gone before you know it. If you think the years have flown by, you ain't seen nuthin' yet. Right now he's figuring out how to be the man he wants to become. So, naturally, he's looking toward the two people who made him for some answers. While he's busy finding his, I can't think of a better time for you to maybe find a few of your own. Like, what kind of man you want to become, when you've only got yourself to fend for and take care of." She patted his cheek knowingly, almost cheerfully, as she stepped back. "Then you'll both be ready for what comes next."

Chapter Six

"That's very sweet of you to offer," Hannah told Jake as she guided her Jeep up the steep driveway that led even higher into Hawk's Nest Ridge. "But Addie Pearl isn't expecting another mouth to feed, and I—"

"She always makes enough to feed twice as many people as she expects."

"And probably depends on those leftovers," Hannah told him, not allowing herself to be swayed by his eager, boyish charm. "So she only has to cook for an army every other night."

Not to be so easily outmaneuvered, Jake said, "Well, I'll only have one serving then, so it won't matter either way." He grinned triumphantly.

"And if you saw how much he can put away, you'd know that extra helping would feed you and two of your closest friends." This from Bailey, who was riding shotgun.

Hannah caught Jake's sheepish shrug in her rearview mirror, as he didn't deny the truth of that statement. She couldn't help it—she laughed. "Very gallant of you, kind sir," she told Jake as she parked the car in front of Addie's beautifully restored log cabin.

They all climbed out and closed their doors. Jake and Bailey started toward the front porch, but Hannah stopped to take in the full impact of her surroundings. "Oh my, would you look at this," she breathed as she took a slow turn around. "The view from inside must be breathtaking," she said, feeling her heart fill as it did every time she stepped outside the farmhouse. Soaring pines crowded the log cabin on either side and filled in most of the front yard, such as it was. The parts of the property that weren't pine-needle-carpeted moss were filled with jutting mounds of dark gray granite boulders and flat, silvery-green shale.

The backyard, on the other hand, was nonexistent. In fact, it appeared as if the ground fell away in a sheer drop right behind the house. There was a deep deck that wrapped from the side of the house around to the back, much like the one Jake had described at his house. The McCalls' house, Hannah knew, was down closer to Blue Hollow Falls, perched on a wooded hill that sloped all the way down to Big Stone Creek. Jake had told her that the wide mountain stream roared right through their property. The sound of it, rushing and tumbling past, was the white noise that Jake said he and his dad fell asleep to every night. Not that she'd ever been there to hear it for herself. Or wanted to go. *Liar.*

"Do you have time to walk down the trail to see my sheep?" Bailey asked, moving back to where Hannah stood.

"It's kind of steep," Jake said, once again glancing somewhat despairingly at Hannah's footwear.

She saw his gaze and grinned, lifting one foot so he could see the bottom of the flat, Teva-style sandals. "Check out the tread," she said proudly. "Good for hiking and, well, just making it around my own property." She looked past Jake and Bailey to where the trees parted beside the house and noticed what looked like a trail leading into the woods, then disappearing rather abruptly as the property dropped off. "I'm not sure about the climbing part, though," she admitted, her smug smile fading. "I have my rubber boots, but though they are great for mud, I'm not thinking they're going to be great on steep terrain."

She knew what she was talking about, at least as far as the mud was concerned. The weather for the previous week had been a steady, thumping downpour, turning the pathways between the rows of lavender bushes into a thick, gloppy, muddy bog. Avery had assured them the lavender would be fine; the drainage system that had been set up as part of the cultivation plan back when the lavender had first been planted years ago would still function as intended now that they'd cleared everything out.

Hannah now knew that the fields had been planted so that the rain and snowmelt would naturally drain downslope, with the run-off flowing into the large pond at the bottom of the hill, and the small creek beyond. If the pond flooded and the creek breached its banks, both of which had happened this week, the pond and creek were situated far enough downhill that the water didn't threaten the plants or any of the buildings on the property. Someone had been very smart when designing the layout of the farm, for which Hannah was continually grateful. She wouldn't have known to even think about such things.

Those same downpours had kept Jake and his dad from finishing up the work on the chimneys at Lavender Blue. Will had been off working one of his indoor jobs while the weather was poor, so she hadn't seen him in over a week. Not that she missed seeing him. *Liar, liar.*

"It's not so muddy up here now," Jake said. "The water runs straight down into the springs, and the wind dries us out pretty quickly. But if you'd rather wait until you get some hiking boots, maybe next time?"

He said it so hopefully, Hannah didn't want to remind him that she was only up there to drop him off, along with a poster she wanted to give Addie Pearl announcing Lavender Blue's big, or hopefully big, "Welcome to the Farm" event slated for the last weekend in June. She'd done the artwork herself, and Avery had helped her with the graphics; then they'd had a stack of them printed down in Turtle Springs.

Hannah had dropped one off at Seth's winery first, as he'd planned to put one up in his tasting room. She'd talked to him the week before about possibly featuring his wine at the event, so they could cross-promote, and he'd readily agreed, all of which Hannah was very excited about.

When she'd dropped it off, he'd mentioned that he could take one up to Addie, who would put it up on the big, enclosed bulletin board outside the mill, where they advertised local events and other places that visitors to the mill might enjoy seeing while in the Falls. He said he'd drop it off when he took Jake and Bailey home, so she'd offered to do it for him. She'd been wanting to talk to Addie about the event, as well as some other ideas she'd been toying with. She'd already been planning to sell her artwork, watercolors mostly, all of local scenery, in the Lavender Blue gift shop, along with their other products. But that wasn't going to be happening for some time yet, and she could only live off the money she'd made from selling her home and her book royalties for so long. So she was thinking about getting her own stall in the mill, too, maybe sooner than later, and wanted to talk to Addie about formally joining the guild. She knew that would entail doing some demonstrations, maybe teaching, as that was what the guild was all about, and she was okay with the idea. Excited, actually.

All of it was exciting. The idea for the community event had been Vivi's. After months of blood, sweat, and tears— all four of them experiencing each of those pretty much in equal measure—Lavender Blue seemed to be suddenly coming together very fast. It was thrilling and not a little daunting. They still had many more obstacles to be hurdled, not all of which would happen by their first big preopening event. The tearoom would have to wait until closer to the fall—who knew you needed that many permits to serve tea and scones—along with other repairs and restorations. But this would be their big start, their first introduction of themselves and their new business venture. New life venture.

"I'm not sure when I'll get back up here again," she told Jake truthfully, not wanting to let him down, but actually unsure just how involved she wanted to be with Will's son. She adored Jake—it was impossible not to. He was earnest and bright, a bit nerdy and apparently quite talented. She identified with all of that. He was at that awkward stage between adolescence and adulthood, when you want so badly to be smooth, and inevitably end up at least a little bit goofy. She remembered those feelings all too clearly herself.

The crestfallen look on his face tugged at a different part of her heart.

Jake had come out to the farmhouse regularly after their serendipitous jaunt through Bluestone & Vine, helping his dad with clearing the chimney rubble. She'd been relieved and happy to discover that the initial little jabs to her heart that had come with the unavoidable comparisons between Jake and Liam had diminished. There were pings, to be sure, but they were tempered now with her sincere fondness for the young man. And that was a good thing, a reaffirming thing . . . she just wasn't certain she wanted to deepen the relationship any further. Selfish perhaps, yes. But for all she worked hard to push herself forward, she'd also learned that it was okay to protect herself. Not everything had to be a test to pass or a battle to be conquered.

"No, that's cool, I understand. No worries," he said.

Hannah caught Bailey shifting her gaze between her and Jake, a considering expression on her young, gamine face, and found herself wondering just what the worldly-wise eleven-year-old thought she saw. Maybe that was something else she didn't need to know.

"We've got some boots you can wear," Bailey said before Hannah could change the topic. Bailey had said it casually enough, but Hannah wasn't fooled. She was trying to help her friend—which was admirable and kind—and possibly also judging the lay of the land with Hannah.

Hannah hadn't spent a lot of time with the precocious youngster. Bailey was lanky and tall for her age, with a wiry build, pretty red hair, and a splash of freckles that Hannah could personally identify with. She was tanned rather than fair, with blue eyes that missed nothing, and was pretty much everything Jake had proclaimed her to be. Bailey had come out to the farmhouse with Will and Jake several times but had spent most of her time out by the paddock, watching Chey's horses. What Hannah had observed about the young girl was that Bailey didn't take anything at face value. She observed, drew her own conclusions, then spoke or acted on them. Given her background in foster care, that was both a wise and understandable approach.

"I have pretty big feet," Hannah replied dryly. She stuck one of her sandaled feet forward. "I often think it would be easier to just buy the shoe box rather than what's inside. I'd have a broader selection at any rate."

Bailey tilted her head. "What, you're like a size nine? Ten maybe?" She nodded. "We've got you covered."

Hannah thought she detected the merest hint of challenge in Bailey's gaze, though there wasn't so much as a thread of it in her tone.

"Well," Hannah said, still hesitating, "you'd better bring a rope, and maybe have a winch handy up here, in case you need to drag me back up."

"Is that a yes?" Jake asked, his eyes wide with surprised glee.

Hannah backpedaled. *You've got a lot going on. Don't*

stretch yourself too thin. What her little voice meant, of course, was *don't stretch your heart too thin; it might break again.* "Well, I really should get inside and talk to Addie Pearl about this poster and be on my way. I don't want to hold up your supper."

"If you want to talk to Addie Pearl," Bailey said, "then you're going to need those hiking shoes." She motioned through the clearing of trees directly behind the house. "She's down with the sheep."

Hannah strained to see where Bailey was pointing, but from where she stood, all she could make out was thin air.

"Yeah," Jake began, "my dad is—"

"Oh, you can't see her," Bailey broke in, talking over Jake. "But she texted me when we were driving up to say she was heading down to look at the old well we found, so I wouldn't wonder where she was." She sent Jake a quick look that Hannah couldn't interpret, but Jake just shrugged and nodded at her and Hannah, agreeing with Bailey's assessment.

Hannah sensed the undercurrent but couldn't have said what they were up to. They looked as innocent and earnest as church mice at the moment. "Well, I don't want to get in the way," she replied instead, knowing if it mattered, she'd figure it out at some point. "Looks like she has her hands full."

Bailey sighed briefly and shook her head in resignation. She looked at Jake and said, "Adults. Always making things so complicated." She arched her eyebrows in a knowing look and added, "Where have we seen this before?"

Jake let out a small, surprised burst of laughter at that, then blushed bright pink as his gaze whipped apologetically to Hannah.

All of which baffled Hannah completely. Clearly she'd been right that there was a very specific secondary plot thread running through this little tableau, one that Hannah was not privy to, but that didn't matter.

Bailey jogged over to the front porch and up the steps, propping up the lid of a big storage chest. She fished around inside for a minute, then came out with a beat-up pair of boots. She grabbed one of the many walking sticks that had been jammed into a beautiful, hand-thrown glazed umbrella stand that filled the space between the bin and the front door.

Bailey trotted back to Hannah. "These should work." She held out the boots and leaned the walking stick against the Jeep. "Addie would be upset if she thought you'd left without talking to her. You could leave the poster up here." Bailey flashed a sudden, wide grin, and it so completely transformed her usually serious, study-the-world face, that it made Hannah almost catch her breath. "Besides, if you think my goat babies are cute, wait until you see my lamb babies."

Hannah's heart started to lean, even as her head warned her not to get more involved. "That's really kind of you," she began, but Bailey took off again before Hannah could say more.

"Be right back," Bailey called over her shoulder. "You're going to need socks."

As Bailey disappeared into the cabin, Hannah just stood there staring, wondering when, exactly, she'd lost the ability to control her own life.

"She means well," Jake said, as the screen door slapped shut behind Bailey. "If you really don't have the time, I can give Addie the poster. I know enough about the event from talking to Avery and Miss Vivienne. I'm pretty sure I could get the gist of it across. You could call her later, if you want. I have her cell number if you need it. I know she'd like to talk to you anyway. She's been saying how much she wants to come out and see more of the place. She's super proud of what you all are doing out there. I've heard her mention it more than once to folks at the guild. She said you mentioned maybe selling some of the lavender things you're making at the mill." He smiled encouragingly. "That would really be great if it works out. The guild is like a big family to her and she'd want you all to be part of it so you feel like you really belong here."

"Oh," Hannah said, feeling a bit chastened, though she knew that hadn't been his intent. "That's truly nice to hear. That's our plan, too. And I'd love to show her around the farm. I've been wanting to invite her out. I've been wanting to invite a lot of people out," she added with a laugh. "I can't believe how many folks I've come to know in such a short period of time. I just kept thinking we weren't ready for company yet."

"Oh, Addie wouldn't mind about the construction," Jake said. "Nobody would. In fact, you'd probably find yourself with more help than you need."

"Oh, I would never presume—"

"Folks out here don't expect anything in return. We all need help from time to time. Snow needs to be plowed, something needs fixing, someone needs a few meals cooked if they've been sick or in the hospital. There's always plenty of chances to repay a kindness." He shrugged. "It's how we all get along."

Truly abashed now, Hannah nodded. "I think that's pretty much the loveliest thing I've ever heard. I've already fallen in love with Blue Hollow Falls, but if any part of me had still been on the fence, that would have pushed me over."

Jake beamed, nodded, and Hannah thought she saw a little bit of a crush forming. It was sweet, more than anything, but it did make her redouble her resolve to step back, put a bit more space between her and the McCall men.

She knew Jake was telling her the truth regarding the

people in the Falls, though. Vivi, Avery, and Chey had all made multiple comments on how everyone they'd met had been so kind and generous. Six months in and Hannah still hadn't gotten used to such genuine warmth. Not that there weren't nice people—lots of them—back where she'd lived in Alexandria. The city was just an entirely different pace, with different energy. Everyone was in a rush, hurrying here or dashing off there. Folks didn't stop to talk like they did out here in the mountains.

If a passing acquaintance in the city asked how you were doing, it was usually just a polite gesture. Out here, folks waited for you to honestly respond. Could be you'd met them once, maybe just a wave and a nod, but a simple "fine, and you?" wouldn't suffice. And everyone said hello, whether they knew you or not. Hannah hadn't realized how isolated city life was, despite constantly being in places packed with people. She'd typically gone about her day without truly interacting with any of them. Other than a polite "please" or "thank you" when shopping or running errands, people didn't even really acknowledge each other. She hadn't ever thought of it as being unfriendly; it was just how life was.

Not in Blue Hollow Falls. Out here where the entire population amounted to fewer people than typically worked in a single high-rise in DC, she'd found herself in constant contact and conversation. Everyone greeted her like a friend she just hadn't met yet. Hannah had discovered she liked that. A lot, in fact. But it had taken some getting used to. She was one of those very folks who'd always rushed around, trying to get more done in less time. Stopping to talk with every person she encountered took a lot of time. It was lovely, was so kind, but boy it could take a chunk out of a person's day.

Now she found she wasn't in such a hurry anymore. And

she was the one stopping to chat, asking sincere questions and waiting for the answers. She really wanted to know how Anna, the postal clerk at the Falls' lone post office, was coping now that her only daughter was old enough to go to sleepaway camp, and whether or not the Jenkins family was going to get their cidery open in the fall. And somehow, she still managed to get the things done that needed doing and felt a lot less stressed while doing it.

"Truth is, they're nosey," Jake offered with a grin. "Everyone is dying to see what you all are doing out there with the old March place. Folks are truly happy you're turning it into something special. I don't even remember anyone living there, not since I've been here, and that's most of my life. All of it that I can remember, anyway."

Hannah was tempted to ask him about his life before moving to the Falls, but that wouldn't help with that whole "putting some distance between her and the McCall men" thing she'd just decided was for the best not five minutes ago. Of course, she'd be lying if she said she hadn't kept her ear a bit more finely tuned when she was running errands, in the hope she'd pick up some tidbit of information about either McCall. She'd even shamelessly worked mention of Will into a conversation here and there, commenting on the great work he was doing at the farmhouse, hoping maybe that would prompt some revelation about his past. Unsurprisingly, she'd heard nothing but praise for his work, and many wonderful comments about Jake. But every time the conversation started to take a turn toward something a bit more personal, someone would invariably interrupt, or the person she was talking to would get called away, leaving her even more curious than before.

"Here you go," Bailey said, breathless from her dash back across the yard. "I texted Addie and told her we were on our way down. Made her happy."

Hannah took the socks, and looked again at the hiking boots, and thought, *well, you can start distancing yourself tomorrow.* She really did want to talk to Addie about the mill and her desire to sell her own work. She'd already started making a mental list of the places she was dying to sketch. The more she thought about it, the more excited she'd become. She'd loved being an illustrator, but the joy she'd taken in it had changed after the accident. She was glad she'd found her way through to the end of her contract, and the work had been cathartic in many ways. But she'd been content to leave that part of her life behind when she'd packed up and left Alexandria. It had been the right time to make that change, along with all the rest of the life changes she was making. But she never intended to leave painting or sketching behind. This would be the perfect way to keep her true passion alive and maybe pay the bills while she was at it.

"Fabulous," Bailey said a few minutes later, when Hannah had finished lacing up the calf-high boots.

"They feel pretty good, actually," Hannah said, surprised, considering they looked like army boots. She looked at Bailey and Jake. "Maybe I've been shopping in the wrong part of the store all along." She did a little turn, letting the hem of her long cotton skirt swirl around the top edges of the boots. "I'm sure this will be trending in no time."

"I think you look great," Jake said, then blushed again when Bailey rolled her eyes and he realized he might have sounded a bit too gushy.

"Thanks, Jake," Hannah said kindly, remembering her own schoolgirl crush on her high school science teacher all too well—knowing it was silly and obviously destined to be unrequited, but crushing nonetheless. Yet another reason it would be smart for her to nip things in the bud.

Bailey led the way and Hannah was proud of herself for

making it all the way down the entire rocky, rutted, and very steep trail without landing on her fanny, or worse, even once. Mostly due to the fact that she'd spent the entire descent silently freaking out about her ability to make it back topside again, without benefit of tow rope. Or crane. By the time they reached the bottom, she'd already come up with a plan to tell them all to go on back up without her, and claim she was going to take her time climbing up so she could take some photos, do some plant research for Avery, plan some future illustrations, or some such. A few hours to make it up the half-mile incline should do it. Maybe.

"Welcome," Addie Pearl called out as they cleared the last of the tall pines and stepped out into an incredibly bucolic, little high-mountain pasture.

"Oh," she gasped, stopping right in her tracks as the vista spread out before her. "Just when I think it can't get any more spectacular," she said on a hushed, almost reverent whisper. The pretty little meadow was framed with tall pines and cedars on either side, not more than a few acres deep and wide, and lined in the distance with a rocky outcropping, before the mountain slope continued its steep descent toward the valley below. She wondered if she walked to the tumble of boulders at the far edge of the field, whether she could spy the Hawksbill River wending its crooked way through the valley floor, maybe see the sun glinting off its surface at every horseshoe-shaped curve. From where she stood, the mountains rising up again on the far side of the valley provided a spectacular backdrop to the vista, with blue skies above.

She had to curl her fingers into her palm against the itch to grab a sketch pad right then, and her watercolors, wondering if she could capture even a hint of the majestic beauty before her. But oh, she wanted to try.

Hannah managed to pull her gaze away as Addie made

her way over to her. "How do you ever get anything done besides staring at that all day?" Hannah asked her, then took Addie's proffered hand in a quick shake.

"I'd like to say you get used to it after a bit, but that wouldn't be true," Addie Pearl said. "I've spent many an hour pondering that landscape and my place in it. Puts the world in perspective." She smiled. "I call it time well spent."

"I'd have to agree," Hannah replied. "I haven't had time to paint a single thing since coming here, but I've a number of views in mind when the time does come." She looked at Addie. "In fact, that was something I wanted to talk to you about. But first, would you mind very much if I came down here from time to time, different seasons perhaps, or times of day? I know I couldn't do it justice." She turned and looked out across the valley again. "But I'd sure like the opportunity to try."

Addie Pearl's lips curved to a very satisfied grin. "Any time. All the time you want. Don't bother calling ahead. Just come when the spirit moves you." She leaned closer. "Those are always the best times."

"Be careful what you offer," Hannah told her with a grin. "You might find me down here living out of a tent."

Addie hooted at that. "Well, if you don't mind watering and feeding a few sheep while you're at it, we might just have a deal."

Hannah laughed with her. "I've heard a lot about these sheep. Can I see them?"

"I imagine you'll do more than that," Addie said. "You didn't think Bailey would drag you all the way down here and let you get off without feeding a lamb or two, did you?"

Hannah's heart melted. "Could I?"

"Of course! We're working on restoring an old well I uncovered when the kids and I were cutting some willow for one of the Bluebirds to use for a basket weave idea she had.

All these years, never knew it was there." Addie grinned. "Buried treasure."

She knew the Bluebirds were what folks called the members of the guild. "I'll say. Is it still functional?"

"Seems like." Addie turned and Hannah finally pulled her gaze away from the vista and looked to see where Addie was pointing.

"Will," Hannah said, stopping, surprised to see him there.

He didn't hear her, of course. He was a good thirty or forty yards away, working on the small, stacked stone well. It was right at the tree line, in the shadow of the mountain face soaring overhead, so it wasn't that surprising she'd missed him. But still, as much as she'd thought about him in the past week, shouldn't she have felt him nearby? Or something?

"Yes," Addie said, glancing from Hannah to Will, then pausing and looking back to Hannah again. "He's just started doing some work on that old thing and it already looks better than I thought it could."

"I know, he does beautiful work," Hannah said, the tiniest rasp tinging the words. She managed to pull her gaze away from Will, only to discover a speculative look in Addie Pearl's unusual lavender-colored eyes. Hannah had no idea what Addie had seen in Hannah's expression. Longing, perhaps. *Abject desire. Unbridled lust?* And not just because the T-shirt Will had on today was plastered to his torso like a second skin. *At least you managed to keep yourself from panting and drooling.* Barely.

"Hannah," Bailey called out, "come on over and see!"

Hannah wasn't ashamed to admit her relief at being saved from having to say anything about . . . well, anything. She looked over to see Bailey standing by the open door of a small stone building that was just beyond a fenced-in paddock. "Coming," she called back. She looked at Addie Pearl.

"I wanted to talk to you about the guild, and Seth said you might be willing to post the notice for our upcoming community event at Lavender Blue."

Addie nodded. "Definitely. Seth already mentioned it to me. Great idea, you two teaming up," she added. Her enthusiasm was sincere, but those eyes of hers didn't lose an ounce of their penetrating power. "You go on and play with Bailey's wee lambs, then come on up and join us for supper. We can chat about all the things you've got on your mind."

"Oh, I couldn't put you out," Hannah said, knowing for absolute certain now that the last thing she needed was more up close and personal time with either of the McCall men. Not with Addie now eagle-eyeing her every reaction to Will. "But it's very kind of you to offer. When you can find the time, why don't you come on out to the farm. I'd love to give you the full tour. Such as it is, at this point," Hannah added with a laugh. "I'd really like a chance to talk to you in more detail about some of our ideas for products and what would be the best way to handle getting a space at the mill. We're definitely interested in applying to become guild members, if you'll have us. And I'd like to talk to you about maybe selling some of my own work there. I'd be willing to demonstrate or give classes. I've been there numerous times now and I just love the place. Very inspiring to be in a place with so much creative talent."

Addie laid her hands on Hannah's forearms and squeezed. "A hearty yes to all of that. I'm so pleased to hear it. Now I really must insist you stay for dinner."

"Oh, I—"

"If you don't have other plans, this would truly suit my schedule perfectly," Addie said. "I've got so much going on, what with getting the amphitheater ready for its big opening, I'm afraid my time is pretty full. Stay and have a bite and we'll get it all sorted out before sunset. Good?"

Hannah could only nod. "Good," she said. "Great," she added with a smile that wasn't entirely sincere. Still, she was truly appreciative of the offer, and she knew Vivi and Avery especially would be thrilled to get this all sorted out so quickly. Her gaze trailed over to Will, who was in the middle of lifting a large, flat piece of stone, which had the effect of bunching and rippling every last muscle he had in his back and shoulders. *And there were so, so many of them.*

"Wonderful," Addie said. "Go on over with Bailey. Come on up when you're ready. I've got a stew bubbling but still have bread to make, so don't hurry."

Hannah jerked her gaze from Will back to Addie, but the older woman had already started back across the uneven, rocky ground toward Will and the well.

"Okay," Hannah said faintly. She really had lost control of her life. She breathed in and let out what she hoped would be a settling breath, forced her gaze away from Will and his amazing T-shirt of wonders, and turned her attention toward Bailey. Who was no longer to be seen. Assuming she'd gone inside the stone building, Hannah headed that way. She glanced around and didn't see Jake at all, so presumably he was inside the little barn or stable or whatever it was, too.

She looked for a gate in the paddock fence, running her gaze along the length of it, and realized she'd have to walk around to get to where she was going. Which would take her right past the well. And Will. She sighed. She didn't know if Will had noticed her yet or not—he seemed pretty focused on his task—but he'd hardly be able to miss her when she was heading straight toward him.

You're being ridiculous, she told herself. *You see him every day at the farm.* Except she hadn't seen him. For six days. *You've been counting, too, I see. Care to name the hours and minutes?* Her sigh this time was one of resignation. So maybe crushes weren't strictly the purview of adolescence. She didn't even know him. Not truly. Sure, she admired and respected the parts she did know. He was a hardworking man, raising a great kid, and did beautiful restoration work. But he was also a man of few words who might be a little overly serious, at least from her observation. *Which you're clearly doing a lot of.*

Every time she'd talk herself out of this silly attraction she felt toward a man who quite apparently had none of the same thoughts where she was concerned, she'd remember that grin, the way it had lit up his entire handsome face, sparking so much life into those gemstone-green eyes of his. *Sucker.* "I know," she muttered.

She should just call it what it truly was. Lust. Bare-bones— bare everything—cut-to-the-chase lust. She should be happy to know she could feel that again, under any circumstances. It meant she was alive. All the parts of her. "Yeah, well, some of those parts need to just simmer right on down there, sister," she said under her breath as she all but marched her way around the paddock fence, as if she could use her size-ten army boots to stomp down all the needy, wanting feelings he'd so easily aroused in her.

"Hannah."

She stopped dead in her tracks. She turned to see him standing not five feet away. Addie Pearl was nowhere in sight. She must have gone back up the path. Hannah swallowed against her suddenly dry throat. "Hey," she said, having already adopted the casual way people in town always greeted each other. She tried to ignore that hint of a rasp that had made its way back into her voice.

"Thank you. Again. For saving me the trip to get Jake and Bailey."

"Oh, it was no bother. Seth said he was going to bring

them up for you and I needed to talk to Addie anyway. She, ah, invited me to dinner. Hope that's okay."

He frowned. "Why wouldn't it be?"

Seriously, it was like she was fourteen again and trying to explain to Mr. McAfee why he should let her do extra credit even though she had an A-plus in his class, all the while trying not to stare into his oh-so-dreamy brown eyes. *Only you're not fourteen any longer. And those green eyes you're looking into now are so, so much better than . . . what was his name again?* She cleared her throat. "Jake said he was staying for the meal, so I assumed you would be, and I just . . . didn't want to intrude."

Will's expression was a bit quizzical and she wished she could dig a hole right where she stood.

"Addie always makes enough to feed an army. Don't worry." His tone warmed as he added, "I'll just get Jake to pass on seconds and you'll have enough to eat a full meal and take home some leftovers."

She laughed then. "Jake made the same offer, earlier."

Will nodded. "He'd probably give up his meal entirely if you asked him," he said. "He likes you." Now his lips did curve slightly. "In case he hasn't made that painfully, awkwardly clear."

His eyes seemed . . . livelier today, and he sounded less guarded. A lot less guarded. She wouldn't go so far as to say he was being chatty, but this was the most she'd ever heard him say, at least that didn't include the words "estimate" or "fireplace." Hannah felt a warm flush fill her as his gaze held hers, never wavering. The pleasurable kind of flush that found its way into all kinds of long-neglected places. "He's a really great kid," Hannah said. "Young man, I should say. I know you're proud of him and you have every right to be."

"That's kind of you to say." Will glanced past her to the stone building where Hannah assumed his son was presently helping Bailey with the newborns. "I'm not sure how much I had to do with that."

He paused then, but Hannah sensed he wanted to say something else, so she waited.

Will looked back to her, his gaze unreadable now. "He takes after his mom. Thinks with his head, leads with his heart. And my mother helped to raise him, too." He looked down for a moment. He'd said it all easily enough, but maybe it hadn't been as easy as he'd made it sound.

Hannah knew a lot about the various signs of grief. She thought she might be seeing a few of them right now. "Sounds like he had a good, strong foundation then," she said, wondering why he'd opened up even that much. Unless it was to discuss the farmhouse repairs, she'd never heard him comment on anything or anyone else.

"The best," Will said, then seemed to let out a short breath before glancing up at her again. His expression was once more serious, maybe a bit impassive.

Hannah wondered if that was how he managed it, whatever it was he was managing, by keeping it tucked behind a sturdy, no-nonsense wall. She knew she should just let it go, steer the conversation back to something less personal, or, for that matter, continue on to the little barn to see the baby lambs. Instead, despite all the internal talks she'd been having with herself all day long about stepping back, about not getting closer to either of the McCalls, she opened her mouth and what came out was, "Someone in town mentioned to me that your mom was from here. Sounds like she was well loved. Did you grow up in Blue Hollow Falls?" *Hannah Joanne.*

He shook his head. "Mom did, and her folks before her. They've all passed on now, but the Lankfords were very well thought of here."

If Hannah had thought finally getting a tidbit about him

would satisfy her curiosity, she couldn't have been more wrong. Now she had a dozen more questions. "That's a wonderful legacy to leave behind."

"Thank you; it is that."

She was dying to ask him about Jake's mom, about why his own mom had helped to raise Jake. About that flash of . . . something she'd seen when he'd mentioned that Jake took after his mom. Bad divorce? Jake had never mentioned his mom to Hannah, and as far as she knew, he didn't head off to parts unknown to see her. But Hannah hadn't been in the Falls all that long. So what did she know about anything really? And why did she think it was any of her business to know?

"You were headed to the lamb house?" He nodded toward the stone building again.

"Is that what you call it? It doesn't look like a barn, but it's bigger than a shed."

"We built stalls in there to help with the lambing and give the babies some time before being pastured, so the name just kind of happened." His lips curved again and Hannah was hanging on his every word.

Like you need help with that.

"Bailey keeps the sheep in the bigger building on past the lamb house during really bad weather." He motioned to a newer looking building. "She only has a handful of sheep at this point, a dozen or so, but she went to auction with the money she'd saved from selling baby goats and bought a ram." That smile teased her again. "So that number is likely to continue to rise."

"Jake mentioned the breed she has isn't all that common. They're small, right?"

He nodded. "Herdwicks. Native to the UK. That's why Addie let her use some of her college money to bid on the ram. It was unusual to see one listed."

"Jake told me her goat business is her college fund. For an eleven-year-old, that's impressive." Hannah laughed. "For any age kid, that's impressive."

Will nodded, and Hannah thought she might get a real deal smile from him then. It was definitely hovering. "Given how she does in school, wouldn't surprise any of us if she was taking college courses by the time she hits her teens, so saving now isn't such a bad idea."

Hannah laughed. "Well, she needs to stop hanging around Chey and the horses and start talking to Avery then. Avery got her first PhD at fifteen."

Will's eyebrows lifted at that. "Her . . . first?"

Hannah laughed again. "If you look up 'prodigy' in the dictionary, you will find Avery's picture, highlighted in gold. She's amazing." Hannah didn't go into more detail. The fearsome foursome had an understanding between them about what was public knowledge, and what was up to the individual to share. Chey was clearly good with horses, Hannah had her paints and illustrations, Vivi had her flamboyant style and Broadway memorabilia, and Avery was undeniably a genius, with her mad scientist lab and mile-a-minute brain. Anything beyond that, however, was their own story to tell.

"I knew she was some kind of science whiz, but I had no idea."

"Actually, she's all kinds of whiz. Her doctorates are in statistical analysis and library science. The whole science lab thing is just her latest hobby, because of the products we want to make. She's very into it." Hannah laughed. "To put it mildly. But Avery doesn't do anything in half measures. The scary thing is she can be doing a dozen different things she's suddenly passionate about, and her brain works so fast, she can keep them all spinning along simultaneously at the same pace."

Will just shook his head. "Intimidating. I think Bailey would be fascinated to know that. And I'd tell you to mention it to her, but I'm almost more afraid of what might happen if we put those two together."

Hannah laughed outright at that, and his gaze caught hers, held . . . and then the skies opened up to reveal heaven above. Or it sure felt like that when the hovering smile appeared and went straight to full on, heart-stopping, sexy-as-all-get-out grin. It was so much better than the first one she'd seen. Which was impossible. And yet . . .

"You should do that more often," she said, then could have kicked herself when the sun ducked right back behind a cloud.

Not fully, but . . . *Stay in your lane,* she schooled herself.

She felt bad for making him self-conscious. "It makes your eyes dance," she said, deciding if she was in for a penny, she might as well just go in for a pound as well. "It's a good look on you."

He ducked his chin then, shook his head as if in surprise, but he wasn't frowning. In fact, she thought she caught the edges of a smile. One of embarrassment most likely but seeing the abashed side of him only made him that much sexier. Whatever the case, she couldn't chastise herself for putting it out there. The reward had been too good.

"I shouldn't keep you from your work," she told him, deciding she'd done and said quite enough for one day. "I'm going to go have a look at the lambs before Bailey comes out and drags me in there."

She thought for sure he'd take the easy out she was offering him and head back to the well. She wouldn't have been surprised if he'd run. So what he actually did shocked her speechless.

"I'm done for the day. I'll head over to the lamb house with you."

"I . . . uh, that would be . . . that would be good," she stammered, having been caught so fully off guard by his offer, she couldn't even string a full sentence together.

She did have the wherewithal to realize that her reaction could be taken entirely the wrong way, but before she could dig herself out of that hole, he clammed her right back up by smiling again and saying, "That's what I was thinking."

Chapter Seven

Jesus, Will thought, *Jake is smoother than you.*

He let Hannah lead the way around the last corner of the paddock, regretting every part of the stupid impulse that had encouraged him to open his mouth in the first place. He should have just let Hannah go on to the lamb house and kept his eye on his work. And not on how her hips still swayed so smoothly, even with those clunky boots on.

Damn Addie and her spooky-eyed wisdom for getting inside his head.

Hadn't it been enough that he'd taken it upon himself to interrupt Hannah's stroll, ostensibly to thank her for playing taxi, again, for Jake? A small gesture, to be sure, but certainly if he was going to move outside his comfort zone, make an effort to reach forward, take a step away from his past, slowly was the wisest way to proceed. Hell, he wasn't sure he had any business taking steps of any size until he sorted himself out a bit more. Okay, a lot more.

He'd been thinking exactly that, especially when he'd mentioned Zoey not five seconds into their conversation. He wasn't even sure why he'd done it. He never talked about her. At least, not until his unexpected gab fest with Addie a week or so ago. Now that he'd put it out there to one person, was he just going to open the flood gates anytime he decided to talk to someone? *Because that's definitely the way to get a woman to notice you. Bring up your late wife at the first possible occasion.*

The truth was, talking about Zoey hadn't been all that hard. It had even made him feel a tiny bit less guilty for not making her a more regular part of his narrative all along, for not paying proper tribute to her memory. *I'm so sorry, Zoey,* he silently confessed. *I owe you so much more than I've been able to give.*

But even with that thought, or maybe because of it, he'd wanted out of the conversation with Hannah immediately at that point. Step taken. Now go back to your lane until you get your stuff straight. But Hannah had just gone blithely along, expressing sincere sympathy, then chatting on, smiling and laughing as if it were all part and parcel of life. And then he was smiling and laughing. Like it was just okay to go on and do that. *Isn't that how it's supposed to work?* And then he was suddenly inviting himself to stay in her company and extend the torture of uncertainty on whether he had any business even considering this.

He'd spent the last week alternately kicking himself for the things he'd revealed to Addie, things he'd never even shared with his own mother, and trying like hell not to dwell on the things Addie had said to him.

Of course, that would have been a lot easier to do if she hadn't made so much damn sense.

"Are you coming?" Bailey stuck her head out just as they reached the wide plank door to the building. "Finally," she said, taking Hannah's hand. "Come on. He just woke up. You can feed him."

Hannah looked a little startled at the suddenness of it all and Will found himself smiling yet again as Bailey dragged her off. He caught Jake's look of surprise and wasn't sure if it was a reaction to Hannah's being caught off guard by Bailey taking charge, or to the fact that his father had come out to the lamb house with Hannah. Then Will saw Jake give a little nod of approval, unaware his dad was watching, before turning back to the two little ones he was trying to herd back into the indoor corral Will and Seth had built over the winter when babies had started coming early.

"Here," Bailey was saying, drawing his attention back to the two of them. She turned and deposited a wooly ball of black fluff into Hannah's unsuspecting embrace. "This is Snowball. He's a rare twin and probably shouldn't have made it, hence the name, like a snowball's chance?" Bailey's eyes sparkled mischievously. "I happened to be out here when his mama was birthing him. The ewe had a pretty tough time—they were her first two ever. We've been hand-feeding Snowball so his mama can concentrate on the stronger one. I don't normally name them, but I'm keeping him." Bailey reached out to stroke the lamb's knobby head. "I didn't think he'd make it, but he's a fighter."

Will noted that Hannah just stood there and blinked through Bailey's whole excited speech, saying nothing. Simply staring down at her armful of soft little lamb. Will might not know Hannah all that well yet, but he knew that wasn't like her. Jake had gone on and on about how Hannah had taken straightaway to watching the baby goats run around and play. So much so she'd said she'd love to have one of her own. So Will knew it wasn't an aversion to or fear of livestock.

Bailey handed Hannah a bottle. "I thought you'd like to give him a feeding." She went about showing Hannah how to hold the baby, how to position the bottle.

Hannah followed along, sitting on a low stool, her back to a stall door, not caring that the hem of her skirt dragged through the dirt and straw on the stable floor. She hadn't said a single word, had barely managed a nod or two, allowing Bailey's chattering to fill up all the available space.

The strands of hair that had come loose from her braid fell forward to frame her face as she bent to the task of feeding the eager lamb, so Will couldn't fully gauge her reaction, but something definitely wasn't right.

Bailey watched for a moment, then turned away to help Jake get the other young ones back in the larger pen with their mamas. Will still stood just inside the doorway and was about to turn to help the kids with the lambs, when he noticed the fine trembling that had Hannah's shoulders shaking. It wasn't in laughter. He saw her knees were shaking a bit, too.

He couldn't have said how he knew to do what he did next. Some protective instinct kicked in, and he didn't question it. Maybe it was his military training to respond quickly and rely on his gut. Maybe it was being a parent, sensitive to the signs that someone was in trouble. Probably a combination of both.

He turned to the kids who were just closing the door to the pen behind the last straggler. "Hey, why you don't you both head on up the hill and help Addie Pearl with dinner," he said. "I'll help Hannah finish up with the lamb; then we'll be up, too."

Jake look a bit surprised but nodded. "If you're sure, yeah, no problem."

Bailey, on the other hand, regarded him a bit more steadily and didn't respond right away. She went to glance past Will to where Hannah was seated, but he shifted, just the tiniest bit, to block her view. Bailey's gaze went immediately back to his, concern clear in her eyes now.

"It's okay," he said quietly, not surprised that the young girl had picked up on the situation, or at least that there was one of some sort. "I've got it."

"I didn't know," was all Bailey said, not in defense, but in apology.

"We can't know what we don't know," he told her. "Go on up with Jake, okay?"

Bailey looked like she wanted to say more, to do more, but she nodded and, to her credit, corralled Jake out of the stables as smoothly as she'd helped him corral the rowdy babies moments before.

Jake pulled the plank door closed behind them, trusting Bailey to keep whatever it was she might be thinking about Hannah to herself. He'd talk to her later. Just as soon as he figured out what was going on.

He turned back to Hannah, took a slow breath, and walked over to her, hoping he'd done the right thing. And, despite his reassurances to Bailey, not at all sure he had this.

He looked around for another stool, found one, and pulled it over beside her. He could hear her quiet sobs before he even sat down. "Let me take him," Will said quietly, as gently as he was able. He reached for the lamb, but Hannah gave just a slight shake of her head, so he withdrew his hands but stayed where he was sitting.

"Sorry," she managed, her voice choked with tears.

"Nothing to be sorry about. Animals do that," he said. "Bring out all our protective instincts."

She ducked her chin in a wobbly nod, her face still cast downward, her gaze on the lamb, who was done feeding now, and dozing in her arms. Hannah was rocking little Snowball, or herself, or both.

Will felt his own chest tighten, his throat, too. He had no idea what had caused this response, but it was no little thing. She wasn't trying to laugh it off or explain it away, as he'd assume she might, given her open and sunny nature. She wasn't embarrassed or even really aware of anything except the warm bundle she was cradling to her chest.

He wanted to reach out, to console her, to ease whatever

burden this had placed on her soul. Because clearly her tears were about a whole lot more than a poor, undersized, struggling lamb. He, better than most, knew about put-upon souls.

He had the thought that his intent to provide solace might instead be an unwanted intrusion, and he shifted his weight in order to stand up, give her some space and privacy.

"I miss this so much," she said on a raw rasp. Fresh tears filled her voice, and he could see them tracking down her cheeks.

He settled right back on the stool again, but at a total loss as to what to say to that.

She sniffled again, and finally turned to brush her cheek against her shoulder. "I'm okay," she said hoarsely. "It's just . . . some things, I can't . . ."

He'd never felt so inept in his life. All his instincts had rushed in to protect her, and now he had no idea how to actually do that. It felt intrusive to make any contact, and yet he simply couldn't sit there, hearing all that pain, and not touch her, try to offer comfort.

He reached up and gently pushed the strands of hair away from where they clung to her damp cheeks. He tucked them behind her ear, then dried the last tears from her cheek with the back of his finger. "I don't think we're meant to shoulder everything all the time," he said, thinking of his own struggles, thinking he could have taken that bit of advice more to heart himself. "We're as strong as we can be, when we can be." Seeing her brought to tears, for reasons he didn't need to know, but identified with nonetheless, made his own voice a shade huskier. "Other times, well, I think it's okay if we just let ourselves feel what we feel when we feel it. Then we pick up and keep going on." He dried another tear. "There's no harm in that, Hannah."

She nodded, and her breath caught in little hiccups as she finally got her tears under control. She lifted her gaze to his, her eyes a glittering, stormy, pain-filled sea of gray. His finger had still been rubbing against her cheek, and now stroked across her lower lip.

Her mouth parted on a little gasp at the touch, her pupils expanding so rapidly they swallowed up the storm but didn't eclipse the vulnerability. The responding roar of raw need and desire that rushed to fill every last part of him felt somewhere just shy of feral. It had been a very, *very* long time—a lifetime—since he'd felt desire on any level. The ferocity of this reaction left him feeling both untamed and a lot untried.

"Hannah," he said, knowing he should let his hand drop away, not take another step forward when he didn't know where the mines were buried in this particular field. Both hers and his. But he continued stroking her lower lip. Felt her shudder in response, almost in abject relief to be feeling anything other than whatever pain it was that had been filling her to the point of overflowing just moments ago. "I'm sorry," he said, searching her eyes for answers, willing his heart to slow down, his pulse, and other parts of his suddenly riled up body to do the same.

She held his gaze, her eyes still swimming, but with teeming, unnamed emotions now rather than tears. She gave her head the slightest shake, as if to say he needn't be.

He traced the side of her chin with the back of the same curved finger, wanting, badly, to lean in and taste her, draw the rest of the pain from her, take it inside himself if need be. Lord knew he was accustomed to it. What was a little more?

"Thank you," she said hoarsely, her gaze intent, as if trying to give back a little of what he'd given to her, making him wonder what his eyes were saying, what answers she was getting. "For . . ." She lifted a shoulder, as if to encompass all of it, and the corners of her mouth finally curved upward, the slightest self-deprecating glint finding its way into her eyes, right before fresh tears filled them again.

This time she let out a little laugh, as if in apology for her continued ridiculousness with the tears.

And that, more than the pain, more than the vulnerability, that moment of "oh well, this is me" was what reached in and clutched a piece of his heart and held on tight. He wasn't even thinking, he was just reacting, as he started to lower his head to hers.

Her eyes widened, then darkened, but in a good way, the way every man wanted to see a woman's eyes change when she looked at him. Her gaze dropped to his mouth, as if in anticipation, and all that primal need and want came raging right back again.

He should pull back, check himself, get way more control over his reaction to her before . . . anything. But her lips were parting, and he wanted to taste them more than he wanted his next breath.

His lips brushed hers, the barest hint, and he felt her swift intake of breath. He started to pull back, but she closed the gap and pressed her mouth to his before he could give either of them the chance to think this step through.

He heard the low, thankful groan, and realized it was his own. But as he moved to join in, a sudden, high-pitched bleat pierced the quiet air, sending them both all but falling back off their respective stools as if they'd just been shocked with an electric prod. Like two kids caught with their hands in the cookie jar. Or their very adult hands . . . somewhere they shouldn't be.

The tiny baby lamb was wriggling in Hannah's arms with surprising vigor, causing her to erupt in watery laughter as she struggled to keep him from flipping right out of her arms.

Will righted himself and helped her with the baby, managing to take him from her as the empty bottle fell to the ground. Holding the still wriggling, bleating baby against his chest, he offered Hannah his free hand as she was still wobbling on her stool, pulling her upright the moment she grabbed his hand.

Off balance, they both stumbled a step or two, taking care to keep the lamb from being knocked around between them.

The baby seemed delighted by this, his bleats becoming more energized and his eyes quite alert and attentive.

"Come here, you little rascal," Will said, letting Hannah go when she got her balance and sheltering the baby lamb against his chest. "Let's get you back to Mama for a bit." He walked over to a stall at the end of the building and lowered the baby over the door. The lamb's sibling bleated in greeting and the two butted heads, which knocked the smaller one over, but he didn't seem to mind, scrambling back up on knobby little legs.

"Look at him."

Will glanced over to see Hannah standing next to him, peering over the door.

"He's so much tinier than his . . . sister? Brother?"

"Brother, I think," Will said. "They're a pretty hardy breed. He certainly seems to be giving it his best shot."

Hannah nodded, then rubbed her palms over her face and pushed back the loose tendrils of hair, as if to scrub away whatever feelings and memories the baby lamb had evoked and regain her control.

Will certainly understood that desire. He was a master of wanting to be in control. *You weren't in control five minutes ago,* his little voice reminded him. *And it didn't seem to bother you one bit.* He opted to ignore that. For now. He wasn't ready to think about . . . any of it.

Hannah took a deep, steadying breath and turned to face him as they both straightened away from the stall door. "That was very kind," she said, her voice still husky and a bit raw. "What you did. Giving me privacy while I fell apart all over the place." She smiled, and even with the splotchy, post-crying face and still-red eyes, her natural warmth was back in her eyes, and to him, she looked as beautiful as ever. "I very much appreciate that."

That was the Hannah he was coming to know. Open, direct, kind. "I wasn't sure what to do," he admitted. "I just figured if it were me, the smaller the audience, the better."

"You stuck around for the performance," she said, but her tone was teasing, her still-glassy eyes bright with humor now.

"I thought maybe the lamb might need some assistance," he offered, feeling his own lips twitch a little.

"The lamb," she repeated, a wry note in her voice now. "I see."

He lifted a shoulder, but the smile came out. He wanted to ask her . . . well, everything. He'd only known her to be happy and upbeat, always a positive air about her, even when the farmhouse was trying its best to fall apart around her and her cohorts. He wanted to know what had brought such an unlikely group of women together, why they'd all moved to a place none of them had ever been before—at least no one he'd spoken with knew anything about any of them—to start up a business clearly none of them had any previous experience running.

Addie Pearl was right that it was kind of confounding that no one seemed to know their story. As outgoing and friendly as each of them was, it was practically a miracle that their life stories weren't already being dissected and analyzed via the Falls' very well-run gossip mill.

Now he wanted to know the parts of her she'd kept so well hidden. And every other thing that made her who she was.

"I should probably explain," she said as the silence spun out between them.

"No," he said, without hesitation. "You don't have to do that. Not for me." Wanting to spare her that. And maybe himself as well. He was already a bit overwhelmed by his reaction to her. His one baby step forward today had turned into a full-on marathon and he wasn't quite sure how he felt about any of it. Now was definitely not the time to deepen whatever bonds were forming between them. She hadn't mentioned their kiss and he was fine with their leaving that subject unexplained as well. For now, at any rate. "I'm just sorry it all came at you like that. Bailey's going to feel terrible about putting you on the spot. She didn't mean—"

"Oh, I know," Hannah said quickly. "I was hoping maybe she hadn't noticed. You were pretty astute to see what was happening yourself. I tried to fight it, I really did." She looked back into the stall, but this time she was smiling when her eyes grew glassy again.

"It just took me off guard and I couldn't seem to get a grip before it swamped me." She looked back at him, her tone gentler now, and though there was a dry note there, too, her eyes were more serious now, or at least they held his quite steadily. "Just so you don't think I'm crazy, I should probably tell you—"

"That's okay," he interrupted.

And he must have sounded a little more emphatic than he'd intended, because her smile faltered, and her gaze immediately shifted downward. Just for a moment. Then she looked at him again. "All right," she said. "Thank you again, though." She was every bit as kind and sincere, but her manner had shifted to something a little more polite now. As if she were speaking to a casual acquaintance, rather than someone she'd just kissed.

He nodded, and the moment stretched. He knew he should say something about—acknowledge the kiss. But now that he'd stuck his foot in it, he wasn't sure how to proceed.

"If there's nothing else we need to do out here, I'll be starting up the trail," she said. She smiled. "It will likely take me half a lifetime to make it up that incline, so please, don't wait for me. At least by the time I get to the top I can blame this on the heat and the steep slope," she said as she gestured to her face. She turned then and walked to the door.

"I didn't think you were crazy," he blurted out before she could walk away. *I knew you were in pain.*

She turned, her expression soft, her eyes kind. "I know." She paused a beat, then added, "I appreciate that you understood what I was going through. I'm just sorry. That you had reason to."

Chapter Eight

Will was in Vivi's bedroom. He'd been in there for days.

"Hannah, darling, could you come in here a moment?"

Hannah's hands paused over the stem of lavender, and the buds she was plucking from it. She swallowed a sigh but wasn't as successful in sublimating the eye roll. She was having a hard enough time being under the same roof with Will. She really wished Vivi would stop finding reasons to send Hannah upstairs to get in his way.

It had been five days since they'd kissed. Kind of kissed. *It had been a kiss.*

Their parting had been awkward. The kiss, what there'd been of it, not so much. She sighed out loud this time. Their lips might have only been pressed together for a few seconds, but that had been long enough to learn that he knew how to kiss a woman. "This woman, anyway," she muttered.

But the awkward parting had happened, too. Ending any chance that that kiss might happen again so she could learn what else he might know how to do with a woman. *This woman.*

She didn't regret what she'd said to him. That she'd at least put it out there that he knew she'd been suffering, and she suspected he knew because he was intimately familiar with the feeling. It was better than dancing around it. She didn't want to get all maudlin with him, and maybe it was just as well she hadn't explained herself. She hadn't been about to talk to him about Liam. Not directly anyway.

She'd merely been about to tell him that she'd suffered the loss of someone some years back and certain things could trigger strong emotions. And she'd only felt the need to tell him that much because she'd seen the pain mirrored in his own eyes, when he'd brushed the hair from her face, soothing her with more than words. He didn't strike her as a man who reached out much, not like that. She'd wanted him to know she understood, and that she was truly grateful to him. The look on his face when she'd tried—both times— had made it clear he'd rather not go there. She didn't know what loss he'd suffered, but she'd stopped trying to learn anything else about him, as that felt like a betrayal of sorts. He'd gone out of his way for her. The least she could do was respect that he had no desire to open up and share his own story.

Of course, she was fairly certain she'd pieced it together and figured it out on her own. The who of it, at least. He'd mentioned Jake's mom, lovingly and with great respect, and he'd mentioned that his own mother had helped to raise Jake. Jake had spoken about his grandmother a few times, alluding to his coming to live with her when he was little. But no mention of his mom. It didn't take a giant leap of logic to assume that Will wasn't divorced, but a widower. And given Jake had been in the Falls for most of his life, that meant it wasn't a recent loss. Will had lost his mom, too, so that might be part of it as well.

Whatever the case, it was none of her business. And he didn't want to make her any part of his business, either. That much had been made clear to her in the past week. He'd honored her request to let her climb that hill alone. He'd gone back to work on the well instead of coming up. By the time she'd gotten to the top, her face was so flushed from exertion she really hadn't worried what anyone might think about her swollen eyes.

Clearly Bailey had seen something and relayed it to the other two, because Addie Pearl had come out of the cabin to greet her as Hannah had exited the shelter of the tall pines and started toward the cabin.

Hannah had begged off dinner and Addie had kindly acted as if that had been the plan all along. Jake had given the poster to Addie, who'd invited her to come out to the mill a few days later to talk about all of her plans. Hannah had been grateful for her kindness and smiled now as she remembered the wonderfully productive meeting they'd shared just a few days ago. She was especially grateful that Addie hadn't once brought up Will or so much as hinted around what had happened in the lamb house. Hannah supposed Will might have told Addie himself, but somehow Hannah doubted that.

He'd been at the farmhouse working on the final chimney and fireplace almost every day since, making up for the rainy days the week before. There had been no sign of Jake or Bailey, and that worried her a little. But hadn't she just been telling herself maybe it was better to take a step back? And that was before she'd kissed Jake's dad.

Will hadn't been rude; he was too polite and well mannered for that. But he hadn't been more than polite, either. Certainly not overtly friendly, and those smiles they'd shared, the laughter, they were a distant memory. He wasn't dour or moody, he was simply . . . focused. Serious. Businesslike.

"A little help please," Vivi called out from the side porch, this time sounding more harried and less manipulative.

Hannah put down the lavender stem she'd been staring at

for a full minute. Her mind had wandered more often of late. Mostly to this same topic. She really needed to find her way past it. So what if Will was the first man she'd kissed since her ex-husband had packed up and walked out less than one year after the accident? And there hadn't been any kissing him either since long before that day. Before the accident, even. And what she'd shared with Will wasn't even a real kiss. It was just a result of a moment of overwrought emotion. *It was a real kiss.*

"Hannah, honey?"

"Coming!" she called out, silently berating herself. She was behaving worse than a lovesick teenager. She hurried out to the veranda and spied Vivi up on a ladder, hanging paper lanterns from the exposed beams overhead. "Oh my word, what on earth?" Hannah ran over, scooting between the round café tables that now dotted the deep side porch. "You shouldn't be up there."

"Honey, the day I lose my ability to balance on my own two feet is the day you can just put me in the ground." Vivi shifted a bit and wrapped the lantern strings around the hook that was already in the beam. "And that's without a twenty-five-pound headpiece perched on my head. Hand me that little rubber-tipped clamp, will you? I dropped mine. There's a pile on the table there."

Hannah grabbed one of the little clamps and handed it up to Vivi, who neatly clipped it on the hook, holding the lantern string in place. She was not at all convinced it was wise for Vivienne to be up there. "I wouldn't trust me on a step stool," Hannah told her, then held the stepladder steady as Vivi climbed back down.

Vivi ignored Hannah's admonitions, brushed her hands, and propped them on her hips as she looked overhead. "There. That's a good start."

Hannah looked up and realized this was not the first

lantern Vivi had hung. In her rush to get to Vivi before she fell on her head, Hannah hadn't really taken in the room. "Oh," she said, instantly entranced. She placed a hand over her heart and did a slow turn. "Vivienne, it's exactly right."

"It was Avery's idea to use the little clamps. She spied all the little eye hooks already screwed into the beams. I'm guessing we won't be the first ones to host events out here. Looks like folks have been stringing up lights and such long before we had the idea."

"It's perfect." Hannah took in the wonderland Vivi had managed to create from their heretofore plain-jane veranda. The enclosed space was quite deep, with plank flooring painted a soft blue gray. The front wall that faced the fields and mountains was a series of French doors, also white, with big, panel-sized windows that afforded a beautiful view when closed. Each of them could be propped open as well, to create an outdoor café feeling, while still being protected from the sun and the elements.

Overhead, the ceiling slanted in a gentle slope from the side of the house, with exposed beams painted white, and freshly stained wood running the opposite direction between. Three ceiling fans were spaced evenly overhead between the beams, their long, broad paddles turning lazily overhead, keeping the air moving without creating a wind funnel in the doing.

In between the beams, strung in a crisscross pattern, were strands of white fairy lights. And from the beams themselves hung a scattered array of pretty little paper lanterns, all in white, in a variety of shapes and sizes. The lanterns closest to the fans were positioned well above the paddles, and others hung at different lengths from the beams, each clipped to the same eye hooks the light strands were strung through.

"It's so pretty and soft," Hannah said. "It really makes the whole space feel quietly festive and roomier."

Vivi's years spent as a costumer had given her a good eye for design and patterning. Who would have thought that skill would lend itself to interior decor, but it seemed the most obvious thing in the world to Hannah now.

"You've created a little wonderland out here."

Vivi beamed. "I thought the fairy lights added just the right dash of magic to our otherwise bucolic little spot. But it needed . . . something more. I want the view of the lavender fields and the mountains to be the focal point, so it couldn't be anything too strong." She glanced up again. "But we needed something beyond what the little twinklers added, in case it's an overcast day, and I didn't want anything industrial looking." She laughed. "I mean, why be functional when you can be inventive?"

"Why indeed," Hannah said with a laugh.

"Do you know it was Chey who came up with the idea of little paper lanterns?"

Surprised bordering on shocked, Hannah pulled her attention away from the delightfully cheerful lighting and looked at Vivi. "Chey? Really? I'm surprised she'd even notice, much less offer interior decorating tips."

"I was fretting over what to add and I wouldn't stop going on about it. I think she threw the idea out there just to shut me up."

Hannah laughed. "That I believe."

"She said some friend of hers back in Wyoming did something similar for her wedding. Hung them from trees or some such. Outdoor shindig. But I knew in an instant she'd hit it right on the head."

"She did indeed."

"I called in a favor with a friend of mine back in Chinatown. I didn't want anything flashy or gaudy. He hooked me up with the right guy and they shipped them last week."

"Well, you've outdone yourself."

Vivi looked from the lights overhead to the arrangement of café tables, and her expression shifted to a look of concern. "I've saved the worst part for last."

Hannah frowned. "What worst?" She looked around. "The place looks amazing. I can't believe you pulled all this together in a matter of weeks."

"Honey, I ran costuming for two musicals that had three-year runs. Each. Throwing some tables and some lighting together?" She barked a laugh. "Child's play."

Hannah happened to know that Vivi had spent a good part of the past few weeks fretting over what kind of café tables to get. Choosing the style of chairs alone had almost driven them all out of the house. She decided it would be prudent not to mention that. "What's left to do? Or do you mean the menu? Because I really love our idea of keeping this welcome party simple and pared down. I think you've put together the perfect—"

"Table settings," Vivi stated somewhat emphatically, talking over her. "Oh, my word, do you have any idea how many choices there are? I've narrowed it down to twenty. And it was painful, I tell you, painful."

"Twenty?" Hannah said faintly.

"There is so much out there today. Stunning, tasteful . . . and the colors?" She clasped her chest and closed her eyes as if overcome, ever the showgirl. "To die for, I tell you."

Hannah grinned. It was impossible not to get swept along on Vivi's demonstrative, ebullient rapture. "Well," she said, looking around again, with a shrewd eye this time. "I've never been one for hostessing parties, but I do know a little about color theory." An idea came to her and she quickly counted the tables. There were six round tables that seated four, positioned centrally, from one end of the veranda to the other. Those were surrounded by close to a dozen smaller, two-person tables. She looked back at Vivi. "Could you maybe just trim your final choice list by a few?"

Vivi's gaze narrowed in speculative interest. "What have you got in mind?"

"The lights, the lanterns, the tables, are all white, in keeping with our summer theme of cool and calm. You're right that the fields, the mountains, the gardens, will provide the big, splashy view, with all the gorgeous colors." Warming to her idea, she said, "What if you picked two to four settings of each of your final choices? Each table gets its own setting? I'm guessing you went floral and cheerful, which is perfect. Floral settings will add just the right splash of color to elevate the background tableau of white tables, chairs, lights, and lanterns, making them feel light and airy. We'll do centerpieces made from our lavender as a unifying theme. As the settings are flat, they won't compete with the view. Patrons will look down and see a pretty table, and up to take in the stunning panoramic view. Does that make sense?"

Vivi immediately swept her up in a tight bear hug. "Darling, you've gotten it right on the first go." She squeezed again, cutting off Hannah's surprised laugh on a gasp. For her age and wiry frame, Vivi had surprising strength. "Oh, I could kiss you." She let go and leaned back to beam up into Hannah's face. "In fact, I think I will." She rose up on her toes and gave Hannah a noisy kiss on the cheek, then blotted at the bright lipstick mark she left behind. "And we thought Avery was the only genius in our fabulous little cobbled together family."

The sound of someone clearing his throat stopped their conversation. "Sorry to interrupt."

Both women turned to find Will standing in the doorway that led to the kitchen.

"The fireplace mantel and fronting is done," he told them

without preamble, "but I have a few questions before I start on the hearth." He gave Hannah a perfunctory nod but kept his attention on Vivi.

For Hannah's part, she nodded back, her smile . . . well, maybe easy wasn't the word, but it was sincere. Yes, that was one way to describe it. He'd been kind to her in the lamb house that day. He didn't want anything beyond that. Also fair. She just wished she could get to the point where she could look at the man without wanting to devour him.

Honest to goodness, he was in filthy dark green canvas trousers and a black T-shirt that had seen better days. Years, even. His hair was caked in white dust from cutting rock, and his face was streaked with more of the same. And if he'd walked up to her right then and cupped her cheek, the way he had that day in the stable, she'd have willingly gone right into his arms, filthy clothes and dusty everything be damned.

Vivi looked from Will to Hannah, then back to Will, a considering look on her exquisitely made up face. "Well, I've got my hands a little full here. Hannah, be a darling and go up and help sort out whatever the questions are." She flashed a smile at Hannah, her eyes alight with intent. "I trust your judgment."

Hannah didn't miss the message. But that didn't mean she had to go along with it. "Oh, I've still got a whole basket of lavender buds to pick, and it's your bedroom, Vivi. Surely you'd rather—"

"You've got great taste, which you just proved by saving me days on those place settings," Vivi said. "It shouldn't take but a minute or two. I've got to get the rest of these rascals organized, so the patterning works. These ceiling fans are throwing my design off." She shrugged. "If it isn't one thing it's another." She waved her beringed hand as if the matter was settled.

When neither Will nor Hannah said anything, much less

made a move to follow orders, Vivi moved the ladder over a few feet, grabbed another lantern and clamp from the café table, and started climbing.

"Ms. Baudin," Will said, immediately concerned.

"Now, don't you go making me give you the same lecture I just gave Miss Hannah. And for the last time, it's Vivi. Now go on, both of you."

Hannah noted the concern on Will's face didn't ease one whit as Vivienne climbed to the top rung of the stepladder. He glanced to Hannah as if silently asking whether they should do something.

"She used to do far more complicated things than this, in spike heels, wearing about thirty pounds of three-foot-tall feathers and beaded crowns on her head," Hannah told him. "I agree with your assessment, but I'm pretty sure she could do acrobatics off the top step that would put us both to shame."

Vivi hooted at that. "You've got that right, sister. Go on now. I'll holler if I need either of you. Avery's back in her lab playing mad scientist, so she can come out here if necessary, but she said something about timing being important so things don't explode and I didn't want to risk that."

"No," Hannah said faintly. "That would be bad."

Despite both Hannah's and Vivi's assurances, Will still had a dubious expression on his face, but rather than risk insulting the woman who'd hired him, he finally acquiesced and nodded at Hannah. "I'm sorry to intrude on your schedule. Should only take a minute."

Hannah nodded and swore she could feel the heat of Vivi's gaze on her back as she followed Will into the house. He didn't say anything as she trailed him down the hall to the main staircase. He paused to allow her to ascend first, but she waved him on. "Go ahead, I'll follow." It was already uncomfortable enough. She didn't need to feel his gaze drilling her in the back—or anywhere else—as they walked up the stairs.

He paused a moment, as if wanting to say something, but in the end, simply nodded and went quickly up the stairs. "Vivienne wants a raised hearth," he said, all business once again. "But I think it would look better to have a small mantel in front of the base, then build in the hearth at floor level. That would have the effect of creating a raised fireplace, making it easier for her to put in fresh firewood, and clear out ashes."

She followed him into the room. Vivi was having electrical work and painting done in the other rooms at the same time as the fireplace restoration, so there were plastic sheets taped to doorways to keep the dust out, her grand four-poster had been moved to the middle of the bedroom, the mattress stripped and draped with cloth. Her antique dressing table, chifforobe, and wardrobe had also been draped. The rest of the furnishings had been moved to one of the other top floor rooms that wasn't presently being renovated.

Hannah knew that Vivi had been sleeping on a daybed in that same otherwise unfurnished room. Well, Vivi called it a daybed. Hannah called it what it was, "the glorious divan of Broadway." What else would one call an eggplant-colored, velveteen settee the size of a modest ocean liner, with a curvy, heavily upholstered back, gold braid trim, and decorative legs that had been elaborately hand painted with a detailed floral pattern. It was an amazing piece of structural art, but challenging to work into a room decor plan . . . unless you were Vivienne Baudin.

Hannah walked over to the fireplace, her mouth dropping open in awe. "That's positively stunning, Will." The fireplace front had been redone in river rock, with a hand-chiseled granite mantelpiece that had been reclaimed from a condemned courthouse down in Rockfish. Will had inlaid the river rock in a pattern that made it look like flowing water. The variety of colored stones had been arranged in curves and swirls, all working together as if the water itself had swept them into the flow of the design. "That's truly a work of art." She turned to him. "I could stare at that for hours. Daily. Is this typical of the kind of thing you do?" She looked back at the fireplace. "I would think something so elaborate would take . . . well, I don't know. I couldn't even imagine." She fell silent as she let her gaze trail along the variety of coils and gentle flourishes that all flowed together to create the overall movement in the pattern. "I was just up here a few days ago, and you hadn't even begun."

"The rocks tell you where they need to go," he said, as if he'd merely been the messenger.

Hannah looked to him. "Has Vivi seen this?"

He nodded. "She wanted something different from the bluestone work of the main fireplace downstairs. I showed her some photos of other work I've done, and she decided on river rock. I was skeptical, but she was set on having it."

"I think it's a wonderful choice. I agree you might imagine it would be too contemporary or rustic contrasted with her big, heavy antique pieces, but it's going to look amazing when this room is all done." She smiled. "I can't imagine any setting that this wouldn't complement, really." Once she'd finished gushing, she realized that he hadn't really relaxed or joined in. The awkward ice hadn't really been broken at all. "Will—"

"Hannah—"

They spoke at the same time, but Will gestured for her to continue.

She nodded, then took a moment to find the right words. "I don't want things to be awkward between us," she said, opting to get straight to the matter in hopes they could clear away the strain and move on. "What happened in the lamb house"—she held his gaze—"all of it . . . I know it was just the moment, the emotional intensity of it all. I don't want you to be uncomfortable, or . . . anything, when we're around each other. And I feel like you are. We both are. I'm hoping we can find our way back to simply being . . . who we are. Talk when we want, laugh when the moment calls for it."

If his impassive expression was anything to go by, maybe she'd misread the situation entirely, and he was behaving exactly in the way that made him comfortable, which was to say, not talking at all.

"Maybe I'm just speaking for myself," she said into the growing silence. "I just don't want you to feel you need to avoid being direct with me or saying whatever is on your mind. I feel as if we're dancing around things. Maybe one specific thing. So, I was hoping to clear the air."

"I was under the impression that maybe you'd just as soon take a step back entirely," he said, calmly but definitely directly. "And that's okay. Your prerogative. I was just trying to give you that space."

She hadn't really known what he might say, but she hadn't expected anything like that. She frowned. "What gave you that idea?" she asked, sincerely confused by his assumption.

"Actually, it was something Jake said."

Now she was completely flummoxed. "Jake? I don't think Jake and I have spoken since then. I haven't seen him. I—" She broke off, trying to think if she'd missed something that might have hurt or insulted Will's son, but drew a blank. The last time she'd seen him had been in the lamb house the previous week.

At her sincere confusion, Will's implacable manner faltered slightly. "That was actually what he mentioned. He said it seemed as if you were avoiding him and he wondered if he'd done or said something to offend or annoy you."

Hannah felt her cheeks grow warm with embarrassment, and maybe a little bit of shame tossed in. She ducked her chin for a moment, gathering new thoughts, then looked at Will and said, "That is on me, and I apologize. It's just . . . given what happened between us, and you not wanting to talk about it . . . I—" She broke off for a moment, unsure just how candid she should be with Jake's father, but what did she have to lose? "I just . . . I could be misreading things entirely, but I think Jake was developing a little crush? Completely innocent," she hurried to add. "Very sweet actually. Endearing. But then I had my breakdown out in the barn, and you and I had . . . our moment. Then you seemed to want to step back, way back. And I just thought maybe it was best to keep my distance. I didn't come out and say that, but Jake is busy with school, and the winery, and the upcoming music festival. I didn't think he'd really notice."

"I can see why you'd figure that," Will responded after taking a moment to think on what she'd said. "I take some of the responsibility for that, too, then." He paused, as if he was trying to decide how candid to be, and admittedly that got Hannah curious all over again.

"My dilemma—and I agree with you that Jake might be a little sweet on you. I appreciate your taking his feelings into consideration." He looked at her directly, and for the first time since they'd kissed, he seemed to be talking to her like the man he'd been that day. The man who'd smiled more, talked more, and offered to accompany her to the stable. The man she'd begun to like almost as much as she'd already begun to lust after him. *Dangerous thoughts, Hannah. Which is it going to be?*

"I wouldn't have brought it up except Vivienne has asked Jake if he'd like to help with serving at your upcoming

Welcome to the Farm party. He wouldn't be serving any of Seth's wine, of course, due to his age, but she did invite him to serve some of his grape juice, along with the food and things you all will be having."

Hannah's lips immediately curved. "That sounds like a wonderful idea. He's a charming young man, Will. I think he'd do a wonderful job." Will didn't look as if he'd been put at ease by her enthusiastic response. Her smile faltered. "Does Jake not want to do it? Or would he rather not serve his juice? I know he's still perfecting it. If so, Vivi won't be offended, none of us would be. I'm sure she just thought it would be a nice fit since he's been helping you out here and we're featuring Bluestone & Vine's wine label. Please don't let him worry if—"

"It's not that," Will said. "He was flattered to be asked. Excited even."

Hannah was confused. "What's the problem then?"

Will looked a little uncomfortable now. "It ties back to Jake wondering if he did something wrong, if you were avoiding him. He wants to take the job, but not if you'd be upset."

Hannah was instantly crestfallen. "Oh no. I'm so sorry. That's not at all what I intended," she said. "I'll have a talk with him, assure him things are fine." She looked at Will then. "If that's okay with you. I just . . . I honestly wasn't sure how to proceed."

"It's not you. I know you were doing what you thought was right. Kids can be really simple, and really compli-cated, all at the same time."

"Don't I know it," Hannah replied with a light laugh, thinking back to some of the brain-bending conversations she and Liam had had, when she'd been trying to get him to understand something and he'd come back at her with his adolescent pretzel logic.

She noticed Will was looking at her then, looking into her, but his expression was completely unreadable.

"You illustrated children's books," he said after a beat, "or still do. Sorry, I'm not prying. I guess you must have come into contact with a lot of them. Children, I mean."

Well, here you are anyway, her little voice said. Avoiding the truth now would just be adding one layer of prevarication on top of another. *Just tell him.*

"I did," she said, a little more softly, but with a steady smile. And it was an honest one. "At book signings and other events. It was an education in and of itself, to be sure." She took a small, steadying breath, hoping she didn't spoil what détente they'd achieved, but he needed to know where she was coming from. She held his gaze steadily and let the warmth of her love for her son shine through in her expression and her voice. "I also know what it's like raising children, young children anyway. I had a son. Liam. He was a delight, a dervish, my perfect child, and a handful, pretty much every day."

Clearly, Will heard the past tense, because she could see the moment he registered what that meant. That flash of bleakness in his eyes, the utter devastation that came right after imagining such a thing, then the fear that was instinctive and normal, personalizing it, imagining what it would be like if that same thing were to happen to you. She didn't like telling people for that reason alone. She didn't want anyone to experience even a moment of the pain she had known, even if it was just imagined.

She continued, saving him from having to find the right words. She needed him to know all of it. "I lost him when he was seven. Car accident. I was in it, too. We were hit by someone who ran a stop sign. I never even saw the other car. It was instant, for him, for which I'm forever grateful." She took a short breath, let it out again. "It wasn't recent, it was seven years ago. Sometimes that feels like yesterday, but I've worked hard in the years since to find a perspective that I can live with, move forward with, that still honors him, but gives me the strength to live a life we could both be proud of." Her expression warmed. "He'd be Jake's age now," she said, and saw Will had already put that much together. "So . . . that's been a bit of a thing for me. I haven't spent time around anyone his age, and the comparisons are natural, of course." She hurried on when she saw empathetic pain on his handsome face. "It's not a bad thing, Will. Your son is so lovely—my hope is my son might have turned out half as well. It's made it a bit rocky for me at times, but that's how life is. There are smooth times, bumpy times, joyous times, and sometimes downright terrible times. Like out at the lamb house. Some of those times are about Liam, but not all. Life doles out pain and joy in regular fashion for all kinds of things." She smiled a bit more widely then. "Take this house for instance."

He looked gutted on her behalf, and she instinctively stepped forward, wanting to make it easier for him to deal with her stuff. "It's been smooth more often than not for a good while now, so I was a little rusty handling the bumpy stuff. That's why I fell apart in the stable. I think I was maybe glossing over a bit more than I thought I was, and I should have dealt with it more directly. Given myself more of a break. But"—she lifted a shoulder—"it's a process. And there is no guidebook. So, I've been all over the map, especially with Jake. And I'm very sorry about that."

She did stop talking then, because she suspected that, while he'd never suffered the loss of a child, he had suffered loss. Of his wife, she was almost certain. Would he say something now? Reveal his understanding? That was up to him. His story to tell now. And she wouldn't be insulted if he didn't, or never did, because that wasn't about her. That she knew all too well.

"You don't have to apologize," he said, his voice thick with emotion. "For anything." He looked away for a moment, and she caught the sheen in his eyes.

"I am sorry, though," she told him. "Jake doesn't need to have his emotions jerked around—even by someone doing it unwittingly. I should have been more thoughtful in how I handled the situation. I would like to talk to him, if that's okay. I won't tell him about Liam, if you'd rather I not. Although . . . I don't know. I think he'd handle it well enough. Kids tend to better than parents do. And it might help put things into perspective." Her expression gentled and a hint of a wry note snuck in. "Probably take care of that crush, at any rate."

Will glanced down, shook his head. "I'll talk to him."

He'd said it quietly, but Hannah wasn't sure how to take his response. Her smile faded. "If you're afraid I befriended him because I saw him as some kind of replace—"

Will's gaze shot up at that, and she broke off when she immediately saw that that hadn't been his thought at all. She immediately relaxed, relieved and grateful for that much at least.

"Maybe I've only made this more awkward," she said. "It wasn't my intent. I just . . . when you brought up children, it seemed wrong not to explain. I didn't want to pretend I didn't understand what you meant. I didn't—don't—share my story lightly though. However you'd like me to handle things with Jake, just tell me and I will. His well-being comes first."

Will nodded and took another moment to consider what she'd said.

She liked that he was thoughtful and didn't immediately jump in before thinking his responses through.

"The only thing I will add is that I know in time people will learn my story. Not from you, but . . . relationships form and conversations happen, like it did today. I don't go around announcing my loss for obvious reasons, but also because I want folks to get to know me as me, separate from that. I will forever be a grieving mom, but I'm so much more than that, too. Unfortunately, but understandably, when people hear about what happened, that one fact tends to overshadow everything else. I want folks to get to know the rest of me, before that information gets factored in, but I know it will at some point. And I only mention that because Jake will hear about it somewhere, from someone, eventually. So, you may want to share it with him yourself. Or I can, if you think . . ." She trailed off then. "Anyway, whatever you think is best. I just don't want Jake thinking that I don't have his best interests at heart and I definitely don't want him thinking that he's done something wrong, or that I'm unhappy with him for any reason. I wish I'd handled it better."

Will nodded, and finally spoke. "Please don't worry about that. I'm just sorry if being around him has made any part of your life more challenging. You've been nothing but kind and generous to him. I can have him stay up at the winery helping Seth while I finish here, so you don't have to—"

"No, no, that's not necessary." Hannah did frown then, realizing she was really mucking this up. "Not at all. Please let Jake be Jake. Tell him or don't tell him, whatever you think best. I can simply put myself in his path and we can be our normal selves, and he'll know from that that I harbor no ill will."

"Okay," Will said, but he was clearly still thinking the whole thing over. "Thank you. For your thoughtfulness."

He looked like he wanted to say something more, and she felt doubly bad for putting him in that unasked for position.

"It's okay, Will," she told him, knowing he'd understand what she meant. "You don't have to tiptoe around me or that particular subject, okay? Just . . . act as you normally would." She smiled, then grinned. "You know, ignoring me when possible and speaking in monosyllabic sentences at all costs. Definitely no smiling, and God forbid we should laugh."

He looked startled at the teasingly offered dig, and finally—finally—a hint of a surprised smile played at the corners of his mouth. She'd meant to shock him out of the moment they'd found themselves in and was happy to see it had worked.

"You're a special force, Hannah Montgomery," he said, almost to himself.

"I try to be," she told him, believing he'd meant it as a compliment. "Keeps folks on their toes. Makes life more interesting."

He met her gaze then, and she had no idea what he saw now, when he looked at her. There was a trace of humor in his eyes, and a healthy dose of respect.

She was relieved.

"I'll talk to Jake. Tell him it was a misunderstanding, that you've just been busy with the event coming up."

She nodded. "Thank you."

Will held her gaze. "And you can stay 'too busy' if that's best for you. Your well-being matters, too. I'll make sure he knows it's not personal."

"Thank you," Hannah said again, touched. "I appreciate that." She smiled. "How about if we just take things as they go?"

He nodded. "That sounds fine."

She walked to the door then, so she could leave him to his work.

"Hannah."

She paused and turned back.

"I just want you to know, if you do spend time with Jake, and a moment happens, and you think it's the right time to mention your son . . ." He broke off, and a hint of that pain, and his empathy for her, shone clearly in his eyes. "Please do," he said. His throat worked then and he added, a bit hoarsely now, "I'd be honored to know you thought enough of my son to share something of yours with him."

Chapter Nine

He was a flat-out coward. Of the white-bellied, lily-livered variety. Will nodded and lifted his hand as Jake turned and waved to him before crossing the gravel lot toward the rear entrance of Blue Hollow Falls' new music amphitheater.

The grand opening festival was still close to two months out, but the local musicians who would be performing that day were already getting together to start working on the program, figuring out playlists, and helping the technicians set up and install all the soundboards, the lighting, and the myriad other minutiae that went into setting up a such a venue.

Jake had invited his dad to come sit in on their jam session but hadn't been at all surprised when Will had begged off, claiming an avalanche of work. The workload was real, but they both knew it was a convenient cover story, as well.

The fact that his son continued to ask him, always casually, never wheedling or demanding, or giving Will attitude at his lame dodges . . . just made Will feel every bit the small, selfish man he knew he'd become when it came to confronting that particular ghost from his past.

He knew Jake understood. Which just made it all the worse. What father wanted his son's pity? Not this father, and yet . . . His son showed courage by continuing to give his father a chance to man up. *Maybe you can reward that courage by mustering some of your own.*

Will climbed back in his pickup truck and his thoughts went, as they seemed to do every single waking moment these days, to Hannah. Talk about courage. Her courage, her strength, her . . . everything, humbled him to his core. His heart clutched in a painful knot as his gaze went back to Jake, and he tried to fathom what it would do to him to lose his only child. He'd never gotten over losing Zoey, but as tragic and awful and utterly life altering as that had been for him, the idea of losing his child . . . ? Not that any tragedy could be—or should ever be—compared or ranked next to another, but he couldn't deny the fact that thinking about the loss Hannah had suffered had helped him to put the loss of his wife in a whole new perspective.

Hannah seemed to have found some way to manage her unimaginable grief. She was a testament to not only forging a brave path forward, but an admirable, purpose-driven one as well. He might have thought her super-human, had he not witnessed the wrenching grief that had swallowed her whole that day in the lamb house. He knew she was all too human, a grieving mom, figuring out her life as she lived it. But something else she'd said had struck him in the days that followed, digging deeper, and deeper still, taking root.

I will forever be a grieving mom, but I'm so much more than that.

Will thought he'd become more than a grieving husband. And he had. He was a father, a son, a good friend, a Marine, and a damn good mason. But somewhere along the way, he'd let the grieving husband take the lead, become the face of who he was. He'd convinced himself he'd put fatherhood first. Being a good provider who was proud of his day's work, and a good friend were also top priorities.

He'd have said those were the focal elements, the purpose on which he'd built his life. He'd merely opted to put becoming a partner to someone new on the back burner. Or on no burner. And that choice didn't affect anyone but him. Right?

Will watched his suddenly too tall and too mature son disappear inside the venue and accepted that he might have become all of those things, but first and foremost, he'd let his grief guide him, control his actions, his decisions. All these years later he was still doing that, as if it was his right, still believing that the only one paying for his grief was him, that how he handled that part of his life was purely his own business. He had the important bases covered.

The truth of it was he'd been the only one benefitting from his choice to let his grief guide him, rather than the other way around. That choice had allowed him to avoid doing the hard work Hannah had done. Had allowed him to simply close off what had once been the most important part of his life. And the ones who'd paid for it had been everyone else but him. His son in particular.

How was it he hadn't seen that?

His son—his teenage son, who should be at an age when he'd be mortified to have him share in some hobby or passion of his—was inside that venue right now creating something he wanted his dad to be part of, but no. His dad would rather cower behind his shield of grief.

He squeezed his eyes closed. "You sorry son of a bitch."

Last summer, when Jake had sung and played the fiddle for the first time, had also been the first time Will had allowed his grief so much as a toehold in him since Zoey had died.

And because he hadn't done the hard work Hannah had, that night his grief had consumed him, swamped him, as if the tragedy had just happened to him all over again. He'd known then that he needed to change. And he'd intended to. But he hadn't initially known how to reach out for help, or where to turn. So he put it off. Then off again. And one day turned into the next, and then another, and then a week went by, then a month, and here he was, almost a year later and he'd made no effort at all. Once again, he'd taken the easy path.

So why didn't it feel so damn easy?

A tap on the driver side window jerked him from his thoughts, startling him back into awareness. He wasn't even sure how long he'd been sitting there. He turned to find Bailey standing beside his truck, an implacable look on her young face. Will glanced around the parking area but didn't see anyone else. He assumed Addie Pearl must have dropped her off but he'd been so lost in his thoughts he hadn't noticed.

He lowered the window. "Yes, Miss Bailey," he said politely enough, as if they'd just bumped into each other on the street. "What can I do for you?"

"Jake asked me to come listen to him play. He wants honest feedback and knows I'll give it to him. You coming in?"

It was clear from the very direct look she was giving him that she was well aware Jake had probably already asked him, and that Will wasn't sitting there in his truck because he'd said yes. It was also clear she wasn't going to be as acquiescent in accepting his lame excuses as his son had been.

Shamed into manning up by an eleven-year-old.

He let out a little sigh and looked back at the amphitheater. *What are you waiting for? Your son's life is passing right before you and you're out here sitting on the sidelines. What are you so afraid of?*

He had an answer for that now, at least. He was afraid he'd fall apart like Hannah had out in the stable. Like he had the night Jake had first played. He was afraid it would always be like that. That he wouldn't find a way through it, as Hannah had. That he'd be giving up control of his life, of himself.

"Here," Bailey said, and she handed him a big, white, linen hankie. "This belonged to someone I cared about." She shook it until he took it. "He took care of me for a few years, but he had some problems from when he was in the army. He was special forces like Sawyer and Seth, and I guess he did things that he didn't know how to deal with when he came back home. Eventually, he had to go somewhere they could take care of him all the time and I had to go back to a group home."

Will just sat there, totally unprepared for the fusillade of information Bailey was directing at him. In the two years he'd known her, since she and Jake had become good friends, he'd never known her to talk about her past.

"I stole that from his nightstand before they came to get me," she said, utterly unrepentant. "His wife—I never knew her—she stitched his initials in it. I wanted something to remember him by. It's clean," she added, as if that mattered.

"Why are you giving this to me?" Will asked, his throat so tight he barely got the words out. His eyes were burning, too, just a little.

"Because I'd like you to come inside and sit with me while we listen to Jake play his fiddle. It's an awful fiddle, by the way. He needs a new one, a much better one, and he won't tell you this, but I know he's hoping you'll get past whatever it is that's keeping you from being able to come and share his music with him, and maybe make him one of his very own like you did for his mom." She eyed him. "He'd kill me for telling you that, by the way, so it would be great if you wouldn't mention it to him. Our secret." She nodded to the linen. "Like the hankie. You can give it back whenever you're done with it." She eyed him flatly. "Clean, please."

That surprised a hoarse bark of laughter from Will and he

nodded. There might have been something in his eye, too, that needed brushing away. Good thing he had a hankie now.

"No one is going to care if you cry," Bailey told him, quite matter-of-factly. "I mean, the way Jake plays, what he can do with that fiddle? It would bring a tear to any music lover's eye." She paused, as if considering her next words. "I probably shouldn't say this, but then I probably shouldn't say a lot of things. It's just, I don't think you need more folks tiptoeing around you, you know? If anyone under-stands what it's like not to have family, it's me, so that maybe gives me a different perspective on what is impor-tant in life, and what's not. So, I think maybe it's okay if I'm the one who doesn't tiptoe around you and just puts it out there."

Will's eyebrows lifted a bit at that, but he didn't stop her.

"What's not important is worrying about what other folks think about you. Besides, I think folks here all know why you don't make fiddles anymore, why you don't play, so even if you do the big, ugly cry, they'll just be happy you're there for Jake. It's just a few of us here today anyway. Friends and family." She gave him another pointed look. "I didn't have either of those things before, but I'm lucky enough to have them both now. So I know that supporting them, being there for them, no matter what my personal deal is? *That's* what *is* important."

If he thought he couldn't be any more humbled than he had been by observing Hannah's courage in the face of what would seem to be insurmountable grief, he'd been wrong. *Out of the mouths of babes.*

"Even if you never play again, or you don't make an-other fiddle, that won't matter so much if you can at least share Jake's part in it. Might be a shame for everyone else, though, because from what I hear, Jake comes by his crazy talent with that thing honestly." She shrugged. "But that's your thing."

He could tell pretty much anyone else that they didn't understand, that he appreciated the kind words and the intent to help him and his son and be sincerely grateful for the effort. Pretty much anyone except Hannah. And now Bailey. He looked past her again, wondering if Addie Pearl had had a hand in this little talk somehow. Will wouldn't be surprised, but he also knew that assumption didn't give Bailey enough credit.

"Jake is very fortunate to call you a friend," he told her.

"He'd do the same for me," she said, seriously and quite deliberately.

Will thought his son probably would. He let out a slow breath.

"We can sit all the way in the back," she told him. "Jake wants a sound check from the cheap seats anyway." She stepped back as if assuming Will was just going to get out of the truck and go with her.

So why don't you?

"Why don't I indeed," he murmured. He inhaled deeply, filling his lungs, clearing his head, then let it go, and tried to let everything else go with it. Then he rolled up the window and took his keys from the ignition. And got out of the truck.

Chapter Ten

Hannah tugged at the edge of her wide-brimmed hat to help block out the June sunshine. She'd already slid over one tail of the scarf she'd tied around the brim and spread it out a bit, so the draped material created a further shield from the glare. That was why she hadn't seen him until just that moment, when she'd turned to squeeze a little more paint onto her palette.

Will was sitting at the very back of the amphitheater. With . . . was that Bailey?

Hannah squinted and shielded her eyes. She shouldn't stare; it was just so unexpected. Not that he would see her anyway. She had positioned her easel and canvas east of the stage, so she could capture the sweep of the broad-beamed awning that extended outward from over the stage toward the seats that had been built into the slope of the hill, amphitheater style. The top of the hill leveled off, providing lawn seating, but the way the pavilion-style stage had been built, down in the hollow, provided wonderful, natural acoustics. The venue was rustic and seemed to fit organically into the lay of the land, as if it was meant to be there, had always been there.

The mill was not quite a quarter mile away, through a

copse of pine, cedar, and sycamore trees that dotted the edge of Big Stone Creek. Cars were parked in a cleared stretch between the two venues for those who wanted to drive in. Natural footpaths and trails that connected the mill and the music venue had been cleared of fallen limbs and leaves, widened where necessary, and clearly marked, so guests could wander from one location to the other. A series of hand-hewn benches created by a few of the mill artisans had been added in several spots near the water. A small number of picnic tables, grills, and fire pits would eventually be added along the riverside trails as well, hopefully before summer's end.

Hannah had wandered the footpaths several times with her sketch pad and pencils, doing some rough drafts of scenes that had caught her attention. The venue itself was beautiful, rich with color, and now with the music filling the warm, late afternoon air, she'd given in to the urge and gone and gotten her paints and supplies from her Jeep, thankful she'd had a small, blank canvas tucked in her large tote along with her watercolor pads. Just in case. She didn't work with oils often, preferring the soft wash of watercolors, but she'd given in to the urge to dabble, and was pleased with her results so far.

At the moment though, her painting was forgotten, as she tried not to watch Will, watching his son play the fiddle . . . and failed miserably. Jake had been onstage several times over the past two hours, playing and singing both, sometimes pairing with Seth's wife, Pippa, other times with various other musicians, and a few times he'd taken that big stage by himself. He was a remarkable talent both singing and playing, and Hannah simply couldn't believe he'd only picked up a bow just a year before. Jake was an amazing musician, and watching him, it was clear his passion for the instrument matched his talent. She remembered his excitement about growing grapes and wondered which passion would win out when it came time to pursue a career path.

Hannah had no idea how long Will had been there, but it filled her heart to see he'd come. She and Jake hadn't spoken much since her talk with Will in Vivi's bedroom, just enough to give her a chance to make sure Jake knew she wasn't put out with him for any reason. Hannah knew, however, that Will didn't involve himself in Jake's musical ventures, and that it apparently had something to do with Jake's mom.

It was funny, Hannah mused, as she watched Bailey talking animatedly to Will after they finished applauding the song that Jake and the other musicians had just finished playing. When she'd been trying to find ways to learn more about Will McCall without coming out and asking, she'd been stymied at every turn.

Now that he had finished the work on the fireplaces and chimneys out at the farmhouse, and hadn't yet begun the other stonework Vivi had discussed with him, Hannah didn't see him regularly anymore. Or at all, actually. Yet, it seemed that all anyone did when they were around her was talk about Will and Jake McCall.

Hannah had told herself it was for the best that he wasn't in her daily orbit, that she'd had the chance to make sure Jake knew she wasn't upset with him in any way, but that he, too, was off doing other things and they no longer crossed paths with any regularity. Will was still dealing with his past, and had his hands full raising a smart, energetic, brilliantly talented young man. Hannah had her hands full, too: Lavender Blue's welcome party was all but upon them; the learning curve of getting the farm up and producing was still an overwhelming factor; and she was painting again, producing work that she, as a full member of the Bluebird Crafters Guild now, would be making available for sale, both at the mill and out at the farmhouse.

Better for the two of them to pursue their own paths forward. That not-kiss-that-had-totally-been-a-kiss was a pleasant memory. Okay, maybe a thrilling memory in many ways. Nothing wrong with that. A good piece of information to know about herself as she moved onward with her life here in her new home. She could feel things again, things a woman felt, separate and apart from being a mother or a businesswoman. That was good to know. Some future time, maybe she'd be fortunate enough to meet someone, and who knew . . . maybe she'd open herself up to that part of her life again. Once the farm was going, and she was more settled into her new routine with the mill and her work. Maybe.

So why does just looking at Will McCall make your heart pound and your mood brighten right up? She was going to stop staring at him, go back to her painting. Any second now.

And then it was too late. He turned his head, and despite the great distance between them, she felt the moment he laid eyes on her as surely as if he'd reached out and touched her. Feeling pinned to the spot by the weight of his gaze, she floundered. *Should I wave? Nod? Acknowledge that we're staring at each other?*

"Should you stop being a complete and utter ninny about the man?" she muttered under her breath, feeling ridiculous and all pent up, all at the same time.

But she didn't look back at her painting. And he didn't look away.

Then Bailey glanced her way, too. They were too far away for Hannah to see clearly any nuances in their expressions, but Bailey lifted her hand and waved. Hannah started to wave back, realizing too late that she still had the brush in her hand, and flung bits of sierra orange onto her shirt and face.

Hannah spluttered and laughed, immediately reaching for her rag to wipe the paint from where it had splattered across her mouth. Bailey clapped a hand over her own mouth, clearly not so far away that she hadn't figured out what had happened. Hannah turned to clean up as best she could, thankful she'd donned her apron and an old cotton shirt before starting. Fortunately, she hadn't splattered the painting itself. When she'd set things right, she turned back toward the duo in the farthermost reaches of the amphitheater, only to discover their seats were now empty.

She scanned the area and finally saw Bailey talking to Jake, who was seated at the edge of the stage, his legs dangling over the edge, fiddle propped in his lap. Hannah scanned the area again, wondering if Will had taken off now that rehearsal was apparently over, wondering why he, too, hadn't stopped to talk to Jake first.

"Hannah."

She spun around, thankfully with no loaded paintbrush in her hand this time, to find Will standing just a few yards behind her. "Will." Beaming at the mere sight of him, her expression faltered as she caught sight of his face. He looked . . . gutted. She immediately walked toward him, her determination to put him in her rearview window instantly forgotten—again—concern for him now the only thing on her mind. "Are you okay? What's happened?"

"I'm sorry to interrupt your painting," he said, his voice a bit rougher, a bit deeper than usual.

"No, I'm just dabbling," she said, waving off her work.

He looked past her at the canvas. "That's more than dabbling." He cleared his throat, kept his gaze on her work. "You're capturing the exact essence of the place."

"Thank you," she said, still looking at Will, trying to figure out what was really going on. "I don't usually work with oil paints," she added as he continued to look at the painting. "But it's something that's been in my mind for a while."

"With good reason, it looks like. What will you do with it when you're finished?"

She started to brush away his polite comments in order to turn the focus back to him, then thought maybe the small talk was helping him work his way to whatever it was he'd sought her out to say. She turned to look at the piece, which was only partly done. "Addie Pearl and the guild have accepted me as a fellow Bluebird. I'll be selling my work from my own spot in the mill. Eventually," she added. She turned back to the painting, which still held his attention. "I'm not sure I'll finish this one, though. I just needed to start it to get the image of it out of my mind and onto canvas." She shifted her gaze back to his. "I know, sounds like a big waste of time and paint, but it's sort of like bookmarking an idea for me. If it pulls me in, I'll keep going. If not . . ." She lifted a shoulder. "I'll move on to something else."

That earned a brief smile as he looked from the painting to her, though his eyes still looked hollow. "How many unfinished canvases do you have?"

Her expression turned a shade wry. "I might have had one or two or thirty stacked up against walls in my studio before I moved out here. I did manage to part with them when I packed up." She gestured to the canvas on the easel. "This might be the beginning of my new unfinished collection."

His lips curved briefly again, nodded, but that haunted look remained.

Hannah was at a loss as to what to say that would help. Should she mention Jake's amazing talent or how wonderful it had been to hear him play and sing? Or be more direct, and ask what had made Will decide to attend the rehearsal? It wasn't something they'd spoken about directly before, so that seemed perhaps a bit too forward.

The silence drew out, but before she could decide on the best path to take, Will finally spoke and made the decision for her.

"I know you have a great many things to do before the welcome party out at the farm," he began. "And now with your guild membership. Congratulations on that, by the way. They don't just accept anyone, though with your obvious talent and career as an illustrator, they're lucky to have you."

"Thank you, that's kind of you to say," she said, briefly ducking her chin. "And I'm not so busy I couldn't find time to waste on a new canvas. What do you need? Is it about Jake? Does he need a ride up to Seth's?" She suspected it was about far more than that, but didn't know how else to help him into a conversation he was clearly struggling to find a way to start.

He shook his head. "Pippa is driving him and Bailey on up. Addie Pearl will get them later and take them both to her place."

"I got here just before Pippa rehearsed. She's amazing."

Will nodded and an even bleaker look flashed across his face. "She is that."

"I understand she donated the proceeds of her last album to help build this entire venue. That's incredible. Jake has spoken of her many times, and all she's done. He's so fortunate to have her as a teacher," Hannah went on, keeping the conversation steady, when what she wanted to do was walk up to Will, wrap her arms around him, and hold on. Let him hold on to her. "I confess I wasn't familiar with her music before. I never listened to much folk music before moving here, but I can understand why she's the big deal she is in the music world."

Will nodded, and if it were possible, looked even a bit more lost than he had before.

Hannah couldn't keep up the pretense of normalcy any longer. She walked to him, put a hand on his arm, and looked him directly in the face. "Will, what is it?" she asked quietly. "Talk to me." She searched his face. "You can, you know. About anything."

He nodded, and a glassy sheen entered his eyes. "It's hard," he said, at length, but held her gaze. "Asking for help."

Her heart squeezed painfully tight at what was clearly a difficult admission from him, and she reached up without thinking that they were in a public place, or what it might look like. At the moment, it was simply the two of them, and one of them was in need. She cupped his cheek with her hand, placed her other hand on his chest. It was a far more intimate gesture than she'd have made had she taken any time to think it through. She'd simply moved to him instinctively, feeling his pain, needing to soothe it. "One of the hardest," she said softly. "I'll help any way I can."

He looked down into her eyes, not moving away from her touch. If anything, he moved into it. "I don't want to drag you through your past," he said, his voice no more than a rough burr, so quiet it just reached her ears. "You've done the hard work. I just . . ." He broke off, searched her gaze, then said, "I want to figure out how to do that, how to be able to listen to my son sing and play the fiddle, and not get swamped with feeling . . . everything."

Hannah's mouth curved into a tender, sad smile then. "That is the hard work," she told him. "Letting yourself be swamped."

She hadn't thought his beautiful eyes could look more bleak. It was the other thing she saw there, though, that tugged her heart even more firmly toward him. Fear. She understood that intimately.

"It feels brutal at the time," she said quietly, "like you're just pummeling yourself, like you're going to drown in sorrow if you don't do something, anything, to keep yourself from feeling like that, from remembering things that are so painful."

"How long?" he asked, and she understood that, too.

If someone could just tell you how long it was going to take until you started to come out the other side, to find a way to manage the tidal wave of emotion, harness it and turn it into something manageable, you could stick it out. But it didn't work that way. At least it hadn't for her. "You can't just suffer through it," she told him. "You have to let yourself feel it, and find new ways to think about what you're feeling, so you'll eventually be able to recall past events in the context of what they meant to you then. If it was a lovely memory before, you need to find a way to remember it as a lovely memory now. Poignant, yes, heartbreaking even, but honor the lovely part, and in time, it helps mitigate the heartbreaking part. At least, that's how it worked for me. Not everyone processes things the same."

He took a steadying breath, closed his eyes tightly for a moment, then opened them again, casting his gaze downward. "I don't know how you did it," he said, sounding overwhelmed by the task ahead.

"I didn't," she said simply. "In the end, I let Liam do it for me."

His gaze lifted straight to hers. "How do you mean?"

"I started trying to live through the avalanche of memories that seemed to bombard me every waking minute of every single day from his perspective, not mine. For example, I used to see kids playing and I'd get hit by this wall of crippling grief, realizing that I would never get to watch my son play like that ever again. A cavalcade of images of him would assault me—that's what it felt like, a physical assault—of Liam laughing, Liam playing, all the most beautiful images of him that I would never be able to add to."

She saw Will's throat work, and he looked away, past her shoulder for a moment. "I shouldn't be asking this of you."

She urged his face back to hers. Her eyes were a little glassy now, too, but that was okay. "Sometimes it still overwhelms me. You saw that up close and personal. But most of the time, I can look at things through his eyes. Remember how much joy he took, like in the example I just gave. Instead of seeing through my sad, grieving lens, I started looking at life through his. How much joy he'd taken in swinging on those swings, sliding down that slide. And I'd hug that joy so tight. Revel in his joy, his laughter, remember all the good and wonderful things he was. Honoring that, honoring who he was, instead of honoring my grief, my loss."

He nodded, and when she went to slide her hand away, he simply covered it with his own, held it there. Maybe her throat worked a bit then, too. His hand was warm, strong, and remarkably steady, and she drew strength from it, even as she hoped he drew strength from her words.

She waited for him to meet her gaze again. "I began making those memories about him, not about me. I told myself it wasn't fair to remember him and be sad." She smiled. "He was a great kid, flaws and all. He deserved to be remembered happily, joyfully. He'd want to bring me joy, not pain. That should be his legacy, you know?"

Will nodded, and his gaze stayed on hers then, as if he was holding on.

"Once I started to think about it that way . . . well, I won't say I began to heal, because there is no healing. Not really. You can't expect to get over it. Nor did I want to. I don't want to forget Liam, or never think about him. This is who I am now, this is my life now. So I had to find a way to live life and keep him in it, but in a way that was good and positive. It was when I started to figure that out, instead of just wishing the suffering would end, that I found a way to move forward. For me, that meant taking Liam forward with me, too. He's not here physically, but that doesn't mean I can't share my life with him." She smiled more fully then, even as she blinked away a few tears. "I guess you could say he's like my guardian angel. I want him to be watching over me and feel happy to see what I'm doing, how I'm living my life. I work hard to be the person, the mom, the whatever, he'd want me to be. Maybe that's nuts, or weird, but I also gave up caring about what my choices looked like to anyone else. If I'm finding a way to live a life that feels good, honest, and positive, then that seems like a healthy outlook to me. It's a livable one, at any rate. And I'll take that."

Will continued to study her eyes, her face, looking at her, into her, and seemed to take her words truly to heart. "You're a remarkable person," he told her, and she saw that the grief, the pain, and the fear had ebbed from his eyes. "I've seen a lot, done a lot," he said, "here, and overseas when I was in the military, and I don't know if I've ever met anyone as strong or as resilient."

She let out a short laugh. "Trust me, I'm not all that. I'm just . . . finding my way." She looked up into his eyes. "I'm like that canvas, a work in progress that never quite gets finished. I just have this vision about how I want my life to be, like a giant painting, and I work toward filling it all in. I wish I could say it stops being work, but it doesn't. Not for me, anyway. I can say that after a while, the work feels normal, and okay. Like doing a good day's work feels good, this does, too."

They were all but standing in each other's arms, and so it shouldn't have surprised her when he pulled her the rest of the way in, but it did. He hugged her, tightly. She slid her arms around his waist and hugged him back.

"Thank you," he murmured against her ear. "I don't know if I deserved the gift you just gave me." He leaned back then but didn't let her go completely. "You've given me a lot to think about," he said, his gaze directly on hers again. "And a new way of looking at things. It's a way forward, or at least a way to start getting unstuck. I don't know how to properly thank you for that."

"If it helps you, then it was my pleasure," she said. "And I mean that. More of that good work, you know?"

He smiled then, and it warmed his eyes. "I do. I can tell you this. If you're trying to live a life that would make your son proud of you, you're succeeding. You're a hell of a woman, Hannah Montgomery, whether you understand or believe that or not. Thank you." He took in a breath and she could feel the shakiness of it, and again when he let it out, but some of the tension left him along with it. "And I hope it's okay to say this, but thank Liam for me, too."

Chapter Eleven

The farm looked good. Will stepped out of his truck and took a moment to take in the house and the fields. There was still work to be done. A lot of it. He hadn't started on the stables, or Chey's stone house, or some of the other work that Vivienne had discussed with him. She'd explained they wanted to focus on the welcome party and their first efforts at a community event; then they'd start the remainder of the restoration and renovation on weekdays, and open the farm up on weekends for the rest of the summer, for folks to pick their own lavender. They'd be working full time on refining their harvesting skills and producing their limited list of lavender products.

If the various permits they needed were issued in time, Vivi hoped to open the tearoom for special occasions by the final fall harvest. Then they'd spend the fall, winter, and early spring of the following year making and packaging the products they planned to sell at the farm and the mill from their harvested lavender and getting all the remaining big repairs and restoration work done. Vivi told him their plan was to have a series of special events that coordinated with the holidays, maybe another open house–style community event after the new year, then launch as a full-fledged business the following April.

He smiled to himself, thinking if Addie Pearl still wanted to know anything about Lavender Blue, he could give her the full rundown. Somewhere along the line, and he was pretty sure he could pinpoint exactly when that had been, he'd stopped working so hard to shut the world out, and started letting at least those people who truly mattered to him in. Listening more, talking more, filling in the spaces he'd never truly realized he blocked out, like some kind of shield between the world and his grief. He'd been surprised to find that the more life he let into those spaces, the more of a cushion they provided. He was so busy being in the moment now, he didn't have to work so hard to block out the past.

And if the number of folks he spied at that moment, already wandering up and down the rows of lush, vivid lavender bushes, baskets over their arms, snips in hand, was any indication of how his fellow citizens of Blue Hollow Falls felt about their town's newest business venture, Will thought the women of Lavender Blue might be a bigger overnight success than they imagined.

"Hi, I'm so glad you could make it."

Will turned to find Hannah standing behind him. Her pretty face was flushed with excitement, and maybe a little by the heat of the late June sun. She wore one of her broad-brimmed straw hats tied with a brightly-patterned scarf, her hair woven into a single plait that swung down her back. Her top was a pretty pale blue with little ruffled sleeves and a scoop neck that was held up with a thin elastic band that dipped down between her breasts. Her floral skirt was long and fell in several sheer layers that swirled around her calves in something of a gypsy look. He grinned when he got to her footwear—purple rubber garden boots with hand-painted flowers all over them—then lifted his gaze to hers. "They suit you."

She laughed and did a bit of a pose. "I figured I'd put those oil paints to better use."

"Looks like you have quite the turnout," he said, intending to shift his gaze back to the fields, but finding himself watching her as she looked at the fields instead. He hadn't seen or spoken to her in over a week, not since their emotional talk at the music venue. By force of habit, his first instinct when he'd climbed back in his truck that afternoon had been to castigate himself for making a fool of himself in front of her while simultaneously dragging her through something he'd had no right to ask of her. Then her words had echoed through his mind.

I gave up caring about what my choices looked like to anyone else. If I'm finding a way to live a life that feels good, honest, and positive, then that seems like a healthy outlook to me.

And she was right. Who cared if he made a fool of himself? He needed help, and he had no earthly idea where to start. Then he'd seen her there, watching him, and knew if anyone understood what was going on inside him at that moment, it would be Hannah. He'd walked to her as if drawn toward her, before he could second guess it or talk himself out of it. And her willingness to help had been sincere and true.

He'd immediately begun to put her words into action, starting on the hard work of thinking about his past, about Zoey, the accident, all of it, in a new light. He'd even taken that same new thought process and applied it to his fiddle playing, and his fiddle making. Watching his son on that stage, he'd found it impossible not to think about that, too. Armed with Hannah's hard-won, been-there insight, he'd started to let the world in around him, and that had caused him to truly start to look at things in an entirely different way. He'd been surprised how swiftly his new life view had changed the makeup of his days, how willing and happy people were to have him take part in the day-to-day conversations he'd simply let swirl around him before, and how sincerely he liked being part of them. He could spend more time castigating himself for cutting himself off from that vital outlet for so long, but that was time he was no longer interested in wasting.

Addie Pearl's wisdom from that day back by the stone well also resonated more deeply inside him, because now he understood what to do with it, how to put it to practical use.

The other thing he couldn't deny was that a great deal of his thoughts about Hannah, before and now, had absolutely nothing to do with his learning how to process his long-held, deeply buried grief. When he thought about her, which was a good deal of the time, he realized it was truly about her, all of her. He was undeniably attracted to her, and not because they shared a tragic happening in their past. His clumsy attempt to start something, a conversation, anything, out in the sheep meadow that day was testimony to the fact that he'd been interested in her long before learning they shared that common thread. If she'd wanted to be known as more than a grieving mother, then he could most assuredly confirm she'd accomplished that goal. That was not what he saw, or thought about, when he looked at her.

In fact, at that moment, looking into her happy face, framed by a backdrop that would stir even the most dormant soul, he could truthfully say that nothing of her past or his was on his mind right now. What was on his mind was the kiss they'd started, but never finished in the stable that day. And how badly he'd like to find out what really kissing Hannah Montgomery would feel like, taste like, when there was nothing else, no one else, standing between them.

Something of his thoughts must have shown on his face because her gaze widened just slightly. Then those soft gray eyes grew a bit stormy and dark, but in all the ways a man would so want them to.

"I'd like to see you," he said, the words out there before he could second guess them. "Not to talk about the past," he added. "Just to spend some time in the now. Getting to know who we are today."

She looked sincerely surprised, and his heart sank. Either he was the only one endlessly distracted by thoughts of them spending more time together, or possibly spending time with him wasn't something she'd be interested in because he'd remind her of her loss, even if he didn't mean to.

"Never mind," he said, before she could respond. "I'm probably jumping the gun, anyway." He tried for a self-deprecating expression, and probably failed by a mile. "Why would you want to get mixed up with—"

"Yes," she blurted out. "I would love to." She seemed as surprised by her response as he'd been about making the offer.

They both stared at each other for a moment, then she grinned, then he did. "Good," he said, feeling a whole cavalcade of things in that moment, but instantly deciding to focus on the one that made him happiest. She'd said yes.

"Very," she replied, and they both stared at each other again, grinning like loons. "I—uh—I'm glad Jake agreed to help out today, with the tearoom," she said, making an obvious attempt to get them back on a normal conversational path, though her eyes were still shining in surprised delight.

"He was happy to do it."

There was a short pause; then she said, "How are you doing?" She hurried to add, "If it's okay to ask. I wish I could have helped more." The moment the comments were made she looked instantly regretful. "You don't need to answer that. I don't know what made me bring it up."

He smiled. It looked like neither one of them had this

whole how-do-you-date-at-our-age thing down very well. Or at all. Something about that knowledge took the pressure off and relaxed him a bit.

"What?" she asked, clearly confused.

"I was just thinking that it appears neither one of us has had much practice with this."

She let out a short laugh then, too. "Is it that obvious?"

"I think it's charming," he said. "At least where you're concerned. I'm sure I'm being far less than the gallant knight here, but given you've seen my soft, white underbelly already, I guess that jig is up."

Her smile turned sweet then, and there was honest affection in her eyes. "I think it's safe to say we've both seen each other at far less than our most confident and in-control selves." She held his gaze. "Maybe that's not such a bad thing, you know?"

"Maybe not," he agreed, then chuckled. "Though, just once, I'd like to at least pretend to be suave around you."

That got an honest laugh from her. "As I recall, the first time we truly talked, you'd just gotten done being the white knight, saving me from immediate death by chimney rock." She beamed up at him. "I think you're pretty gallant. In fact, I think that's one of your core traits. And I'll tell you something else," she said, leaning closer as if she was sharing a secret. "Men who are too smooth? Sound like they're trying to sell a used car. A little rough around the edges rings far more sincere."

He gazed down at her pretty face, into her pretty eyes. "You're being very kind."

"I'm being very honest."

He nodded, as if accepting the compliment, even if he wasn't quite sure it was all that true. But if it was to her, then what else mattered? "Well, for the record, you can ask me anything. Anytime. You've certainly earned that right. I guess I'd like to think if the unique way in which we started to get to know each other is worth anything, it's that we can bypass a lot of those more formal dating etiquette rules."

"Is that what we're doing?" she asked, seeming quite cheerful about the prospect. "Dating?"

"I'm not sure what the kids are calling it these days, but given I asked you out and you said yes . . . I think that's the right term."

"I guess that's right," she said, sounding quite pleased.

"At least one date, anyway," he added, with a wry grin of his own. "I suppose we should figure out exactly when and where it will be, but—"

"Hannah, honey?" Vivienne called to them from a distance, then waved a long, silk scarf over her head in case they'd missed her. "If you're done flirting with our very handsome and capable stonemason, could you maybe come give Chey a hand in the lavender fields again?"

Hannah flushed a bright pink, but Will just smiled and wiggled his eyebrows, which made her laugh in surprise, and her embarrassment fled.

Maybe you have one or two suave moments in you after all, he thought, and decided making Hannah laugh, and maybe even making her blush, wouldn't be a bad goal to add to the list of others he'd set for himself.

"Care to join me and pick some lavender?"

"I thought I'd go find Jake, see how he's doing," Will said. "Maybe try one of those lavender cupcakes. Then I'll come out and find you."

Those gray eyes of hers flared again, and he had to curl his fingers in to keep from reaching for her. He'd bet all the money he had that she'd taste a damn sight better than pretty much anything Vivienne could cook up. And having tasted Ms. Baudin's amazing cooking, that was saying something.

"Sounds like a good plan," she told him.

"Hannah, honey," Vivi said, sounding a bit more impatient this time.

Will winked at Hannah as her cheeks filled once more with the most delightful shade of pink, and then she turned and headed toward Vivienne and the rows of fat, brilliantly blooming lavender bushes.

Will's smile remained as he watched her go, his nerves maybe a bit jittery, but not in a bad way. He'd often recalled what Hannah had said about still talking to her son, sharing what she was doing with him, as if he were her guardian angel, watching over her. So he didn't feel as silly as he thought he would have when he murmured, "So, what do you think, Zoey? Is this what I'm supposed to be doing? Is it okay to move on . . . honor your memory by living a full life?"

He stood there another long moment, as if he half expected her to appear next to him, like some wavery, heavenly figure, and chat with him about how he was supposed to court another woman. The two of them had talked about everything under the sun in their time together, so it seemed the most natural thing in the world, on the one hand. He ducked his chin then, shook his head, smile still in place, but a decidedly self-deprecating one now. "But on the other hand, how does this work, exactly?" he murmured. "And just how badly am I kidding myself that I have any business dating anybody."

Well, it's taken you damn well long enough, my fiddle-playing man, so get on with it already. You like her. Jake likes her. Hell, I like her. But then, you always did have good taste.

Will went stock-still. Maybe he was hallucinating. Maybe he was just having a really bad case of wishful thinking. Because damn if he hadn't just heard Zoey. Like *heard* Zoey.

Of course, if you don't mind, when it comes time for the two of you to hit the sheets, I'm gonna bow out. I mean, I love you, and forever will, but . . . you understand. Three's a crowd.

Will grinned then, almost laughed out loud. *That* was most definitely Zoey. "Understood," he said, as if it was the most natural, normal thing in the world. Having a conversation with his late wife. About a woman he might possibly be falling for. Okay, quite probably falling for.

And maybe it was natural. Or maybe he'd finally lost his damn mind. In the end, as Hannah had said, if it worked for him, then who the hell cared? *It doesn't really matter what anyone else thinks.* "Indeed, it doesn't."

He started walking toward the farmhouse, wondering why in the world he hadn't just talked it over with his best friend sooner. Of course Zoey knew the right thing to say. When hadn't she? He might have avoided wasting one hell of a lot of time trying to duck life.

"Here goes nothing," he said under his breath, and entered the fray of life. All of it.

Chapter Twelve

"This is a much bigger turnout than my projections determined. Even accounting for the weather report being off by a greater margin than statistics would have indicated, and an overperformance of word-of-mouth engagement, my numbers are still way off." Frowning, Avery looked from her clipboard to the fields beyond the veranda, which were still teeming with people picking lavender, despite the event's having formally ended two hours ago.

Hannah smiled, knowing how much it annoyed Avery to be reminded she was human and therefore not perfect. Hannah poured them both more tea from the pretty floral-patterned china service that had been positioned neatly between them on the café table. "Well, as long as we're out-performing, not underperforming, I think we can live with the projection error."

Avery looked at Hannah, her eyes appearing bigger than usual behind her round, horn-rimmed glasses. "It wasn't an error. I couldn't possibly have predicted—"

Hannah laid her hand on Avery's arm, then handed her a scone. "It's okay," she said. "We're doing well. Really, really well. Have a scone. Celebrate."

"I should have started with a greater baseline figure

given there is no charge for the lavender picking and tea service today."

"Scone," Hannah repeated, and put it into Avery's hand.

Avery munched absently as she skimmed her numbers again. "So, you and the mason, huh?" she said, still mulling, calculating, recalculating.

Hannah, who had just taken a bite of her own scone, might have choked slightly. She quickly sipped some tea, swallowed hard, then tried to pretend that Avery's surprising comment hadn't caught her off guard. Too late for that.

Avery looked up from her clipboard, her lips curving dryly. "What? You don't think anyone notices the two of you all but jumping each other every time you're within eyeball distance? The whole town is talking about you two now." She batted her eyelashes. "Apparently you shared a 'moment' together at the amphitheater?" She made air quotes while still holding her partially eaten scone, then fanned herself with her free hand. "Steamed up more than a few pairs of glasses from what I heard."

Hannah just sat there, slack-jawed. If she'd taken the time to think about it, she supposed it wasn't all that surprising. Only she hadn't been thinking about it, not that way. She hadn't been thinking about the town or what everyone might or might not be talking about. She'd been too busy trying to sort out her feelings for Will and what she wanted to do with them. Not that all her pondering and decision making had done her a whit of good.

After their talk at the music venue, she'd admitted that she was drawn to Will in ways that had to do with a lot more than how he filled out his white work tees, or the fact that he was struggling to figure out how to manage his own tragic past. If anything, the latter was what had convinced her to steer clear of him, at least in any personal way. He had a lot he was trying to figure out; she'd done a lot of that work already. So the last thing she needed was to be dragged through it again and again as he dealt with his own issues. She had told him the truth, that she'd always be there to help, to talk to, but the occasional conversation was not the same as becoming involved with him, where she'd be a part of the process full time. That would be supremely foolish. If she was really interested in getting involved with some-one new, exploring that part of her life again, pretty much any other man would be a better candidate than Will McCall.

Which totally explains why the moment he asked to see you socially, you all but fell on top of him in your rush to say yes.

Yeah, she was going to just have to get over trying to get over him. That plainly wasn't working. All day long she'd found herself searching for him in the fields, or watching him talk to Jake, or wandering over to the stables to look at Chey's stone house and check out the horses. Yeah, had anyone asked, she could have pretty much pinpointed where Will McCall was at any given moment. A flying drone couldn't have kept better tabs on his movement than she had.

"I'm going to take that besotted look on your face as a yes, then," Avery said, her eyes dancing when Hannah flushed at being caught mooning.

"I don't know what I'm doing," Hannah said, being honest. "He's a really good man dealing with some tough issues that I know a little bit about. We've talked about them a few times. It's nothing more than that." *Except there was that kiss. And how much you would really like to finish it.*

"Right," Avery said dryly, once again pulling Hannah from where her gaze had naturally turned to search for him. Again. "And hey, I'm not saying it's a bad thing. He's not hard on the eyes. For a guy his age."

"Hey now," Hannah said jokingly.

Avery raised both hands. "I'm just saying, if you were to do an emotional to physical ratio chart, the two of you would likely get an eighty-five-percent compatibility rating. Possibly higher. I'm not entirely sure as I'm missing data."

"Missing data?" Hannah repeated. "You've worked some kind of chart for us?"

Avery shrugged, unrepentant. "It's just a hobby. I'm trying to apply some of my mathematical theories to human behavior." She grinned. "I needed some guinea pigs and you two were just ever-so-conveniently making goo-goo eyes at each other."

Hannah's mouth dropped open, then snapped shut. "We do not make any kind of eyes at each other."

Avery merely raised her eyebrows over the rims of her glasses and sent Hannah a pointed look, then popped another morsel of scone in her mouth.

"In fact," Hannah went on, "I could hardly get the man to crack a smile, much less—" She broke off as Avery immediately flipped a few pages on her clipboard and scribbled down something.

"What—" Hannah asked. "What are you doing?"

Avery looked at Hannah and beamed sweetly. "Gathering data."

Hannah sighed in defeat and munched on the rest of her scone.

"So," Avery asked at length, after sipping some tea and sighing in disgust once again as she continued to review her welcome party statistics. "Is it the wife thing holding you back?"

Hannah had just taken another sip of tea and almost sprayed the table with it. Dabbing at her chin, she very deliberately set her cup and the remains of her scone down and gave Avery one of her own pointed looks. "The wife thing?"

"Will's wife," Avery said. She put her clipboard down and looked at Hannah, her expression serious now. "His late wife. I asked a few questions, and it's not like it's a secret.

His wife was killed in a car accident on Christmas Eve when Jake was a toddler. Will hasn't made the kind of progress we have in dealing with it, despite its being over a decade ago." She folded her hands on top of her clipboard. "I was just wondering if that was why you're ambivalent about pursuing him." She raised her hands, palms out. "Not data collecting."

At Hannah's narrowed gaze, a hint of a sheepish look crossed her face. "Okay, well, I'll at least wait until later to write it down. But I'm serious. Are you worried that his loss will, you know . . . pull you back?"

That was the thing with Avery. For all her geekiness and need to dissect and put everything into some kind of equation or projection chart, she was a true friend, and was sincerely concerned for Hannah's well-being.

Hannah relaxed, knowing Avery would always be Avery, but she'd also always have Hannah's back, and her heart was forever in the right place.

"Yes," Hannah said, opting to be honest about it. Maybe talking would help her sort things out once and for all. "I didn't know all the specific details you just mentioned, but I knew he was dealing with loss and was pretty sure it was his wife. On the surface, Will seems a pretty foolish choice, you know? And with the details you just filled in, even more so. I mean, none of us have been involved with anyone for some time. We've just moved out here, launched this joint venture, which isn't fully launched yet, and . . . so many other things. I just feel like it's not the right time, in addition to his being quite probably not the right guy."

"Yes, well, try as I might to organize and chart human emotion, pretty much the only thing I've determined so far is that emotional investment outweighs intellectual rationale pretty much every single time when the heart is involved."

"I'm not saying my heart is involved," Hannah said,

trying not to feel alarm when just saying that felt like a lie. "I'm attracted to him, because, well, you've seen him. He's not hard on the eyes." She grinned. "For an old guy."

Avery rolled her eyes, but grinned. "I would concur."

Hannah laughed at that. "See? And he's got that whole quiet, alpha male thing going. But then there's the emotional stuff he's dealing with, which shows his vulnerable side, and I'd be lying if I said that wasn't at least a little sexy, even if I don't wish suffering on him, or anyone. He clearly loves his son and has done a great job with him. He's hardworking, makes art out of rocks, and . . ." Hannah trailed off. She wasn't exactly talking herself out of anything here. "And yeah, okay. I've got it bad," she admitted sheepishly. "So bad that even his pining for his long-deceased wife just makes him that much more . . . I don't know. Human, and flawed, and yet loyal. Kind of proof that when he loves, he loves fully." She looked at Avery and lifted her shoulders. "How am I supposed to fight against that?"

Avery held her gaze, and Hannah could see her mind whirring behind those rapid-process eyes of hers. "Maybe you don't," she said, at length. "I mean, yes, there is definitely that emotional quicksand of his past versus yours. You're out on the green now and he's still in the sandpit. You don't want to be dragged back into the sandpit."

Hannah nodded and smiled despite the seriousness of the conversation. "Since when do you make golf metaphors?"

"Golf is a game of mathematics," she replied, as if that explained everything, and it essentially did. "I've always wanted to learn to play, but I'm not the most coordinated person. Doesn't keep me from studying it, though." She shrugged. "What can I say—the golf channel is my white noise when I work."

"I never knew that," Hannah said, amused.

Avery's cheeky smile resurfaced. "New data. Maybe you should jot that down."

Hannah laughed, then responded to Avery's earlier assertion. "You're right, though. I don't want to go back to the sandpit. I also can't seem to shrug off this attraction, much less make it go away." She hesitated to say the rest of it, then decided it didn't matter at this point. "He asked me out. Earlier today. I keep trying to put distance between us until this . . . whatever it is, simply dies out. Then he shows up and . . ."

Avery looked at her. "You couldn't say yes fast enough."

Hannah hung her head, then raised her hand. "Guilty as charged."

"Good," Avery said.

Hannah lifted her gaze back to Avery. "Good? Why? It's like I'm asking to get hurt. Or, at the very least, emotionally bruised."

"I think you need to take the edge off so you can feel things as clearly as you're seeing them."

"Take the edge—" Hannah's eyes widened. "You mean go to bed with him? I'm not even sure I want to date him, much less—"

"Pheromones and hormones can really cloud one's judgment. I've got a chart for that I'm developing, too. Well, I'm starting by mapping out what would constitute the perfect kiss. I haven't worked my way beyond that because . . . you know."

Hannah did know. Avery had dated or tried to. She'd had her first kiss, and quite a few more after that, with different guys she'd gone out with. But nothing beyond that. At twenty-four, Avery might be a certified genius, but she was also still a certified virgin. She was adorable and funny, sharp and forthright, and beautiful in her own right. But she also possessed a brain that ran at the speed of light and never shut down, and most men simply couldn't compete with it, much less keep up with it. Those first kisses—which Avery had deemed complete failures—had never led to anything more, because either the gentleman in question took off not too long afterward, or Avery sent them packing.

"So, I'm not telling you from personal experience, but everything I've read on the subject does back up my assertion."

"He has a teenage son and is a central figure in this town," Hannah told her. "The very last thing I'm going to do is simply jump in bed with him. Not that I would anyway."

"Because of the late wife thing."

Hannah gaped. "No, because of the I-just-don't-jump-straight-into-bed-with-men thing."

"That, too," Avery agreed.

Maybe Hannah should have thought it through a little more before having this talk with Avery.

"It was just a suggestion," Avery added, looking not remotely sorry for making it. "Who knows, maybe he's lousy in the sack, and you'd get over him anyway."

"I'm not having this conversation with you anymore," Hannah said on a half laugh, putting her linen napkin on the table next to her plate.

"Suit yourself," Avery said easily, ever unflappable. As Hannah pushed back her chair Avery picked up her clipboard again. "But, if you do, I'd really appreciate some direct anecdotal data for my research."

Hannah shook her head on a helpless laugh. "You'll be the first person I call."

Avery just grinned and started making new notes.

Hannah walked back into the kitchen, but the crew they'd hired to help with the tea service had already cleaned up and left. The place looked spotless. They'd stopped serving a half hour before the end-time of the party, so it wasn't surprising, but even without the food and drink, the festivities had continued. Folks had gone on arriving all afternoon, and others had lingered even after they were done picking their lavender. A few of the locals had pulled instruments out of their cars and trucks and struck up an impromptu combo, which had added the perfect finishing touch to the warm, breezy, summer day. Pippa had come down to support the winery and help chat up the wines that were being served under a tent they'd erected for a special tasting. She'd joined in with the other musicians, much to everyone's delight, and Vivi had happily given Jake a few breaks to sing a bit as well.

Hannah had looked for Will at those times, both to see if he was watching Jake sing and to see how he was handling watching and listening to his son sing. Will had said Jake sounded a lot like his mom, which had to be why it was so hard on him to listen.

The first time Jake had sat in with the musicians, Will had been out at the horse stables helping Chey with some youngsters who'd wanted to pet and feed the horses carrots, under Chey's supervision of course. There were no amplifiers and the musicians had no mikes, which was what had made it all so perfect and natural, but Hannah was sure the sounds of the music and the singing had carried at least as far as the paddock.

She'd watched as Will had paused, looked up, and turned immediately to watch his son and listen. Then he'd surprised her by unerringly finding her gaze and holding it, too. As if he'd been keeping track of her every bit as much as she had him. He'd nodded, as if in thanks for her concern. She'd nodded back, smiled, and he'd returned to watching Jake, smiling, too. Hannah had been too far away to see his expression, but he'd seemed good with all of it, or at least very willing to be part of it, and Hannah had been happy—and relieved—to see that.

She'd lost track of him though when she'd taken her break on the veranda with Avery, and a quick scan now didn't show him anywhere in sight. The number of people still picking lavender began to dwindle sharply. Vivi was out there with them now and waved to Hannah that she was fine and didn't need help. A glance at the stables showed that Chey had put the horses inside, so the paddock was empty of animals and people, and Chey. Maybe Will had already left. Hannah didn't see Jake, either, so it was probable they'd gone on home. She told herself it was silly to feel . . . well, not miffed. He certainly didn't owe her anything, but she was disappointed that he hadn't come to say good-bye, or at least to comment on the event. *Or maybe set a day and time for your big date.* "That, too," she murmured, then smiled, amused at herself. For a woman who wasn't all that sure about getting tangled up with a man, she was certainly tying herself into knots over his every little move. "Or lack of one," she added dryly.

Other than her short break with Avery, she hadn't been off her feet all day. It seemed Vivi had the final stragglers in hand, so Hannah decided to head over to her place. As comfortable as they were, she'd love to get out of her garden boots, shower the day off her skin, and maybe even play a bit with her paints before heading back over to the house later for a previously agreed upon meeting with the others, to go over the day and celebrate their first big event.

Hannah was looking forward to it, expecting there would be champagne, given how successful the day had been. She knew Vivi had concocted some special treat for them to celebrate their official launch. Well, maybe not the official-official launch, because this had been a party, not business, but the response certainly boded well for their big day when it happened next spring. Hannah was pretty sure their ideas about having other holiday-related events were a definite go now.

She sighed happily. It had all seemed such a distant dream, with so much to do before they actually turned Lavender Blue into anything resembling a money-making venture. Today's event had taken that distant dream from the horizon right up to front and center, giving her a renewed rush of anxiety over whether they could possibly get everything ready in time for their real launch. It was a good kind of anxiety, though, the happy, anticipatory kind. They were really doing this. And for the first time, her optimism about their chances for success felt truly warranted.

Thirty minutes later, she stepped out of the gloriously long, hot, steamy shower she'd taken, dried off, then pulled on a pair of comfy floral leggings and a billowy, Indian cotton top. Comfort would be king for the remainder of the day, she decided, leaving her hair loose to dry. She wandered over to her current painting in progress, studying it, trying to work up some energy to dabble a little. She felt soothed by the shower and pleasantly tired from the long day. As much as painting relaxed her, the truth of it was, she just wanted to get off her feet for a bit.

She was contemplating opening the bottle of Llamarama wine that Pippa and Seth had given to each of them as a thank-you for their joint venture that day when her doorbell buzzed.

Surprised, she went to the windows first and peered down, but didn't see a vehicle parked below. If it had been Vivi or Chey, they'd have just knocked and stuck their heads in. Avery would have texted first with her specific time of arrival. "So, who is at my door?" she murmured as she crossed the room. There were no peepholes in country doors, so she cracked it open, then paused in utter surprise. "Will."

From the looks of him, he'd gone home and cleaned up, too. His hair was damp and clung more closely to his head, much wavier than it was when dry. He was freshly shaven and wore a clean, soft green, button-up shirt and black jeans that did amazing things for his flashing green eyes and equally dangerous things to her no-longer dormant libido.

Then she realized what was happening. He was here to pick her up for their date. "Oh no," she said apologetically. "I guess I must have misunderstood. I didn't know you meant tonight." She glanced down at her exceedingly casual apparel, barely one step up from pajamas. "I just showered, and I was going to—but I can go—"

"No, no," he said, stopping her from further stammering. "I'm not here to pick you up. I just dropped Jake off at Seth and Pippa's—they're going to do some work up there this evening. I thought since I was driving right by, I'd just—I wasn't sure when or where I'd see you, to make plans. I would have called, or even texted, but . . ." His smile was sheepish and endearing and, oh boy, were she and her very overactive libido in a whole lot of trouble. "I don't have your number."

"Oh!" she said. "Right." She realized she wouldn't have been able to contact him, either. She laughed. "We're definitely rusty."

"So we are," he replied, flashing that heart-stopping grin.

She stood there for another moment, just taking him all in, trying not to drool, when her manners finally made a return appearance. "Oh, I'm sorry. Come on in." She stepped back and opened the door. "I'm sorry, the place is a bit of a mess," she said as he stepped inside, and remained there, as if unsure whether he was welcome to intrude further. "I'd like to say that it's because I haven't fully unpacked yet—and I haven't—but I'd be less than honest if I pretended to be a neatnick." She spread her arms. "What you see is pretty much the real me."

"I think I read somewhere that a cluttered space is the sign of a creative mind."

She laughed. "I'm not sure if that is true, but I'm totally going to claim it."

He looked around the open floor plan. "Great space," he said. "Bigger than you'd think."

"Thanks, I thought the same. The light is perfect for painting."

He nodded, his gaze shifting back to her, and they stared at each other some more. "Your hair," he said, causing her to reach up in a panic, wondering what state of post-shower fright she must look like. His embarrassment over causing her panic was at odds with the flare of heat she thought she saw in his eyes as he said, "I've never seen it down. You always have it braided."

"Oh," she said, reaching up to smooth it, then letting her hand fall by her side again, suddenly not quite as relaxed as she had been a moment ago.

"I like it," he said. "It's wavier than I thought it would be."

"Yours, too," she blurted, and they both smiled, then grinned. "Man, we really are out of practice."

Will chuckled and nodded. "I was just thinking that Jake is probably smoother than I am."

She laughed. "I know. I had Avery giving me dating tips earlier."

His eyes widened in surprise. "Really? Did you think you needed some?"

Hannah realized that was the last thing she should have mentioned, considering what Avery's advice had actually been, but it was too late now. She shook her head. "No, it was unsolicited. Apparently . . ." She trailed off, wondering if she should tell him what Avery had told her, or if it was best to let that lie, given they were already acting like awkward, untried teens on their first date.

He stepped further into the room then, but stopped at her kitchen counter, still a few yards away from where she stood. "Apparently?" he prodded, his gaze looking very, very adult at the moment.

She swallowed against a suddenly parched throat. Maybe

she should offer him some wine. *Maybe you should just listen to Avery and jump him. He certainly looks like he'd be receptive to that idea.* She broke their gaze and turned to open one drawer, then another, looking for the wine bottle opener. Striving for a casual, breezy tone she was far from feeling at the moment, she said, "According to Avery, everyone in the Falls is laying odds on whether or not we're going to be an item."

"An item," he said, and she stilled. He was right behind her. And the very idea that she was in arm's reach of him made every inch of her body sing with delight.

She kept searching, not even looking at what she was digging through now. "Mm-hmm. She said it was pretty clear to everyone that we, uh . . ." She broke off then, redoubling her search efforts as she remembered that what had been clear to everyone according to Avery was that they wanted to jump each other. She was all but throwing things out of the drawer when he reached around her and put his hand on hers, stilling her action.

She pulled in a shaky breath, feeling the warmth of his own on the side of her neck. Not only did he look like heaven, he smelled heavenly, too. She wanted nothing more than to lean back against him, have him wrap his arms around her, and pull her tightly to him.

Her body ached with need—to the point she almost wanted to weep. She couldn't remember the last time she'd felt this way. Far longer than her divorce. Since before the accident even. She and Steve had already been having issues and intimacy had been one of them. She enjoyed it; Steve had grown indifferent. She found out later that that was because he had been flirting with a coworker and his guilt had caused some performance anxiety. Nothing more than that, he'd sworn, when Hannah had discovered the suggestive text messages. He'd confessed that he enjoyed the thrill of doing something new, that he felt the two of them were missing that spark and spontaneity since they'd started a family. Then the accident had happened, and . . . after that, moments like the one she was having now had been the last thing on her mind.

But that was then. And long in the past. So, very, very long.

"Hannah," he said, his voice a rough whisper that skimmed along the tender skin of her neck, leaving a rippling of awareness in its wake.

She turned and found herself in his arms. Unlike before, this time neither one of them was an emotional wreck. The emotions running high now had nothing to do with their past and everything to do with the very immediate present.

She looked up into his eyes, knowing she was failing miserably at trying to disguise the want and need she was feeling. If she hadn't been sure, the way his pupils flared to life proved it. "Will, I think we should—"

"We should take this slow," he said, his voice a low rumble.

She nodded. "Yes," she said, and heard the breathless note in her voice. His gaze dropped to her mouth and the muscles between her thighs clenched painfully tight, almost making her gasp with the suddenness of it.

When he looked back into her eyes, the hunger in his matched the voracious need ramping up inside her.

"We've both been through things," he said, and she nodded, trying not to look at his mouth, at those lips, the ones she'd only tasted once, and far too briefly. Failing. "And alone for a long time." His throat worked, and when he continued, his voice was even rougher. "So it makes sense that we're feeling . . . what we're feeling. It's just the circumstances driving this."

"Probably," she managed, though she was no longer certain. It was hard to imagine that she'd ever not want him like she wanted her next breath, no matter what had happened to her leading up to this moment.

"So it's smart for us to take things one step at a time," he said. "Make sure of ourselves, of—"

He broke off and she finished it for him, unable not to. "Of this."

He nodded. "This."

Then his mouth was lowering to hers, and she was closing her eyes, her body thrumming in almost anguished anticipation of his touch, his taste.

He brushed his lips softly over hers and she moaned, long and low, utterly incapable of keeping her longing silent.

"Hannah," he said, almost a growl now, resting his forehead on hers briefly, their breaths mingling, their bodies so close.

"Will, please," she said, her voice breaking.

He groaned then, and whatever willpower he had, whatever control she thought she could exert, seemed to leave each of them at the exact same time.

Chapter Thirteen

She was heaven, reaching all the way down inside him and hauling him up from the depths of his self-imposed hell, all in one single, perfect kiss. He might have been able to pull back, hold back. Had, in fact, kept himself from taking her mouth as fully as a man could after that one brief sip. Then she'd said his name, and her voice had broken when she'd let down all of her barriers and revealed that her want matched his. He was lost to it then, lost to his need and want of her, her equally hungry want of him.

He framed her cheek with one hand, tipped her mouth up to fully meet his, and sank into her. She took him into the soft warmth of her mouth, suckled him, kissed him, then searched for the same from him. Their first honest kiss was slower, sweeter, than he'd have thought, given the rage of need pounding through his veins. He felt as he had their first time, bordering on feral. He'd gone so long without this kind of touch, feeling this kind of need, having the opportunity to do something to assuage it. He wanted to sink in, wallow in it, let it wash over him, drown him in all the sensations, the pleasure, the ecstasy. Then he wanted to take, to consume, to sate every last one of his most carnal impulses. His hunger for her was primal.

He was fully in the moment, and maybe that's how it needed to be this first time, an overwhelming force of nature so strong that the power of it made it impossible for him to think about anything else. Anyone else. Any fear he might have had that he'd make some inevitable comparison, or worse, feel a sudden jolt of genuine guilt, never had a chance to manifest itself.

"Will," she whispered against his lips, her fingers sliding into his hair in a languid slide of nails against his scalp that set what was left of his control on fire. He pulled her more deeply into his arms, backed up blindly until he was pressed against a wall, or a door, he had no idea, pulling her fully into his arms, wrapping himself up in her.

He slid his hands down her arms, then down the lush curve of her torso, until he could bracket her hips in his wide palms, and urge her forward, so the softest part of her pressed against the hardest part of him.

Her sharp gasp at the contact was followed by a swift moan and a shudder that seemed to rock them both. She kept herself pressed there until she shook with the need for more.

He wanted nothing more than to scoop her up and carry her to the nearest soft, flat surface. He wanted to spend hours, days, a lifetime, mapping every inch of her body. With his tongue.

She was squirming against him, testing his own limits, not to mention the fit of his jeans. "Hold on," he murmured against the side of her neck as she teased his earlobe, pulling it gently into her mouth, then nipping it with her teeth. He'd never known before that was an erogenous zone, but he almost dropped her for wanting to give himself fully over to her playful manipulations.

Gripping her hips while he still could, he lifted her up. "Wrap your legs around me," he all but growled in her ear.

"Will, no, you can't pick me up, I'm too—oh!" she said, ending with a gasp as he did indeed pick her up. He felt another shudder rocket through her as she wrapped her legs around his hips, pressing him as fully into her as their clothing would allow. He made a mental note to buy her a drawer full of those stretchy pant things she was wearing; it felt almost like no barrier at all. His jeans, on the other hand, were coming dangerously close to cutting off his blood flow entirely.

She kissed the side of his neck; then he could feel her lips curve into a grin as she whispered in his ear. "I should have taken up with a man who tosses big rocks around for a living a whole lot sooner."

He turned his head and caught her lips in a deep, searing kiss. "I don't know," he said as he slid his lips along the line of her jaw, then nipped her earlobe before whispering, "If you ask me, you picked the perfect time."

She smiled against his mouth when he took it again. "You make a good point," she said when he finally lifted his head. They both realized the double entendre at the same time and laughed. Somehow, rather than diminish or jerk them out of their passionate trajectory, this injection of the humor that had gradually become such a natural part of their give and take only served to deepen the intimacy between them. It wasn't until that moment that Will realized he missed that connection more keenly than anything else. Some part of him wanted to pull back in caution at the realization. The deepening of affection that came with that kind of intimacy would open him up to a level of vulnerability he wasn't sure he was ready for. Sex might be sex, but that . . . that connection was what held the true power. He spent a split-second thinking maybe he should put the brakes on. Now. Hard.

Then she tugged his head down to hers, and led the way

into their next kiss, teasing his tongue into an intimate duel, nipping at his bottom lip. Their gaze, when it connected, showed her eyes dancing with joy as well as drenched with desire. The tug in his heart was hard and insistent, and he knew then that he was way past the point where he could protect himself.

He carried her past the series of hand-painted screens she'd set up to create a wall of sorts, between the area she used as a bedroom and the main living space. He was surprised to see what looked like an ocean of bed. It was low to the ground, but she'd made up for its knee height with a thick mattress pad, a puffy, sky blue duvet, and more pillows than he'd seen, collectively, in his entire life. "I'm not sure there's room for us," he said, keeping her wrapped around him.

"What, a man who throws boulders around for a living is going to let a few pillows stop him?"

He grinned. "Fair point," he said, then tossed her on the bed, surprising a squeal from her as she landed among pillows on the duvet, sending several of the former bouncing off the bed and almost getting swallowed up by the latter.

He followed her down, pushing pillows aside, and her hair from her face. She was spluttering and laughing as he pinned her to the bed with the weight of his body. Affection for her rose up so sharp and deep it caught his heart in a tight fist and held it there. The power of the feeling allowed the first tiny slivers of guilt to niggle their way in. He knew this was not wrong. In fact, other than marrying Zoey and having Jake, this felt like one of the most right things he'd ever done in his life.

"It's okay if you need more time," she said softly, reaching up to stroke the side of his face, clearly having seen his moment of doubt.

That her first instinct had been to take care of him, put

his needs first, undid him. His gaze moved to hers and he searched her eyes, soft as fine cashmere now. She was smiling up at him, her eyes filled with support and affection . . . no worry, or worse, pity, to be found no matter how deeply he searched.

"The only thing I want more time for is this," he said, and turned his head to capture her finger between his lips.

She gasped, then moved under him, her hips lifting into his when he drew her finger into his mouth. He slid her finger free, then pinned that hand to the bed, leaning down to take her mouth again, only this time the intensity was meant to assuage physical need, finally giving lust and desire the upper hand. She accepted the change in tempo readily, almost greedily.

She tipped her head back, her lovely eyes closed now as she gave him access to the tender skin on the side of her neck, and lower still, as he nudged the wide neckline off one shoulder, shifting his weight to trail kisses downward. By the time he slid her shirt up and she all but wrenched it over her head, she was writhing beneath him. She was completely new and foreign to him, and he reveled in learning her body, finding her sweet spots, her erogenous zones, her sensitive places. He made her gasp, made her moan, and even laugh when he found a ticklish spot, which charmed him even as it ratcheted up his need for her.

When he started to roll down the waistband of her leggings, she laid one hand over his wrist and tipped her head up to look at him. His chin was resting on her belly button, and he smiled at her wild hair and even wilder eyes. "You look like someone has been ravaging you," he said.

"God, I hope so," she replied, and they both laughed.

"Do you want me to stop?" he asked when her hand stayed his.

"God, I hope not," she said, and he chuckled. "I just

thought I'd point out the rather stark inequity between the amount of clothing I have on, and the layer upon layer of clothing you're still wearing."

"Ah," he said, and moved back up her body, laughing outright when her bottom lip plumped out in a pretty pout. He kissed her mouth, then took that plump lower lip between his teeth before kissing her again until she was writhing once more. "I promise I'll return to what I was doing." He rolled to his back. "Just as soon we resolve that inequity issue."

Her eyes lit up as she rolled to her side. "Oh, well, that is a plan I can get behind."

He reached for her and pulled her across his chest.

"Or on top of," she said, and leaned down to kiss him.

It was remarkable to him how comfortable this was. The heated, no-holds-barred hunger that had driven them to this point had somehow settled in to a more thoughtful, slower-paced, intentional seduction. He wasn't holding any of himself back, couldn't have if he'd wanted to. It was that certainty, that deliberate intent that kept any sense of guilt or wrongdoing from creeping in. Nothing about making love to Hannah Montgomery was ever going to make him feel anything less than exultant.

She began to unbutton his shirt, kissing his chest through the T-shirt he wore underneath. "So many layers," she murmured.

"I could help with that."

She raised her head and caught his gaze. "Fair is fair," she said, and continued on her path down his torso. "Besides, I've had too many fantasies about this white T-shirt." She glanced up again, grinning boldly. "Well, to be exact, the fantasies were more about you out of this T-shirt, but either way . . ."

His eyebrows climbed at that revelation. "Fantasies," he said. "About me?"

She laughed. "You say that as if you can't fathom what about you would make a woman fantasize." She tugged his shirt free from the waistband of his black jeans. "Yet another one of your endearing qualities."

He let his head fall back to the bed as if in shock. "Endearing? Are you sure you know who you're in bed with?"

She giggled and climbed up his body then, kissing him quite deliberately, and so very tenderly on his mouth. It tightened his throat and tugged once more at his heart. She waited for him to open his eyes; hers were shining when he did.

"I'm very, very certain about that," she said softly, then kissed him again.

He reached for her face, rolled them both to their sides, and slowly moved on top of her.

"I wasn't done with my T-shirt fantasy yet," she murmured against his mouth between kisses.

He reached behind his neck and pulled off his T-shirt and his unbuttoned shirt in one smooth motion. They joined her cotton top . . . somewhere. Then he lowered himself back down on top of her, his bare flesh meeting hers for the first time. "God, you feel good," he said on a long, satisfied groan.

"I was just thinking the same thing," she said with a deep, satisfied sigh, and nestled more snugly against his chest. She slid one legging-clad leg between his still jean-clad legs. "Imagine what it will be like when . . ." She slid her leg higher between his.

He all but growled then, and pinned her leg before she could rub it any higher. "About that," he said, letting his head fall back and closing his eyes as he realized something else.

"What? What is it?" she asked, shifting a little so she could look at him.

He opened his eyes and lifted his head just enough to meet her gaze. "When I dropped by here, I wasn't expecting . . ." He nodded to their current entanglement. "Let's just say

I'm not as prepared as I'd hoped to be when this moment finally arrived." He let his head drop back to the bed and gave it a little shake.

To his surprise she laughed. Actually, it was more of a giggle, and he cracked open one eyelid and peered up at her. "I'm definitely not doing this right if you're amused rather than disappointed. Crushed might be too big an ask, but—"

She giggled all over again and he found himself grinning as well, and rolled her to her back, pinning her underneath him as her giggles turned to breathless laughter.

"Some men might find your laughter a bit emasculating," he said, right before capturing her mouth with his.

Her eyes were still filled with mirth, but it was the other things he saw there, too, that made him realize how much more was really happening between them right now than the discovery of naked bodies and how they might bring each other pleasure with them. She looked confident and joyful, two of the traits that had pulled him toward her from the beginning, like a cold, dormant plant seeking the warmth of a bright, shining sun. But it was the sincere affection that went along with that shining light that grabbed hold of the final part of his heart. Because he understood that feeling. Intimately. He had no idea if she saw that when she looked at him, but it didn't change the fact that he felt it.

"You just looked so forlorn, like someone had taken away your favorite toy." She kissed him again. "I appreciate that protection is important to you. It is to me, too." She kissed him again, and yet again. Short, sweet kisses. "I'm guessing—hoping—we'll find ourselves in this particular situation again." She waited for him to look at her. "I want you, Will McCall," she said, quite simply. "And it's thrilling to know you want me back. So, I'm okay if we don't do everything all at once."

He was struck silent by her honesty and her willingness to simply say what she was feeling. "I don't know what I did to deserve you," he said, determined to show her the same courage and trust she was showing him. "Your kindness, your patience, your generosity." He leaned down and took her mouth, slowly this time, and as tenderly as he was able. When he lifted his head, saw the desire and happiness in her eyes, nothing else existed for him in that moment. It had been a very, *very* long time since he'd felt this particular type of contentment. He hadn't thought to ever feel it again. It was both terrifying and utterly humbling.

To give himself time to process the myriad of thoughts and feelings ricocheting around inside him, he slowly began kissing his way down her torso.

She laughed and squirmed beneath him, gasping as he continued his foray downward. "Will, you don't have to— we can wait."

He glanced up and wiggled his eyebrows when she looked down at him. "Are you sure?" he asked, the words muffled as he was clenching the waistband of her leggings between his teeth.

She erupted in giggles, but didn't push him away, then arched off the bed hard when he finally reached her most sensitive spot. She reached for him then, but only to tangle her fingers in his hair, writhing against him now, alternately whimpering and moaning. "Will," she gasped, as he dipped his tongue inside her. A moment later she shuddered, then shattered, her moans turning to shouts as she climaxed, then climaxed again, until she was shaking with it.

He pulled her leggings the rest of the way off, then moved up the bed and gathered her into his arms, holding on, kissing her hair as she curled into him, aftershocks still vibrating through her, her breath coming in short pants.

He didn't realize it until she finally looked up at him, her eyes still hazed with pleasure, but he was grinning. Like a mad fool. Like he'd just accomplished the most amazing feat in the world. It said a lot that despite the enormous level of discomfort he was feeling in his lower extremities, the only thing he was thinking about at that moment was when he could do that for her again, and what other kinds of pleasure he could give her.

Then she was sliding her hand down his torso and unbuttoning his jeans. "Hannah," he said, his gaze shooting to hers. "It's okay, really—"

"It certainly is," she said, slipping her hand under the waistband and edging the zipper downward.

Now it was her turn to wiggle her eyebrows, and if he hadn't been using every last shred of his self-control to keep from going off in her hand like a rocket, he'd have burst out laughing at her sweet payback. As it was, he simply did his best to keep his eyes from rolling back into his head as she took her sweet time kissing her way down his torso. He made one last halfhearted effort at stopping her, then he gave up, gave in, tilting his head back and letting her take him all the way there, and growling right over.

When he could manage to open his eyes again, he caught her highly satisfied look and thought, *Yeah, I can identify with that.* "You're looking very cat and canary," he told her, his voice hardly more than a rasp.

"I'm feeling quite accomplished at the moment," she said, sounding a bit smug. "I won't deny it."

"Come here," he said, grinning as he pulled her up next to him. She slipped her arm over his waist and rested her head on his chest. He wrapped her in his arms and felt his eyes slowly drift closed. "Thank you," he said drowsily, for reasons that had nothing to do with the pleasure she'd so generously just given him.

He felt her yawn, then reach back and flip part of the duvet over them before snuggling in more deeply. "Oh no," she mumbled, as he felt her body relax, "thank you."

He grinned sleepily at that. He'd been grinning a lot lately. There were a lot of ways he might have seen himself finally getting to this point again in his life, he thought as he let sleep claim him. All of them awkward, challenging, potentially mortifying.

Not a single one of his imagined scenarios would have come anywhere close to this. He supposed that was because he just hadn't met Hannah Montgomery yet.

Chapter Fourteen

Hannah was a little late to the champagne celebration. Okay, a lot late. But she was too blissed out to care. Later she would overexamine and overanalyze, then hyperventilate about every single moment, breath, word, and sigh she'd shared with Will. But just for now, while she could still feel where he'd touched her, where he'd kissed her, how he'd pleasured her, she'd hold on to that buzz and hug it close. The real world would surely intrude soon enough. "Like, in about thirty seconds," she said as she walked around the side of the house to the veranda.

She looked up at the chimneys Will had restored and rebuilt, admiring the beautiful work he did. Strong, honest work he enjoyed and was proud of, as he should be. She understood that, supported that. Lived that. She turned toward the lavender fields, warmth filling her as her eyes adjusted to the dusky light of sunset. She was surprised to see there was still lavender left out there, given the crowds that had come through that day.

She took in a deep breath, enjoying the scent and letting the serene beauty of the endless, lush rows wash over and through her. The ripples and folds of the blue mountain backdrop behind them, highlighted by the last rays of the sun, settled her, grounded her as they always did, making her feel anchored to something strong and infinite.

Her smile grew, because, honestly, she could stand out there all night, but the moment she walked inside that house, there would be zero chance the rest of the fearsome foursome would not know what she'd just spent the past few hours doing. She felt like she was a walking neon sign of sexual satiation. And they hadn't even had actual sex yet.

Her grin remained unchanged as she finally turned toward the house and reached out to open one of the French doors. As wondrous as it was to find that part of her still worked and worked just fine, thankyouverymuch—it had been all the rest of it that had left her feeling giddy and buzzy, like a girl experiencing her first big fall.

Slow down there, missy. This is still lust. Not that other L word.

"Yeah, but I think it could be," she murmured, still too hopped up on endorphins to be properly terrified by the very idea. That would come in time. She'd learned to leave those things until it was their time to be dealt with. Nothing to be gained from worry. "Except losing this delightful little pheromone buzz I've got going on." And she deserved that much, didn't she?

Hannah discovered she'd been quite wrong about the rest of the fearsome foursome being all over her the moment they got a look at her face. She didn't even make it inside the door, much less look at them, before all three of them stood up and said, "So?" in unison. Though the tones in which that one word had been delivered varied wildly.

Vivi had her hands clasped under her chin, her eyes sparkling with glee. Avery pushed her glasses up the bridge of her nose with one hand and had her trusty clipboard and pen at the ready in the other. While Chey stood there with her arms folded in front of her, as if challenging Hannah to be anything other than completely forthcoming. In case

Hannah needed proof of that assumption, Chey turned and pulled out one of the chairs by the kitchen table. "Sit. Spill. Leave nothing out."

Chey McCafferty was of average height, about five-foot-six, with an average, though toned and athletic build. Those were the only average things about her. She was a former barrel racer and darling of the rodeo circuit, descended from a long line of rodeo riders, bull riders, and a number of other livelihoods that could possibly get a person trounced, tossed, or gored. She had nerves of steel, an uncanny ability to take in a room at a glance and read everyone in it with frightening accuracy, and an absolute zero tolerance policy for bullshit. Her word, not Hannah's.

Chey also happened to have one of the softest hearts of anyone Hannah had ever met. She was a big, sappy, heart-on-her-sleeve romantic. A truth she guarded fiercely and shared with very few as it wouldn't have served her well in her previous occupation. So Hannah knew there was no point wasting time trying to deflect or demur.

Hannah sat; then Vivi, Avery, and Chey took the other three seats. Vivi poured Hannah a fresh glass of bubbly and pushed it toward her. "Cheers," she said brightly, then propped her elbows on the table and braced her chin on her hands, wrist bangles jangling and rings flashing like sparks under the ceiling lights. "Tell us everything."

Hannah and Will had shared a half bottle of the Llama-rama wine by the time he'd left, so she really shouldn't, but this was a celebration, after all. She picked up the glass and tipped it in each of their directions. "Cheers to us," she said, and took a sip, then giggled when the bubbles tickled her nose.

"Not your first glass then," Chey said dryly.

"First glass of champagne," Hannah said. She looked from Vivi to Avery and finally to Chey. "I'm sorry I wasn't here to toast our first success. We did really good today."

Vivi lowered her chin and her perfectly painted lips pursed in a dry, perfectly painted curve. "Honey, if I had a man who looked like that dropping by for a little—"

"He didn't drop by for a—what do they call it now?"

"Bootie call," Avery supplied, eyes on her clipboard, already jotting down notes.

"Yes, that," Hannah said. "That was not what this was. He asked me out on a date earlier today and he wanted to set the day and time."

"Well, y'all must have had some hearty disagreements or really conflicting schedules," Chey said. "Because, by my count, he was there 'setting a time for your date' for so long that it qualified *as* your date." She'd used air quotes and a seriously-don't-even-try-me look that normally would have had Hannah telling all.

But Hannah was still pleasantly blitzed on a lot more than good wine, and though the fearsome foursome had shared pretty much every last detail of their lives over the past six years, Hannah suddenly decided she really didn't want to offer up details about her time with Will. That was intimate and belonged to her, to the two of them.

Avery spoke up before Hannah could find the words to politely decline their champagne-laden inquisition. "Your pupils are dilated, your cheeks are flushed, and not from prolonged sun exposure or embarrassment." She leaned closer and peered at Hannah's face through her glasses, then jotted a few more notes. "Some slight inebriation is my guess." She peered again at Hannah's neck this time. "Along with some razor burn." She jotted more notes. "His."

Vivi's and Chey's gazes shifted immediately to her neck, which Hannah wasn't fast enough to cover with her casual hand gesture.

Chey lifted one brow. "Setting a time and place, huh?"

"Can I just ask," Avery said, quite seriously, "about the progression of events that led from a casual discussion of date plans"—she waved the tip of her pen at Hannah's neck—"to that?"

Hannah laughed self-consciously, but didn't directly reply. "I appreciate that you care about me and want to make sure I'm okay." Her expression turned a bit wry. "But you're insatiably nosey."

"You're the first one," Avery said. "So of course we are."

Hannah didn't have to ask what she meant by that. The four of them had discussed all manner of logistics before deciding to launch this grand experiment, and one of the major topics had been what would happen when or if any of them ended up in a serious, long-term relationship.

"Although I will admit the algorithm I used to predict the progression of this was way off." She blinked owlishly at Chey. "I had you ranked at almost even odds." She looked from Chey to Vivi. "And you were three-to-one." She looked at Hannah. "I had you at five and me at eleven."

"Eleven?" Hannah said, not surprised at her ranking, but dismayed that Avery had so little faith in herself. "Oh, Avery—"

Avery raised a hand to stop her. "My schedule doesn't have me pursuing anything of that nature for another two years, ten months, and, well, it doesn't matter now, because you've blown my projections all out of whack, so I'll need to completely redo them."

"Sorry?" Hannah said with an overly sweet smile.

"Har, har," Avery said, but she had already flipped to a fresh page and was scribbling madly. Hannah had asked her once why she didn't use a digital device for her note-keeping and had gotten a thirty-minute dissertation on organization and the brain's greater capacity for organization when items were both noted and written.

"First," Chey said, still stuck on Avery's initial comment. "Me?"

Avery nodded, not fazed at all by Chey's intense look of

dismay. "It's not a reflection on your character. Not a bad one, anyway. It's just, of the four of us, you are the most forthright and confident in your decision making. You're attractive, smart, funny, and your capacity for love is pretty much boundless, though why you're so determined to keep anyone from knowing that, I don't know. While you may not be actively looking, you strike me as the one who, when presented with the irrefutable evidence that you've met 'the one'"—now it was her turn to use air quotes—"will not waste time playing any sort of societally imposed mind games." She smiled brightly then. "You'll just lasso him, jump him, and rope him."

Vivi and Hannah laughed outright. Chey just rolled her eyes. But Hannah didn't miss the speculative look on her face. Avery was a champion overthinker, and common-sense conclusions eluded her from time to time, but she was rarely wrong in her endless projections. Hannah had asked her about that once, too, her constant need to analyze everything, and she'd dryly responded that given how fast her brain processed things, she either had to constantly feed it data to keep it happy, or become a drug addict to dull it into inactivity.

Hannah had laughed, but she'd privately worried just a little that Avery hadn't been completely kidding.

"But Hannah jumped a guy first," Avery said sweetly. "So no pressure."

Hannah's mouth dropped open at that, but she wisely closed it again because she *had* just kind of jumped Will. More than once. And it had been glorious.

Something of that truth must have shown on her face, likely in Las Vegas–style lights, as the other three all swiveled their attention back to her. She lifted a hand to stall further interrogation. "First of all, I want to thank you for your concern."

"You said that," Vivi told her. "New info please. This old woman needs to live vicariously through you young folk."

Chey gaped. "Avery had you second, need I remind you."

Hannah laughed and, to her credit, Vivi wiggled her brows, smoothed her lavender locks, and touched her be-ringed hands to her face as if checking her makeup. "Yes, well, be that as it may, sweetie, since Hannah here is being the overachiever, perhaps I could use a few pointers on how she managed to snag the most eligible and unattainable man in Blue Hollow Falls."

"He's not unattainable, he's—it's complicated," Hannah said. "I can't say why we connected the way we did, but somehow we have. We've been very open and honest with one another about a wide variety of things." She lifted a shoulder, then smiled. "And, you know, there was all that screaming sexual tension." She looked at Avery. "So, to par-tially answer your question—and this is as much as I plan on revealing—you put that kind of emotional bond in a room with that kind of sexual tension and—"

"Jumping happens," Chey supplied.

Hannah grinned and took another sip of champagne, then nodded at Chey. "What she said."

They laughed and Avery, bless her, did make addi-tional notes.

Vivi was the first one to take a slightly more serious tone, but it came from a caring place. She reached out and covered Hannah's arm. "It's still a big step, honey," she said.

Hannah could have passed off Vivi's concern by claiming it was just sex, but each woman at that table knew different. A few awful attempts at first dates notwithstanding, none of them had trusted themselves enough to take any kind of serious step with a man since they'd met each other.

"I know," Hannah said, putting her other hand on Vivi's and squeezing. "And you all know I appreciate your con-cern and your love. I'm not sure what this is, or what it will become, or if I really want it to become anything more. All I know is . . ." She trailed off and thought about the wholly unexpected evening she'd just spent with Will McCall. "We talk, about important things, and frivolous things, and I make him laugh, which I don't think he's done very much. You'd be surprised how much he does both of those things when he lets his guard down and opens up. He's actually very funny."

That statement earned varying degrees of dubious looks in response.

"I was surprised, too," she admitted. "Beyond that, I will tell you that this particular evening was unexpected, unplanned, and a sincerely glorious surprise." She looked them each in the eye and added, "And no, I'm not talking about sex." She lifted her glass. "I promise I'm not leaping off any cliffs, but I do plan to revel in this bit of unexpected bliss. Then I'll get my head back on straight and do my best not to make unwise choices."

"A sound plan," Avery said. "Although I can share with you research that shows the effect pheromones play on using good judgment. It's not promising."

Hannah laughed. "I appreciate that, and frankly, I'm not surprised." She raised her glass. "To getting blitzed on pheromones, a little wine, a sip of champagne, and a man who does things to a white T-shirt that . . ." She simply closed her eyes, ducked her chin, and lifted her glass a little higher. "Am I right?"

"Show-off," Chey muttered.

"I knew it," Avery whispered fervently.

"Go get him, honey," Vivi said, clinking her glass to Hannah's.

"To new paths taken, and new tests yet to be determined," Hannah toasted. "Go me! And that's all I'm saying about it."

Chapter Fifteen

Hannah was ready to eat every one of those words not three days later. "See?" she told her reflection in her rearview mirror. "This is why you shouldn't do impulsive things." She realized she was checking her face and the stupid makeup she'd put on—again—in case she bumped into Will. The same Will she hadn't heard a peep from since the day of the party. Seventy-two very long hours ago. Which, objectively, didn't seem like a lot. They'd routinely gone longer than that between talking before they had . . . done whatever it was they'd done. She wasn't sure what label to attach to it now. She knew Will hadn't come over with that purpose in mind. At the very least, he'd have brought a condom with him if that was the case. Surely he hadn't expected she'd have one handy. She truly didn't believe that had been his plan anyway.

They'd exchanged their contact information before he left, had even laughed about how odd it was they had done what they'd done and then swapped phone numbers. Later that night when she'd climbed into the very bed where they'd done what they'd done, she'd thought back to how unexpectedly comfortable it had been. They'd been so open about it all, had even teased each other about it. The whole thing had felt healthy, natural, and very real. To her, anyway.

Hannah couldn't say with any confidence how the evening might have ended if Jake hadn't texted Will, asking where he was. They'd completely lost track of time, and Will was a half hour late for his and Jake's predetermined pickup time at the winery. Hannah was late for the celebration, too, so they'd said their good-byes a bit more hurriedly than maybe she would have hoped and had parted on a laugh that they hadn't managed to do the one thing he'd come by to figure out. He said he'd contact her soon and they'd pick a time and place for their "real date," as he'd called it.

"Soon," she muttered as she got out of the Jeep and went around back to get out her painting supplies and the canvas she'd begun at the music venue weeks ago now. She felt like an idiot for being so moony over a man at her age, pining away for him to call her or text her. She felt even more like an idiot for being all walk-on-air ridiculous after their little interlude in the first place, thinking it was the beginning of something potentially wonderful and how amazing it had been for them both.

Only clearly it had only been wonderful for her. Because, if it had been up to her to set that date, she'd have had a hard time waiting until the next morning to contact him, hear his voice, make plans. Obviously Will didn't feel the same. Even if he'd worried about seeming overanxious, one day, maybe even two days, was being cautious. Three days felt like rejection, no matter how you looked at it.

Hannah had wanted to talk to Vivi about it, ask her advice, but that still hadn't felt right. "And, be honest with yourself," she said under her breath, "you're not ready to admit to anyone just how big a fool you were ready to make out of yourself for him, after just one time together."

She continued the silent castigation, a familiar routine that had evolved into its own pattern over the past several days. She could have talked to Chey, but Hannah knew what she would say. Chey would ask her why the hell she hadn't just picked up the damn phone and called him. If Hannah wasn't sure what was happening? Then just ask. And Chey would have had a point, Hannah admitted. She'd even picked up her phone several times the first day to do just that. Call, or send a text. Something casual, but showing she was thinking about him, looking forward to seeing him again. Only she'd dithered too long, and now it wouldn't seem casual no matter what she said.

Instead, as day three had dawned, Hannah had packed up her paints and her canvas and had come out to the music venue, not because she was so enamored of her painting-in-progress that she was dying to continue with it . . . but because the musicians were rehearsing again today, and that probably included Jake. And where Jake was, his father would probably follow, at least at some point.

So, what better way to gauge the lay of the land than to casually bump into each other. She'd established her reason for being there before they'd had their little whatever it was—she refused to decide on a label now—and so it wouldn't seem needy or stalkerish. "Even though it's totally both of those things."

Hannah had played endless rounds of the stupid "maybe he had a good reason" game. Jake had gotten sick. Will had gotten sick. Will had been swamped with work. But she knew if a person wanted to connect with someone, they would. A text took two seconds. She'd worried that maybe he'd jumped too soon, had had second thoughts; after all, he was still actively dealing with a lot of baggage from his past. That possibility was the winner most often, except they'd been honest with each other about not rushing. And she felt, at the very least, he'd have contacted her to say he was having second thoughts rather than leave her hanging, wondering what had gone wrong.

Whatever the case, this radio silence wasn't sitting well with her. And she was just old-fashioned enough, traditional enough that she wanted him to reach out first. Not that she had anything against a woman reaching out, or asking for what she wanted, but in this case, he'd been the one who had asked her out. It was his date to set, not hers to chase. The ball, she'd decided, was firmly in his court.

"Hannah."

She paused for the briefest of moments, then swallowed the disappointment that had sunk in a split second after the momentary rush of joy. She pasted a polite smile on her face as she turned. "Addie Pearl," she said, "it's a pleasure to see you. I'm sorry I haven't been back to the mill this week. Since our event—well, you were there, you saw the turnout." Hannah's lips curved more naturally now. "I know I thanked you on Saturday, but I can't tell you how much it meant to us that you helped spread the word. Many of our guests told us that they'd found out about our event at the mill. And not just the poster, but from your artisans talking us up. That was very, very kind."

"They're your artisans, too, now," Addie reminded her happily. "We all benefit when we support each other. Like you all linking the event with Seth and Pippa's new label." She beamed, but her unusually colored eyes were keenly assessing Hannah. "It's good neighbors and good business."

Hannah laughed. "It is at that."

Addie looked past her to the canvas she'd just lifted out of the back of the Jeep. "Nice work. You didn't mention you also worked in oils."

"I don't really, which is why I'm not sure where I'm

going with this." She smiled as she shrugged. "But it's good to try new things, right?"

"Actually," Addie said, even as she nodded in agreement, "that's why I interrupted you just now. I hope you don't mind."

"Of course not," Hannah said, her expression faltering a bit at the serious look on Addie's face. Hannah sat her wooden case of paints and the quilted roll that held her brushes down on the open tailgate of the Jeep. "What's up?"

"Care to take a little walk?" Addie pointed toward one of the walking paths that led from the music venue to the mill. She handed Hannah an extra walking stick Hannah hadn't realized she'd been carrying. "This is for you. A little present from me."

Hannah took the stick and her mouth dropped open on a delighted gasp. Her gaze flew from the hand-carved stick to Addie. "This is stunning." The stick was a stripped and polished tree branch—Hannah couldn't have said from what kind of tree—and the end had been carved into intricate lavender stalks and blooms, each bloom beautifully hand painted. "One of the mill artists? I haven't had the chance to meet them all yet." She turned the stick around and looked at all the detail. "It's gorgeous."

"I saw it and thought of you." She smiled. "You'd mentioned wanting to paint the view behind my place. I thought you'd like having your own walking stick for making the trip up and down the mountain."

"This is so very thoughtful," Hannah said. "I will treasure it. I do still want to come out and paint. I'm not sure when that will be, though. Things at the farm seemed to have picked up speed overnight with our renovations, and we're starting in on making our inventory of products, but I would let you know first no matter."

Addie Pearl shook her head. "No need. Just come on out

and head on down. The only precaution I'd give you is that if it looks like rain, you might want to give it a pass. Getting back up that trail is a bear when it's muddy."

Hannah laughed. "Like it's otherwise easy? I thought I was going to collapse pretty much every ten or twenty yards."

"You get used to it," was all Addie Pearl said. She nodded toward Hannah's painting gear. "If you have extra supplies, please feel free to store them in the shed down by the sheep paddock, so you don't have to haul them up and down."

"Thank you," Hannah said, having not thought that part through, and grateful for the suggestion. "That would probably be a good idea." Hannah set her supplies back in the Jeep and closed up the back, then marveled a bit longer over her brand-new walking stick, before turning and gesturing for Addie Pearl to lead the way on their little stroll. She was very curious to find out what the older woman was about.

They set out and had walked just a short distance when Addie Pearl sent her a knowing look and said, "I'd hazard a guess you could probably get the help of a certain young man I know to help you lug your equipment down my hill."

Hannah grinned. "Jake is a sweetheart, but I could probably manage. I know his time is tied up with rehearsals and working for Seth."

"Yes, that is true, but I wasn't talking about the younger McCall."

Caught off guard, Hannah almost tripped over her new stick. "Oh," she said, wondering what Addie Pearl knew about her and Will McCall. Of course, what didn't the whole town know about everything? *Not that there's apparently anything to know in this particular case,* she thought.

"Will's mother and I were lifelong friends," she told Hannah.

"You were?" Hannah said, her curiosity sparked. "That's lovely."

"She was a delight, Dottie was. We told each other everything. She's been gone a number of years now, but I still miss her every day."

Hannah nodded. "It's hard, losing people we care about." She said it easily enough, her thoughts naturally going to Liam, but not in a hard way. "I try to think about their importance to me in a way that honors how much they meant to me. I think about the laughter we shared, those inconsequential moments that otherwise had no real importance, but sum up everything that made that person special to me." She smiled at Addie Pearl. "Like we still share those personal things that only the two of us understood or laughed about, you know?"

Addie Pearl nodded and seemed to regard Hannah with a new light in her eyes. "I don't think I've thought of it in quite that way." Her eyes shone when she looked at Hannah. "But I will from now on. Thank you for that."

"My pleasure," Hannah said.

"I won't ask," Addie Pearl said as they continued their walk, and Hannah understood what she meant and appreciated her tact. "That's your story to share, and we don't know each other that well as yet. But I am aware you know of Will's loss." She glanced at Hannah, then back at the trail. "It's common enough knowledge around here."

"I do, yes," Hannah said, a little warier now as she realized that Addie Pearl wasn't just making small talk. This was all somehow connected to what she'd come to talk about. She'd thought it likely had something to do with her new guild membership, and that Addie was going to ask her to give a seminar or something. Apparently not. "In fact, Will and I have spoken about it directly."

Addie Pearl looked up at her, her gaze searching Hannah's briefly, but then she looked back at the trail, and Hannah was left wondering what it was she'd been hoping to see.

"That's good," Addie said, almost as much to herself as to Hannah. "I'm glad to know it. He's had a lot to shoulder."

"He has," Hannah agreed. A thought struck her—that maybe Addie had come to warn her away from Will. Not for her sake, necessarily, but because she was protective of him. She could ease Addie's mind and tell her that Will had already distanced himself, so she needn't worry. "I know it's still something he's struggling with," Hannah said.

"He doesn't talk about it much," Addie Pearl said, glancing up again, just enough to keep Hannah in her peripheral view, keeping her attention mostly on the rutted path through the woods in front of them. "If he's talked about it with you, he must trust you. Or trust that you'd understand. And I can see now why he might feel that way." She surprised Hannah by stopping and looking directly at her. "That's a good thing for him. You've done some hard work in that area, I can see, and I'm sure he'd benefit from your wisdom, as I have in just the short time we've spoken."

"Thank you," Hannah said, a little taken aback, but not in a bad way. "That's very kind of you to say."

Addie Pearl didn't say anything else right away, and Hannah felt compelled to add, "I don't mind, if that's what's worrying you. It's okay, that we're talking about this."

"He knows your story then," she asked.

Hannah nodded. "He does. And I'll be honest and say it's not something I share lightly. Nor do I spend time discussing the past. But . . . regarding where I am now?" She smiled then, as she most often did when she thought of her son these days. "That I'm happy to share if it helps. Sometimes we just need a different perspective, a new way to look at an old thing. I know that approach helped me so much. So if I can help someone else find their own path through grief, I'm happy to do it."

"It does help," Addie said readily, reaching out to lay her

free hand on Hannah's arm. She squeezed lightly, then let go. "And you have."

"Good," Hannah said, and they were walking again.

Addie didn't say anything for a few minutes, but the silence was more comfortable now. They were nearing Big Stone Creek and the sound of rushing water complemented the chatter of the birds flitting between the branches overhead, and the drone of the summer locusts. It was cooler in the shade of the trees. Hannah tried to let her surroundings soothe her as they always did, but she couldn't seem to tamp down the sense of trepidation she felt about what Addie wanted from her, or wanted to tell her. Warn her?

She didn't know, and was just about to come out and ask when Addie pointed to a wooden bench that had been carved into a fallen tree trunk, probably by one of the guild crafters. It was situated in a little clearing, facing an opening in the foliage that lined the boulder strewn banks of the big creek beyond. "Wow, that's gorgeous," she said, gesturing to the bench. "And what a view."

"Care to sit for a few minutes?"

"Sure," Hannah said, her heart rate picking up as it seemed they were about to get to the point of it all. She was probably being silly, worrying about nothing, especially since it was likely going to be moot when she explained to Addie that Will wasn't as interested in her as she and the rest of the town apparently thought he was. Then another thought struck her. What if Will had sent Addie Pearl to break that news to her, to explain his reasons for backing away? But that didn't ring true to her, either. Will might have dug himself into a hole of grief that he hadn't managed to climb out of until now, but he didn't strike her as the type to ask others to do the hard work for him. Far from. On the other hand, he'd been silent for going on three days, so . . . what did that say about him? Maybe she really didn't know the man she was getting involved with. Or had started to get involved with. Maybe he was doing her a favor after all. *And maybe you're really not as ready for any of this, with any man, as you'd hoped,* her little voice added.

Hannah had let herself get all worked up. Yes, she'd spent intimate time with Will, something she hadn't done since long before her divorce, long before she'd lost Liam. So of course, to her, that was a very big deal. But to a great many people, what she and Will had shared could simply have been considered a spontaneous moment of giving in to immediate desires and wants. Nothing more, nothing less. It was just . . . she hadn't wanted to believe it could be that for Will. It had been a long time for him, too. Even longer than for her. And what they'd shared had had a far more direct connection to his own loss than to hers. She'd been the first woman he'd been intimate with since he'd lost his wife. He hadn't come out and said that, but it had been intimated in all the little jokes they'd made about how rusty they were. Surely that had meant something. Surely she'd meant . . . something.

Hannah had been staring silently at the rushing waters of the creek and came out of her thoughts to see that Addie was looking at her with kind regard.

"Sorry," Hannah said. "I always feel reflective when I'm in the woods." She looked back to the creek again, hoping that her expression hadn't been broadcasting the turmoil she was really feeling. "Actually," she continued, "I feel that way most of the time here in the Falls. Living out here, up in these mountains, it's been very . . . grounding for me. I feel settled in a way I haven't before." She smiled at Addie then. "I'm truly grateful for that. I don't think I'll ever take it for granted. The view from my own porch makes my heart swell." Just thinking about that calmed her. "I think that's why I've been so excited to paint again. I'm grateful for that, too."

Addie Pearl nodded. Then they both settled back on the

bench, leaning their sticks against the curved back of the fallen tree and relaxing as they let their surroundings lull them a bit. The silence this time was more relaxed, and Hannah decided whatever it was Addie needed to say, she'd let it wash over her like the water was washing over the rocks in the stream in front of her. *Let it flow, let it go.*

"I wasn't sure I wanted to talk to you about this," Addie Pearl said at length, her tone easy, gentle. Kind. She let out a little chuckle. "That's unusual for me. I tend to be a pretty bullheaded sort, charging ahead when I think I know what's best." She glanced briefly at Hannah. "Which is pretty much all the time."

Hannah let out a short laugh. "I admire your confidence. I often wish I had more of it. I don't dither, exactly, but I do tend to spend far too much time weighing options and analyzing things."

Addie's smile broadened. "And see, I could probably stand to do a bit more of that."

"To future goals," Hannah said, and they both shared a chuckle.

"I'm sorry if I've alarmed you or made you worry," Addie Pearl said. "That was not my intent at all. I thought maybe if we talked a bit first I could get a better sense of you, and whether or not my idea held merit."

Hannah looked surprised. "Okay." She smiled then. "So, did I pass muster?"

Now Addie looked surprised and delighted at the same time. "Surpassed it," she said, nodding and looking quite pleased. "I should have trusted that you were something quite special when Will took such a keen interest in you."

Concern shadowed Hannah's face once again. "That's very kind of you to say," she said. "But I should tell you that though Will and I have shared some things, I'm not sure if I'm the right person to help with . . . whatever it is you need me to do." She lifted a hand. "Not that I'm not willing, I'm

just not sure I'm the woman for the job." She held Addie
Pearl's gaze. "I haven't heard from him in a few days, so
we're not in any kind of constant contact. I'm not sure . . .
what we are." She hadn't intended to say that last part aloud.
It had just sort of slipped in there with the rest of it. Even
she had heard the hint of a plaintive note in her words, so no
doubt Addie Pearl had, too.

"Oh," Addie said, then nodded contemplatively. "I see."

"I'll be happy to try," Hannah said, not wanting to disap-
point Addie after all she'd done to help launch Lavender
Blue's first community event and also because she liked and
admired the woman.

"Why don't you tell me what it's about, and I'll let you
know if I think I can be of any help." She placed a hand to
her heart. "I wouldn't say anything to anyone."

Addie reached out and patted Hannah's arm again. "I
didn't think you would," she said. "You're too thoughtful for
that." She took in a long, slow breath; then, decision apparently reached, she said, "As you know, Jake is playing the
fiddle, and he's singing, and he's quite something."

"He is that," Hannah agreed, thoroughly confused now.
This was about Jake?

Addie Pearl took her gaze from the creek, shifting to look
at Hannah directly. "You might not know this, but Will's
grandfather taught him how to play, and how to make his
own instruments by hand. Will was named for him, actually,
though everyone around here called him Mack. And oh my,
Mack was a gifted crafter. Turned out his grandson was a
chip off that old block."

"I knew Will had played once upon a time, but I didn't
know about his grandfather, or that they'd handcrafted their
own instruments. Was Will's mother his only child?"

Addie nodded. "She was. Went and married a military
man she met when she was off at college, traveled the world,
had a wonderful son, and was blessed with a remarkable

life. Only came back to the Falls after her husband was killed in the line of duty. He rose to the rank of colonel and that's what everybody called him. Will used to come spend summers at the Falls with Dottie's folks when he was school age, but we didn't see him around here again after that until Dottie moved back full time. He enlisted in the marines just out of school, just like his daddy did, and was off on his own adventures by then."

"I see," Hannah said, admittedly interested in having some of the holes in Will's story filled in for her. But she still had no idea where Addie was going with this.

"I'm going to share this because I think it's important, and I think the timing is as well."

"Okay," Hannah replied, equal parts curious and wary now. "It will stay in my confidence, I promise." She wasn't at all certain she was ready to hear what Addie was about to share, especially if it was some new piece of Will McCall's life story that she'd be better off not knowing. She was already turned around and half upside-down because of the man as it was.

"Last summer, Jake played the fiddle for the first time. Sang, too. With Pippa, when she resumed her singing career. Right over yonder at our very own mill. It was a big night, I can tell you that."

"Yes," Hannah said. "I've had the chance to hear her sing and play. I'm not surprised she's reached the level of success she has. She's supremely talented, and I happen to like her a lot, too."

Addie grinned. "She's quite a bright presence and has been a welcome addition to our little community. She's also been a dear to teach Jake personally as she has." She looked to Hannah. "When Jake expressed an interest in wanting to follow in his father's footsteps with the fiddle, and his mother's footsteps with his singing, Pippa approached Will and asked if he'd be willing to join her on the road back to the stage and performing. She'd been overcoming the effects of surgery and he'd been a long time away from his passion for music, due to his wife's passing, but . . . he wasn't ready for that yet."

She'd said it matter-of-factly, but Hannah could see the reflected pain and sorrow Addie felt at Will's reluctance to find a way past his grief. "It's such a challenging thing," Hannah said, feeling comfortable enough now to speak her mind even more directly. "Everyone processes grief in their own way, and sometimes that way is to bury it so you don't feel like you're being just bludgeoned by it every day. It's an exhausting thing to contend with, and not as easy as all that to get on top of. I don't hold it against him, how he decided to get through it. He had a child to raise and a whole life to reconfigure. And if he was in the service at the time, then he had that responsibility, too." She looked at Addie. "After all, if you're not actively suffering every day, why ask to bring that kind of pain into your life on a regular basis?"

Addie had been nodding in agreement the entire time, and Hannah wondered if she were preaching her hard won wisdom to the choir. She had no idea what kind of personal losses Addie might have suffered. She'd lost her good friend when Will's mother had passed away, but it seemed to Hannah that her understanding ran deeper than that.

"And yet he was still suffering all the same," Addie Pearl said. "He'd just made it manageable."

"I would agree. Nothing about grief is ever easy, though. Even when you do find perhaps a healthier way of coping, of moving your life forward, it's something that requires ongoing attention. There will always be things that will remind you of that time, or of that particular event, or person. So . . . you have to give it the necessary thought, make sure you're truly finding a productive way to handle it, even when it's inconvenient." She smiled. "Because those moments never happen when it's convenient."

Addie nodded thoughtfully. "I see Will trying to do the work now," she said. "He's been coming to Jake's rehearsals, and we've talked about it a time or two. I know he wants to handle his reactions better, be a part of this new phase in his son's life. I commend him for it."

"We've talked about it, too," Hannah said. "I feel the same as you. I've let him know I'm here to talk if he needs to. The same as I would for anyone," she added, lest she give Addie Pearl the wrong idea. Although she wasn't even sure what the right idea was at this point.

"He made a fiddle for his late wife," Addie told her, and Hannah's full attention went right back to her. "The last one he ever made. He'd been teaching her how to play. It was to have been her Christmas present from him."

Hannah gasped. "And she—her accident happened on Christmas Eve. Oh, that's . . . that's even harder. No wonder Jake's music is so hard for Will to hear. He told me Jake sounds like his mom, too." She shook her head, her heart going out to Will all over again, despite his leaving things hanging between them.

Addie nodded. "She was coming back from a local holiday performance on base. Jake was with a sitter. Will was on a mission with a unit of special operatives." She waved a hand. "I don't know those details, as they are not up for public consumption, but suffice it to say he wasn't sitting in a tent in the desert somewhere. Despite the tragic circumstances, it took some time to extract him and get him home. I think that added to his pain a great deal, that he hadn't been there for her, or for his son. Mercifully, she didn't suffer. It happened in an instant. . . ." She looked to Hannah. "He never played again. Never worked on another fiddle. Understandable, even so many years later. But now, Jake is growing up. And he wants to connect to his mom, and to his dad, in this very particular way."

"Will lost so much that day," Hannah said, her heart

breaking for Will all over again. "I do understand why he closed off that part of his life. I had a hard time painting for a very long while. My publishers and the authors I was working with were very understanding, of course, and made all kinds of allowances for me at the time. Honestly, though, if it hadn't been my sole source of income, I can't say whether I'd have found my way to keep going." She took a breath, paused a moment, and went on. "The only reason I ended up working with the author of the second series I illustrated was because my son loved her books so much when he was little. I heard she was doing a signing near where I lived, so the two of us went, and I was surprised to learn she knew of my work on the other series I'd been illustrating. We stayed in touch, and she eventually asked me to collaborate with her. It was one of the most enjoyable projects I ever did. Liam was getting old enough by then that we really shared the whole process of my illustrating. They had long been some of his favorite characters. After I lost him, it wasn't something I ever wanted to look at again. I honestly didn't think I could."

Addie's entire countenance crumpled. "Oh, honey," she said, devastated. She just reached right over and wrapped Hannah up in a surprisingly strong hug. "I didn't know," she said. She held on for a good long while, and when she finally let go, they both had damp eyes. "I'd have never . . ." She broke off, shook her head. "I'm a foolish old woman. I thought you'd both lost a spouse. It just made perfect sense . . . and you hit it off so well with Jacob, and—" Her expression went slack again as an additional wave of guilt washed over her.

"It's okay, Addie Pearl," Hannah assured her, wiping her eyes. "I'll admit, there are parts of being around Jake that are challenging. Liam would be his age now. But to be honest, he's such a delightful young man and I've spent enough time in his company now that I can see how utterly different he is from Liam in pretty much every way. So . . . that makes it easier. I've decided to think of Jake as a friend I'd hope my son would have made."

Addie wiped her eyes, then finally withdrew a hankie she'd had tucked in one of the many pockets of the cutoff canvas coveralls she wore that day. She blew her nose rather noisily, which made Hannah's expression warm even further. Now it was her turn to pat Addie's arm. "I didn't mean to upset you, but I thought, given everything we're talking about here, that you should know. It's okay to be sad, but he was a great kid, so I try to think of how he'd love something, instead of how much I miss him not getting to see it or do it. You know? He'd have loved the Falls and would have talked your ear off."

Addie sniffled rather inelegantly and nodded. "I can't . . ." She didn't finish, shook her head again, then put her hand on Hannah's arm and held on this time. Finally she made a little sound of disgust and said, "Here I barge into your day with all these grand plans of mine, certain I'm going to save the world, or a small part of it anyway, and instead I drag you through—" She broke off. "Now I'm blubbering all over the place and you're the one giving comfort."

"It's never foolish if your heart is in the right place," Hannah said, meaning it. "It really is okay," she went on, patting Addie's arm. "What is it you thought I could do for Will?" she asked, deliberately changing the subject for both their sakes.

Addie's voice was a bit throaty. "As I said, I can see Will is making strides, and I couldn't help but notice that you seem to be a part of that. I'll apologize for sticking my nose in, but I saw the two of you in the parking area at your party the other day. The way you were looking at each other . . . maybe I drew the wrong conclusions."

"You didn't," Hannah said, seeing no reason to sidestep

anything now. "We are interested in each other. But I'm not sure he's really ready."

"Or he'd be in more regular contact," Addie finished, then let out another little snort of disgust, but not self-directed this time. "Men can be such dolts."

Hannah laughed at that even as she dried the last of the dampness from her eyes. "I think we can all claim doltish-ness on our personal resume. I should probably just call him. It's silly that I haven't. I just . . . he was the one who asked me out—so I thought he should do the calling, you know?"

"I do," Addie said. "But if there is one thing I've learned in this long life, it's that there's nothing to be gained by sit-ting around, wishing and hoping."

"I don't know," Hannah said. "I don't want to be chasing someone down who doesn't want to be caught. Maybe if I had contacted him right after we—after the last time we saw each other, we both could have easily sorted out where we stood. Now I feel the deafening silence is speaking for itself."

"Men have weird logic sometimes," Addie said. "I could tell you stories about the man I married, but I won't bore you. Suffice it to say, a man can rationalize pretty much anything if it suits his purpose. Men hate conflict, so if said rationalization helps avoid an emotional confrontation? That's the direction they will inevitably go and convince themselves they're being noble for doing it." She shifted to look directly at Hannah. "If Will asked you out and is reneging on the offer, then the least he owes you is a polite explanation. And I'm disappointed to hear he hasn't done so. That's not the man I know."

"I was thinking the same thing, on both fronts, but honestly, Addie Pearl, at this point, I'd really rather just let that sleeping dog lie. He's got a full plate, and so I think it's best if I just go on about my business. Things are only right when they're right for both people involved. Maybe it's not quite time for intimacy, for him. Baby steps aren't always a bad thing."

"He keeps moving this slow, he'll be taking baby steps right on into the Hereafter."

Hannah spluttered a laugh at that.

"Just calling it like I see it," Addie said, unrepentant. "Sometimes a swift kick in the hind quarters can help a man get his head on straight. In fact, that was exactly what I was hoping you could help me with. He wasn't ready last year to contemplate taking that next step, getting back to his work as a fiddle maker, much less playing one. But a year has passed now, and with Jake's progress and love for fiddling, it seems like Will could use a good nudge before he talks himself back into his safe little hidey-hole."

Hannah didn't necessarily disagree with her, but she frowned in confusion. "How did you think I could be of any help with that? I have zero musical ability. I'm happy if I can keep time by tapping my toe."

"I wasn't thinking of anything that direct," Addie Pearl said. "I just thought, if he was lowering his walls a bit, letting you in, and you seemed to be a force of good, maybe you could, you know"—she made a little shooing motion with her hands—"urge him to take his support of Jake's fiddling right up onstage. With you there rooting both the McCall men along, it might actually happen."

Hannah nodded now that Addie's whole scheme had finally come to light. "Actually, he told me that it was Bailey's tough love that got him into that arena the first time. I was really only there to add encouragement after the fact."

"That works, too," Addie said.

"Well, it's a lovely idea," Hannah told her. "But I don't think I'm going to be the one rooting him on from the front row. I mean, I'll always cheer for anything that brings him and Jake closer and deepens the bond they already share." She paused, trying to decide if she wanted to offer her opinion on the plan. "But as well intentioned an idea as it is—and I agree it would be a wonderful thing for both of them—Will might never want to play again, much less up on a stage. Unless it's something he truly wants to do, I think that needs to be okay, too. He made a huge stride being there in person to support Jake." She smiled and let her honest affection for Will shine through. "His love for his son will push him forward. But it may have some limitations, and Jake might need to accept that. I guess I would just caution that support can sometimes come across as pressure, and I'd hate for Will to feel like folks are sitting and waiting for him to do things he truly doesn't want to do."

Addie Pearl listened intently, truly seeming to take what she'd said in the manner she'd intended. Addie took a few moments when she'd finished before speaking.

Hannah hoped she hadn't overstepped. Addie Pearl had a lifelong relationship with the extended McCall family and was certainly in a position to know a great deal more about Will than Hannah did. She could only speak to the aspect of dealing with grief, and other people's ideas about how she should handle things and when she should be ready to move on. Her parents being two of the worst offenders, love them though she did. Establishing new boundaries and making fresh connections had been two of the reasons why she was now living in Blue Hollow Falls.

And, as to those new connections, though Hannah was hopeful to deepen her relationship with Addie, her loyalty was to Will in this matter. Whatever he thought of her, or whatever kind of friendship or relationship they might go on to have, she cared about him, and for him. So her protective instinct extended most strongly in his direction.

Addie's smile came slowly, but it spread into something ebullient. "You'll do, Hannah Montgomery," she said. As if reading Hannah's thoughts, she said, "It speaks well of you that you look out for his best interests, no matter where things stand between you."

"He's a good man," Hannah said simply, and she meant it. This talk with Addie had also made her rethink her decision to wait for Will to contact her. She didn't want to push him into anything he didn't want to be involved in. This was a big step for her, too, so if they both weren't up for giving it a go, she wasn't interested. But given what they'd shared with each other in her home, in her bed, she felt she did at least deserve to know where he stood. Maybe he was taking those baby steps Addie had just joked about, and that wasn't necessarily a bad idea, given the first time they'd been alone together, they'd ended up in bed. She just wanted to be part of the conversation, that's all.

"Well, I won't keep you from your canvas any longer," Addie said. "I appreciate your spending some of your precious free time with a nosey old woman."

"A caring woman," she corrected warmly. "And I'm glad we talked. I hope that's something we can do often. Whatever the subject matter." They stood and grabbed their walking sticks from their resting perches on the back of the bench.

It was only then that Hannah saw Will standing just a few yards away, at the edge of the clearing. She had no idea what he might have heard of their chat, but from the look on his face, he hadn't just arrived.

"Ah, Will," Addie Pearl said, a smile creasing her weathered face. "Right on time."

Chapter Sixteen

Will and Hannah both looked sharply toward Addie, who merely shrugged.

"Well, if the two of you can't see past the end of your own noses, then I wasn't just going to sit around on the sidelines and let you screw this up."

Will noted Hannah's mouth drop open, which answered any lingering question he might have had regarding her knowledge of this little setup.

Addie looked at Hannah. "Our little discussion was truly my reason for coming to talk to you." She looked to Will, then back to Hannah. "But you can't blame an old woman for having a backup plan."

Will's jaw might have been clenched, but he was polite when he said, "I can't speak for Hannah, Addie Pearl, and I appreciate that you have our well-being in mind. But if it's okay with you, I'd prefer to see to my own affairs in the future."

Unfazed and undaunted, Addie braced her palms on the top of her walking stick and held his gaze directly. "Well, you can't rightly do that if you don't actually do anything about them. You might be a bit out of practice at this dating business, but even all the way back in my heyday, a gentleman didn't leave a young woman hanging for several days—"

"Addie," Hannah said, in hushed shock.

She looked at Hannah, as undaunted as ever. "And today's woman doesn't just sit around waiting for her white knight." She lifted her stick in Hannah's direction. "You want something? Go out there and get it." She nodded toward Will. "Though if this one can't get his act together, you might want to broaden your scope a bit."

Hannah's expression was somewhere between stunned disbelief and abashed embarrassment.

"Sound advice, Miss Addie," Will said. "All around," he added, when Hannah swung her questioning gaze to him.

"Glad you can take this in the spirit intended," Addie replied. "Now, I'm going to pull my nose back out of your business. This here park bench is officially available. It's a lovely summer day. Perhaps the two of you could make good use of it." She walked over to the trail that led back through the copse of trees to the main path. She glanced back at both of them, neither having moved so much as an inch. She made a shooing motion toward them. "Go on now. I've got a guild to run and mill business to oversee. I don't have time to be running around after you two, trying to get you on track." She pointed the knob of her cane at them. "But don't you think I won't." She smiled then, quite merrily actually, and with a wink at them both, she was on her way.

"Well then," Hannah said, once Addie had retreated far enough down the trail that her steady, striding figure could no longer be seen. "I guess we've been told."

"It would appear that way."

Hannah turned to face him, her expression unreadable for the first time since he'd met her. "Addie's lecture notwithstanding, you don't need to stick around. I'm sorry she set you up. Both of us up, apparently. I would like to ask one thing though."

"Hannah," he began, knowing he deserved that somewhat frosty, dismissive tone. "I owe you an apology."

"Actually, you don't owe me anything. Although a little respect would be nice. You did ask me out, and you did say you'd contact me. Granted, you didn't say when, but I guess my estimation of the window of opportunity was a bit shorter than yours."

He let his chin drop, knowing he deserved every last one of her gently said, but decidedly pointed words. Then she undid him completely by letting her annoyance drop away, and adding, "I'm guessing it was a lot too much, a lot too soon, and I'm sorry for that, Will." She took a step closer. "Sorry it felt that way to you." She took another step, then stopped and spoke slowly, as if choosing her words cautiously. "I don't know if it will help matters or hurt them, but I'm not sorry for me." She paused and waited until he met her gaze directly. She smiled then, fully, honestly, and he swore he felt his heart physically shift toward her inside his chest. "In fact, I was downright giddy after you left the other night, propriety and restraint be damned."

He had to resist the urge to clap his hand over his heart, as if he could physically keep it from giving itself to her. He wanted nothing so badly as he wanted to close the distance between them, pull her into his arms, and make her giddy all over again.

"I was wrong not to get in touch with you," he said, hearing the rasp of regret and a bit of shame along there with it. "I know that, knew that. I was just trying to . . ." *Get in control of the feelings I have for you, which can't be wise or smart, or real. Too much, too soon, and then some.* "It is a lot," he admitted. "But none of it bad. The opposite of that." He held her gaze again. "I didn't want to leave you that night, and I've thought about pretty much nothing else since then."

Her eyes widened at his heartfelt and raw admission. He saw his own confusion mirrored on her face, along with a flash of awareness that made his body leap and catch right up with his heart. That's what she did to him, how she affected him. And it scared the ever-loving bejesus out of him.

"I'll be honest," he said. "I'm not sure how to—I wanted to call, but I didn't know how to explain. And I don't want to be anything other than candid with you. But . . . I haven't explained it to myself yet. I didn't want to say the wrong thing. But by not saying anything, it ended up being just as wrong anyway. I—"

"It's okay, Will," she said softly, and sounded like she meant it. "I understand. I mean that. It is overwhelming. Not in a bad way, not for me, but overwhelming is still overwhelming. You have other things you're dealing with, different from me. So . . . I get it. I guess, if I can say anything, it's that I hope the friendship we have, or that we've begun, would always be front and center. If you need to talk something out or figure something out, then let me be a sounding board and trust that I'll understand what you mean. Even if what you're trying to figure out is about me. Maybe especially then. We're adults." She grinned then. "Though I will cop to feeling a lot like a rejected high school girl the past few days, so we're none of us without our faults. I could have just called you and dragged it out of you." Her tone grew more serious again. "As long as we remain candid and honest with one another, even if we end up on opposite sides of an issue, even if that issue is what we want from whatever it is we've started, then . . . that has to be better than leaving things unsaid, or unexplored, or unexamined."

He nodded as she spoke, agreeing with everything she said. Putting her suggestion into practice, however, was an entirely different thing. "I'm used to being in charge, whether it be in my former career as a marine, or raising my son—at least for the past twelve years of his life—so I haven't had the luxury of discussing things or getting a second opinion. I've spent my life making unilateral decisions—some of them with deadly consequences—with little to go on in some cases other than my gut." He smiled briefly. "And when my gut has nothing for me, I am on the record as being very good at just burying my head in the sand rather than dealing with issues that I'd rather leave unexplored and unexamined."

She took another step forward, but he lifted a hand, just enough to stop her, and swore silently at the flash of hurt he saw in her eyes.

"I am very attracted to you," he told her. "And that is a weak adjective I'm using that doesn't come close to describing the impact you've had, are having on me."

She went still then, but rather than show hope or sunny optimism, as was her usual default position, her expression shuttered once more, and he realized she was preparing herself for what came next and assuming it wasn't going to be good.

"I don't want to stop," he told her, and some of that wariness in her expression lifted. "I'm just not sure how to go forward when I don't know what I want, or am capable of giving, or having, or . . . so many other variables I can't even organize my thoughts around them. I don't want to lead you on, and at the same time, I want you so badly it makes it hard to stay focused on anything else but that."

Her eyes did flare then, leaving no doubt that she understood, intimately, what he meant. He had to dig his nails into his palms to keep from reaching for her right then.

"I should have contacted you right away. I should have trusted you, that you'd understand my being all over the map with this." He lifted his hands, let them fall to his sides, and let down whatever walls he had left. "I don't even know what the next step looks like, Hannah."

"Maybe there is no map to guide us," she told him, her

voice a little husky with emotion now, too. "I certainly wouldn't have predicted that what happened at my house the other night would have come anywhere in the next dozen steps, and yet . . ." She lifted her shoulders in a simple shrug; then a hint of her sunny smile edged out. "It sure felt like a pretty darn good next step at the time."

He smiled then, too, and nodded. "I would have to agree with you there."

"So . . . what if we don't worry so much about where this is going?" she said. "We're on the record now as being complete idiots without a clue what we're doing, so no harm, no foul if one of us ends up wanting something more or different from the other." Now it was her turn to lift her hand to stop him. "I'm not saying that we couldn't get hurt. I do know we've both been through unimaginable pain before and survived. I also get not wanting to ever experience hurt of any kind ever again. I guess it comes down to asking ourselves if we're willing to risk it to figure out if we can have something worth working for. There is no way to have one without risking the other, so it comes down to figuring out if this is worth that risk. Only you can figure that out for you; only I can figure that out for me. And I don't know either, Will."

His heart took a little hit at that, and he realized that was what she'd been feeling the past few days, being on the receiving end of his uncertainty. It was a fair point to make and put things in a different perspective for him.

"It was thrilling and exciting what we shared the other day," she said, which only served to ramp up the chaos inside his head as he tried to separate his desire for her from his ingrained tendency to protect himself at all costs.

"I've enjoyed all of my time with you, clothed or not," she added with a brief, cheeky grin. "Enough that I am willing to see where it leads. I'm willing to risk that. There are no promises either of us can make on that score, except one.

Honesty. And I can promise you I will always give you that. Jump in, dive headfirst into the deep end, or dip your toe in and wade around in the shallow waters for a bit. I'm willing to go at whatever pace works for you, at least until it doesn't work for me. And then I'd tell you that. All we can do is be honest and forthright about how we're feeling. I'm a confronter, a talk-things-through-er." She grinned now. "You're a bury-er. A maybe-if-I-don't-give-it-energy-it-will-go-away-er. There's something to be said for both approaches. I would love to be better at shrugging off the small stuff."

"I don't know if I can say I'd rather spend more time confronting stuff I'd rather not deal with, but I will say that I won't let things go unspoken that have to do with you, or us." His lips curved more deeply. "I may have to drag myself to doing it kicking and screaming, but I'll at least give you a heads-up that the battle is in progress."

She laughed at that. "Fair enough."

Everything he was coming to love about her shone clearly from her soft gray eyes. He wasn't any less utterly terrified after their little talk. If anything, he was more scared than he'd ever been in his life. He'd fallen hard and happily for Zoey, had just gone gung ho, full tilt into his relationship with her, as had she. They'd remained that way for the duration of their time together. It had been a wild ride he'd loved with every part of his heart, and he'd felt lucky to experience every single second it had lasted.

That was before he knew the deep, soul-crushing, gut-leveling pain that losing something like that, losing someone like that, could do to him. So, while he'd love nothing more than to dive in the deep end with Hannah, and it was definitely beckoning, calling his name, with every sweet smile and dry laugh she shared with him . . . he just couldn't. He knew too much about the dangers that lurked in the depths of those dark, all-encompassing waters.

But how did he dip a toe in? How did he wade his way in slowly? Test the waters? Was that even possible?

His gut told him if he was going to wade in or dive in, ever again, Hannah was it; she was the one worth entering those swift waters for. Of that he had no doubt. So, he was already in the fast-moving currents, already on the way to being in deep over his head. Could he handle that? And more importantly, could she? Because he simply wasn't cut out to wade in.

And the words just came out of him then, because if not right now, then when? "Here is my truth," he began. "All of it." His throat threatened to close over and he had to clear it, more than once, before he could continue. "I want you in my arms, and in my life. I want you beside me, I want you under me, and on top of me, all around me. I'm not good at sticking my toe in. In fact, I suck at that. I think that's why it's taken me so long to climb out from under my grief. I don't know how to do things in stages, so it feels all-consuming to me right from the get-go. I find something I connect to, and I'm in. I don't know how to moderate that, and I'm well aware that that kind of intensity isn't for everyone. I can sit back and let you dictate the pace, and, unlike the past few days, I can promise that as long as you let me know what they are, I will put your needs above mine, always." He paused, tried to get his suddenly pounding heart under control. This was why he hadn't called her, because of all of this, and it was a lot. "Patience isn't an issue with me. I apply it every day in my current job and most decidedly in my past career. I would never pressure you to do anything you didn't want to do, and you don't strike me as a pushover anyway."

She smiled at that, and he wanted to smile, too, but he felt like he was putting his life on the line here, and he needed to get the rest of it out there, so he could find out if he'd just ruined the best thing to happen to him in a very long time. But laying himself bare was, in a way, the only protection he had left. If she couldn't handle who he was, then now was when he needed to know.

"All that said, however we proceed, it will be next to impossible for you not to know that I'm so hungry for you it feels like I'm starving. All the time. For all parts of you, not just the physical. Hearing that probably scares the hell out of you, which is why I'm saying all this. Because it scares the hell out of me." He lifted his hands, let them drop by his sides. "That's as down-to-the-bone honest as I can be." His heart was beating so hard, his pulse thrumming so loudly, he could barely hear himself speak, much less think. Surprisingly, now that he'd put it all out there, he did manage a brief, wry look. "You wanted forthright," he said. "Be careful what you wish for."

Chapter Seventeen

Hannah wanted nothing more than to close the distance between them and quite literally fling herself at him. Let him wrap her up and keep her close for the rest of his days. Let her do the same for him.

Hearing him say those words to her, bare himself to her as he had, was both wrenching and breathtaking. Wrenching because she could see the fear, hear the barely contained nervousness. This putting yourself out there, being vulnerable to someone, wasn't for sissies. And maybe she'd been so caught up in the rush of pheromones that she hadn't truly given that part a thorough look. It had been so very long since she'd even had to think about it. She'd met Steve in college. She hadn't been involved with anyone else since.

Their relationship had been over a long time, and she had no ghosts there, no baggage. Not about her marriage, anyway. Losing her son had pretty much eclipsed any pain she might have felt regarding the end of her already dysfunctional marriage. It had been a relief more than anything, not having to devote any more of what she had left of herself to trying to save it.

Once it was over, she'd realized almost immediately that she'd been trying to save it because that's what you did when you made vows, and they had a child together. When the truth was she should have been trying to save it because it was something she actually wanted. But she hadn't. Nor had her ex, who'd proven that by his quick remarriage and immediate production of a whole new family. She'd stopped asking herself what else she could have done, and wishing she could help to ease Steve's pain over their joint loss when she'd learned he'd been assuaging it with someone else all along.

So it was a bit of a shock to her system, standing there now, to realize that the risk she was running by getting involved with Will wasn't really about putting her heart out there and possibly getting it stomped on. Her heart hadn't broken, but had actually finally begun to mend when Steve left.

No, the far scarier part for her now was that she would have the power to hurt Will. And that was something she'd never forgive herself for doing, even if she'd never intentionally do so. She saw his chin dip, and realized she'd let her silence go on far too long. "My truth," she said, not entirely surprised to hear the shakiness in her voice, "is that I am afraid."

His gaze jerked back to hers.

"About a lot of things. The idea that you have found something in me to connect to, so strongly, thrills me. Down to my toes. That you're willing to stand there, right now, and bare your soul to me, knowing that you might scare me off, that grounds me, steadies me. That takes real strength." She smiled briefly even as she blinked away the wet sheen over her eyes. "And these past few days of silence notwithstanding, it tells me you won't back down from saying what needs to be said, not when my well-being is at stake, anyway. I respect that, and I happen to like it a lot, too."

His gaze turned wary rather than relieved, and she knew he heard the "but" coming. She wished there wasn't one.

"I'm just not sure that . . ." She trailed off, wanting to find the right words, and not insult him, or worse—far worse—his late wife. She took a steadying breath and simply put it out there, as he had. "You have held on to your grief for your wife a very long time. I ache that you suffered for so long. But . . . I worry that—"

"I'm replacing her with you?" he said, no accusation, or worse, condescension, in his tone.

"I would never presume that," she said. "What I mean is that sometimes the easiest way to deal with a big, huge, hard thing is to transfer it onto something else, hopefully something better and happier, healthier. Sometimes, that's a good way to deal with things, but other times it can just be another way of avoiding the big, huge, hard thing."

"And you worry that you're behind door number two."

She nodded, a brief curve hinting at the corners of her mouth.

He didn't immediately deny it, which would have worried her more, not less. Instead he seemed to take her words as intended and appeared to be truly thinking them over. "I'm sure there has to be some truth to that," he said at length.

She wanted him, but she wanted his desire for her, his need and want of her, to truly be about her. So, his honest assessment was a good thing, even if it pricked at her heart at the same time.

He did step closer then, stopping when he was just in front of her. He held her gaze unswervingly, and every part of her responded to him, to his proximity.

"But just so you know, while in some ways this all seems very sudden," he said, searching her eyes as he did, "you've captivatd me since I first saw you. All of this didn't happen because we both suffered a major tragedy, or because of the time we spent together in your bed. That last part just made it impossible for me to duck it any longer."

"It?" she asked, maybe a bit breathlessly, and not caring.

"This," he said, looking deeply into her eyes. "You had my attention even before that day I pulled you out from under a crumbling chimney. But that was when I knew for sure something was there. Your soft eyes, the pretty smile, your unswerving optimism no matter how many setbacks you all faced with the farmhouse, your willingness to just say what's on your mind. All of it got to me. All of you." His gaze remained intent, but the rest of his oh-so-serious expression split into a grin that made her knees actually wobble. "The upward trajectory from there has been sharp."

She laughed at that, wishing it would relax some of the tension mounting inside her. "I can identify with that," she admitted. "I admired your work ethic, your focus, your steady and calm demeanor even when our house was literally crumbling around us. And it's possible I might have spent a lot of time watching you toss big rocks around when I should have been picking lavender." She grinned broadly when his abashed grin was matched with a bit of a blush. "I've never been so fond of white T-shirts before in my life." His cheeks grew a bit ruddier still, and she delighted in discovering yet another thing she hoped to make him do more often.

They held each other's gaze and she couldn't seem to stop trembling in anticipation.

His grin peeked out slowly, and his gaze never left hers. "So, if I promise to wear a white T-shirt . . . does this mean our date is still on?" he asked, breaking the taut silence.

That made her laugh even as her heart pounded. *Were they going to do this after all?* She nodded. "Can we set the date and time now, though?"

He ducked his chin, chuckling as he did. "I deserve that."

"A little," she said, wondering when it would be okay

for him to just kiss her already. She was dying for him to touch her.

He lifted his head and she might have gasped just a little because the fear was gone now, the nerves, too. Leaving only the heat. "Is tonight too soon?"

Her pulse leapt. "I guess I can wait that long."

His grin was slow, and not a little wicked. "I was thinking dinner down in Turtle Springs. Maybe take a boat out on the Hawksbill River. You get a very different view of the mountains from the middle of the river. If you'd like to bring your sketch pad, I thought maybe some of the scenery would be inspiring."

Touched at his thoughtfulness, she nodded. "That sounds lovely."

"I was hoping you'd think so. I also figured being in a tiny canoe on a big wide river might give us a fighting chance to spend some time talking about more inconsequential things. Getting-to-know-more-about-you things."

She laughed. "With our clothes on this time."

"Though I kind of liked the things I was getting to know before, too."

His husky voice and the way he was looking at her, coupled with all the things he'd said to her, made her want to beg off the river trip and drag him back to her place right then and there. *And you were worried he was going to be the intense one?*

"Then we have a lot to look forward to," she said, thinking if he didn't kiss her inside the next five seconds, she was just going to go full on Addie Pearl and take what she wanted. Right there on the park bench if need be.

Something of that must have shown on her face, because he took a step closer still, all but eliminating the rest of the space between them, yet still not touching her. "That hunger I mentioned is the only thing keeping my hands off you."

She trembled and had to forcibly keep herself from simply

leaning into him, against him. "Maybe . . . maybe dinner and the canoe trip could wait one more night," she said against a suddenly very dry throat. "You know, just so we don't jump each other right there in the restaurant. Might upset the other diners."

"So considerate," he said, murmuring now as his head bent imperceptibly closer to hers. "Always thinking of others."

"That's me."

"How badly did you want to paint today?" he asked, his gaze dropping to her mouth.

She wet her lips and his throat worked, hard.

"I couldn't hold a paintbrush steady right now if my life depended on it." She looked from his eyes to his mouth. "Didn't you want to sit in on Jake's rehearsal?"

"I caught the first song. He knew I had a meeting with Addie Pearl."

"Right," she said, her gaze fixed on his mouth now. "Addie Pearl. We might owe her a thank-you."

"It would go right to her head," Will said, and leaned in so close now he was whispering into her ear.

"She earned it," Hannah said, barely able to get the words out, she was shaking so hard with want.

"True."

"Could we go somewhere, anywhere more private? To, ah, continue this conversation?" Hannah asked. *Begged*. "Because one more second of this torture and we might end up giving the youngsters that frequent this trail an entirely inappropriate nature demonstration."

His chuckle was raspy and deep, and she wanted to rub her hands up and down her arms to stop the tingling sensation it sent skittering over her skin before it reached other places that needed no additional tingling right then. None. At all.

"Again with the thoughtfulness," he said, and finally,

mercifully touched her. But not in the way she'd anticipated. He took her hands in his, then wove his broader, warmer fingers through hers.

It was more shockingly intimate than she would have expected—their palms united, warm, bare flesh against flesh—as he rubbed his fingertips over her knuckles.

He tugged her that infinitesimal bit closer and shifted his head to take her mouth. Gently, but oh so fully. She almost whimpered in relief as his warm lips covered hers, parted them. Then he slipped his tongue inside, teased hers, suckled her. She heard a long, low groan from somewhere inside him when she did the same in return. Then he broke the kiss, pressing his forehead to hers. She could barely hear the sound of the creek behind them for the sound of her pulse throbbing inside her ear. Everything was throbbing.

"Maybe dinner tomorrow is a good idea," he said roughly. "Jake can stay at Addie's tonight." He opened his eyes and lifted his head enough to look down into hers. "If you'd like."

"I would very much like."

"Seven?" he asked.

"What time is it now?" She leaned in close and nibbled his earlobe and had the satisfaction of feeling him tremble. She whispered in his ear, "Would now be good?"

Hannah pulled into the garage under her loft and shut off the engine. She couldn't get out of the Jeep fast enough. It was only because they'd driven separate cars that they'd managed to make it all the way to their destination at all. If there had been any concern that their brief time apart would have allowed the heat to cool or second thoughts to rush in, she needn't have worried.

Will pulled in right behind Hannah. The dust hadn't even settled on the driveway behind them as they raced up the stairs. She might have been giggling madly and he might have been chasing her, and maybe, just maybe, she let him catch her right inside the door, grinning and breathless, just so she could feel what it would be like for him to back her against the nearest wall and finally, mercifully, thank-you-Lord, feel the entire length of his wonderfully warm, hard body pressed up against every last one of the soft, and quite damp, parts of hers.

There were gasps and moans, and there was laughter, always laughter, which somehow thrilled her and seduced even more fully than his very skilled mouth and his oh-so-clever hands.

When they couldn't stand any longer, her carried her to bed—*carried her*—making her feel young and free, beautiful and desirable. Addie Pearl might have schooled her not to wait for her white knight, and Will McCall had more than a few dings in his armor, but he was all the knight Hannah needed.

This time they undressed each other fully before tossing off pillows and climbing into the delicious coolness of her soft linen sheets. He was hard planes and bunched muscles and she was soft curves and ample everything, and yet they seemed to fit into each other's arms with very little angling and rearranging.

"I need to find my pants," he said, when he lifted his head from where he'd been doing the most amazing things to her nipples. He grinned then. "I did come better prepared this time."

Her head was still arched back, eyes closed in bliss, her hips pinned down by the weight of his arm. So she flung her hand somewhere in the general direction of her nightstand. "So did I."

"So thoughtful," he murmured, returning to his task.

"So needy," she replied, then moaned in appreciation when he finally began making his way down her torso.

One thrust of his tongue and her most immediate need

was met with a loud and guttural shout. So was her second. And her third. "Come here," she said breathlessly, reaching for him. "I'm dangerously close to being climaxed unconscious."

His grin bordered on smug. She figured he'd earned that right. "We wouldn't want that." He grabbed a condom from her nightstand, finally ripping the packet open with his teeth. Maybe she wasn't the only one shaking with anticipation. He turned to her, pulled her into his arms, then shifted his weight until he was on top of her.

"True," she said, still short of breath, thinking her blissed-out grin might be permanent. "This next bit would be more fun for you if I were an active participant."

"Hopefully for you, too," he said wryly, then bent his head and nipped at one earlobe while settling in between her legs.

Hannah felt a sudden rush of emotion, feeling his weight finally fully on top of her, wanting to feel him inside her, wanting him to fill her. More than once since her divorce, since the accident, and all that dealing with both of those things had entailed, she'd thought she should just find someone decent who wouldn't mind a friends-with-benefits arrangement, leap that hurdle, and put it behind her, so it wouldn't gain any unnecessary importance. Now, lying here, in her bed, with only the second man she'd ever been with, she was so very glad she'd waited. She looked up into Will's beautiful green eyes, and knew, no matter where this led, for this particular part of her forward journey, she wouldn't have wanted it to be anyone other than him.

Given their urgency to this point, she'd expected him to take her in some breathless rush of heat and need. Instead, he lived up to his word, about putting her needs first. He took his time. His wonderful foreplay had relaxed her and she certainly couldn't have been more ready, but after years of celibacy, she was a bit snug, and he was a bit above average, so he entered her slowly, letting her body adapt to him. She closed her eyes and focused on the feeling, for so long not a part of her life, and at the same time, so wonderful. She opened her eyes in time to see him close his as he sank fully inside her. She arched up to meet him, holding him tightly. He groaned so deeply she could feel his chest vibrate against hers. He stopped moving and she spent a split-second wondering if he was trying to hold himself back from climaxing, or if he, too, was having to adjust to the idea of being with someone new. And if it was as positive for him as it was for her. She didn't want those thoughts to intrude now but couldn't stop them.

Before nerves or doubt could take hold, his eyes opened again, and his gaze pinned immediately on hers, and stayed there as he began to move inside her. She wrapped her legs around him and arched into him, moving with him as they slowly found their rhythm. Any and all comparisons to any other part of her life vanished as she gave herself completely over to him, to this new life she was living now. This was who she was now, who she was with now, and it was glorious. Nothing else mattered.

Chapter Eighteen

Will hadn't been exaggerating about his desire for her, his hunger. But that hadn't meant he hadn't been worried—okay, more than worried—about how it would feel to make love to her. He'd actually been thankful—mostly—that they'd been forced to stop short the first time. No pressure to do more than get used to being with each other in a fully intimate way.

But following her to her place that afternoon, knowing they would be taking that giant step—to his mind anyway—he'd still worried. Not performance anxiety so much as whether he'd be able to stay in the moment and keep his past where it belonged at a time like that: in the past.

He'd been with no one else in all that time. Surely there would be hurdles, obstacles, mental all of them, but that just made them all the more challenging. Maybe it had been their utter and complete openness with each other. Not just about taking a step forward together, but about their respective pasts. He knew she was fully aware of what he'd been dealing with, so there was nothing to fear there. He knew, because she'd told him the first time that she'd also been celibate for her entire time as a single woman.

And that had made it easier for him. Because he was

more worried about taking care of her needs, about making it as easy as possible for her, releasing him from having to overthink his own potential issues.

Her humor and openness charmed him, her responsiveness to his every touch turned him on, and the way she gave herself over to him when he was fully inside her had had him falling even harder and faster.

She lay asleep now, sprawled across his chest. She was delightfully unselfconscious about her body. Not because it was perfect. She'd joked when he'd undressed her earlier that afternoon that she'd wished she'd thought to wear leggings again as they kept things from jiggling that shouldn't, and when he'd bared her breasts that first time, she hadn't tried to hide the stretch marks, or explain them away. He admired that.

She'd lived a full life in her body, given birth, nursed a child, worked, played, and now made love again with that body. His was banged up and marked up, had been shot at more than once, and worked his body hard every single day in his job. He bore the aftereffects of his life, too. And life would continue to do that to both of them. He wasn't turned off by that, he wasn't seeking perfection, and thank God neither was she. Perfection was ephemeral and impossible to maintain. They weren't kids anymore, and he discovered he liked the comfort there was to be had in being fully, naturally themselves when they were together, scars, stretch marks, and all.

"Penny for your thoughts," she said drowsily, as her eyes blinked open to find him watching her. Her eyes were soft, and full of happiness and affection. He didn't think he'd ever tire of looking into them.

"I was just thinking that there are some parts about getting older I don't mind."

"Like what?" she asked, folding her arms on his chest and propping her chin there.

"Like not having so many hang-ups about the things that don't matter. And really appreciating the things that do."

She thought that over, nodded. "Agreed." She tilted her head to the side slightly and said, "Although I'm not so sure how I feel about not being able to sustain that one position we tried because my knees just weren't having it."

He laughed in surprise and she just shrugged unrepentantly.

"I happen to really like that position," she said.

"Well," he said, "maybe we'll find some use for those pillows after all."

She grinned at that. "Problem solver."

Now he shrugged, the smile still there. "Like I said, you make me aware of your needs, I'll do my best to meet them."

She sighed and kissed him right on the heart. "My hero."

This, he thought. *This is what I want in my life. Making love to a woman I hunger for, laughing and talking about nothing at all, then finding our way right back to pleasuring each other all over again.*

He shifted her off his chest and rolled her to her back, having to shove several pillows out of the way. "Speaking of small things, knee pads notwithstanding, we might have to have a conversation about the pillow population. I'm pretty sure they procreated when we weren't looking."

"It's true," she told him. "I stopped trying to control the population explosion years ago. They kept me company, though, so we both got what we wanted."

"Sounds reasonable," he said. "But perhaps we can cull the herd from time to time."

She looked up at him. "I rather like the pillow I was just sleeping on moments ago. We can banish the lot of them if you'll keep me company and give me a place to rest my head." Her smile spread. "I'm easy like that."

He chuckled and marveled at the same time. He'd expected to have a lot of heavy lifting to do when it came time to be with someone new, making endless bargains with himself to make it okay to move on, to not feel guilty for doing so. Maybe it was true that all it took was meeting the right person to put one's life in perspective. But he felt remarkably okay. Stunningly so, in fact.

The oddest thing of all was that being with Hannah helped him frame his past the way he'd always wished he could. Instead of feeling like he was replacing Zoey, which he could never and would never do, he felt like his life with her had prepared him for the life that losing her had pushed him into now. He was a better lover, a better partner, and a better person because of his wife. She'd have hated the man he'd become after her death. And now . . . now he thought maybe he'd finally found his way forward. Allowing love to grow inside him again celebrated rather than diminished the love he'd felt before, as if he was building on that very sturdy foundation they'd begun.

"You're staring, again," she said a bit sleepily.

"I was just appreciating the things that matter," he said.

Her expression softened, and she blinked her eyes open again. "You say the best things."

He leaned closer and kissed her. "I blame you."

She giggled as he shifted her so he could kiss the side of her neck and nibble her ear.

"For this part, too." He worked his way down. "And this part."

She gasped as he closed his mouth over one nipple, but before he could start yet another exploratory journey in learning the wonders of her body, she tugged him gently back up to her.

"What is it?" he asked, when she took a moment to search his eyes.

"We're okay?" she asked him, so sweetly, but also honestly, that he knew she wanted a real answer.

He also knew exactly what she meant. Maybe something

of his thoughts had shown on his face after all. "We're better than okay," he told her, without hesitation.

Her expression broke into a wide, happy smile. "That's exactly what I was thinking."

"Look out," he told her, wiggling his eyebrows and making her laugh, "maybe tomorrow we'll actually go on a date."

"You sound awfully confident that I'll say yes," she teased.

"I've come to discover a few rather persuasive techniques that might weaken your resolve," he replied.

"Is that so," she said, appearing to ponder the validity of his boastful claim. "Maybe you should demonstrate."

He grinned. "I thought you'd never ask."

Chapter Nineteen

"Knock knock," Hannah called through the front door to Will's house. She'd been there numerous times the past two weeks while Jake had been away at camp. He'd just gotten back home again, though, and she didn't think it would be right to simply knock and go in as she'd been doing recently.

Jake answered the door. "Hannah, hey!" he said, grinning broadly as he opened the door. "Let me help with that." He took her easel and her toolbox so she could pick up the over-sized pad of watercolor paper she'd leaned against the house.

She followed him into the small foyer. "I swear you got taller while you were gone."

"Actually, I did. I was getting cramps, or what felt like cramps, but like my bones hurt. Dad took me to Doc Hamilton when I got back yesterday and it turns out I've grown over an inch since March. He said growth spurts happen sometimes and when it goes fast it can make your bones hurt. Or, something like that."

"Ouch," Hannah said, and started to share a story about Liam being tall for his age and experiencing growing pains, too, but stopped herself. She knew Jake was aware now that she had a son, and that he'd died. Will had talked to him before he'd gone off to camp. But she and Jake still hadn't talked about it directly. She knew she needed to find a way to bring the subject up, so Jake wouldn't feel awkward about it, so he'd know it was okay to talk about it, and that had been the perfect moment. If she were honest, there had been a few other moments before he'd left for camp, but she hadn't been able to just go ahead with it. She wasn't entirely sure why.

Hannah had asked Addie to use her judgment in talking about Liam with Bailey. Only because if Jake knew, then it was better if they both did. And she and Will couldn't really move forward with that piece of information hanging over their heads. She'd offered to talk to Bailey herself, as she had with Jake, but Addie agreed it might be easier for her to have that conversation for the same reason Will had decided it would be best if he told Jake. That would allow the kids a chance to process the information without her sitting right there in front of them. They could ask any questions they wanted without fear of hurting her or making her sad.

Hannah smiled inwardly as she directed Jake to take her easel and supplies out to the big screened-in porch off the back of the house. True to form, after Addie had talked to her, Bailey had waited until Jake had left for camp, then she'd sought Hannah out. The first time Hannah had gone down to Addie's meadow to paint, Bailey had simply run right up to her and hugged her tight. She'd told Hannah she was very sorry and apologized about the baby lamb. Hannah had hugged her right back, sniffled a lot, and thanked Bailey for being the good-hearted person she was. She'd assured Bailey she owed no apologies of any kind. She'd half expected Bailey to ask her some questions, but she hadn't. Oddly, that had made it easier for Hannah to bring Liam up on occasion when the two of them happened to be alone in the meadow together. Liam's name hadn't come up often, just once or twice, but Bailey had simply taken it in stride, and responded as she would if Hannah were talking about any other part of her family. It had been . . . freeing. *Who knew that your safe space would be with an eleven-year-old girl?*

Hannah watched Jake set up her easel, and wished she knew why it was easy with Bailey and so hard with him. Of course, Jake hadn't said a word about her loss, but Hannah wasn't surprised. He wasn't like Bailey that way. Hannah knew it would be up to her to bring it up. She just . . . hadn't. Yet.

"Thanks," she told him. "This is going to be a wonderful place to paint. I'm grateful to you and your dad for letting me set up shop here for a bit. Your view of the creek is spectacular. The trees, the downhill slope, painting while listening to the water, all the birds, the frogs. I've taken a ton of photos, but I knew being here would make it that much better."

Jake nodded, liking her excitement. "I like it out here, too. I used to sleep out here sometimes in the summer when I was little. Grandma Dot would burn those candles that keep the mosquitos away."

"Oh, I would have loved that," she told him. "What made you stop? Too tall for the wicker couch I'm guessing," she teased. Too late Hannah realized her gaffe. It was quite probable that Jake had stopped sleeping out here when his grandmother had passed away. "Jake, I—"

But he responded before she could try and fix it. "Oh, I went through this lame phase after my grandma died where I thought that kind of thing was for babies. I know that's dumb, but I guess by the time I figured that out I just never really thought about doing it again." He shrugged and grinned and she saw the beginnings of a squarer jaw, more angles in his cheekbones. "Maybe now I will."

Hannah nodded, relieved she hadn't put her foot in it as badly as she'd thought. "Don't forget the candles," she said. "The mosquitoes have been little beasts this summer, and with you being so close to the creek, they'd probably eat you alive."

Jake nodded, and she thought he looked like he wanted to say something else, but instead he said, "Is there more stuff in your car? Do you need help?"

She shook her head. "This is it. I've got some old baby food jars I put water in to wash out and mix with different colors of paint, so we'll need to fill those up."

"I can do that," he said easily enough, but Hannah had seen him freeze, ever so slightly, at her mention of the baby food jars and realized that the time for dancing around the subject of Liam was over.

"Thanks," she said, then summoned a sunny smile. "You know, that was one of the first things my son got big enough to do for me. He had this little stool he climbed on and he had to use the bathroom sink, but it made him feel so important."

Jake went completely still then, and Hannah's heart ached for him. She didn't want this to be awkward or hard, but she knew it was both, and that she was partly to blame for making it harder.

"It's okay to talk about him," she said gently, but easily. "I should have sooner, but I didn't want it to be weird, or make you feel uncomfortable. I realize now that it's only made it more of those things, not less, and I'm sorry for that."

There was a moment of silence, and then Jake said, "Bailey told me she's talked to you about it—him—and you're cool with it. I wanted to. Before I left. But . . . I don't know. I guess I just didn't know how."

"That's okay," Hannah said. "I had the chance a few times, too, but I didn't. It's not an easy subject to bring up the first time, but if it helps, the thing I choose to do is think about all the good memories. Like with the baby food jars. I want to be happy when I think about Liam. He was a happy kid, and he'd want me to be happy when I think about him, not sad." She lifted a shoulder, her tone gentle. "Sharing memories with other people is a good way for me to do that." She waited for Jake to finally look at her and her heart broke a little at the lost look on his face. "You can ask me about him or talk about him. It's—I really don't mind. But I also don't mind if you'd rather I don't bring him up when we're together."

"It's not that," Jake said. "I guess . . . that would feel disrespectful."

Hannah's heart squeezed a little. "You're a very kind and thoughtful young man, Jacob McCall. I appreciate your saying that."

He nodded but didn't say anything else.

Hannah's expression warmed further. "If it helps, it's not like I talk about him all the time. Just when something sparks this memory or that, like just now. It's nice to be able to say it, laugh over it, whatever, then keep on going. The more I do that, the better it is."

Jake nodded, and seemed to think about her explanation. "I'd be okay with that," he said, then looked at her. "If it helps you."

"So, enough about that," Hannah said, thinking the conversation hadn't gone too badly.

"Can I just ask one thing?" Jacob asked. "Then I promise I—"

"You can always ask me anything, Jake. About anything, including Liam."

"That's a cool name," Jake said, then paused, as if testing how it would be to just talk about him.

"Thank you. It was my favorite uncle's name. Actually, my uncle Liam and aunt Penny pretty much raised me, kind of like Addie is doing for Bailey."

"Do you not have a mom or dad, either?" he asked, then immediately she saw the tips of his ears turn pink and he hurried to add, "My mom didn't have parents. Well, she did, obviously, but it was just her mom who raised her. Her mom was in the military like my dad and his dad, my grandpa. I never met my grandpa—he died in the war before I was born. My mom's mom did, too, but my mom was older when it happened, like in college. So, she really didn't have a family after that until she met my dad."

"She was really lucky to find him," Hannah said, grateful and relieved that Jake felt completely natural talking about his mom with her. She felt honored and trusted. "I know she was really loved by your whole family."

Jake nodded, then kind of looked at her expectantly.

Hannah remembered he'd been asking about her parents. "My mom and dad are alive, and even though they weren't around a lot when I was growing up, we all love each other very much. They both traveled extensively for work, still do, so my aunt and uncle helped to take care of me when I was growing up. My uncle was really tickled when I named my son after him." Hannah grinned. "He'd stop people on the street when we'd be pushing Liam in his stroller and boast about it. To complete strangers."

Jake laughed at that.

"Liam's middle name wasn't nearly as cool, though. Theodore, for my dad."

"I don't know," Jake said. "Theo might have been all right."

"You know what, you're absolutely right." They shared a smile and she could see Jake relaxing. She blew out a shaky, relieved breath of her own.

"Where are your mom and dad now?"

Hannah nodded. "They are presently in South America. My dad is an archaeologist, and my mother is a language teacher. She teaches English to kids in other countries, usually where my dad is working."

Jake's eyes widened. "Wow, that's pretty cool. Did you ever get to go with them when you were little?"

Hannah shook her head. "They weren't really in places that would have been good for me, but I have since I've gotten older."

"That's cool. Where do your aunt and uncle live?"

Her expression was filled with fondness as she replied, "Oh, they're both gone now."

"I'm so sorry," Jake said. "That's rough."

"It was, but it wasn't sudden. My uncle had been ill a long time, so it was merciful. My aunt got sick not long after." Hannah smiled. "She used to tell me she was worried my uncle wasn't taking good care of himself in heaven, so God thought she should get on up there and straighten him out."

Jake laughed at that, then ducked his chin. "Sorry," he said.

"No, it's okay. We laughed about it often. Aunt Penny was pretty amazing, really. And that all happened before the accident with Liam, so that was a blessing, too. I feel like they're all up there watching out for each other." She laughed a little. "Probably makes me sound weird, I know, but it's kind of comforting."

"Not weird," Jake told her. "I think about my grandma kind of like that. I probably would my mom, too, but I don't remember her. I was too little. I grew up with my grandma, so I guess it's like you and your aunt and uncle. Then she got sick and my dad came back full time."

"That's a lot for a young person to handle," Hannah told him. "I'm really sorry. I was a grown-up when I lost my aunt and uncle, and it was still pretty hard. It sounds like you had a lot of people who loved you and were looking out for you, though, and that part is really good." She smiled. "You still do."

Jake nodded. "My dad told me pretty much the same thing. I still miss Grandma Dot, though it's different now. Not as sad." He looked at Hannah. "I kind of like your idea about remembering the good times and being happy when you think about them. My grandma did that when she talked about my mom. She told me so many stories. Funny ones and cool ones, all kinds of things. I know I don't remember her, so it's not the same, really. Remembering her doesn't make me sad, but it does make me feel closer to her. Like I know I would have loved having her for my mom, if that makes sense."

"Perfect sense," Hannah said, and blinked away the tears that wanted to gather. For all the sorrow in his young life, Jake had indeed had some wonderful people loving him and taking care of him, helping him become the kind and thoughtful young man he was.

There was a short lull in the conversation and Hannah went back to unpacking her paintbrushes.

Jake sat and watched for a moment, then said, "My dad . . . he loved my mom so much, he just really couldn't talk about her when I was little. I didn't get it then, but I didn't really notice, either. My grandma talked about her a lot. I get it more now, I guess. Bailey says I'll understand it better when I'm older and fall in love with someone."

Hannah nodded, and felt her eyes grow even mistier despite her best efforts to fight it off. She continued to blink tears away and smiled, not wanting Jake to think he'd made her sad. "It sounds like you all took good care of each other, and that's the best anyone can ask for."

He nodded, and she could see he still had questions, so she continued giving him space and time, setting up her easel and stool, unpacking her tools, knowing he'd ask whenever he was ready.

"Can I ask what happened to Liam's dad?" His face colored a bright pink even before the words were out. "You don't have to say, I was just—never mind."

Hannah slipped her brushes into the mason jar she used to hold them and set them on the little fold-out stool she always carried. "It's okay," she told him, and sent a reassuring look his way. "We were college sweethearts, but it turned out we grew up into very different people. We had

Liam, and that was important to us, so we tried really hard to find a way to make the marriage work." She paused and looked for the right words for a fourteen-year-old who didn't need the details, just the overview. "We weren't really having much luck figuring that out. Then the accident happened. And afterward . . . well, we just decided that it would be better to go on and live our lives separately, and maybe find that person who was the right fit for the adults we'd become." She went back to unpacking her things, glancing at Jake, praying she'd handled that right.

He nodded, seeming to accept what she'd said. Hannah sighed in relief and finally started unpacking her watercolors and the baby food jars.

"Do you think my dad is the right fit? Or will be?"

Hannah almost dropped every jar she was holding. As it was, she managed to bobble them onto the stool without breaking any.

Jake had asked the question with no pro or con overtones that she could read, so Hannah had no idea what his thoughts were on the matter. She knew Will had talked to his son about them on the drive back from camp. Will had told her that Jake seemed fine with it but hadn't asked a lot of questions. Hannah had been relieved, but she suspected Jake probably had lots of questions now that he'd had time to think it over.

Today was her first time seeing Jake since that conversation. She and Will had thought today's visit would be kind of a test to get the true lay of the land. Hannah had no idea where Will was at the moment, *but now would be a really good time for you to join us.*

Hannah knew a lot was riding on how she answered this question. What Jake might have said to his dad on the topic didn't necessarily reflect his true feelings. Will and his son were very close, but this was brand-new territory for both of them. For her, too.

"Bailey says she thinks you're the right fit for him," Jake said when she didn't respond right away.

Hannah turned to look at him and decided to just take a seat right there on the porch floor, with her paints and tools scattered around her. Grounding herself. Literally. "I'm very flattered she thinks so." She smiled then, hoping to cover her nerves. "She's a pretty good judge of character."

"She is," Jake said. He didn't appear defensive, or at all upset, but neither did he seem overjoyed at the prospect.

If anything, he seemed to be a bit anxious, and she wasn't sure how to read that. *Anxious, I want you and my dad together? Or anxious, I really wish you weren't?*

"I like and admire your dad a great deal," Hannah began. "I'm happy we're becoming friends. I enjoy spending time with him." Her tone grew even brighter as she added, "And that feeling seems to be mutual, which makes me happy, too." She lifted her hands, then let them drop to her folded legs. "I don't know more than that, yet. Figuring this kind of thing out takes time." That might not be the steady assurance he was looking for, but Hannah thought he was old enough to understand. One thing she was certain about was that she'd always be up front with him, and honest. He'd been through enough in his young life to know there were no guarantees. So she'd never make him a promise she couldn't keep. "But I want to figure it out, if that helps."

Jake nodded, and seemed to be thinking it all through.

Hannah drew her knees up and circled them with her arms. *As armor goes, I don't think that will help you much,* her little voice helpfully supplied. She ignored it, but also stayed just as she was. "Is it okay if I ask you how you feel about it? I know you and your dad are used to being a tribe of two. I don't want my spending time with your dad to change that. At all."

"It kind of already has," Jake said; then when he noticed her worried expression, he hurried to add, "Not in a bad way."

She almost slumped over in relief.

"I just meant that since he's been hanging out more with you, he's become a lot better about things."

Hannah's eyes widened in surprise. "What kind of things?"

"Well, he's been trying harder for a while now. Like, he talks about mom a little. And I appreciate it. I tell him it's okay if he doesn't want to, if it makes him sad, but I'm glad he does. They're always stories I didn't already know. I guess it's kind of like how you talk about Liam. If something comes up and it makes him remember something about her, he'll just say it now. I really like that." He looked at Hannah. "It makes us feel, I don't know, like a more normal family. Even though she's gone. You know?"

She nodded. "Completely. It is much the same for me. I'm glad Will's doing that and that it's been good for you."

Jake frowned then, as if something had suddenly occurred to him. He looked worried. "Maybe I shouldn't have told you about all that. About my mom, I mean. Like if it makes you feel uncomfortable."

"No, no," Hannah said immediately. "I'm glad you did. I think it's a good, natural thing to be able to talk about. I'm glad you feel comfortable enough to share it with me. I'm happy I can share my family with you, too."

Jake smiled. "Okay. Good," he said, clearly relieved.

"Your dad and I have talked about your mom, too."

He looked surprised. "You have?"

Hannah nodded. "I'm glad about that, too. I'm glad he's figuring out how to be more comfortable with it."

Jake looked down at his hands, which he'd folded together, his arms braced on his knees. He lifted just his gaze to hers, as if he wasn't sure about this question, either. "Do you think . . . did you help him with that? Because you both . . . ?" He let the question trail off but kept his gaze on hers.

"Lost someone special?" Hannah said, helping him

out. "Maybe. But I think it's something he's wanted for a long time."

Jake nodded. "I think so, too. But it's gotten a lot better since he met you." He lifted his head, looked at her directly then. She didn't miss the gratitude and the sincerity in his green eyes. So like his father's.

Hannah felt humbled and relieved all at the same time. "Well, that's good then."

"I think so." Jake smiled. "He talks more now, too. You know, about normal, regular stuff. And not just to me, but like when we're out in town running errands." His tone turned a shade dry. "Like a lot more." Jake laughed even as he rolled his eyes a little. "I used to wish for that all the time. Now, I don't know."

Hannah laughed with him. "Well, sometimes you don't get to pick and choose. When you get one thing, you get all the things. Ultimately though, I'm guessing it's worth the chattier part if it gets you the other part."

"Definitely true," Jake said.

The anxiety she'd noticed before seemed to be gone now. He looked more like the kid she'd gotten to know. That helped her to relax all the way, too. Maybe this wasn't going to be as hard on either of them as she'd been afraid it might be.

"Is it okay if I say that I like that you're seeing my dad?"

Hannah nodded and tried not to cover her heart with her hand. He was really good at just sliding those big questions right in there. This time the answer was easy. "Very okay," she said. "In fact, it would only be okay for me if it was okay for you."

Jake looked surprised

Hannah lifted her shoulder as if it were a simple enough thing, but held his gaze directly when she spoke, wanting him to see her sincerity. "You and your dad are a package deal. He takes that very seriously, as he should. So do I. I'd be exactly the same way if it were me and Liam letting someone new into our lives."

"That makes sense," he said. "I'm glad," he added. "Bailey said Liam would be about my age." Jake's gaze lifted to hers as if he'd realized too late that might not be a good thing to say.

"It's true," Hannah said, giving him a reassuring look. "You two are very different though. He was more like . . . well, I was about to say Bailey, but no one is like Bailey."

Jake laughed at that. "Right?"

Hannah laughed too. "I guess if I had to pick a person we both know, I'd say Liam was most like Seth. Very outgoing, almost to a fault. He would talk to anyone, anywhere, and he was an outrageous flirt. Even as a baby."

Jake's laughter was half boyish giggle, half teenage croak. "Definitely Mr. B. Even now that he's married, he's still like that with Pippa. It's embarrassing."

Amused, Hannah thought Jake wouldn't find it embarrassing for much longer. Like, any day now. "I like to think maybe he'd have had a friend like you. Someone more grounded, a thinker, someone who asks all the questions and figures things out first, then leaps." She grinned. "He'd have definitely needed that."

Jake grinned. "That's cool." He paused. "And thanks. For saying that stuff."

"I mean that stuff," Hannah told him, her smile affectionate and sincere.

"Well, I hope that's what I am," Jake said. "And yeah, maybe we'd have been buds." His smile was so endearing and sweet just then, it made Hannah's eyes well up all over again.

I wish you two could have met each other, she thought. She caught Jake looking and laughed as she sniffled. "Sometimes talking about him does this, too," she said, pointing to her eyes. "But that's okay. I'm not sad, not really. Just . . .

missing him. And I think that's normal. Like, it would be weird if I didn't, right?"

"Right," Jake said, seeming relieved, and kind of surprised, as if that was a new way of looking at it, one he could work with.

"I should probably let you paint," Jake said, rubbing his palms on the legs of his shorts, perhaps belying just how nervous he'd truly been.

Hannah uncurled herself and pushed to a stand. "I'm glad we talked," she told him. "I'd wanted to. I just . . . didn't know how."

"Me either," he said, letting her see the relief on his face, "and I am, too." He reached down and grabbed the jars. "I'll go fill these up for you."

"Great, thanks."

Hannah happened to glance through the window set in the wall between the porch and the kitchen, and caught Will framed by it. She didn't have to wonder how long he'd been standing there, or what he'd heard. The tear silently tracking down one cheek said it all. He brushed it away as Jake walked into the kitchen and she watched as Jake quickly did exactly the same thing. Father and son had a very manly exchange about nothing in particular; then Will left him to fill the jars and came out on the porch.

Will didn't say anything. He just walked up and pulled her into his arms for a long, solid hug. "Thank you," he whispered roughly in her ear, and there was a world of emotion in those two words.

"Thank your son," she whispered back. "That's one great kid you've got there."

She thought he'd been about to say more, but he let her go and stepped back as Jake left the kitchen juggling half a dozen half full baby jars pinned together with his fingers. Will slid open the porch door so Jake could carry them in, then he announced that the two of them were making a run to the hardware store in town, and would leave her to paint in peace.

Hannah laughed and waved them off. But the moment she heard Will's truck pull out of the driveway, she sank down on her stool, let out a long, tension-releasing, shuddering breath, then covered her face with her hands and indulged in a good, cleansing cry.

Chapter Twenty

Will had to yank the handle a bit because the wood had warped over the years, but eventually he dragged the thing open. He pulled on the string attached to the overhead bulb, not surprised when it snapped off in his hands, but a little surprised that when he reached up and grabbed the end of the pull chain, the dusty old workshop was instantly bathed in a pool of soft yellow light.

He'd braced himself before walking out to the old building down at the bottom of their property. He wasn't sure what its original intended purpose had been. It was bigger than a shed, smaller than a barn. A boathouse maybe. His grandfather had refurbished the ramshackle old thing and turned it into a really nice workshop long before Will had been born. Will had worked out there with him for many a summer, honing his own skills, until he could make an instrument as beautiful as his grandfather did. Will had gone on to set up makeshift workshops in every base housing location he and Zoey had called home, but none anywhere near so perfectly designed for making instruments as this old place.

Will hadn't been inside the workshop once in all the time since he'd come back to the Falls to live full time. He'd thought about clearing out the place and turning the old building into something more useful for his current life. He certainly didn't plan on ever making another fiddle. But he'd never been able to bring himself to do it.

He took in the musty interior, pleasantly surprised to find that rather than causing a stab of sadness and guilt, looking at the familiar bits and pieces instantly filled him with some of the best memories of his childhood. His smile grew as he ran his gaze over the special workbench his grandfather had designed and made specifically for building a fiddle from the ground up. Mack's array of tools were neatly stored in wooden boxes with the labels that had been carved directly into the wood by his grandpa's own hand. A few dozen of Mack's favorites hung from hooks on the peg board that lined the wall above the shelves.

"Will?"

"In here," he called out.

Hannah stepped inside a moment later. "Wow," she said. "This is amazing." She stepped closer and he draped an arm over her shoulder and pulled her near.

"Thanks for being willing to do this with me," Will said. "I ended up deciding it was maybe better to come in on my own first."

"No, that's fine. Whatever works for you." She slid her arm around his waist and leaned into him as she took a slow look at the place.

He liked that, the way she instinctively tucked herself in and relaxed against him. Zoey hadn't been much of a snuggler, which had been fine with Will, too. This was just new to him. He wouldn't have guessed that he'd like it; he'd never been much of a PDA kind of guy. Although, come to think of it, he'd been pretty much unable to stay out of Hannah's personal space since he'd met her, no matter where they happened to be. Maybe that was just how he was with her.

Whatever the case, feeling her soft curves pressed against him made him happy.

"Your Grandpa Mack built all of this?"

Will nodded. "Not all at once. He kept refining things as new design ideas came to him, but this is pretty much how it's looked for as long as I can remember. I think his father had a hand in the original remodel, if I remember correctly. My great-grandfather was a carpenter and a wood-carver, so that would stand to reason."

Hannah slipped out from under Will's arm and explored the room. "I can't even imagine the set of skills you'd need to make something as intricate as a fiddle." She glanced at him and grinned. "I had a hard time making Popsicle stick houses with Liam when he was in kindergarten."

"It's maybe a little more complicated than that," Will said with a laugh. "But it's still one step at a time. Once you learn the procedure, it's time-consuming, but not particularly hard. With experience you can put in new design ideas that are more challenging, that you'd need experience and a real feel for, but the basics stay the same."

She looked at the antique fiddles and several other stringed instruments, an old banjo, a mandolin, a few others, all mounted in various spots around the shop. "He was a collector?" she asked. "Or did he make these, too? They look too old for that, but I guess depending on his age—"

"He never saw an instrument with strings he could keep his hands off," Will said, sincere affection in his tone. "Especially in old antique shops and flea markets. I think half the reason my grandmother agreed to him choosing this house was so he could turn this old building into a workshop and keep his junk, as she called it, out of her nice, pretty house."

Hannah laughed. "I can understand that. Steve was pretty fastidious. He loved having my art hanging on the walls, and was properly appreciative of my skills, but he dreaded coming into my studio or getting a speck of paint on his clothes. He hated the old clothes I wore when I painted." She grinned at Will. "I will admit to being small enough that I kept several of his best shirts after I found out he'd been cheating on me. I used them as painting smocks for years."

Will nodded. "Sounds more than fair to me. I'd have probably doused them in turpentine and set his whole wardrobe on fire."

Hannah laughed. "I might have considered that, too," she said, then continued her exploration, careful not to touch anything, but taking her time as she looked in all the nooks and crannies, of which there were many.

Will turned the other way to look around the room so Hannah wouldn't see his expression. It was ridiculous to feel so protective of her. She could certainly take care of herself and had, through some incredibly daunting times. In fact, he should probably be thanking the asshole ex for not realizing what a treasure he had, so she'd wound up right here, right now, with him. But he'd be lying if he said he wouldn't have enjoyed taking good old Steve out to the shed, and not to show him his antiques. Will couldn't even wrap his head around what it would have felt like to find out Zoey had been unfaithful to him.

All that said, he was grateful she felt comfortable enough to talk about her life with him now. He'd overheard her comments to Jake about her family, her parents, her upbringing. They'd both shared numerous stories now of their childhood and formative years. She'd encouraged him to share stories of his time in the military, his life with Zoey, having Jacob, and in turn, she'd shared stories of her life, too. Some were hard, some were easy, many of them had them both laughing. Above all, those stories were all part and parcel of who they were now, and the more he knew, the more he appreciated her. She'd often said the same.

Will had been the one to bring up the fiddle. Hannah knew

it was a tough subject for him, and he knew Addie had told her why. She never poked, never prodded—neither of them did. But as they revealed more of themselves to each other, he'd found he wanted to talk about it. So many other barriers were crumbling, and he'd found the process freeing rather than inhibiting, or worse, guilt producing. The example Hannah had set of how she'd handled her loss, her grief, had shown him the path out of his own muddled thinking.

Hannah came to the harp in the corner and let out a little gasp. "Oh, Will, look at this." She walked around it. It was pretty banged up and the strings were mostly broken, but the grand scope of the design was undeniably beautiful. "She's seen some hard times but look how magnificent she is. I can see why your grandfather had to have her, despite her condition."

Will nodded, but chuckled. "All of the antiques in here looked like that or worse. Mack had something of a hobby restoring old instruments. He always claimed he'd sell them and use the money to buy supplies for his fiddle making, but it was rare that he parted with one." Will laughed and gestured at the walls. "Clearly."

Hannah's mouth dropped open and she looked once more around the room. "So they looked as bad as this once upon a time?" she asked, gesturing at the harp. "Wow."

"That bad and worse. He said restoring them taught him almost everything he needed to know about making his own instruments. Craftsmanship skills that had otherwise been lost over time, and I think he definitely had a point."

She walked around the space again, looking at the instruments. "That's amazing. They're all beautiful." She turned to him. "You were so fortunate that he took the time to pass all those skills down to you." She looked back at the walls, at the instruments hung there. "They might have been lost forever, otherwise."

Will nodded even as guilt plinked at him. He'd earned it.

"He took care to restore them but not refurbish them, so what you see is exactly how they looked when they were made, with original materials only. It would take him years sometimes, to find the right pieces or parts to finish them. He spent most of his spare time prowling antique shops, auctions." Will grinned. "My grandmother wasn't much for any of that. She abhorred dust. But my mom, she loved it. Like a fish to water. So my grandpa would take her off with him on big adventures on the weekends, give my grandmother a break."

Hannah turned to look at him, delight on her face. "How lovely. Did your mother play? Or join him restoring or building the instruments?"

Will chuckled again and shook his head. "No, she just became a champion shopper."

Hannah laughed. "Nothing wrong with that."

"She did learn to have a good eye for antiques. She hunted antique shops in every state, every country we lived in. We never had much room, so she shopped a lot more than she bought, but the hunt made her happy. Every once in a while, she'd discover a piece she just couldn't pass up and she'd have it shipped home. Most of the furniture in the house were pieces she found on our many travels. Some of them in good condition, others my grandfather restored for her. I think it was one way they stayed close to each other, sharing that, despite her living the vagabond military life."

"That's wonderful," Hannah said, then turned to look again at the various pieces. "I love everything about that."

And I love everything about you.

Will turned away and walked over to the workbench before she could see that expression, either. It was too soon. Way too soon. They were still all hopped up on pheromones and spent half their time with their hands all over each other like teenagers discovering sex for the first time. Only with a very adult knowledge about how things actually worked and happy to put it into practice again. It was lust, more than love. It had to be.

But every time she smiled, every time she laughed, the words were right there. *Slow your roll,* he schooled himself. *There will be plenty of time for declarations.*

He tried to push off his other niggling worry, certain he was making something out of nothing. He wanted to talk to her about it, as they did about everything else under the sun, but he hadn't been able to find the right time, or the right words. She'd been so wonderful with Jake, the day he'd first asked Hannah about her son. She'd said all the right things, straight from the heart, leaving him no doubt she'd meant every word. Any last reservations he might have had about this giant step forward he'd taken had vanished that day. He was all in. And he was pretty sure he'd look back later and know for certain that was the moment he realized he loved her. Pheromones and lust be damned.

But, since that day, they hadn't spent much time together as a trio. When he'd come back that afternoon, she'd already packed up and gone, leaving a note that she'd been needed at the farm. They'd talked several times about her coming back to paint, but it had never been the right time. She had only been out to his place once since then, for dinner, but Jake had been staying up at Seth and Pippa's that night, because they were in a crucial stage with Jake's latest batch of grape juice. Will had been hoping, now that they had Jake's blessing, to start moving toward doing things together, the three of them. Not always, of course, but some of the time, at least. Will wasn't sure how else things were going to work.

Hannah truly liked Jake—that he knew. She still spent time with him. Happily, so it would appear. Her affection was honest and pure and right out there on display, clear for anyone to see. Will knew, and was sure Jake did, too, that Hannah would never do or say anything to hurt him, or challenge his rightful place as Will's number one concern. She'd even said as much, to Jake and to him. Will couldn't ask for more than that.

If she hadn't been so obviously okay with spending time with Jake, Will would have immediately assumed that as the three of them grew closer, she'd found it harder than she'd anticipated to be around a child who was the same age as her son would have been. But that definitely didn't seem to be it.

He'd started to think that maybe it wasn't Jake, per se, but the whole vibe of their doing things as a threesome, like a family would, that was hard for her. That would be understandable, but he sincerely hoped that wasn't the problem, either, since he came to their relationship as a family unit.

But if not that, then what? And where did that leave them?

He felt a tap on his shoulder and turned around. She slid into his arms and right up against him as if she'd been doing it for years. And to use one of her favorite phrases, he loved everything about it. She tipped up on her toes to kiss him, smiled, then kissed him again, her gray eyes shining. And he loved everything about that, too.

Surely there had to be a way to make all the pieces of his life fit with all the remaining pieces of hers.

Chapter Twenty-One

"I cannot believe you let Bailey talk you into boarding goats out here." Hannah scattered another pitchfork full of hay around the cleaned out, previously unused stall, then laughed. "What am I saying? Of course I can believe it. Bailey Sutton could talk a shepherd out of his sheep."

Chey grinned. "She's a girl after my own heart. Sees what she wants, gets it done. I like her."

"I know. It's impossible not to. But will those little guys really be able to get through that brush? It's acres of thick, twisted vines with thorns the size of ice picks."

"I've done some reading on it and it sure seems to be the case. I've never worked with the wee beasties myself, but there are whole businesses now dedicated to using goats to clear overgrown property. If it's green and it grows, they can eat their way through it."

Hannah shook her head. "Amazing."

"Beats paying someone to bush hog it, then someone else to come back and reseed it." She shrugged. "I've got the time and I'm willing to give it a go."

Hannah shook her head. "The things I'm learning, living in the mountains."

"Me too," Chey said with a laugh.

They worked in silence for a bit, with Hannah prepping the unused stalls they were dedicating to the goat crew, while Chey cleaned out the tack room and reorganized the gear she'd never gotten around to unpacking.

"So, you and Mr. Stonemason seemed to have gotten pretty tight pretty quickly." Chey laid a saddle pad over the stall door, then walked back over to the tack she was getting ready to clean. "How's that working out?"

Hannah had come out to get another forkful of straw but propped the pitchfork against the bale instead and leaned on the handle. Chey didn't often pry, so Hannah was admittedly curious where this was coming from. "Well," she said, "it's funny, because in some ways I can't quite believe I'm truly in a relationship with someone. But then when I'm with him, honestly, it feels like we've been friends a very long time. It's . . . comforting."

Chey rolled her eyes. "Comforting. That sounds like the two of you are in a retirement home and happy to have companionship."

Hannah laughed. "Fair point." She snagged another forkful of hay and carried it to the stall. "Would it make you happier if I said it's exciting and new and all of those heart-pounding, giddy kinds of things? Because it is all of that, too. I feel ridiculously happy all the time." She stuck her head out of the stall and wiggled her eyebrows at Chey. "And I will admit that dusting off the old libido and taking her out for a regular spin has been pretty terrific, too."

"Show-off," Chey said, then gave her two thumbs-up and flashed Hannah one of her dazzling smiles. "And that's more like it. Because if you can't be giddy over a man who looks like that? And, more importantly, who looks at you the way he does?" She shook her head. "You might as well put that libido in cold storage, sister."

Chey was usually a somewhat serious person, at least that was how she presented herself to the world most of the time. It had come in handy in her former occupation, and being somewhat guarded also came to her naturally. So, most folks didn't know she had a wicked sense of humor, or a heart as big as the moon. And her smile, when truly unleashed, would knock your socks off with its completely transformative ability.

She wasn't flashy and gave new meaning to being down to earth. Her idea of dressing up was to knock the mud off her boots and put on a clean pair of jeans. But Hannah saw Chey as a beautiful force to be reckoned with, which she most definitely was. When things got tough, there was no one Hannah would rather have in her corner.

Hannah laughed. "Agreed. But giddy heart palpitations aside, at the core of it, we're very solid together. That's the part that calms any nerves I get, wondering if this is all just too much of a good thing."

"Darlin'," Chey said, tipping down her chin and affecting her strongest, rodeo girl drawl, "there is no such thing as too much of a good thing. That's just a myth the unlucky in love put out there to cover their mistakes."

Hannah's mouth dropped open on a choked little laugh. "A little harsh, don't you think?"

Chey waved it off. "You know what I mean. Here's what I've learned from all I've seen, and we both know that I've seen a lot. You find something good that makes you happy? I don't care if it's a job, a man, the perfect place to put down roots, or a really good horse. You get lucky enough to stumble into one of those? Grab on to it, sister, and hold on for dear life."

Hannah nodded at that and gave Chey a little salute. "A valid observation."

"Of course it is," Chey said, taking the compliment in

stride, then shooting Hannah a wink. "I'm one of those unlucky losers I spoke about, so I know whereof I speak."

Hannah had been about to grab another forkful of straw but paused, surprised by the admission. Shocked, actually. Early on, the four of them had shared pretty much every raw detail about the loss each of them had suffered. As they'd become true close friends over the years since, they'd shared a lot more of their lives with each other. Vivi had regaled them with more stories from her time on Broadway than Hannah could recount, all of them colorful, memorable, and oftentimes hilarious.

Avery had shared the struggles she'd had being a smart kid in an adult world, her take surprisingly droll. She hadn't wasted time feeling sorry for herself for being "the oddball in a room full of squares" as she called it. She'd been too busy absorbing everything she could get her hands and eyes on. Her stories had been refreshing and empowering, and Hannah had often found herself wishing she'd had a tenth of Avery's moxie.

Chey regaled them with stories of life on the rodeo circuit, all of them pretty raucous. She'd been born into the life and, until a few years ago, hadn't known any other kind. It was both a grueling and fascinating lifestyle that Hannah couldn't begin to fathom, and the risks involved made her hair stand on end. But Chey, at least up until she'd lost her brother, had honestly loved every second of it.

For her part, Hannah had talked about her life as an artist and an illustrator. A random art class she'd taken in school for fun, when her focus had otherwise been on a future in finance, had taken her life on a completely different trajectory. Thanks to a college art professor with contacts in the world of marketing and graphic design, Hannah had been exceedingly fortunate to find a way to market her surprising skill set, and that, in turn, had eventually led her to becoming a book illustrator.

Hannah didn't have the colorful stories Vivi did or face anything like the challenges Avery had, much less anything in the universe of the risks that Chey had taken on a daily basis. In fact, for all that Hannah's career was unique, she'd had, by far, the most average life of the lot. The classic yuppie, she'd married young to her college sweetheart, started a family, had a nice house in the suburbs of the nation's capital. The other three had often told her how sorry they were for her that she was so boring. She smiled, thinking about that, and where she was now. *Not so boring anymore.*

One thing Chey hadn't ever shared with any of them were stories about her love life. She'd had plenty to say about some of the men on the circuit, but nothing about any man who might have claimed even a part of Chey's big heart.

"The only loser in that equation would be the guy in question," Hannah told her. "Not you." Hannah said it partly out of loyalty, but mostly because she thought it was true. It would definitely take a certain kind of man to be enough for Chey, but if she deemed him worthy, he would be getting one hell of a return on his investment.

Chey jokingly sketched a bow, gesturing with a flourish using the grooming brush she happened to be holding. "Very kind, very kind." She straightened and shot Hannah a wry grin. "And oh, so very, very wrong." She tucked the brush into the tool bin she was sorting through, her back to Hannah as she continued to speak. "I did some really stupid things when I was young—young*er*," she added with a wink over her shoulder, "and trying to impress all the wrong guys. If it hadn't been for Cody, Lord only knows where I'd be now or who I'd be stuck with."

"Well, I'm glad you had him to fend off the bad apples,"

Hannah said, knowing that Cheyenne and her brother had been closer than most siblings, largely due to their lifestyle, but also because they'd genuinely loved and looked out for each other. "But something tells me you'd have never been stuck with anyone you didn't want to be with, not for the long haul."

"Fair point," she conceded dryly. "What I was referring to, actually, was the one I let get away."

Hannah forked another batch of straw into the stall, surprised by that piece of information, too. "I'm truly sorry for that, Chey," she told her. "We all make bad decisions in our lives, but that doesn't make living with the regret any easier to deal with."

Chey nodded. "True enough. In this case, I was sixteen and so full of myself. I'd spent the previous half dozen years trying to straight-out scare every boy I knew, so hell-bent on proving to myself and them that I'd earned my place on the circuit. But, boy, sixteen hit, and those hormones surged on up and suddenly all those obnoxious boys of my youth were the sexy-as-hell bad boys I wanted to be with in my future."

Hannah laughed. "I think we can all identify with that, but given the kind of testosterone they must have had to do what they did for a living?" She fanned herself and fluttered her lashes. "My, my."

"And then some," Chey said with a laugh. "Lucky for me and probably them as well, Cody beat most of them off with a stick despite my lovesick protestations."

Hannah grinned. "So, who was the one who got away? Did Cody chase him off, too?"

Chey shook her head. "No, not at all. I had a really good friend in those days, who happened to be a guy. To me he was like another brother, only one I didn't feel like punching every other minute. I mean, I loved my brother and God help anyone who tried to step in between us or so much as look at him sideways. We had each other's back at all times. But that didn't mean we didn't squabble like squirrels caught in a blender."

"Ew," Hannah said, making a face even as she laughed.

Chey smiled. "You can thank my dad for that visual. That was his favorite line. And it was true—we could be pretty rough on each other, when we were adolescents, anyway. But me and Wyatt Reed? We never fought. He was tall, and brawny, with the kind of blue eyes that made you shut up and listen when he talked."

"Hubba-hubba," Hannah said, wiggling her eyebrows.

"Oh, most definitely," Chey agreed. "And then some. But stupid me, I didn't see it. Not then, not like that anyway. To me, he was just good ol' Wyatt. For all his looks, he was definitely not like other guys on the circuit. He was quiet, and sweet, so smart, and so damn funny. He had no business being out there and no heart for it, but his old man . . ." She trailed off, shook her head and turned away, back to her gear. "To this day I wish there was some way I could have put a plug in that man's ass and a bullet through his shriveled heart."

Hannah looked up, startled. "Chey, that's awful."

"He was mean as a snake, Hannah. He deserved far worse."

Hannah walked over to the closed stall door and leaned on it. "What happened to him? To Wyatt. Do you know where he is today?"

Chey shook her head. "No idea. His daddy got in trouble with the local law pretty much every town we went to, and trouble tended to follow him as well. They left the circuit just before I turned eighteen."

"You didn't keep in touch?"

Chey shook her head, and her expression shuttered a bit then. "That's the part where I was really, *really* stupid."

Hannah didn't say anything, just let Chey find her own words.

"Right before they were kicked out, Wyatt found me and told me he was in love with me." She let out a deep, remorseful sigh, then shook her head. "I'd had my eye on one of Cody's friends for a while. Just hadn't figured out how to turn his head without Cody warning me off. They were friends, but Maverick was definitely a bad boy."

"Maverick?" Hannah said, cocking one eyebrow. "Really?"

Chey laughed. "I know, right? Even at sixteen, how did I not get that? And, of course, I knew Cody would pitch a fit if he found out I'd set my sights on him." She smiled. "Did eventually, too. And then some. But when Wyatt put it all out there, my head was still so turned about by Mav, and I was so surprised, stunned really, I didn't see it, see him, see all that we had, for what it was."

Hannah's heart squeezed with empathy for her. Chey seemed so tough and bulletproof, but Hannah knew better. "What did you say to him?"

"I wasn't mean or anything, but there is no good way to break a person's heart, and I'd never had to do that before. It was godawful and I felt so awkward and horrible. I told him I loved him like family, but not in the way he loved me. It wasn't just like kicking a puppy; it felt like shooting one."

Hannah flinched at that, but she understood what Chey meant. "I know that had to be hard, but what you told him was the truth, Chey. And it doesn't sound like you were thoughtless in the way you explained it to him. You shouldn't beat yourself up for that. If that's how you felt, then—"

"The thing is, I'd never even let myself consider that it could be anything else. It just . . . that lightbulb never went off for me, you know? He was my friend and that was that. It was like a line you didn't cross, so I never even considered it. . . . I just didn't know it was even a possibility."

"And once you did . . . did you realize that maybe you could have loved him back? The same way?"

"I think I would have," Chey said. "I mean, I did love him, in all the ways that matter, but I didn't know that. And I didn't deserve to know. He put himself out there, risked it all. He was two years older than me, but light-years more mature. I was a hot mess of hormones looking to get in trouble with exactly the worst kind of guy. I grew up, too, eventually, but . . ."

"You always wondered what-if, I'm sure," Hannah said sympathetically. "But that seems like a pretty normal thing to do, Chey. To feel. Not that it makes it any easier, but you shouldn't be too hard on yourself."

Chey didn't respond, just continued sorting through the tack bin. "I think about him from time to time. To this day. I still miss him. I missed him terribly when he left, and it was all the worse for how we parted. I knew I was his one safe place, and I blew it. I really, really blew it. I tried to get in touch, to say I was sorry, to see if we could salvage the friendship, but my few attempts were met with utter silence. And he was right to do that, to just move on and put me in his rearview mirror. I wasn't trustworthy any longer. At least he had every right to believe that about me. I truly hope he's happy somewhere, living his best life. And that he found a way to get far away from that sadistic son-of-a-bitch father of his sooner rather than later. If I had to guess, I'd say Old Man Reed is behind bars or six feet under, and I don't feel bad for thinking it or hoping it's true."

"Understandable," Hannah said sadly. "I hope Wyatt is doing well, too. On all fronts."

Chey closed the lid on the bin, then turned around to rest her weight against it and looked directly at Hannah. "I don't talk about Wyatt," she said. "It's like a bruise that will never heal. But I brought him up today for a reason. I see how happy you are, and I know how solid Will is. You two are good with each other and to each other, and for each other." She paused, as if choosing her words carefully. "But I've watched you with Jake, too. And you're great with him, which is easy because he's a pretty spectacular kid. But I know being around him is hard for you. I see it when Jake isn't looking, when you think no one is."

"Chey—" Hannah began, then stopped. Startled by the statement, the insight, she'd been about to tell Chey she had it all wrong, to duck confronting that truth, which she'd been doing for weeks now.

"I can't imagine all the ways being around him must be challenging for you," Chey said more gently. "I'm not so sure I could do it, if it were me. Even as awesome as Jake is, as his dad seems to be. I know it would be easier if Will was flying solo and this wasn't a thing you had to face. But I also know a big part of the man you're falling in love with is the father that he is. Painful or not, poignant for sure, it's a connection you two share."

Chey pushed off the box and walked over to lean by the stall door, resting her arms on the edge next to Hannah's. Her voice was quieter when she went on, her heart clearly in every word. "I can't tell you what choice to make, and I sure as hell can't tell you what kind of suffering you should work through to be okay with this. What I can tell you, with everything I know, and everything I am, is that living with regret sucks. Hard. And I think that you'd regret this for the rest of your days if you didn't find a way to make it all work out."

Hannah's eyes stung with gratitude even as her heart clutched with a sudden surge of panic, that her secret was out, that she'd have to confront it now. "Thank you," she said. "For revisiting your own regret just to try and help me. I'm sorry you felt you had to. And . . ." She paused, then blew out a long, shaky breath and ducked her chin. She owed Chey the truth. Owed it to herself, too. "You're not wrong." Hannah looked up at her friend, her other sister of the heart. "I do want to figure it out. And I am trying. I don't want to hurt Will, but I know he suspects things aren't one-hundred-percent. He knows, and Jake knows, how much I care for both of them. You're right, Jake is the best, in every way. I couldn't ask for more, in terms of stepping into a ready-made family."

"But?" Chey asked kindly.

Hannah shook her head. "I don't know."

"Is it that ready-made part?"

Hannah shrugged. "I don't know. I don't think so. I mean, partly, it's Jake I'm worried about. He doesn't need me getting all entwined in their lives, only for me to discover I just can't find a way to manage this . . . whatever this is that I'm feeling. It's not grief, or even sadness. It feels more like . . . I don't know. Anxiety, maybe? But there's nothing wrong with any part of the equation. Not in my head, not in my heart. I'm truly happy."

"Maybe it is the idea of being part of a family again. Something tangled up in that. It would make sense, Han."

Hannah lifted her shoulder. "Maybe so. Being around Jake is not wrenching. Quite the opposite. In the moment, we're fine together. Just like Will and I are fine. But when I go home, when I'm alone . . ." She looked at Chey, her eyes clouding over. "I cry. A lot. Not about anything specifically, just . . . as a way to let it all out."

"Let what out?" Chey asked. "I mean, specifically, what are you thinking about when you cry? Maybe if you could pinpoint that, it would give you some insight into what the trigger is."

Hannah shook her head. "That's just it, I don't know. I just feel this overwhelming . . . pressure. Like my chest is too tight, and my heart is being squeezed. I cry, I get it out, and I feel better. And I think, okay, it will get better the more I'm around him, around them both. But . . . it's not. Will wants us to spend more time together, the three of us, and I've been ducking him, because I can hide it from Jake when we're together, but I know I won't be able to with Will. And I don't want to hurt him or insult him."

"He wouldn't be insulted, Han," Chey said gently. "He knows you care about Jake, that you two are building a really good foundation. Anyone can see that. Will knows you would never wittingly do anything to hurt him."

"But maybe I already am," Hannah said, feeling the anxiety start to build. "Will and I spent so much time talking about his wife, his loss, and I shared a lot about how I'd handled mine. We talked about me and Jake, and how my loss might affect that relationship. We literally talk about everything under the sun. But we never really talked about the three of us. Together." She shook her head. "I mean, I know that sounds silly. Like, if Will is good with me and I'm good with Jake, and Jake is happy with the whole situation, then what is there to talk about? You'd think I'd be looking forward to it. But then that . . . thing just rears up."

"Do you feel like you're being, I don't know, untrue, to Liam somehow? Being in a new family?"

Hannah shook her head. "I don't. Truly. I honestly don't know where all the emotion and the anxiety comes from, but it's exhausting, Chey. It's not like before; it's not grief. It's just . . ." She ducked her head and rested her forehead on her arms. "This big, heavy weight on my chest. And it's getting heavier, not lighter. I should be able to figure this out."

Chey rubbed Hannah's shoulder. "Maybe you need to

talk to someone. I mean, we've all done that. You know it can help."

"I know," she said, and sniffled at the wetness that wouldn't leave her eyes. "I've thought about it. I guess I just . . . it feels like a big step backward." She waved her hand. "And I know that's not how it works." She shook her head. "I'm afraid if I don't get a handle on it, I'm going to start finding ways to duck seeing Will, too. Or spend less time together, until I can get a grip. Only, he's not stupid; he knows something isn't right. If I don't figure this out, there won't be anything left to get a grip on."

"Then go talk to someone who can help you figure it out," Chey repeated. "It sounds like you're fighting off panic attacks. They happen for a reason, Han, but not necessarily one you can obviously see. Even if you've never had it before, you know it can be a thing. We've all had enough counseling to know that grief can be pretty insidious. Even when you do the hard work. You know how to look for help, how to ask."

Hannah nodded. "I know. And you're right. I've been avoiding facing the truth because I just don't want it to be true." She looked at Chey through tear-filled eyes. "I'm tired of having to fight for things. Normal things. I don't want to ruin this, Chey. It's better than anything I could have ever hoped to have again. I'm truly happier than I've been in so long." She laughed as she sniffled. "Can't you tell?"

Chey laughed with her and they hugged over the stall door. "You'll do fine. You'll figure this out. Go talk to someone, Han. Okay? And I really think you need to talk to Will about it, too. So he knows you're working on it. That you want to fix it. If he can't be there for you with this, then you need to know that, too. Right?"

Hannah nodded. "You're right. About all of it."

Chey gently tipped Hannah's chin up until their gazes met. "Promise me." She didn't make it a question.

Hannah nodded. "No regrets."

Chey beamed and kissed her on the forehead. "That's my girl. Now, dry your face, and grab a bottle of water to rehydrate. You're coming with me. I need to get these horses out to pasture, which means I've got to go see an eleven-year-old to negotiate a deal for those goats." She shot Hannah a wink. "And I'm pretty sure I'm going to need backup."

Chapter Twenty-Two

"Hold the vine here, then snip," Jake said as he showed Will how to prune the grapevine.

"How can you tell which ones to cut and which ones to leave?"

The two continued walking the rows of vines, and Jake explained the pros and cons of overcutting and undercutting, and how the weather could make it all a moot point.

Will shook his head. "I do understand how the weather can make a difference in a person's business. It affects mine. But this seems like an awful lot is left up to Mother Nature."

Jake grinned. "I know—that's what makes it such a cool challenge."

Will chuckled and just shook his head. In the past year or so since he'd gotten interested in grape growing, Jake had shown Will pretty much every step of the process once the grapes were harvested, but they'd never had the chance to walk the fields like this. "I'm proud of you for pursuing something you enjoy."

Jake shot him a proud smile. "You can thank Mr. B for that," he said. "For letting me bug him to death and hang around until he showed me stuff just to shut me up."

Will chuckled, knowing exactly how insistent his son

could be when he got fixated on something. Like wanting to know more about his mom. Will saw the same passion and determination now when he was playing the fiddle, when he was singing. "Seth has had nothing but good things to say about you, your work for him. Between your school-work, working for Seth, helping out with the sheep and the goats, then doing all this, and now your music, too, I have to say I was kind of worried that you've been taking on so much. You've impressed me a lot with how well you manage all of it, but maybe you need to lighten the load, just a little."

Jake flushed with pride at his dad's praise. "Thanks, Dad. But none of this feels like work to me. I enjoy doing all of it. Like, what else would I be doing?"

Will shook his head again, but he was grinning. "Well, then you're definitely doing something right."

They continued to walk the rows, with Will doing some of the trimming, under Jake's supervision. It hit him as he watched his son, listened to him talk, and not for the first time, just how fast his teen years were going to go. It seemed as if yesterday he was dropping Jake off at grade school. Before long, they'd be filling out college applications and talking about dorm supplies. Will was excited for Jake, and the opportunities his hard work would provide him. That he had an aptitude for music and a love of farming would hold him in good stead, even if he ended up taking a completely different path. Will knew what it was to be pas-sionate about something, and he hoped Jake used his own current passions as a barometer of sorts when making his future decisions.

On the other hand, Will wasn't ready for the empty nest. Having Hannah in his life would mitigate some of the feel-ing of loss, he knew, but it didn't change the core fact that it wouldn't be like when Jake went off to summer camp. He wouldn't be coming back, at least not in the traditional father-son roles they'd shared up to that point. Will wanted, badly, for Jake to choose a life that would allow him to stay in the Falls, but he couldn't, and wouldn't, stand in his way. As a Marine, Will spent years away, and he'd support his son no matter what, but that didn't mean he didn't have his own dreams, his own desires, about how he hoped it would all turn out.

He and Hannah had even talked about that, and she'd asked him if he'd be willing to uproot and live elsewhere if Jake settled in some other part of the country, or the world. Will hadn't really thought about that before. He didn't rule the possibility out, he supposed, but he truly hoped it wouldn't come to that. Not only because he couldn't see himself living anywhere else now, but he'd be less than honest if he said Hannah wasn't already factoring in to his future thoughts. He wasn't so sure about what she was thinking. On the surface, things seemed fine. Better than fine. But something wasn't completely right. He'd wanted to bring it up, but then he'd convince himself he was just borrowing trouble, that whatever it is, Hannah would tell him when the time was right for her.

"Is Hannah going to come to rehearsals with you later?"

Pulled from his thoughts, he turned to Jake. "She wants to work on the last part of that painting of the amphitheater, so she may come and set up for that. It's been pretty hectic out at the farm lately with the end of the season coming."

Jake nodded, understanding more than most about harvesting things. But Will caught the troubled look in his son's eyes before he turned his attention to the next vine in need of trimming.

"Is something the matter?" Will asked, trying for as casual a tone as possible. "We could ask her to come by for dinner after rehearsal if you want."

"I doubt she would," Jake said, sounding disappointed.

"What makes you say that?"

"I know she's super busy and all, but it seems like she

doesn't do things with us. I mean the three of us. Together. She does things with me and I know we're cool. You two are always doing stuff together, and there's no doubt she's really happy when she's with you. But she doesn't hang out with us together. And I know you've asked. So have I."

The niggle that had been bothering Will now became a full-fledged nudge. So he wasn't the only one who thought there was trouble in paradise. "You have?"

"Sure. I mean, I like her, Dad. I like her a lot. I always have. So, yeah, I think it would be cool to do stuff together." Jake paused, and Will could see he was working up the nerve to say something else.

"What else?" Will asked, ducking his chin to make eye contact with Jake. "Whatever it is, it's okay to say it. I'm not going to take sides, Jake. I truly want to hear your thoughts. If it affects you, it affects me."

Jake still paused, then finally looked directly at his dad. "Do you think maybe being with us together makes her sad? Because of . . . you know."

"Because of Liam?" Will asked, understanding Jake was trying to be sensitive, wanting to reassure him it was okay to speak directly about things, even when they were hard. "She's never said anything like that to me." But Will knew the instant Jake had said it, that the pattern was pretty clear. Hannah's excuses had always been valid, and he didn't doubt their veracity, but at the same time, she had never once actually taken him up on a single family-style get-together. "She doesn't seem like that when we talk about you," Will said. "I don't doubt her affection for you is anything but sincere."

"I think so, too," Jake said. "That's why I wondered. I guess . . . I don't mean that she doesn't like to be around me, or around you. I just think she has a problem with us looking like a family. I think maybe it makes her miss the one she had." He turned away. "I don't know. I could be completely misreading it. I just . . ." He looked back at Will. "I don't want to hurt her, Dad. She's been through enough, you know? Maybe she likes us, but she just isn't ready for anything more." He cast his gaze down for a moment, then back to Will. "With what happened to her and all, maybe she never will be."

Will didn't answer right away, but all he could think was *out of the mouths of babes.* He suspected Jake had hit it right on the head. Everything did seem fine between him and Hannah, and he'd only heard positive things about the times Hannah had hung out with Jake and Bailey at Addie's or at Seth's, and the times Jake and Bailey had come to Lavender Blue to handle the goats. He knew both of the kids often hung out in the kitchen with Hannah, Vivienne, and Avery, and that Bailey had bargained horseback riding lessons in exchange for her goat brush-clearing services. So Hannah and Jake saw each other pretty regularly, and Will felt he'd know if there was any problem there.

That wasn't the problem.

"I don't know," he told Jake, understanding it was imperative not to build false hope. Jake might have had a little crush on Hannah way back in the spring, but he'd shifted gears when Will had started seeing her. He knew Jake was becoming very attached to Hannah, and why wouldn't he? They were great together. But if what Jake suspected were true, Will needed to find a way to talk about it with Hannah. In a way that would hopefully come with a solution.

"Maybe if we both talk to her together," Jake said. "Tell her it's okay to keep things like they are."

Will shook his head. "I appreciate what you're trying to do, but life doesn't work that way. Relationships aren't stagnant things. Any kind of real relationship grows and deepens as it matures, as time goes on. And not just the romantic kind. All relationships. Yours and Bailey's, yours and Hannah's, mine and Addie's. The more time we spend with people who are important to us, the more we share, the more we grow."

"I get it," Jake said. "I know you're right."

They fell silent for a long minute, the vine trimming completely forgotten. Will finally drew in a long breath and let it out slowly, trying like hell to keep the ball of anxiety that had already begun to form a knot in his gut from getting any bigger. He'd lost the first woman he'd ever truly loved to circumstances far beyond his control. He wasn't about to lose the second if there was something he could do about it. "She's going out to Addie's tomorrow, to paint down in the meadow. I'll rearrange my schedule and go down there and talk with her. She likes it there, and it's . . . well, it's a special place. I know she'll be honest with me, and I promise to be honest with you about whatever is said."

Jake nodded solemnly. "Just . . . don't say anything wrong. Okay?"

Will smiled at that, even as his heart broke a little. Jake wasn't getting attached to Hannah, he was already all in. *Like father, like son.* Will just hoped they wouldn't be handling heartbreak as father and son, too.

He tousled Jake's hair, which he used to love, but these days barely tolerated with a grimace. "I'll do my best."

Jake reached out and tousled Will's hair, then grinned at the shocked look on his dad's face. Right before Will raked his fingers through his hair to set it back to rights.

"It's so not cool," Jake said wryly.

"Yeah," Will agreed. "Point made." They both laughed, then finally turned their attention back to the vines.

Don't say anything wrong.

Yeah. If only Will could figure out how the hell to be sure he didn't do that.

Chapter Twenty-Three

Hannah checked the slowly darkening skies, made a few more strokes to finish up a corner of the stone lamb house, then reluctantly began packing up her tools while the watercolor dried. She raised her arms and stretched. It was cooler up here, but not by much. She slipped off her straw hat and mopped her forehead with one of her clean rags. "Come on, rain," she murmured.

It was hard to believe it was August already, but there was no doubting the late summer heat. It hadn't rained except a little cloudburst here and there for close to a month. They'd had to invest in a different kind of sprinkler setup for the lavender fields just to keep them from dying out completely before the final harvest. Most of the fields were done, but that final culling was critical to their plan to lay in stores big enough for the quantity of product they'd wanted to make over the winter months. They'd decided on throwing another community party in September before the weather turned cold. No lavender picking this time, but definitely some music, the tearoom would be open, and they would have a wreath-making workshop and another wine-tasting combo with Bluestone & Vine. After that, they'd hold a two-day open house between Thanksgiving and Christmas to do a preview launch of their product line. Vivienne was planning on holding weekly teas through the winter before the actual launch of the tearoom in the spring. She'd secured all the proper permits now, so she could hire staff and operate as a full-fledged business.

It still felt as if they had five million things to do, and on top of that, Hannah was trying to get enough artwork done to fill her stall in the mill, which she'd start manning on a regular schedule once the farm wound down at the end of summer. She'd already taken a few commissions from people who had seen her painting at the amphitheater rehearsals or in various other spots around the Falls. And what time she wasn't spending tending the lavender fields and painting, was spent with Will. Or with Jake.

Her phone buzzed with an incoming text and she smiled. "Speaking of those McCall men." She reached down and saw it was from Will. He'd initially intended to join her down in the meadow for a picnic supper. She'd thought it was a bit buggy and hot for that, but was so charmed that he'd thought of it, she'd agreed without hesitation. Now with what looked like a change in the weather, he was telling her it would be best to get up the trail before it became a mud slide. "I couldn't agree more," she said, and texted him the same. Seeing her phone was close to dying, she searched in her bag for her external battery pack—something she'd taken to carrying since she had a habit of losing track of time when she painted, and realized she'd left the unit charging back on her kitchen counter. She hurried to let Will know that, and that she was packing up and would text again when she was heading back to the Falls and had a chance to charge her phone in the car a bit.

She glanced up at the sky again and frowned. It was definitely looking dark over the distant peaks. She finished stowing her gear and carefully stored her painting in her art valise. She hauled the lot of it over to the shed, never so thankful for Addie's offer to store her work there. Because Bailey stored feed and some medical supplies in there, the shed was temperature controlled by a big solar energy panel mounted to the roof, so her supplies stayed in good condition.

The bleating of the babies coming from the lamb house beckoned her, and after she closed up the shed, she took another glance at the sky and decided she had a few minutes to indulge herself. She'd apologized to Snowball many times for blubbering all over his soft, wooly curls. The lamb wasn't being bottle fed any longer and no longer resembled the scrawny little bundle he'd been several months ago. He would always be Hannah's favorite, and she kept a small little something in her pocket for the lamb to nibble on, when she could sneak it to him without being stampeded by the whole herd.

Hannah stepped inside the dimly lit interior, immediately sighing in relief at the cool, dank air, even if she had to take a moment to get used to the various barn smells that came with it. She marveled over how big the last batch of babies was getting and covered her heart with her hand at the sight of two new ones in the far stall. "Seriously," she told them, peering over the stable door. "Stop it with the cuteness." It was a miracle Bailey hadn't talked her into taking one or a dozen of them home to Lavender Blue with her already. As it was, Chey was already talking about getting a few of Bailey's pygmy goats to keep full time. Not because they needed them anymore for clearing purposes. And that had been an amazing lesson in animal power right there. But because in that miniature size they were just so stinking cute.

"Hey, Hannah," a voice called from somewhere outside the building. "Are you down here?"

Startled, Hannah went over to the door. She was shocked to see it had turned almost dark as night, and big fat raindrops had just begun to fall. Apparently, her eyes had adjusted to the growing darkness so well she hadn't noticed. Peering into the gloom and through the rain fog, she made out the form of someone coming around the paddock fence on a mountain bike.

"Jake?" She called his name a second time more loudly but realized there was no way he could hear her now that the wind had picked up. She stuck her head out of the barn and waved to him, so he'd see where she was. Raindrops pelted her face and she quickly withdrew back into the stable. "What on earth is he thinking?" Will hadn't said anything about Jake or anyone else coming down to the meadow.

Even with the rain, Jake made it to the stable in short order and shoved his bike between the building and the bushes that bordered it on one side; then he hopped over the swiftly growing puddles and met Hannah in the doorway. She stepped back to let him inside. "What are you doing down here?" she asked, still surprised to see him. "They say it's supposed to storm."

"Yeah," he said, with a short laugh, but his eyes showed nothing but worry.

"What's wrong?" Hannah said. "I told your dad I was coming up, but I guess I stayed in here playing with the babies too long. We can just wait out the storm in here. Do you have your phone? I'm sure mine is dead by now. Just let your dad know. We'll come up when it's over." She thought about what the trail would be like, then looked down at what she was wearing and grimaced. "Oh well," she said, "another pair of jeans will bite the dust." At least she'd stopped wearing skirts for her jaunts up and down the trail. She'd learned quickly that having strong fabric for the occasional slips and falls was a much better plan.

"No, it's not that," Jake told her. "I mean yes, we can ride it out in here, but we have to get the sheep in. That's why I came down. Bailey is all the way over at your place and they're saying it might be a derecho. High winds, maybe hurricane force gusts, and heavy thunderstorms."

"Does your dad know you're down here doing this?"

"I sent him a text but haven't checked to see if he wrote back. I've got to get them in. You stay in here." He looked at the stone walls, and up at the roof. "This will probably be the safest place for us, too."

Alarmed now, she said, "If it's as bad as you say, I don't think you should be out there."

"I've got at least thirty minutes. Don't worry." Then he was out the door before she could stop him.

"Jake!" she shouted, running out into the rain to call his name again. He was already inside the paddock herding the sheep toward the chute that would lead them to a side door into the largest building. There were pens in there to hold them for this exact purpose.

"Well, if you're doing this," she muttered, "I'm going to help." She ran through the downpour, sending plumes of mud puddle slop flying in her wake. She could feel it hitting the backs of her jeans, right up to her butt, but there was nothing for it now. She got to the chute gate at the paddock end and opened it, then climbed into the chute and ran, slipping and sliding, to the other end, and fought with the gate there. Her straw hat was snatched clean off her head, the scarf she'd tied under her chin slipping away with it as it went sailing through the sky. She'd forgotten she still had it on and was surprised it had lasted that long. She couldn't take the time to chase after it now. The scarf and hat were probably already damaged beyond saving anyway. She ended up having to bang the darn chute latch with the side of her fist. It popped open just as the sheep started in from the other end.

"Look out!" Jake hollered, and Hannah climbed up on the fence as the dozen or so sheep scuttled past her into the indoor pen, bleating their displeasure the entire way.

Hannah closed the gate behind them and turned to run to the other end of the chute to help Jake close the paddock fence, but he was nowhere to be seen. The rain was stinging her eyes now. The drops had gotten smaller and the wind fiercer. Much fiercer. She scraped her hair from her eyes and tried to peer into the deepening mist and gloom. A flash of white caught her eye and she saw Jake, or his white T-shirt anyway, at the far end of the paddock. It took her another second, using her hands to try to shield her eyes from the pummeling rain, to realize that one of the little ones had apparently panicked and somehow gotten itself stuck. When the wind blew the right way, she got snatches of its panicked bleating even this far away.

The first crack of lightning made her jump and let out a short scream at the same time. "Dear sweet—" She swallowed the rest along with more rainwater and made the split-second decision to run and help Jake. No way would he leave that baby and no way was she leaving him.

He'd freed the lamb before she got halfway across the long field and motioned for her to turn back to the stone stable. She waited to make sure he was getting across the field okay, the lamb tucked firmly under his arm, before she turned and started running. She slowed and glanced over her shoulder several times to track his progress. Each time he would wave her to go on. As he drew closer, Hannah could see the baby was thrashing, and Jake was trying not to slip and slide to keep from either falling on the baby or inadvertently dumping it free again.

"Come on, come on, come on," Hannah urged him under

her breath. He was getting closer, so she turned back again, never so happy to see the stable was close. She turned back one last time and motioned for him to hurry. The thunder was cracking regularly now and the lightning strikes made her blood run cold with their bold, flashing intensity. Way too close for comfort.

She stood in the doorway, arms outstretched to relieve him of his bundle the moment he got to the door, even though he was still a good twenty yards out. "Come on, Jake," she said, willing him to get there faster.

The chain of events that happened in the next fifteen seconds occurred so swiftly, with such vicious precision, it took her breath away before she could even register the shock, much less scream, and she could feel each separate beat of her heart.

The bolt of lightning shot down with such sudden fury, she jumped back a full two feet. The resulting crack when it hit the tree sent her instinctively right to her knees in the packed dirt, arms over her head, as if ducking from an incoming bomb. She'd barely hit the floor when she jerked her arms down and looked through the door as a loud CRACK followed the lightning strike. That sound was still echoing in her ears, and ricocheting around inside her heart, as she scrambled toward the door, half crawling, half stumbling, trying in vain to get to her feet. She clawed her way up the doorframe, clutching it to regain her balance, and felt her heart stop dead in her chest, watching in horror as a tree several times taller than the building she was standing in came crashing down, straight across the pasture, heading right toward Jake.

She might have screamed Jake's name, or maybe the scream was inside her head. Jake tried to run faster, but the mud hampered his efforts.

"NO!" Hannah screamed, quite certain that one had been out loud. *No no no no no!*

Jake outran the thick, heavy central trunk of the tree, but the widespread branches, many of them heavy enough on their own to do critical damage, took him and the baby lamb down.

Hannah lost sight of him and the lamb as the heavy, leaf-filled limbs obscured what view she'd had through the rain.

She didn't waste a single moment, not so much as a second. She went tearing across the muddy meadow toward the paddock. Slipping and sliding, she grabbed the paddock fence in both hands, not even feeling the splinters that gouged her palms and shredded her fingertips as she literally launched her entire body up and over the thing as if she'd suddenly gained a superpower.

No, she thought, the terror of what was happening right in front of her boiling down into a single, blistering ball of anger and fury. *No, no, NO!* Her inner voice screamed until she felt so raw she shook with it. *You took one child from me, but I'll be damned if you'll take another!*

And just like that, every unnamed fear she'd had, all those crying jags, the anxiety bombs, her utter inability to control herself every time she got home after spending time with Jake, every moment spent wondering what in the hell was wrong with her and why she couldn't accept her place in the lives of the two people she loved most crystallized in a moment of clear, pure realization.

She hadn't been grieving her lost family. Being with Jake hadn't resurrected her grief for Liam. No, the reason she'd been worried sick, reduced to sobs of exhaustion, was because of the possibility of having to live through a moment exactly like the one she was living through right that very second. She hadn't been able to save Liam. Her beautiful little boy that she'd loved more than life itself.

And some deep-seated part of her, still overcome with that desperate, helpless, god-awful terror, had so fiercely resisted allowing her to ever put herself in a position where she could possibly risk that kind of loss again, it had literally made her sick.

Only it was too late for that. Too late to protect herself, protect her heart. Jake hadn't been born hers . . . but in her heart, he was hers now.

Hannah was racing toward the tree limbs as if her life depended on it, because it did. She was screaming Jake's name; she couldn't seem to stop. *Please be okay, please be okay, please be okay,* she prayed, the words running on an endless loop inside her head. *Don't you dare be dead.* She slowed so she could work her way through the heavy limbs to the spot where she thought she'd seen him go down. The high winds whipped the slender ends of the branches against her face, torso, and arms, leaving cuts and bruises. She didn't notice the sting or feel the pain. Her eyes were hot and dry as the fury built inside her. Rain lashed her cheeks, stinging her eyes. Once she was among the massive tangle of branches, her vision blocked by the leaves and the driving rain, she immediately lost all sense of where to look.

The tree was so big, the sprawl and tangle of the limbs alone were taller than she was. Some of the branches were as big around as tree trunks, far bigger and heavier than anything she could lift or even move. As she worked her way closer, the bark and sharp twigs caught at her clothes and scratched her skin. *Please, please, please,* she silently begged, pleaded, and bartered. *Not Jake. Take me. Not Jake. Come on!* she demanded. *COME ON!* She was all but clawing her way through as the wind sent twigs whipping across her torso and arms like whips, sending one stinging across her cheek. She ducked her head, still calling his name, her voice raw now, hardly more than a rasp.

And then finally, *finally,* after what had probably only been a few minutes but had felt like endless panic-filled hours, she saw him, and she instinctively convulsed, like she was going to be violently ill. He was lying on his side, drenched to the bone, blood matted in his dark hair, his skin so pale it looked translucent to her. The bleating lamb was still clutched in his arms, screaming in its own fear and panic. She looked at Jake again, trying not to be sick, praying for the least little sign of life.

Then, her gaze jerked back to the lamb. It was thrashing, but Jake was holding on tight, not letting it go. *Oh, thank God!* she thought, and almost crumpled to the ground when her legs threatened to give out under her, her relief was so all consuming. Good. *Good, good, good.* If he had a grip, he was still alive. *Focus on that.*

When she got closer, she could see the side of his face was bloodied, but the rest was covered by twigs and leaves, so she couldn't see clearly whether his eyes were open or closed. *Be closed, be closed,* she prayed. She'd seen open, sightless eyes once in her life, and she didn't ever—could not ever—ever, ever, ever see that again. "Jake," she said as she drew close enough that she thought he might hear her. "Don't move, honey, don't move."

Hannah didn't know if he was conscious, but she kept talking to him as she finally got to his side. She saw that one heavy branch, almost trunk-like in size, was lying across his lower body. The rest of the limbs around him were smaller and had likely caused the gash on his scalp, and the scrapes and cuts.

"Jake, I'm right here," she said, her voice raspy from shouting and sucking in too much rainwater. "I'm right here, and I'm not going anywhere. You're going to be okay." *Nothing.* She bent or snapped off the smaller twigs and branches, until she could wedge herself right up next to him.

"Here, honey," she said, "let me have the lamb." The squalling baby was wild eyed, but its bleats had become hoarse little squeaks now. She needed to remove it from Jake's arms so she could see his face. "Don't move until we make sure you're okay. Just relax your grip and I'll get her, okay? I promise I won't let her go."

Jake moaned softly, then started to move.

Tears of abject relief gathered in her eyes. "Lie still, sweetie," she gently cautioned him. "Don't move. Just let her go."

He tried to move anyway, still groggy and unaware of the circumstances, then yelped in pain, and went still.

"Jake," Hannah said, finding some rare, untapped center of calm, now that she knew he was okay. "It's all right," she said easily, her tone soothing, but sturdy. "You're caught under a tree limb, so you need to stay still."

"Hannah?" he croaked, his eyelids fluttering, then finally blinking open.

She knew her smile was downright beatific at the sight of those beautiful dark green eyes. "I'm right here."

"Hurt," he croaked. "My hip. Leg."

"I know. Don't worry, you're going to be okay. You need to lie still, as best as you can." She leaned over again. "I'm going to take the lamb, okay?" She reached for it, but Jake's hold went instinctively tighter, as he was still fighting to understand what was happening. "Jake?"

"Mm-hmm," he said, still not really fully with her.

"I'm going to take the lamb now—it's going to be okay."

"Mkay," he said, and his eyelashes fluttered a bit.

"I'm right here," Hannah said, finally able to ease the lamb from his death hold of a grip. "I've got her," she told him. "She's okay, she's just fine. You did really great saving her." She kept up a calm, running commentary, hoping to steady him, keep him from panicking once he became more alert.

The moment the lamb was free from being clutched so tightly, she simply trembled, but lay limply in Hannah's lap, panting, but quiet now. Hannah shifted until she sat cross-legged and tucked the lamb into the well created by her legs and body. She gently stroked the baby's sodden, clumpy fleece while continuing to talk to Jake in the same calm, soothing tones. The baby finally quieted, its head drooping drowsily against her leg, plum worn out even though Hannah could feel its thrumming heartbeat.

"Hannah?"

Hannah's gaze flew from the lamb back to Jake. He looked and sounded alert now. *Thank God.* "Right here."

"What happened?"

"Lightning strike," she told him. "You've got a bit of a tree on top of you."

He glanced down and she started to shift toward him, not wanting him to see his predicament and panic, but he solemnly took in his situation and said, "So I do."

She didn't know whether to laugh or cry. "Hey, Jake," she said softly, all the affection and love she had for this boy right out there, no more holding back.

He managed to shift his head just enough to look directly at her. "Hi." His smile was crooked, and she could see he was in pain, but that dry note was all Jake. Her Jake.

"Hi," she replied. "I want you to focus on your breathing, all right? Slow and steady. I know it's hard, with the rain and everything, but try to do that for me, okay?"

He started to nod, flinched, and said, "Okay," instead.

He looked like he wanted to go back to sleep, which she knew wasn't good given he quite probably had a concussion. "Look at me, Jake. Talk to me."

"About what?" he said, still hoarse, but otherwise sounding fully aware now.

She smiled at him. "Whatever you want. But first, let's take inventory, okay?"

He started to nod, and she tried to warn him, but he stopped before he flinched this time. "Sure," he said. "Of what?"

"You," she said, trying really hard to focus on the moment and stay positive. He was going to be all right. He needed her to be calm. So she would be. "We're going to work from the head down, okay?"

"Okay."

"Tell me, does your head hurt? Focus just on that. Don't move it. We know it hurts when you nod, so don't do that. Just relax as best you can and tell me what you feel."

"It hurts. On the side." He started to reach up but aborted the move on his own. He didn't flinch, or appear to be in more pain, which was good, so Hannah assumed he was just trying to follow her instructions. "I think . . . it hit the ground."

He sounded steadier now, and Hannah took in a deep breath to help maintain her calm. The aftereffects of the adrenaline punch were making her feel jittery now. "How about your jaw? Eyelids?"

The latter earned her a quick flash of his trademark dry smile. "Okay."

"Good," she said, and blinked away the tears that kept forming at the corners of her eyes. Happy tears, in this case. He was handling this really, really well. "Don't move it, but your neck, how—"

"I think it's okay." He definitely sounded stronger now. "I think . . . I think I blacked out when I hit the ground."

"You might have," she told him, deciding it was better to be straight with him. He was too smart to try and fool.

"That's why it's important to stay as alert and awake as you can, okay? In case you have a concussion."

"Okay," he said. He grimaced a little, then said, "I can move all my toes."

Hannah blew out a huge sigh of relief. "You kind of jumped down the inventory list a bit," she teased, trying to distract him a little from the pain.

"Pretty sure it's mostly my hip," he said. "Maybe my right leg a little."

"Okay, that's good. Not about the hip," she added, "but the rest. You're doing really great, Jake."

And then he did the damnedest thing. He smiled at her, truly smiled, rain soaked, scratched up, injured and all, and said, "You are, too."

Her breath hitched just a little as a fresh threat of tears gathered, even as she laughed. "Thanks. So, let's say we get ourselves out of here."

"I'm good with that," he said gamely.

"Your phone, is it on you?"

"Yes. But . . . in my right shorts pocket."

She looked and realized which one he meant. The one with a tree on it. "Ah. Okay. Plan B." Maybe her phone still had a shred of charge in it. She squinted through the tree branches in the direction of the stone building and suddenly realized that the rain had slowed, and the wind had died down completely. No more thunder or rumbling skies, either. The storm had passed over the meadow like a blade scraping along a flat surface, only with a lot of violent turbulence following along in its wake. "I think the worst of the storm is over," she told him.

She shifted slightly, careful not to disturb the sleeping lamb, and was surprised at how quickly she was able to get her bearings now that the storm fog had lifted, the rain had lightened up, and the wind wasn't whipping things around any longer. From her spot in the middle of the branches, she could actually see more clearly. The leaves had all been flattened by the rain—the ones that hadn't been torn off by the wind—so that helped, too.

She immediately spied a far more direct route out of the tangle of tree limbs and thought, *Now you tell me.* In her panic to get to Jake, she'd just gone flying and crawling in, but the path out looked fairly simple if she just moved directly toward the main tree trunk. She looked back to Jake, who was watching her with surprising calm. "Okay," she told him. "I'm going to take the baby to the stable and get my phone, call for help." She didn't tell him that it might be dead. They'd deal with that when and if the time came. "You are not to move. Do you hear me?" She gave him a pointed look, affection and love right there for him to see, too. "*No* moving."

Jake smiled again, even as he winced. "Got it. No moving. I swear. It's not much fun anyway."

Her heart clenched a little at that. "I'd lean down and kiss you on the forehead, but—" She gestured to the lamb. Instead she pressed her fingers to her lips, then pressed them to his forehead. She was actually just trying to feel whether he was cold or hot, not that she was sure what she'd do about either one. It was just the mom instinct in her. To stroke foreheads and soothe.

She saw color steal into his cheeks at her action. She'd probably embarrassed him. "Sorry," she told him. "It's a mom thing. It's what we do."

She saw a flicker of some unreadable emotion pass through his eyes, and they grew a little glassy. Hannah realized then what she'd said, how it might have sounded, and worried that he'd thought she was trying to take his mom's place or something. She opened her mouth, to say exactly what, she didn't know, but to try and fix her gaffe, but he spoke first.

"Thanks," he said, looking straight at her. And that was when she saw it, right there, shining from his green eyes. A look she recognized, one her heart recognized in an instant. One she had missed, so much.

"I like it," he added, and his voice broke in that post-adolescent croak.

"Good," she said, and maybe her eyes were glassy then, too. "Because you might be getting more of them." She gave him a wry wink. "Fair warning."

He closed his eyes briefly, then opened them again and looked right back into her eyes. If there was any doubt about what she thought she'd seen before, he left no doubt now. "I'm good with that," he told her. "Really good with that."

She hoped he saw the exact same emotion in her eyes, because it had filled her heart up to overflowing the instant that tree had started to fall. *I love you, too,* she said silently. "Hold down the fort," she told him, and got an eye roll and a smile. "I will be very fast."

Hannah scooped the lamb up in her arms and carefully held it against her body. She'd expected it to wake up and start thrashing, but it was well and truly exhausted. *Poor thing,* she thought, but was glad. It would make the task ahead a lot easier.

It turned out not to be all that hard now that she'd found the easier path out. Once she was clear, the mud and carrying the lamb kept her from flat-out running, but she made it through the paddock gate and over to the lamb house fairly quickly. She gently deposited the baby in the first empty stall, hoping it wouldn't wake up and be frightened to be alone, but she figured Bailey would want to check her over and make sure she was okay, and this way it would be easy to know which lamb it was.

The minute she was free of her little burden, fresh adrenaline coursed through her. Hannah turned and all but fell on her backpack, finally having to force herself to slow down and make her fingers stop shaking so she could pull the clasp down the cord and open the drawstring top. Her phone was right on top. She said every prayer she knew and pressed the button.

When the screen lit up, she cried out in relief and immediately punched in 911. *They would have to come by helicopter*, she thought, silently willing the operator to pick up. When nothing happened, she pulled the phone away and saw there was no signal. She bit back a scream of frustration.

She looked outside, saw there was still a steady, though much calmer rain coming down, and quickly dug in her bag and found the baggie she'd used for her sandwich. She jammed the phone in the bag and zipped it up, then ran back into the rain, searching for a signal. Then it hit her. She always had a signal where she set up her easel and stool to paint. Naturally it was in the opposite direction from the fallen tree, but it was her best shot. If she ran back to Jake and got no signal there, her phone would surely die before she made it all the way back across the field.

Slipping and sliding as she ran around the paddock fence, she skidded to a stop the moment she got close to her spot and hit the call button again. "Come on, come on," she murmured. "Do this, phone. Do this." And then 911 picked up. "Oh, thank God." Hannah quickly explained the situation, giving their location as best she could. She explained it all twice, and they told her a medivac helicopter would be coming, but with the storm still in the area, they couldn't give her a clear time frame. Hannah wanted to get back to Jake, but the operator told her to stay on the line, and she knew if she moved, she'd lose the signal. However, right then her phone finally died, freeing her from having to make that choice.

She prayed the chopper would get to them sooner rather than later, and that she'd given them enough info to find the meadow easily. Hopefully they got her GPS coordinates before her phone died. There was nothing else to do now but get back to Jake, keep him calm, and wait.

By the time she made it through the tangle of branches to his side, taking the much easier way in this time, the rain had stopped completely. "We're all set," she told him, and lowered herself carefully beside him once more. "I'm sorry it took so long, but help is on the way."

"Did you tell Dad?"

"I told the operator your name and his and gave them all the information they needed, but then my phone died. I know they'll contact him."

"Good," Jake said, then let his head relax back now that the rain wasn't stinging his face. He slid a hand across the dirt, palm open.

Now that neither of them had the lamb to contend with, she reached for it immediately and held on to it with both of hers.

"I'm okay," he told her.

"You're better than okay," she said with a grin, feeling almost giddy with relief. *Help was coming. Jake was going to be fine.* "So, while we wait, I want to tell you something," she said, thinking talking would distract him from the pain. And because of that moment they'd shared before she'd gone to make the call, she didn't want him going another moment without knowing, without understanding. "I know I haven't been real great about spending time with both you and your dad. At the same time."

"Hannah," Jake said, his expression instantly alarmed, "you don't have to—"

"No, it's all right, Jake," she said and smiled. "It's going to be fine."

He closed his eyes briefly. "Okay. That's good." He kept them closed another moment and then looked at her again.

She felt bad for alarming him. She'd been trying to do the opposite. She had no idea what she looked like, probably not good, but hoped he saw the sincerity in her eyes if nothing else. "I was having kind of a hard time," she began.

"I know," Jake said. "Dad and I talked about it. He was going to talk to you out here. Today."

Surprised, and feeling worse now knowing she'd really worried them both, she said, "You did? He was?"

Jake nodded, then gritted his teeth.

"You know what, maybe we shouldn't be talking about this now. Rest as best you can. Keep your eyes open, but try and do that slow, steady breathing thing I talked about before. It will help manage the pain. I can talk, but you probably shouldn't. I'll . . . tell you a story."

Jake looked at her. "You can finish the one you started," he said.

She hesitated, and he said, "Does it have a happy ending?"

She let out a short laugh at that and nodded.

"Then that one," he said, and smiled at her. "Please."

She dashed her fingers at the corners of her eyes even as she flashed a brief grin. "Okay," she said, then tried to find the right words this time. "I didn't mean to worry you, or your dad, but I guess I did. I wanted to talk to your dad about it, but . . . I wasn't sure what was really bothering me." She laid her hand over Jake's again and he turned his over so they could hold on to each other. "It wasn't about Liam," Hannah told him. "Or anything to do with not wanting to be with you. I love being with your dad. I love being with you. I wasn't sad. In fact, you two make me the happiest I've been in a very long time. I just had this really bad, really

weird anxiety, whenever I thought about us all together, and
that was really confusing to me, because I want to be with
you guys. Very much."

"Was it because you were afraid of being part of a
family again?"

"In a way, but that's not it, not exactly." She shifted carefully around in the small space until she could lie on her
stomach, propped up on her elbows, so her face was more
level with his, and so she was closer to him. She shifted her
weight so she could put her hand back in his and he immediately held on tight. That made her heart fill right up and
she squeezed right back. "I didn't figure it out exactly until
I saw what was happening, with the lightning and the tree."
She held his gaze then. "I realized I wasn't afraid of having
a family again." She squeezed his hand. "I was afraid of
having one, and losing it again. I think some part of me
thought I shouldn't risk caring so much that I could get hurt
again and, in its own weird way, it was trying to protect me
by making me feel yucky enough that I wouldn't try."

"You won't lose us, Hannah," Jake said, his gaze searching hers.

She could have told him that she was talking about the
kind of loss no one could control, but there was no need for
that. "What I realized was that if that part of my brain, or
my body, thought it could somehow protect me by not letting me get attached to you two, well then, it didn't do a
very good job."

Jake looked confused.

"Because it's too late for that. That ship has sailed."

Jake flashed her a grin. "You mean it?"

"I'm afraid you've lost your chance to get rid of me.
You're stuck with me now. At least for as long as you'll
have me."

Despite the pain, and the fear, Jake's eyes were bright

now, and there was more than a little relief shining in them, too. "Good."

Hannah was really glad she'd told him now. She hated that she'd made them worry. "Yeah," she told him. "I think so, too."

They both heard the vibrating sound that pulsed through the air. Hannah shifted onto her knees, then stood and scanned the skies the best she could. She saw the medivac helicopter a moment later and waved her arms overhead. "The cavalry has arrived," she said. "Looks like you're getting a free hop to the top of the hill." She shot him a grin. "The things people will do to keep from having to pedal their mountain bike up that trail."

"Right now, I'll take it," he said, his smile tired, but brave and still there.

She sat back down beside him. "Won't be too much longer now." She reached out and gently brushed his hair from his face, careful to avoid the injured area, then ruffled the front a little bit, just wanting, needing to touch him, soothe him, if she could.

"Why do adults do that?" he said. Now she was smiling.

Chapter Twenty-Four

Will found her in one of the triage cubicles in the emergency area of the Turtle Springs hospital. "Hannah," he said, relief instantly replacing the worried expression on his face as he spied her behind the half-drawn curtain.

Hannah slid from her seat on the end of the hospital bed and went straight into his arms.

He didn't say anything, just wrapped her up tight and held on. He finally loosened his hold enough so he could look at her. Hannah had seen herself now, so she knew she looked worse than a fright show, but you'd never know it from the look in his eyes. If she hadn't already figured out she was head over heels in love with him, that look would have done it.

He kissed her bruised and scratched up face, then pulled her right back against him, burying his face in her hair. "Let's not do this again, okay?" he said, and she heard both the residual fear and the abject relief in his voice.

"Deal," she said, wholeheartedly. "How is Jake doing?" Her phone was still dead, so she hadn't been able to communicate with Will directly, but the EMTs had told her Jake was on his way in, and she knew Will would have gone straight to Jake's side the moment he got there.

"He's okay. Banged up pretty good, but amazingly, nothing was broken. The cut on his head ended up not being as bad as it looked. No stitches or anything."

Hannah felt almost woozy with relief. "Oh, thank God."

"Addie Pearl and Bailey are in with him now. The doctor ran a few other tests and we're just waiting for the results, but he should be cleared to go home in an hour or two."

"I'm so thankful he's okay." Hannah slid her arms around Will's waist and nestled against his chest, her cheek pressed against his heart. *Boy, do I need a lot of this.* "He was really amazing, Will. You'd have been so proud of how he handled himself. I know he was in pain, and he had to be scared, but you'd never have known it." She looked up at him. "He was smiling, even joking with me. Though I should tell you he's really over having his hair played with."

Will barked a hoarse laugh at that. "Yeah, so I learned." His voice choked up with emotion when he added, "Thank you, Hannah. For what you did for him, for getting help, for keeping him calm. When I got that call—" He broke off, then just leaned his head down and kissed her, gently, intently, as if trying to pour out of him everything he was feeling and couldn't put into words.

She understood every bit of it.

He lifted his mouth from hers, then tucked her close again, as if trying to offer her shelter, and protection, and whatever else he could offer of himself to help shield her. "I'm so, so sorry you had to go through that."

Hannah kissed his chest right over his heart. "I'd do it again," she said without hesitation. "For you. For him." She'd known the truth of that the moment lightning had struck that tree. But if she'd had any doubts, they'd vanished when Jake had looked at her with all the love in his heart, right there for her to see, right there for her to take. And she knew she wanted all of it.

Will loosened his hold, cupped her tender, bruised cheek

in his hand, and searched her eyes. "We would do anything for you, too. You do know that, right?"

Hannah nodded, sniffled, then laughed and dabbed at the corners of her eyes. "I promised myself I was all done with those."

He slid his thumb over and dried one for her, then another, making her sniffle all over again, and they both laughed.

She looked into his eyes then, and her breath caught. Her heart might have skipped a beat, too. Because right there was the same emotion she'd seen in his son's gaze, only this time it was all grown up, but every bit as much all for her. "Will," she said, and now her voice was choked with emotion. She wanted to tell him she felt the same way, say the three words that she'd been wanting to say for weeks, but couldn't.

But now that she had talked with Jake, he needed to know that part first. "I told Jake something today, when we were waiting for the EMTs. I need to tell you, too."

Will looked immediately concerned. "What is it?"

"He told me you two talked, and that you were planning to talk to me. About my not spending time with the two of you together. That's why you planned the picnic."

He looked alarmed at that, as if she might be angry. "Hannah, I—"

"No, Will, it's okay," she said. "I'm really sorry I worried you both." She smiled briefly. "I worried me, too. I wanted to talk to you about it, but I honestly didn't know how to explain it without really alarming you since I couldn't even explain it to myself."

"You can always talk to me," he told her. "Even if we don't understand what we're dealing with, it's got to be better finding a solution together than suffering on your own." She nodded, sniffled again, and he gently stroked her face. "So, tell me now. What was going on?"

She should have gone to him, talked to him, as Chey had

suggested. She realized that now. She might not have fully
trusted that he'd be there for her, no matter what, but looking into his eyes right now, she knew she'd never doubt it
again. "I was having these, well, I guess you could call them
kind of anxiety attacks with crying jags."

"Aw, Han," he said, his voice now more a hushed whisper. He tilted her face to his. "You should have told me."

She nodded, eyes swimming again at the love and concern clear on his face. "I didn't say anything because they
made no sense to me. I love being with you, and I love being
with Jake. I just figured it was some kind throwback to
dealing with losing Liam—though it didn't feel like that. I
wasn't sad; being with you both didn't trigger that grief. If
anything, being with you and Jake made everything better.
I knew what I wanted, and I honestly thought it would get
better, sort itself out, but it didn't."

"If you don't or can't be with us—we understand. Today,
seeing Jake get hurt, must have been pure hell for you. I'm
so glad you were there to help him, but I hate that you
had to be there, to see that, deal with it."

"I'm glad I was there for him," Hannah told him. "And
I do want to be with you. I love being with you both, want
to be with you both. But something was really messing with
me when I thought about us spending time all together, and
I couldn't understand why. I even called the therapist who
helped me after the accident, but she'd retired and closed
her practice. The only reason I'm telling you this now, all
of it, is that I want you to know, I was determined to fix it,
Will. I wasn't giving up, not on you, or Jake, or us. I was
going to figure it out." She looked up at him. "And then
today, out in that storm, I did."

His worry ebbed and what she saw take its place thrilled
her right down to her toes.

"I'm glad we're worth fighting for," he told her, "because
we weren't going to let you go without a fight either. That's

what that picnic was about. I should have said something
to you sooner, offered to help you, but I was afraid I was
borrowing trouble. We definitely don't need to be doing that
again, either."

"Agreed," she said, and drew in a shaky breath. "We see
something, we say something."

"Deal." He brushed his thumb over her lip, gently
soothed the bruised skin on her cheek, and looked deeply
into her eyes, letting her see the truth of his words before he
spoke them. "I love you, Hannah Montgomery. With all of
my banged-up heart. You came into my life, our life, and
gave mine back to me."

Her eyes filled and so did her heart. "Good thing," she
said, "because what I figured out today, what I told Jake,
was that it wasn't that I was afraid of being in a family with
you. I've always known that. I want that." She looked into
his eyes, wanting—needing—him to believe she understood
now, that she was okay now. "When I saw that tree come
down today, when I thought I might lose him—" She broke
off, shook her head. "I realized that what that thing inside
me was fighting so hard against, wasn't finding a new
family, but putting myself in the position to lose one."

"Aw, honey," he said, and there was a sheen covering his
eyes then, too, as he hurt for her, for how hard she'd had
to fight.

"The thing is," Hannah said, "I knew the moment I
thought I might lose Jake that it was already far too late to
save myself from risking my love." She reached up and
cupped his cheek now. "I've already gone all in, Will. You
both are already so very dear to me. I would have moved
heaven and earth to get to Jake today, done whatever it took.
And that's all we can do, all we can be. We fight for the
ones we love and pray like hell nothing bad happens to
them. But I can't—won't—deprive myself of all the good
there is in loving you, loving Jake, and being loved by you,

just because I might lose it. Lose you. That's a risk I will take. Every single day. Because I do love you, Wilson McCall, with every part of me. And I love your son." She grinned through her tears. "So, I really hope you're good with that, because I'm pretty sure you're stuck with me."

Hannah pulled his head down to kiss him, but he was already meeting her halfway. And wasn't that really what love was all about?

"Finally."

Hannah and Will broke their kiss to find Bailey standing by the half-open curtain, a very satisfied look on her face.

"Jake wants to see you," she said. "Both of you." Then she turned and was off without giving them a chance to reply.

Will looked at Hannah. "You ready for this?"

Hannah smiled up at him. "As I'll ever be."

They wound their way through to Jake's curtained off cubicle on the other side of the ER. Bailey and Addie were nowhere to be seen now. The moment Will pulled back the curtain, Hannah immediately went to Jake's side without hesitation. The only anxiety she felt was for the condition he was in. Will hadn't been kidding about him being banged up.

From the look on Jake's face, he was thinking the same of her.

"We're quite the pair, aren't we?"

Jake nodded, but his expression was more tentative. "Are you okay? I asked the EMTs about you, but they didn't tell me anything. They said I could see when I got here. But then we had to run like a million tests."

"I'm fine, just a little scratched up."

Jake looked from her to his dad. "Did you guys talk?" he asked, keeping his voice low, directing the question only to Hannah.

Hannah realized he was worried that maybe what she'd

told him out in the field had not come to fruition. "We did," she said. "I'm really happy to report that he's on board with me hanging out with the two of you. Which is good, because it might have felt kind of awkward with me showing up at your house just to see you if he didn't."

Jake's face split into a wide grin, even as he winced and reached up to touch the cut on the side of his head.

She leaned down to inspect it. It didn't look nearly as bad as it had in the middle of that hell storm. "Looks like they did a pretty good job of cleaning it up." She glanced down at Jake, then leaned in and pressed a kiss next to it. She smiled at him and winked. "But now you're the rest of the way good to go."

"More of that mom magic power?" he asked.

"Don't you know it. I've got loads stored up, so prepare to be embarrassed frequently."

He groaned at that, but Hannah saw the secret thrill in his eyes and felt a rush of love that she'd only ever felt for one other person. It was scary, yes. Petrifying really, but she'd take on that and more just like it if it meant she got to have that kind of love in her life again.

She felt Will step behind her and slide his arms around her waist. He pressed a kiss to the side of her neck. "Is this a private party, or can dads join in?"

Hannah glanced back at him. "I think we can safely say, finally, that sometimes three really is the perfect size crowd."

They were laughing at that and Hannah was thinking she'd never felt so wrapped up in love at any other point in life than she did right at that moment. Then the curtain parted again and one of the EMTs from the medivac helicopter stepped in. "Sorry to interrupt," she said. She pulled something out of her pocket and handed it to Jake. "I know it's probably beyond saving, but I thought you'd want it back."

Jake held up his phone. The case and the phone were not only smashed, but kind of twisted in an odd angle.

"Doc said that phone was what kept your hip from being broken." She nodded toward it. "That shape probably matches a pretty hefty contusion you'll be sporting for a few weeks."

"Thanks," Jake told her, motioning with the phone.

She smiled. "You three take care," she said, and ducked back out.

Hannah and Will turned from the departing EMT to look at Jake, who was turning his phone back and forth, looking at it in a mix of disappointment and amazement. He lifted up the fresh T-shirt Bailey had brought for him and edged down the waistband of the shorts she'd brought him, too, sucking in his breath as the fabric scraped over a rather spectacular mark that was already turning a deep shade of purple. He positioned his phone above it. "Well, what do you know," he said.

It was a perfect match.

"So," Will said, "I guess that's what they mean by 'saved by the bell'?"

Jake and Hannah looked at each other, then they both turned and each gave Will a pitying shake of the head.

Then the three of them looked at one another and burst into laughter, cuts, contusions, phone-shaped bruises, and all.

That was the moment Hannah knew the McCalls had just become an unbreakable tribe of three.

Actually, four. Hannah stepped back as Will and Jake started talking phone upgrades and whether or not they should mount the twisted phone on a base and call it modern art. Hannah listened to their manly chatter, punctuated by laughter, and took a moment for herself. She closed her eyes and drew in, then let out a deep, cleansing breath. No panic attacks. No crying jags. She allowed herself a slow, satisfied

grin. She'd met this most recent life test, and she'd kicked
its ass. Of course, she was pretty sure she'd had a little help.

She curled her hand against her heart and pressed it there.
*I know you were looking out for us today, Liam. Now you'll
have all three of us looking out for you.*

She opened her eyes to find Will's gaze, looking right
into hers. He nodded, as if he knew, and she didn't doubt for
a moment that he absolutely did.

Look what you got, Hannah thought, and knew they were
worth any risk.

Epilogue

Will's palms were sweating, and he couldn't seem to make them stop. He'd be worthless up there if he didn't get his nerves under control.

Hannah lifted up on her toes and kissed his cheek, then when that didn't work, she took his face in her hands and kissed him soundly on the mouth. "You got this," she told him, then held his gaze until he nodded. "I'm going to hustle out of here now so I can get to my seat in time to see everything."

"I should have told him," Will said, certain now, after all his hard work to keep his big secret, that it was exactly the wrong thing to do.

"Jake surprised you a year ago, with his fiddle-playing prowess, and his beautiful voice." Hannah grinned. "I'd say this is a perfect full circle. He will be on the moon."

Will nodded, nerves seriously trying to eat him alive. "Won't be much of a surprise if I can't keep my hands from sweating."

She took them both and held them in her own. "You've

been practicing for ages now. Like you even needed to," she added dryly. "'Have you heard yourself? You're amazing."

That got a chuckle out of him. "You might be a little biased."

Hannah was undeterred. "And Jake is amazing. Where do you think he got those chops? Get out there and show him how it's done." She gave him one last deep, soul-searing kiss, then scooted out from behind the curtain they'd put up off to the side to keep Will hidden, and made her way to her seat. Will knew exactly where it was, exactly where to look, in case he found himself in need of a little emotional support.

He paced the small space, wanting time both to speed up and slow the heck down. He wanted to get it over with. He wasn't ready to go out there. *Get a grip, man.* The rest of the musicians onstage not only knew what was going on, they'd been rehearsing in private every chance they got. Usually when Jake had been up at Addie's or out at Lavender Blue with Hannah.

I'm so proud of you I could burst.

Will went stock-still, dipped his chin, then closed his eyes. *I'm doing it for Jake,* he told her. *He deserves me at least trying.* He opened his eyes, wiped away the moisture that had gathered at the corners. Then he smiled, and the smile spread to a grin. "I mean, look at what he's done, Zoe. Our son. I've got a lot to live up to."

I never doubted you would.

Will's palms still weren't dry when he heard Pippa take the stage to announce to the festival crowd that they had someone who wanted to join the group onstage. "Why don't you come on out here and show these boys, and this girl, how it's really done," she said, and the crowd roared in delight.

Will picked up his fiddle, the one he'd made for himself,

under his grandfather's tutelage when he'd been barely older than his son was right now. Then he picked up the case holding the one he'd made for that very same son. "Just don't make a fool out of yourself," he muttered under his breath.

Then he stepped out from behind the curtain, and the crowd erupted in wild cheers so loud Will almost had to take a step back. His gaze registered the shock on Jake's face first, then Will shifted it to the third row, dead center, and found her, blinding stage lighting and all. Hannah's happy, pretty face. He nodded to her, then caught Jake up against him when his son wrapped him in a hug so tight, he thought he might have bruised a rib. He'd take one of those, every single day. "Here," he said, handing the case to Jake. "Bailey mentioned something about you needing a new instrument. I hope this is a good fit."

Jake's mouth fell open and he just stared at the case, then up at Will. "Dad," he said, clearly at a complete loss as to how to handle the moment.

"Well, open it up and let's take her out for a spin. Pippa tuned it for you, just like the one you've been playing." He smiled. "You might like the sound this one makes a little bit better though."

Jake open the case and his eyes went round as saucers. He looked down at the fiddle, which was a beautiful piece of craftsmanship with Jake's own name worked into the swirl of the wood, then wrapped his father in another tight hug. Will held on just as tightly as the crowd cheered, clapped, and whistled in thundering delight.

Every nerve-wracked moment, every sleepless night spent wondering if he had lost his damn fool mind, thinking he could, or even should, try to pull off something like this after all those years. All of those fears were put to rest in that one priceless hug.

Jake's eyes were shining wet when he looked up at his dad, his grin so wide Will thought it would split his handsome face in two. Will might have been sporting one to match.

"You might have to take it easy on me," Will told him. "I'm a little rusty."

Pippa, who was wiping away a few happy tears of her own, shifted so Will could take the spot next to Jake. Then she nodded to the other players behind them and lifted her own fiddle. The bass player started them off, then Pippa nodded to Will, who looked at Jake. "You ready?"

In answer, Jake put the bow to the strings, grinning like mad, and started right in. Will joined him, while Pippa leaned in and sang into the mic, a song she'd written about fathers and sons, about redemption and love.

Pippa smiled at Hannah, too, including her in the moment.

And Hannah, who was surrounded by Chey, Avery, Vivi, Bailey, and Addie Pearl, led the savvy sextet in a toe-tapping, hand-clapping, and—thanks to Chey—wolf-whistling cheering section as they all rooted on Hannah's tribe.

Holiday treats abound when Donna Kauffman and
Kate Angell get together for Halloween in

THE BAKESHOP AT PUMPKIN AND SPICE.

Please read on for an excerpt from
Donna's delightful novella,
"Sweet Magic."

All Hallows' Eve was fast approaching and Abriana and her grandmother were hard at work creating Bellaluna's Bakeshop's trademark special treats for their favorite magical, mystical holiday season. The Bellaluna women were known to be somewhat . . . special themselves. A visit to their shop, nestled in the little town of Moonbright, Maine, was guaranteed to cure any craving your sweet tooth might have. But there was a chance that one of their special treats could cure any craving your heart might have as well.

Abriana Bellaluna—Bree to everyone except her Grandma Sophia—loved this time of year most. The harvest season was ending, the leaves on the trees were turning into a rainbow of beautiful colors, swirling in the air like party confetti, celebrating the holiday season ahead. The temperatures dipped, the sounds of logs being split echoed in the crisp morning air, and smoke wafted from chimney tops, scenting the air as fireplaces warmed the hearths of their cozy little village. Sweaters were pulled out of storage, gloves were fished out of coat closets, and Bree could feel the excitement begin to build as everyone's thoughts turned toward their very favorite time of year.

Thanksgiving, Christmas, then Valentine's Day, each one a festive time, filled with traditions and joy, kept things bustling for the Bellaluna's family-owned bakeshop. But for the residents of Moonbright, none was as festive and eagerly anticipated as the holiday that launched the season, Halloween.

There were parties, contests, not to mention the trick-or-treating. But one of the most anticipated events, and what drew so many outsiders to their little coastal town, was the grand Halloween parade.

Every man, woman, and child—and a fair number of their household pets to boot—dressed up in costumes that ranged from handmade creations by the very youngest, to elaborate concoctions that looked like something from a Hollywood movie set, and joined in the parade. Floats were made, and cars, fire trucks, along with a few tractors were decked out as well. The whole town got in on the fun. The parade grew as it progressed, like a giant, costume-festooned conga line winding through the streets. Music filled the air from the high school marching band and those who brought along their instruments and played as they strolled. Impromptu sing-alongs happened on every corner, and the shops that lined the main street through town stayed open until the wee hours, offering treats and specials to everyone who cara-vanned by.

Even though she'd always been inside the shop working on the actual holiday, looking out at the passing parade as she handed out treats and rang up sales, Bree looked for-ward to that night all year long. She loved the sense of community, of everyone she'd known her entire life coming together on one night to celebrate, sing, laugh, and have a good time. It was a no-pressure holiday. No gifts needed buying, no family ties needed testing. It was simply a night to play dress up, enjoy a few sweets, and sing and dance.

Bree spent all year planning her costume, and the night itself always flew by. She loved working side by side with her grandmother and the other seasonal help. Her mom, too, when she wasn't galivanting around the globe with Bree's dad, as she was this particular season. Above and beyond all of that was the other thing that made Halloween her favorite holiday. Every year for as long as she could remember, or at least as long as she'd had a romantic bone in her body, Bree spent the evening in happy anticipation, waiting with what felt like bated breath throughout the night for those moments when Sophia or Bree's mother would reach for the special trays of treats behind the counter. That was when Bree knew the Bellaluna women were about to work their magic.

At twenty-eight, Bree should have long since been able to dispense a few special treats of her own. Alas, that had yet to happen.

Bree was currently holding the proof that this year, apparently, wasn't going to be any different. She stared in disgust at the Italian iced cookie in her hand. "How can something that looks so good taste so bad?" She tossed the nibbled cookie in the trash, still grimacing at the tart, acrid taste on her tongue. Trying to remain optimistic, she picked up another one she'd just finished icing and examined it more closely. As if somehow the naked eye could see what her taste buds had already discovered. And deeply regretted.

The cookie appeared to be perfect in every way, something she could proudly display in the old-fashioned glass cases that ran the length of Bellaluna's Bakeshop. Perfectly brown around the edges, plump in the middle, with a dollop of their special family-recipe Italian cream icing on top. A delicate array of sprinkles added the perfect final touch. It looked like a little piece of bite-sized heaven. She'd followed her Grandma Sophia's recipe down to the tiniest detail. Just as she had every one of the dozens of other times she'd tried—and failed—to perfect the Bellaluna women's trademark "special treat." Bree had even tasted every single ingredient as she'd added it, so there was no logical way it could taste bad. What was not to love about butter, sugar, and Italian cream?

She took a determined bite out of the soft, creamy cookie, then immediately grabbed a napkin and spit it right back out again. It tasted like she'd used two cups of baking soda instead of cake flour. She tossed the napkin and the cookie in the trash, then glared at the remaining ten on the tray, as if they'd personally ganged up on her to dash her hopes and dreams.

"Abriana, dear, I need you to cover the front for a few minutes," Grandma Sophia said as she pushed through the swinging door that separated the public part of their shop from the extensive kitchen area in the back. "Ah, *bella*," she said, as she spied what her granddaughter had been up to. Sophia's voice was still softly accented from a childhood spent in the sunflower fields of Tuscany. Sophia was seventy-six, but had the timeless beauty of her namesake, Sophia Loren. She had luminescent skin that always held a natural glow and had remained remarkably free of creases and lines. Well, except for the ones that fanned out from the corners of her soft brown eyes when she smiled, which was often. She kept her hair the same rich brown she'd been born with, always in a pretty French twist, with carefully styled tendrils in front of each ear, accenting the cheekbones of her heart-shaped face. Her "vanity curls" as she called them. She wore little makeup other than eyebrow pencil and a bit of lipstick but didn't need anything more and never had. Her figure remained trim despite the fact that she'd never tired of sampling the treats the Bellaluna family had baked and sold for more than fifty years in

Moonbright, and another generation or two before that in the old country.

Bree could only wish she'd been as fortunate in the gene pool department. She'd taken after her Irish poet father in coloring, her hair somewhere between auburn and brown that never managed to capture the luster of either shade, with hazel eyes that couldn't quite decide between brown or green, pale skin that only glowed for its absence of any color except for the bane of her existence, the freckles she'd never grown out of. They didn't just sprinkle her nose in some cute, perky, delightful manner. No, they'd splashed themselves with gay abandon on every part of her body early on, and decided they were there to stay.

Along with her dad's fair coloring, she'd gotten her mother's soft curves. Okay, maybe "soft" was just another way of saying "plump." It wasn't from oversampling the wares, or from lack of exercise. In fact, Bree was healthy as an ox. A fact she was proud of, and reminded herself to be grateful for, every time she tried to find a blouse that would button over her ample bosom. But was it asking too much to want her spirit animal to be more gazelle than beast of burden?

"I've told you not to worry yourself with this, *mio dolce*." Sophia, who was a good six inches shorter than Bree's five-foot-eight, even in sensible pumps, gave Bree a little squeeze around the waist. "Your time will come, *bellisima*."

"I'm twenty-eight," Bree reminded her with a dry smile. She hugged her back and pressed her cheek to the top of her grandmother's head. "Now would be a good time."

Bree had understood from a young age that she wouldn't come into possession of the special gifts the Bellaluna women each had until she'd been in love herself. A true love. Bree had had numerous crushes as a young girl and had been in several decent, but ultimately short-lived relationships. She'd even thought she'd been in love once or twice. But true love? She looked at the cookies and sighed. *Apparently not.* "But shouldn't they at least taste good?" she asked her grandmother. "I checked each ingredient."

Sophia tipped up on the toes of the sensible black pumps she'd worn every day of her adult life, and kissed Bree on the cheek, then immediately wiped off the lipstick print left behind with the handkerchief she kept tucked in her apron pocket. "Looks can be deceiving," she told her granddaughter. "Taste, too. Bellaluna magic isn't to be wielded lightly. You can't go dispensing what you don't understand yourself."

Bree nodded as if she understood, but her logical, culinary-school-trained mind warred with her soft, romantic heart. If you added up good-tasting ingredients, the result should taste good. Magic or not.

Sophia untied her apron as she bustled around the corner of the shiny, stainless steel worktable. She was nothing if not a constant bustler. She lifted the neck loop over her head, careful not to muss a single strand of her twist, and hung the apron on one of the rows of antique teaspoons that had been fashioned into hooks. They lined a long breadboard that Bree's great-grandmother had hung on the wall outside the little office tucked in the back corner of the shop. "I just have to run down to the pharmacy for a moment."

Bree glanced over, brows furrowing in concern. "Is anything wrong?"

Sophia might look and behave like a woman a good decade younger than her actual age, but Bree kept an eye on her grandmother all the same. Sophia wasn't getting any younger and, at some point, surely time would start to catch up to her.

Sophia waved away her concern, and Bree sighed in relief, happy that time was not today.

"I promised Janice Powell I'd help her pick out some lipstick and nail color, and some sunscreen for the cruise Hank surprised her with on their tenth anniversary last week. I'll be back in a blink." She slipped the tube of lipstick out of the apron pocket and took a moment to refresh the pretty rose color, using the tiny locket-style mirror that she'd clipped onto the lipstick cap before blotting on a tissue that somehow magically appeared from the sleeve of her dress.

"What a wonderful anniversary gift," Bree said, marveling as she always did at her grandmother's effortless ability to always look perfectly put together despite the fact they spent a large part of their time in a warm kitchen.

Sophia stepped into the office and snagged her handbag from the corner of the desk. It was the size of a small piece of luggage and dwarfed her slender frame. She never went anywhere without it. Bree wondered if maybe that was the key to her grandmother's fountain-of-youth fitness. Maybe Bree just needed to get a bigger purse.

Sophia beamed at her. "Isn't it, though? Hank even dropped by and picked up a quartet of profiteroles to go with the tickets he surprised her with over dinner. Given this is where they first met, it was a lovely touch."

Bree smiled even as she gave her grandmother a considering look. She knew the Powells were just one of the many couples who had fallen in love after meeting at Bellaluna's Bakeshop. Sophia took a certain proprietary joy in their ongoing happiness, as Bree supposed she should, considering she'd played at least a partial role in their love story.

Bree had long thought it was a marvelous thing, being even a small part of one of the most important, magical moments in a person's life. She wondered what it would be like when it was her turn.

"Excuse me," came a deep voice from the doorway. "I hope I'm not intruding."

"I'll be right out," Bree said automatically, without turning right away. "So sorry to keep you waiting," she added, a cheery note in her voice. She looked at her grandmother. "I'll clean up in here after you get back. Tell Mrs. Powell I said hello."

But Sophia had already stepped past her granddaughter and was waving for the gentleman to join them in the back. "Come in, come in," Sophia said. "I'm so glad you could stop by."

Confused now, Bree turned as a tall man with a shock of dark curls, each one seeming to have a mind of its own, stepped fully into the kitchen. He had a lean build and wore a tweed jacket and pale green button-down, over casual khaki trousers. It wasn't until he glanced at Bree and nodded that she noticed he wore glasses. Glasses that framed maybe the softest blue eyes she'd ever seen. She'd never thought of blue as a warm color until that moment. In fact, she felt all kinds of warmth when a slow, almost shy smile curved his lips. Which was odd, because he wasn't the type that typically caught her eye.

"I know you told me to knock at the back door," he said, that deep voice something of a surprise coming from his otherwise quiet-looking demeanor. Well, except for that hair.

She realized she was curling her fingers into the palm of her hand against the sudden desire she had to walk over and sink them into the riot of black silk and see if those curls of his felt as glossy as they looked. That made no sense at all. She wasn't normally a fan of wild manes and shy, bespectacled smiles, either.

"But I thought it might be best to introduce myself out front," he finished.

Bree looked from the man to her grandmother. What was she up to now? Bree groaned silently and hoped this was not her grandmother's latest setup for a date.

"Nonsense," Sophia told him. "We're all shopkeepers here. And cooks, too, I suppose. Our kitchen is your kitchen," she said with a smile, then turned to Bree. "This is Caleb Dimitriou."

Connect with U(s)